WHEN
WE
WERE
YOUNG

DAWN
GOODWIN

HEAD
ZEUS

An Aries Book

First published in the UK in 2022 by Head of Zeus Ltd,
part of Bloomsbury Publishing Plc

9 7 5 3 1 2 4 6 8

A catalogue record for this book is available from the British Library.

ISBN (PB): 9781803283708
ISBN (E): 9781800242197

Cover design: Matt Bray

Typeset by Siliconchips Services Ltd UK

Printed and bound in Great Britain by
CPI Group (UK) Ltd, Croydon CRO 4YY

Head of Zeus Ltd
First Floor East
5–8 Hardwick Street
London ECIR 4RG

WWW.HEADOFZEUS.COM

To Bear. Those were the days.

I

PRESENT DAY

It was supposed to rain at funerals. Like it did on the television, everyone clad in black, weeping and wailing into a hole in the ground, the sky as sombre as the outfits.

At least that's what Stacey Maxwell had thought.

But on the Thursday they buried Valentina Mackenzie, the sun was making her squint and the sky was inappropriately blue, not a cloud to be seen.

Of course, choosing an outfit had been difficult. Not least because Valentina wouldn't have been seen dead in head-to-toe black. Stacey giggled, then clamped her hand over her mouth, even though she was alone, sitting on the edge of her unmade bed, clothes tossed around her, staring out the window at that ridiculously jaunty sky.

She fired off a 'what are you wearing' message into the newly formed WhatsApp group, aptly named 'Val's funeral'. Bev Powell was admin on the group, naturally. She'd uploaded a photo of the Powerpuff Girls as the

I

group's icon. It didn't really fit – they'd never watched the cartoon together and, as far as Stacey was aware, there were three Powerpuff girls, not four – but maybe Bev was being ironic. She could be obtuse sometimes. Well, she used to be, but Stacey didn't actually know what she was like now. She hadn't seen any of them in nearly thirty years. Facebook friends, sure, but not real friends. Not anymore.

Her phone buzzed. Bev's reply said that she was wearing a black dress. Stacey sighed and grabbed the navy dress that was almost black that she had tossed onto the pile of rejections, all the while feeling strangely traitorous to Valentina, who would've at least managed to slip some glitter in somewhere, maybe a spot of leopard print.

Stacey wriggled and contorted herself to get the zip up over her muffin top, then had to bend her arm unnaturally to get it all the way up the back. There was probably a hack for this, designed just for single people. If there wasn't, there should be.

She stood in front of the full-length mirror impassively, tilting her head this way and that, examining the shapes and angles that had changed so much over the years, the extra flesh that padded out the bones now. What would they think when they saw her? Anxiety sucked the moisture from her mouth. She nearly knocked over one of the many used mugs stashed on her bedside table as she twisted and turned.

Then the doorbell went, announcing the taxi she had booked extravagantly. It was now too late to change.

As the taxi pulled up outside the church, Stacey was regretting her choice of dress even more. The material was too thick and beads of sweat were running relays down her spine. The rolled neckline, combined with the opaque tights that now felt a size too small since the last time she'd worn them, were making her feel claustrophobic. She kept clawing at the neckline in defiance of suffocation. The taxi driver had a strong whiff of sweat about him and was blasting out an inefficient air con that served only to circulate the rancid air around the car. He'd spent most of the twenty-minute journey with earphones in, talking loudly over the radio in a language Stacey didn't understand. Occasionally he'd bark out a laugh and she'd jump, her nerves on high alert. She stepped out of the taxi in relief, inhaled deeply and tugged at the crotch of her tights where they were pinching.

The irony that she had lived only twenty minutes away from Valentina without knowing it was not lost on Stacey. Three of their group had grown up in and around the village of Shilbottle, known locally as 'Shitbottle' after someone graffitied the town sign years ago when she, Bev and Paula were kids. The graffitied sign was still there today, standing proud and still making people snigger. Every time it was replaced by the council, the graffiti came back.

Valentina had been the odd one out, the stranger who had burst into their lives in their last year at university, all bright colours and wild Italian hair. Stacey had spent the years after graduation trying to get as far away from Valentina as possible and yet here she was, twenty minutes down the road after all that.

It was a postcard Northumbrian church, with a beautifully maintained rose garden in front and the graveyard tucked neatly behind, a respectable distance away. Birds chirped, bumble bees buzzed and the air was fragrant with summer. It was twee and English and everything Valentina was not.

Stacey noticed Bev standing to the right of the church entrance, shuffling from foot to foot, wearing a dress that the Women's Institute would've approved of wholeheartedly. Bev had not noticed her yet, so Stacey had a moment to take in the sensible flat, slip-on, black shoes and neatly blow-dried helmet of hair. She looked like a Lego figurine with her handbag clutched in front of her.

Hay fever tickled at Stacey's eyes, making them twitch and water. She reached into her small, black handbag to find a tissue. Everyone was going to think she was crying because of Valentina rather than the high pollen count. Stacey's bag was a pewter colour with a bright pink, leopard-print strap, not really funeral-friendly but it hadn't crossed her mind to change it for something more subtle. She found a packet of tissues and pulled it out, snagging her little finger on her house keys at the same time. The keys pinged free and clattered to the tarmac. Bev looked over sharply, then waved.

Stacey flushed and scooped up the keys, feeling her freshly painted and yet already smudged nails scrape the tarmac, as Bev walked over.

'Did you pick that one specially?' Bev said, pointing at her bag with its jaunty strap.

'Yes, yes, I did,' Stacey lied.

'She'd have liked that.' Bev looked like she may have been crying already. 'Sorry, I haven't even said hello to you yet. How long has it been? Too long. How've you been?'

'Oh, you know. You?'

'Yeah, all good. You look good.' She was lying. Stacey knew she looked swollen.

They loitered outside the church, making small talk about the warm sun, then another taxi pulled up and Paula Dunne climbed out. As Bev and Stacey watched, she adjusted the jacket of her black trouser suit, then crouched down to tie the laces on a pair of white trainers. Her hair was still very short and no-nonsense, tucked behind her ears. It was now jet black rather than the white blonde she had dyed it at university. Stacey remembered how she would leave peroxide stains on the towels, which would drive Bev mad.

Stacey's own hair hadn't changed that much in the thirty years since university other than the invading army of grey that was marching across her scalp. It was still long, but only because she never had the will or budget to get to a hairdresser. Today she had pulled it into a low ponytail at the nape of her neck.

Paula came over to join them and they stood awkwardly, the silence between them weighed down by all the years that had passed in between conversations, before Paula pulled each of them into a brief, pat-on-the-back-type hug.

'Here we are, the three of us back together again. How long has it been?' Paula said, her smile tight.

'Too long,' Bev repeated.

Stacey fully expected Valentina to come running in late, like old times. Then it hit her that Val wouldn't be running anywhere anytime soon and she giggled. Bev threw her a look and Stacey pretended to cough to cover it up.

'We should... you know...' Bev nodded towards the church door, her eyes wide, hesitant.

Stacey expected other people to already be inside, sitting patiently, hands clutching packets of tissues, eyes downcast, but the church was empty. The vicar nodded at them as they filed into a pew a few rows back. When it became apparent that no one else was coming, he urged them to move to the front, his hands waving like a parking attendant, his voice soft and comfortingly Geordie.

The casket was closed thankfully, but it shouted at them all the same, demanding their attention. Stacey avoided looking at it. Paula was looking at her phone, tapping the screen like she had a twitch, while Bev dabbed at her eyes with a tissue and sniffed. The air was pungent with incense and the scent from large, opulent arrangements of pure white lilies. Stacey could feel a sneeze building and blew her nose into the tissue she was still clutching. Bev patted her arm sympathetically, obviously thinking it was grief that was making Stacey's nose run and not the excessive allergens.

The vicar began to speak about a woman Stacey didn't know, a woman so different to the girl they had known all those years ago. Someone kind, benevolent, well-liked. Stacey hoped he wouldn't ask anyone to say some words. She wouldn't know where to start. With how Val could start a fight with herself if there was no one else there? How she misguidedly thought she could drink anyone under the table, but was prone to nastiness when she'd had too much? How she was fiercely loyal to her friends? Too loyal. Or how things could so easily spiral out of control when she was around?

How she'd ruined Stacey's life?

There were more awkward moments than special ones. Valentina had apparently requested they sing a hymn, but with their three voices and the vicar's, it had sounded absurd in the cavernous church. Someone had put a photo on the casket of Valentina from thirty years ago. She was smiling into the camera, cat's-eye sunglasses holding her hair back from her face, her cheeks pink and alive. Stacey realised with a jolt that it was a photo Paula had taken one day when Bev had suggested a picnic because the sun was warm and they were bored. They'd gone to sit in the woods, their feet dangling in the river, the water serenading them as they laughed, ate crisps and drank bottles of cider that they'd stashed in the shallow water to keep them cold.

Then a wasp that Valentina had swatted one too many times had stung her, so they had to leave. Most things in those days had ended with Valentina ruining it.

A few weeks later, they had packed up their secrets and gone their separate ways.

While the vicar said his final prayers, Stacey looked around the church. There was a gallery above her and she thought she could see a shadow of someone sitting there, but when she stood up to leave, it was empty. They filed out into the blinding sun and stood apart but together, no less awkward than before.

Now Stacey could see how the years had left their mark on each of them. All that time following the rules on skincare and diet had only resulted in Bev looking drawn and haggard, the skin on her neck hanging in crinoline folds, but she had avoided the middle-aged gut that Stacey could feel straining against the fabric of her ill-judged dress. Stacey's knickers and tights had rolled down while she had sat inside the church, exposing a belly overhang that was even more uncomfortable than her underarm sweat patches. In contrast, Bev looked neat and ironed, her Lego hair smooth in its sensible bob style. Bev no longer wore bold, colourful glasses, instead opting for a sensible tortoiseshell frame. It used to be that they could tell her mood from the colour of the frames she had chosen on any given day. Stacey was disappointed to see that conformity had finally taken over.

Of the three, Paula had fared the best – or was better at hiding it. She hadn't changed much at all, apart from the frown lines on her forehead, but there was a rigidity about her now, like she was wound a little too tight, and her fingers constantly pecked at each other. Her body looked hard and wiry, her movements stiff.

'Did you notice the photo?' Stacey said. Paula and Bev nodded.

'The day with the bee sting. God, she made a fuss that day,' Paula replied. 'Was convinced she was going to have an allergic reaction, do you remember? That she was going to die from anaphylactic shock.'

'Turns out she was wrong,' Stacey said bluntly.

Paula's phone vibrated in her hand. She flicked her eyes at the screen, her lips a tight line.

Bev shuffled from foot to foot again, betraying how on edge she was. 'Right, well, what happens now?' she asked.

Stacey thought about the letter she had shoved in her handbag as she left her flat. 'I got a letter from her. Valentina, I mean,' she said. She expected the other two to say, 'Me too,' but they didn't. 'She wanted us to reconnect, at least have a drink or something after the funeral. Like old times.'

Paula guffawed. 'Like old times, my arse. So she sent you a letter about her own funeral?'

'Yeah, I got it the other day.'

'Why you?' Bev said.

'What do you mean?'

'Well, you weren't exactly the closest out of the four of us, were you?' Bev sounded vexed.

'I don't know, she just... The point is she wanted us to at least have a drink, put the past behind us for one day. What do you say? Might be nice? Do you both have to rush back?' Stacey swallowed. She desperately wanted a drink.

Bev shrugged. Paula checked her phone yet again, then said, 'Yeah, okay.'

The pub was walking distance from the church and as soon as they rounded the corner and saw the name of it, Paula muttered, 'For fuck's sake.' The sign was freshly painted, the name standing out against a bright white background: *The White Horse*. The same name as their local when they were at university.

A couple of people milled around outside the entrance, sucking on e-cigarettes and pints, their arms exposed in T-shirts and the skin on their cheeks pinkening in the sun. Stacey suddenly wanted a cigarette herself, but knew Bev would disapprove. Funny how after not seeing her for thirty years, she still worried what Bev might think. Like smoking was the biggest sin she'd committed. She followed Paula and Bev through the door of the pub.

Inside it was a lot more charming than the White Horse they had frequented. The walls were painted an intensely dark green and the fixtures were copper-coloured, with table lamps giving the room a heady, 1920s feel. Framed black and white photographs from days gone by were arranged along the walls above a white dado rail and muted conversation hung suspended below the high ceiling. Pubs no longer smelled like cigarettes and sweat. This one was airy and cool. Stacey approved of the way they had made the lines of the place work to give it a sense of light and space despite the dark décor.

A substantial man greeted them, a voluminous ginger beard hugging his chin. He wore a thick beanie on his head despite the heat of the day and had an immaculate tea towel slung over one shoulder. Bowls of olives, lemons wedges and cucumber slices were laid out in front of him, ready to make the perfect artisanal gin and tonic, and he posed behind a row of beer pumps that carried the labels of obscure craft beers with names like Beaver's Whisker Ale and Elephant Snout Stout.

Paula marched straight up to him and ordered a bottle of white wine without asking anyone's preference. She looked like she wanted to get all of this over with as quickly as possible. She snatched the bottle from him. Stacey and Bev followed her as she weaved through other punters, with their rustling crisp packets and mini buckets of salt and vinegar chips, to the beer garden.

Stacey was conscious that they had barely said more than a few words to each other so far. Would they still have things in common? She had followed them all on the socials over the years, but those were just stolen moments of perfection. What were their lives really like? She knew full well the image she had been portraying over the years – and what the stark reality was. She needed to watch her tongue once the wine was poured, didn't want them getting too close again.

Paula found a table perilously close to the bins at the far end of the beer garden and dumped the ice bucket onto it. The table wobbled as Stacey cocked her leg over the picnic bench and sat down. She could feel her tights catch on a rogue splinter.

Paula paused, then sat down next to Stacey. Bev took a seat opposite.

'Warm, isn't it?' Bev said for about the fourth time.

Paula rolled her eyes and put her phone on the table in front of her. The screensaver showed her with her arm around a large woman with a round face, wide hips and an enormous smile.

Stacey filled their wine glasses to the brim.

'We should say something, shouldn't we? About her, I mean,' Paula said. Her accent had mellowed over the years from a gruff Geordie to just a soft twang now.

'Okay, well...' Bev cleared her throat. She raised her glass. 'To Valentina. Irrepressible, larger than life, knew how to fill a room—'

'—and empty one,' Stacey said.

'Yeah, that too. She was unapologetically Val, fiercely protective of those she loved, only wanting love in return. Wildly misunderstood. Cheers to you, Valentina, wherever you are. I hope you found happiness.' They chinked their glasses together and each took a long drink.

'There was no one else there,' Paula said.

The statement fell onto the table between them.

'Yeah,' Stacey said.

'Did she not have a family then? Husband?' Bev asked.

'I don't know. There were photos on Facebook of Australia for a while, but I didn't… not that I was stalking her online or anything. I just kept an eye, you know, after what happened…' Stacey said.

'Better the devil you know, right?' Paula said bitterly.

'I didn't realise she lived so near to me,' Bev said. 'Do you live far from here, Stace?'

'Um, no, twenty minutes or so. I'm back near my mum's, actually. Didn't really get very far in the end. You?'

'Not too far either. How is your mum?'

'She died a few years back.'

'Oh, I'm sorry.'

Stacey shrugged. 'She wasn't well for quite some time. Her lungs – the smoking.' Stacey's mother had never been without a cigarette dangling from her bottom lip, the smoked curling up into her squinting eyes.

'Do you remember how proud she was that you were at university?' Bev said with a fond smile. 'She'd go on about you all the time – the first in your family to get a degree.'

Stacey kept quiet. There was nothing her mother should've been proud of. She was a complete fraud.

'None of us really left that university, did we? Always keeping an eye on the place. Like we couldn't tear ourselves away.' Paula's voice was coated with frost. She gulped at the wine. 'So what else did the letter say – and when did you get it?'

Stacey rummaged in her handbag and pulled out a crumpled envelope. 'It came a few days ago. I think maybe she was ill and knew it was coming? So neither of you got a letter then?' The other two shook their heads. 'Don't know how she knew my address, to be honest. Came as a bit of a shock. The letter, I mean.'

Stacey smoothed the letter out on the wooden table, her hands a little unsteady. Val's familiar scrawl raced across the page like spider legs. Sharp edges and spiky lettering, the ink soaking into the paper in parts.

Dear Stacey,

How are you? Your Instagram squares tell me you're married and have what looks to be a lovely life with your husband. You look happy.

Things haven't quite worked out that way for me and I'm writing to you because Paula probably doesn't read her mail until there's a pile of it and Bev would find this all too overwhelming.

If you are reading this, then I am dead.

Happens to us all eventually, I guess. I would like to think I died in a blaze of glory, but the truth will not be as rock and roll as that.

I know you will make the effort to be at the funeral and I'm hoping that Paula and Bev can put the past behind them and be there too. You all live so close and yet so far from one another, and that's a shame. The biggest regret of my life is how we left things. I've missed you all and wish things had ended differently.

So I need one last favour from you. A lot to ask, I

know, all things considering, but I need you to make sure Paula and Bev are at the funeral and that you meet up for one last drink. There's a pub down the road from the church – The White Horse. Not a coincidence.

Go there, order a round of shots from Dave, the ginger barman, tell him they're for Val. They're already paid for.

And then I want the three of you to talk. Listen. Laugh. About when we were young and foolish. Bury it all in the past. Forgive.

Love,

Valentina xx

Stacey's voice cracked as she finished reading the letter. The sudden swell of emotion took her by surprise, considering that she'd had a few days to come to terms with the shock of all of this coming at her out of the blue. She grabbed her glass and drained it.

A table of men next to them erupted in loud, jarring laughter, their pint glasses clinking as foam spilt over onto the wood.

'I better get those shots in then,' Paula said.

'I'll come with you,' Bev added.

Stacey stayed where she was and poured herself more wine. Paula's phone shuffled on the wooden table as an alert lit up the screen. Stacey peeked, saw a few missed calls and text alerts. She looked away. A young couple walked into the beer garden and headed over to an empty table, a portly French bulldog on a bejewelled lead at their heels. The woman was brilliantly blonde and immaculately made-up, wearing skin-tight white jeans; the man was wearing white shorts and trainers with invisible socks. Even their dog was white. Their hands were clasped tightly together and when they sat down, they were so close their hips touched. The dog immediately lay down under the table, tongue lolling as it panted in the warm sunshine. She sipped on a Pimm's overflowing with more ice and fruit than liquid; he tugged on a pint of craft ale as he gazed at his girlfriend. Stacey desperately wanted to knock the Pimm's from her hand onto her spotless jeans.

This was definitely not like the White Horse she was used to.

Stacey fiddled with the wedding ring on her finger, twisting it around as she watched them. The ring was tighter these days, the skin around it bulging. She couldn't get it off, even if she wanted to. Someone would have to cut it off – or her finger. She looked away from the happy couple as Bev and Paula returned with a tray of shot glasses.

Bev clattered it down, the glasses teetering. She looked annoyed.

'What's wrong, Bev?'

'Nothing,' she said sulkily. There it was. The Bev pout, usually brought out when there was a blatant disregard for the rules.

'So why do you look like someone has pissed on your pasty?'

'She's annoyed at Valentina,' Paula said with an eye-roll.

'It's just all this drama – for what? We haven't spoken to her in thirty years – for very good reason, I might add. We haven't spoken to each other either – and that was all her fault. Yet here we are, going out of our way to follow her final wishes like it might mean something,' Bev said, her voice shaking.

'It's just a drink, Bev,' Paula said tightly. 'We can go our separate ways again soon enough.'

'Yeah – besides, is there somewhere else you need to be?'

Bev's eyes strayed towards her phone, which had not made a peep while it had been on the table – unlike Paula's, which seemed to be buzzing and vibrating constantly.

'It's not that.' Bev sighed. 'I guess I'm still angry about it all. She's still managing to dictate what we do. And actually, I've missed you both – a lot.' Her eyes were misting up. 'I know we promised to keep our distance, but we shouldn't have had to in the first place. You were my best friends.'

Stacey could feel old emotions rumbling in the back of her own throat too. The truth was she'd missed Paula and Bev as well, could've done with them in her corner in the last few years especially.

'Fu—' Stacey stopped herself from swearing as a young child ran past, heading for the climbing frame in the far corner of the beer garden. 'You're right. She can't even die quietly, can she?'

Despite her annoyance, Bev immediately replied, 'Don't say it like that.'

'Oh come on, Bev. Let's not be coy. We know what happened, what we did, why we did it.'

'But she didn't force us. It was our choice,' Paula said quietly, her eyes fixed on her wine glass. 'If you remember, I didn't want to come today, but I did because you both persuaded me.'

'But it's weird, right? Sending letters, buying us drinks from the grave. How she is still forcing our choices?' Stacey said. She slurped more wine greedily and wiped her mouth with the back of her hand.

'Yeah, it's a bit weird.'

'How did she die?' Bev asked quietly.

They looked from one to the other.

'I just got a DM through Instagram from a random woman with the details of the funeral a day or so before I got the letter. It didn't have any details other than where the service would be. I assumed it was a family member who had sent it, but the name seemed vaguely familiar,' Stacey said.

'Yeah, I got a DM too,' Paula said.

'Me too,' Bev added.

Silence again. Then Paula said, 'Well, we don't have to drink it.'

'Course we do!' Bev replied.

'It's not like she's going to know!'

'For fuck's sake, Paula,' Stacey said, then giggled. 'Look, it's the last round of drinks Val will ever buy us and I never turn down a free drink.'

'She used to buy us stuff all the time, do you remember? Too much stuff in my opinion. It got awkward sometimes,' Paula said.

'God, yeah, but I happily accepted it – I had no money,' Stacey said. Paula's phone buzzed again. 'You going to get that? It's driving me nuts.'

Paula flicked her eyes at the screen, but didn't move to pick it up.

'What's going on, Paulie?' Bev said. The old nickname seemed to slip from her lips with ease.

Paula opened her mouth to reply, but a waiter came over to their table and collected up the empty wine bottle, humming to himself. 'Who died, ladies?' he said cheerfully after noticing their silence.

Paula glared at him. 'Our best friend actually. This is her wake.'

He paled, his hand hovering over an empty wine glass. 'Better bring you another bottle then,' he said and rushed away.

Stacey reached over and handed around the shot glasses.

'Sod it. To Valentina.' She held it aloft with an unsteady hand.

The glasses tinkled together obscenely. They knocked back their shots and grimaced in unison.

The waiter approached again, this time sheepishly brandishing a fresh bottle of wine. 'On the house,' he said. 'Sorry.'

'Our lucky day,' Stacey said.

He dumped the bottle and retreated.

Stacey looked over at the couple's table again as the heat of the shot worked its way down her throat. The dog was now asleep, the couple still perilously close to each other. She noticed the woman inch away a little, but the man just moved with her. He had one arm around her, his hand playing with the ends of her hair. She was like a possession he coveted, always touching, stroking, holding onto her, as though he was worried she would make a run for it.

'Come on then, Paulie. What's going on?' Bev persisted. Stacey dragged her eyes away from them.

'What do you mean?' Paula snapped.

'You're all jumpy and your bloody phone hasn't stopped all day.'

'It's just Sue – she's a bit... overprotective. Anyway, never mind that, what's going on with you two? Tell me everything. Are you still teaching, Bev?'

Bev paused, looked away and said, 'God, no, gave that up shortly before Bethany and Jasper were born. I'm a good old housewife these days.' She smiled widely. 'Besides, Malcolm is so busy with his business that he needs me at home to sort everything else. I dabble in arts and crafts, make homemade greeting cards that I sell at the local church and in local shops, cupcakes for the school, that kind of thing. Keeps me busy. What about you, Stace? What are you doing?'

'Um, I'm working for a young, dynamic IT company. It's great – really interesting and a vibrant group of people. There's always something going on, you know, socially. I'm never home.'

'So no architecture then? That was the dream back then. You were always sketching out some idea or other. And Alan – it is Alan, isn't it? – he doesn't mind you socialising with work?' Bev asked, her eyes like spotlights focused on her.

'No, why would he?' Stacey tried not to sound defensive, but she felt like a bug under a magnifying glass. 'How old are your kids, Bev?' she said to refocus the spotlight.

'They are seventeen and fifteen. Teenagers – quite the challenge, but we have a wonderful relationship. Very close. What about you, Paulie? I saw you got married too. You looked very happy in the wedding photo you posted on Facebook. You ever talked about having kids? I'm sure it's on the cards – it's so much easier for same-sex couples these days.' Bev had a habit of asking a question, then answering it for you. It made for rather one-sided conversations from which you emerged feeling like you had managed to say everything and nothing at all.

'We haven't been married that long – and I'm not sure I want kids,' Paula replied.

'Oh, you should. It's such a blessing!'

Stacey resisted the urge to retch.

'It's so lovely that you are married,' Bev continued oblivious. 'I love that we've all ended up happy, considering.'

'Yeah, sure,' Paula replied.

Another empty wine bottle littered the table and the air was finally cooling on their skin. They had outlasted the couple with the dog, who had left a little while ago, their hands still clutching at each other. As they had walked past, Stacey had noticed a joyous brown smudge on the back of the woman's jeans and it looked like the man had dripped ketchup in his lap. It had made Stacey smile. The woman had misunderstood and had smiled back politely as she passed. *Schadenfreude*, it was called, that feeling of joy derived from someone else's downfall. It was a feeling Stacey was all too familiar with.

The blokes at the table next to them were stubbornly sticking around, their voices even louder now, their language getting coarser and falling harshly on the ears as they discussed football, rugby, anything that involved men in shorts chasing balls.

Stacey, Paula and Bev kept their voices quiet in

comparison, but their combined mood had lifted as the wine flowed. They thankfully veered away from talking about their current lives to laughing about their past one – shared memories from university and before. Stacey noticed how they all avoided talking too much about Valentina. It was as though every time her name came up, a shadow fell over them, so they would move on quickly, keeping it light and frothy, the banter loose and easy. There were plenty of moments that felt familiar, that reminded Stacey of the friendship they used to have, the ease with which they could be in each other's company.

She was reminded of how much she missed it, but also of how dangerous getting close to someone could be. Once, she had thought that being surrounded by people was the most important thing in the world.

Now she knew solitude was safer.

I sit in the far corner of the beer garden, obscured by a large potted fern, my cap pulled low. Look at them, raising a glass to a woman they didn't really like. I can't hear what they are saying because a table of loud, laddish types next to them is drowning out their words.

I lean in closer, but a branch of the fern catches the peak of my cap and nearly pulls it off, exposing the face I am trying to obscure. I run my hand through my short hair, then secure the cap firmly in place again.

The three of them look angry and sad in equal measures, each of them still wearing the effects of the funeral on their skin.

But as they pour more wine, they start to laugh at what I

assume are stories from before and shared experiences. The laughter is crass, inappropriate, vulgar. They don't deserve to laugh or joke or reminisce, the stories embellished with the passing of time.

Stories from before that weekend. A time when everyone was friends and everything was new and exciting.

From before they were murderers.

2

Valentina dropped the bags at her feet, then took a minute to pause, breathe. She chewed on the skin around her fingernail, caught herself, took another breath. Stupidly nervous. She could hear voices coming from a small open window, louder than her father's voice in her head telling her that she better pull herself together and make this work because he wouldn't be bailing her out again.

'Where did you find her, Bev? Do you know anything about her at all? It's a bit weird that she's moved to a new university in her final year, isn't it? She could be an axe murderer or anything,' a voice said.

'Please blow your smoke in the other direction, Stace. You know I hate it. And she's nice – she answered the ad we put up in the Student Union.'

'Anything is better than that last one – God, she was boring. Never came out of her room. Let's hope this one is a bit more interesting,' a third voice said, huskier and gravelly, the Geordie accent strong.

'Well, if you two got a job, then we wouldn't need another flatmate and it could be just the three of us, like it should be.'

Valentina swallowed nervously. They didn't know *she* had chosen *them*, not the other way around.

She had seen them on her first day on campus when they were pinning the ad up on the noticeboard, how they'd laughed together, then walked away arm in arm, forcing others to part in front of them to let them pass. She had followed them around for a bit, then had gone back to the noticeboard and taken the ad down so that no one else could answer. Then she had phoned her father and told him she would be sharing with friends rather than living alone in the flat he had paid for.

They are going to like me. I'll make sure of it. Note to self: be interesting, not boring.

She smoothed down the front of her emerald green top and knocked harder than intended on the peeling door.

Seconds passed and the door was flung open.

The woman standing on the other side of it was Bev Powell, who Valentina had met last week. Her light brown hair framed her face in a precise bob, a face that wasn't smiling today. Her eyes were magnified behind a pair of ridiculous, Sue-Pollard-style, red-framed glasses.

'Hi, Valentina,' she said flatly.

'Hi, Bev.' Valentina smiled warmly, hoping her friendliness would be infectious.

It wasn't. Did she have the wrong day? The wrong time? Her paranoia burst straight out of the starting blocks and started cantering away.

Bev stepped back and nodded for her to come in. She shuffled past, dragging her bags behind her.

The flat smelled like hot, buttered toast.

'Leave those there,' Bev said dismissively and walked through a doorway to the right, off the hallway.

Valentina had been expecting a warmer welcome. Last week Bev had been all smiles, warm and friendly after Valentina had called to look at the room. The flat was on the far side of campus, a fair walk to the social sciences block where most of Valentina's lectures were going to be, but that didn't matter.

She stepped over an abandoned pair of running shoes on the floor and followed Bev into the kitchen with trepidation, not sure what to expect from the other two girls who lived there. She hadn't met them yet.

They were sitting at a breakfast bar tucked into the corner of the cramped kitchen. A girl with a blow-dried mass of long, wavy blonde hair sat with her feet up on the bench, hugging her knees and scowling at Valentina. The other girl at the table was very pretty with high cheekbones and a white-blonde pixie cut. She wasn't even looking at Valentina. Bev walked over to the sink, which was full of dirty dishes, and stood looking out of the window at nothing in particular, her back to Valentina.

'Er, hi, I'm Valentina. Um, you can call me Val. Most people do eventually.'

Nobody called her Val.

Silence.

The girl with the pixie cut finally looked at her, then slowly raised her hands from below the table, her eyes never leaving Valentina's. The other girl did the same, like a robotic clone, just as Bev spun round. Valentina instinctively stepped back.

A series of loud bangs went off in her face. She flinched and jumped before realising they were all holding party poppers. Paper strings hit her face and clung to her hair.

'WELCOME HOME!' they shouted in unison and started laughing.

Valentina's heart was banging in her throat and she felt nauseous, but she laughed awkwardly.

Bev rushed over and hugged her. 'Sorry, we couldn't resist! Stacey's idea, of course.'

The girl with the long hair waved and said, 'You're welcome.'

'Shit, you got me,' Valentina said, relaxing a tiny bit in Bev's firm hug. 'I thought you were going to kill me or something.'

'No, we'd wait until you were asleep and put a pillow over your face,' the pixie-cut girl said. 'But not before you'd paid your rent for the month.' Her face was still deadpan and Valentina actually believed her for a second.

'Paula! Stop it,' Stacey said.

'Sorry,' Paula said and her face relaxed into a grin. 'I'm pulling your leg. I'm Paula Dunne.' She slid across the bench and Valentina stretched her hand out, expecting a handshake, but Paula reached past her to open the fridge. Valentina blushed and dropped her hand. 'Right, let's welcome you properly,' Paula said as she grabbed a bottle of wine.

'Whoa, let her at least put her bags in her room,' Bev said. 'Come on, I'll show you around.'

Valentina swallowed, her pulse still tripping over itself, and followed Bev to where she had left her bags. Bev grabbed one and struggled under the weight of it towards the double glass doors just past the kitchen. This was the room Valentina had seen last week. Essentially, it was the lounge of the flat, but with a bed, desk and wardrobe taking up one half of the room and a couch with a low coffee table and a small television taking up the other half. A long glass window stretched across most of one wall, with a door out to a balcony that overlooked the car park below and the woods beyond that stretched out behind the campus.

'Okay, here you go – as we said, this is our lounge and your bedroom, but if you want, we can look at all of us rotating every few months so that you aren't always the one having to put up with Stacey and her *EastEnders* addiction when you're trying to study,' Bev said.

Valentina took in the Athena posters on the walls, an abandoned game of solitaire on the coffee table, the cards discarded and jumbled up, and the view out of the window, the woods dark and brooding as the river cut through the middle confidently.

'It's fine. It's perfect. And I like *EastEnders* anyway,' she said with what felt like her first genuine smile. Valentina hated soap operas, but she wanted to learn to like what they liked. If her disastrous stint at boarding school had taught her anything, it was that people didn't really warm to her easily. She needed to be a chameleon, to wear the skin of those around her if she wanted to fit in.

'Great!' Bev said. 'Dump those there and let me show you where everything else is.'

Valentina did as she was told and followed Bev.

'This is my room – excuse the mess,' she said, throwing open the door of a tiny box room at the far end of the corridor. It wasn't that messy, but smelled vaguely damp and musty. The walls were painted in a pale pink; the bedspread also pale pink and covered in tiny flowers, with a teddy bear sitting on the pillow.

Bev turned back and pushed open the door to the room next to it. 'And this one is Paula and Stacey's. Even messier than mine, but there's two of them, I suppose.' The largest room was a maelstrom of clothes, shoes, bags and books. The wall on one side was covered in anatomy posters while the wall on the other side was covered with a handful of photographs of the three girls and posters of famous architectural landmarks.

Bev shuffled her out again. Valentina followed like a puppy, her eyes wide and curious. 'Here's the bathroom – we have a rota for cleaning it and the kitchen, but be careful because Paula has a way of avoiding her turn.'

'I heard that!' came a voice from the kitchen.

Bev rolled her eyes. 'Your room is your responsibility obviously. And that's it! That's the grand tour.' They headed back towards the kitchen. Bev pointed out the telephone sitting on the floor just outside the glass doors to the lounge. 'There's a pad of paper under the phone. Just write down how long your calls are and we will work out the phone bill when we get it. Same with food – we put money in the kitty every month and like to cook and eat together as much as possible, but obviously if you want to buy your own stuff, that's also fine. Just label it carefully though, 'cos Stacey is a pig when she's pissed and will eat anything that's not strapped down.'

Stacey grinned and raised a now full wine glass proudly. 'She's not wrong.'

'Here.' Paula shoved a glass into Valentina's hand. 'Sit down, we won't bite... yet.'

Valentina slid onto the bench at the breakfast bar and exhaled.

'To a new chapter. Partners in crime,' Bev said and raised her glass.

They clinked glasses and Valentina began to relax.

I think I'll fit in here after all.

3

Bev swayed slightly as they stood outside the pub in the still-warm darkness. Paula was glued to her phone, monitoring the Uber app and giving constant updates on her driver's ETA. A street lamp was illuminated behind her, giving her an ethereal glow. Looking from one to the other, Stacey felt a warmth rush over her that could've been mostly from alcohol, but was also nostalgia.

And then melancholy pushed the nostalgia away.

What happened to us bright young things? Where did it all go wrong?

But she knew the answer to that, didn't she?

Stacey thought about what was not waiting for her at home and heard herself saying, 'I would love to have you both come back to mine! I feel like this shouldn't be it for another thirty years. But Alan will probably be in bed already – he has a big project on at work. Can we come to yours, Bev? Maybe order in some food or something?'

'It's nearly ten o'clock!' Bev said.

'So? What happens at ten o'clock? Do you grow horns?'

'No, it's just... it's *late*.'

Stacey snorted. Paula looked up from phone, her forehead wrinkled. 'She's right, it is late. We should go home. My Uber is nearly here.' She looked nervous suddenly, like she really was worried about growing horns.

Stacey sighed. 'You both used to be a lot more fun.'

'So when will we see each other again?' Bev asked as a black Prius pulled up to the kerb.

'Hopefully before thirty more years have passed. Bev, I think your Uber is that one over there,' Paula said as she got in the back of the car.

'Oh, thanks,' Bev said. 'Bye then, Paula.' But Paula's Uber was accelerating away already. Bev leant into Stacey for a hug and Stacey hugged her back, then didn't want to let go, felt like she was clutching on, hugging her for longer than was appropriate.

She watched, alone on the pavement, as Bev's Uber pulled away. She rummaged in her handbag for her keys, tucked her front-door key between her fingers so that it was poking out like a weapon and headed to the bus stop, her heels dragging.

Paula looked back once at Bev and Stacey hugging goodbye, then settled into the back of the Uber and finally looked at her missed calls. Fifteen calls from Sue and a number of WhatsApp messages and voice memos.

She sighed and rested her head back against the seat, feeling a headache settling in behind her eyes. She was tempted to tell the driver to take her somewhere else, anywhere else. Just not home. She would need to provide answers, reassurances, excuses and all she wanted to do was crawl into bed, alone, for a restful and deep sleep. The kind of sleep she hadn't enjoyed in quite some time.

Instead, she turned her phone off and focused on the soft rock playing on the radio over the rumble of the tyres, her eyes taking in the bodies walking along the pavement, their faces artificially illuminated by yellow street lamps, and the car that pulled up next to her at the traffic lights, the driver shuffling in his seat to whatever music was playing on his radio.

She could've gone along with Stacey and pressured Bev into having them back at hers, but then her perfect marriage and perfect family would've been on display and Paula couldn't deal with that right now.

Stacey had changed a lot, as they probably all had. She still had those amazing blue eyes and Paula had to remind herself not to look too closely, to keep a sense of distance in case she fell down that rabbit hole again. Today had been a day for old wounds to itch, but scratching would only leave a scar.

Stacey probably thought Paula had been prickly and rude, but it was self-preservation really. Paula had been an expert at faking it when they had lived together and it was a skin she stepped back into fairly easily today.

While at certain moments it had felt like things hadn't changed at all and that so much time hadn't passed, at other moments she had been acutely aware of the polite space between them, like the last thirty years had been an awkward pause in their conversation, with none of them wanting to be the first to speak again, to share their realities. They were all guarding their secrets and protecting themselves, keeping the others at arm's length.

For that reason alone, it was for the best that they never see each other again after today. They'd said that thirty years ago too.

The Uber pulled up outside her front door. The hallway light was on, but the rest of the maisonette was in darkness. Maybe Sue had gone to bed.

Paula thanked the driver and walked very slowly up the path. Closing the front door gently behind her, she pulled off her trainers and carried them in one hand as she tiptoed into the lounge.

The lamp in the corner of the room lit up suddenly and she cried out. Sue was sitting in the armchair in the bay window, looking like a Bond villain.

'Why were you sitting in the dark?' Paula said, swallowing down a nervous giggle.

'Where've you been?'

'To a funeral. You know that.'

'I was worried.'

'So you thought you would sit in the dark and wait? It isn't late.'

'I called you a few times. You never answered.'

'My phone was running out of battery, so I turned it off to try and make it last as long as possible because I knew I had to book an Uber. It was flat by the time I got in the Uber, so I couldn't message you to say I was on my way.'

Sue glared at her.

Paula walked into the kitchen and turned on the light

before peering in the fridge. 'I'm starving – do you want anything? I might make an omelette – or cheese on toast,' she called over her shoulder.

Sue came up behind her, stood so close that Paula could feel her breath on her neck. Her fingers grabbed onto the top of Paula's arm, squeezing painfully. 'You should've called and let me know where you were. I was worried.' Sue released her arm and moved away. 'I'm going to bed.'

Paula exhaled.

Bev was concentrating on not throwing up as she walked up the path to the house. The car journey had shaken up her stomach, making the wine curdle with the cheese and onion crisps she had eaten earlier. She took a few deep breaths, put one hand against the wall of the house to steady herself. It wasn't that late, despite what she'd said to Stacey, but it was unusual for her to be out on her own at all, let alone after 10pm at night. She hoped Malcolm and the kids had fared okay without her.

The cul-de-sac was quiet, many of the houses already in darkness. She noticed Malcolm hadn't put the milk bottles out yet. Movement behind her made her spin around. A fox ambled across the road. It stopped, glared at Bev, then sloped on.

Her keys were in her bag somewhere, but it was too dark for her to see them. She usually left the outside light on for Malcolm when he was out. It must've slipped his mind to do the same for her.

She gave up on looking for them and rang the doorbell. Walter, her little fox terrier, barked fiercely in response.

A gruff voice from inside said, 'Shush, Walter! You'll wake the whole street up.' Malcolm flung open the door, looking annoyed.

Perhaps he'd been worried, she thought with a weird delight.

'Don't you have your keys with you? I'm watching the news,' he snapped and headed back to the lounge with impatience.

She followed him in, petted a bouncing and still yapping Walter, and slipped out of her shoes. She stood for a moment, letting her toes curl and uncurl in the thick carpet.

Jasper emerged from the kitchen, munching on a share-size bag of tortilla chips, the smell of artificially orange cheese pungent. 'Hi, Mum,' he said.

'Hi, honey. Shouldn't you be in bed? School tomorrow.' She reached towards him but he slipped past her, straight upstairs.

Malcolm was reclining in his chair in the lounge, his feet propped up on the footrest, a plate of cheese, ham, pickled onions and French bread at his elbow on the small, marble-topped side table.

'Sorry, I couldn't find my keys in the dark. The light wasn't on.' He said nothing in return. She could hear his teeth crunching down on a pickled onion. 'Is that your dinner?'

'Well, we had to have something.' He pierced another pickled onion with his fork.

Her stomach growled in a Pavlovian response, the nausea temporarily overshadowed, and she realised she had had next to nothing to eat all day. They had shared some chips from a tiny bucket at one point and a couple of packets of crisps, but that was it.

She turned away just as he said, 'So how was it?'

'It was okay – sad, I guess. There was no one there but us. But seeing Paula and Stacey again was lovely. They haven't really changed.'

'Hmmmmm,' he said, his head tilted to the side so that he could see past her to the television screen. Then he looked at her and she smiled at him expectantly, but all he said was, 'Um, you're in the way – would you mind…?'

Bev sighed as she moved away. This was their lives – him either at work, sitting with his feet up in his favourite chair (which she loathed because it was a black leather hulk of a chair that did not suit her other pale grey, handmade sofas) or sweating it out on his Peloton bike, which took up most of the free floor space in their bedroom so that she had to bend like a contortionist to get clean knickers out of her drawer every day. No conversation, no laughter. He only saw her when she was in the way of the television.

Stacey had asked her about teaching earlier and she hadn't wanted to tell them the truth. That she'd realised very soon after starting her first placement that she actually didn't like other people's children. That she had wanted to scream at their annoying little faces. That actually some days she didn't even like her own. Jasper was an entitled, slovenly kid who was rapidly turning into his father and Bethany was a moody, sullen child. Neither of them seemed to notice she was there unless they needed something and even then, they treated her with impatient contempt much of the time.

A bit like Malcolm. She looked over her shoulder at him impassively.

Her stomach rumbled again. Malcolm didn't notice when she left the room.

Stacey opened her front door and flicked on the hallway light. Her cat, Nemo, slinked over to her and immediately wrapped himself around her legs.

She knelt down, feeling her knees crackle, and tickled Nemo under the chin. He purred, then glided away into the kitchen to stand next to his bowl in a subtle nod that his dinner was late. Her eyes came to rest on the wedding photo on the wall, as they always did, then she followed Nemo.

She dumped her keys and bag on the small, round kitchen table and opened the fridge. She took out an open bottle of wine and a tin of cat food, putting one in a glass and the other in Nemo's bowl. They both tucked in greedily.

Glass in hand, she kicked off her shoes and left them where they lay, then wandered into the tiny lounge and sat in the shadows cast by the light coming from the hallway, her gaze on the window and the night sky beyond it. Her face was opaque in the reflection and she watched herself drink from the glass, the wine cheap and acidic. Her stomach gurgled. She didn't need more wine – she'd certainly had enough with Paula and Bev – but she wanted it because her brain was threatening to go into overdrive, dipping and diving in and out of unwelcome memories.

Nemo wandered in and sat in the middle of the carpet to clean his paws. She watched him dispassionately. He smelt like cat food.

She put her glass down on the carpet at her feet and wandered into the kitchen. Cupboard doors were flung open and the fridge was inspected until she settled on a bag of tortilla chips and a half-empty jar of salsa. That was dinner sorted then.

Back on the couch, she propped the salsa jar between her knees and tucked into the chips with one hand, leaving the other to flick through the options on Netflix. She settled on *Interview with a Vampire* with Brad Pitt and Tom Cruise, because she remembered going to see it with Valentina, Bev and Paula once. She had always preferred Brad Pitt, but Valentina preferred Tom Cruise, while Paula was more interested in Thandie Newton. Bev had never liked to pick favourites. Stacey smiled as she remembered trying to persuade Paula that there was no choice to be made between Brad and Thandie. Then there was the night Paula gave Stacey her first and only hickey after trying to convince her that she would have more fun as a lesbian.

That had set off a chain of events that had hurtled them to—

A dollop of salsa dripped from the end of her chip onto the front of her navy dress. She scooped it up with her finger, her eyes fixed on the screen, not prepared to follow the memory through to its conclusion.

Stacey woke to a throbbing headache, a weight on her chest and a rough sensation on her cheek.

She opened one eye to see Nemo filling her vision, his sandpaper tongue licking what she assumed was salsa off her face. She groaned and lifted him to one side, tried to peel open both eyes, but the sunlight pouring into the room was not helping the rhythmic thuds behind her temples.

She was still on the couch, still wearing the navy dress from yesterday's funeral. She lowered her feet to the carpet and felt moisture soak into her tights. Praying Nemo hadn't peed on the carpet, she looked down and saw that her wine glass had toppled over. Pinot grigio was a lot easier to get out of a carpet than cat piss. She sat for a moment with her head in her hands, one foot in the wet patch, feeling her stomach eddy and trying to work out what day it was.

The funeral was yesterday, which meant today was Friday and she was supposed to be at work.

She leapt to her feet. She had taken yesterday off and in her head it had felt like the weekend, what with the trip to the pub with Bev and Paula, her dinner of nacho chips, the crumbs of which were scattered across her couch cushions.

She looked around for her phone, then reached down the side of the couch cushions, finally feeling her fingers brush against her phone case. The screen refused to light up when she tapped it. Flat battery. The clock over the oven was no help; she never remembered to reset it when the clocks went back, so she didn't trust what time it said. It could either be 08h15 or 09h15 and neither was good news as that meant she would be late either way.

Fifteen minutes later she was throwing on a jacket, grabbing her phone from where it was charging and thrusting into her handbag the pile of letters that the postman had just deposited through the letterbox. Nemo had watched uninterested from the middle of her bed as she had stood under a cold shower for all of two minutes, hurriedly brushed her teeth and slapped some mascara on her eyelashes before throwing on a dress that lay discarded on her bedroom floor from where she had left it when she wore it on Tuesday. She hoped no one at work would notice she had already worn it this week or the slightly sweaty smell coming from it. She spritzed some cheap perfume over herself just in case.

The bus was packed and she had to stand for most of the journey, the nautical motion of it making her feel even more peculiar. She sipped on a bottle of water she found in her bag in the hope that it would stop her from leaning over and vomiting on the weary-looking woman sitting in the seat next to her.

Eventually, with only a few minutes left of her journey, the woman got off the bus and Stacey flung herself into the vacant seat before anyone else could nab it. A woman with greying hair and sensible shoes scowled at her for stealing the seat, but she avoided eye contact and pretended to rummage in her handbag. She pulled out the letters she'd shoved in her bag.

She recognised the handwriting on the top envelope immediately.

It was another letter from Valentina.

The bus pulled to a sharp halt that flung her forward in her seat and she looked up in time to notice that this was her stop. She shoved the envelope back in her handbag and pushed through the bodies blocking the way to the door.

She stood for a moment on the pavement, a stiff breeze blowing her fringe from her forehead. People rushed past, coffee cups in hand; a pigeon pecked at a dropped croissant; a man stood in front of the vaping shop in a cloud of scented fog. She took it all in as a sense of unnatural calm settled over her, like a weighted blanket.

She had waited thirty years for the truth to come out. Finally, this might all be over soon.

I wonder what they are doing now. Will they stay in touch after they reconnected over a coffin and some overpriced chips? I'm curious to see how this plays out now that the sticking plaster has been ripped off.

I look over to where their pictures are on show, taped to the bare white wall with Sellotape that will probably remove a layer of paint when I tear them down. Layer upon layer of paint – strip one layer away and there is another beneath.

Just like lies.

I will probably miss all of this when I am done. It has brought me comfort, like finally getting to know the family you were separated from prematurely. I have collected these photos slowly and methodically over the last twelve months, watching, collecting information, planning. And in the middle, there is one around whom everyone rotates. The mastermind; the puppet master; the conductor.

She is the key to all of this – and she will be left until last.

4

Pulling her leopard-print dressing gown cord tight, Valentina wandered into the kitchen in search of a cup of tea. Paula, Bev and Stacey were sitting around the breakfast bar, eating cereal and listening to Radio 1.

'There she is! She's alive!' Bev proclaimed.

Valentina smiled awkwardly. 'Sorry about yesterday.'

'Did you have a hangover? We didn't notice,' Stacey said with a smirk, then slurped milk from her spoon.

Yesterday was brutal. Valentina had never felt so ill. The day before, when she had officially moved in and the first bottle of wine was empty, Valentina had brought out a couple of the bottles of champagne she'd stolen from her dad's wine cellar because she thought the real stuff might impress them. He wouldn't miss them anyway. They had drunk the champagne out of cheap mugs and then necked shots in the kitchen. They had talked about their courses and she found out that the three of them were all friends from before university, having grown up in the same town. They had a shared history and were really close.

Thinking about it made her fizz with a sense of longing, of wanting what they had so badly that she could taste it. She heard herself pretending to know the people they were talking about, the places they had been, and she had laughed at the anecdotes and sympathised when they complained about the awful lecturers, the terrible food. Even so, she was keenly aware of being the outsider again.

Then they had asked her why she had transferred in her final year and she had to tell them the first lie.

She told them she had started at Sheffield University, but hadn't liked the city university vibes, so had transferred to this university for a change of pace and the campus vibe. They didn't need to know what had actually happened, why she had to transfer. They didn't need to know about the lecturer and his accusations of harassment, the suspension or her father's well-timed payment in return for keeping it off her record.

More drinks followed and they had moved into the lounge. Someone put some music on. She remembered standing in the middle of the room dancing around them as they watched and laughed. Then, it had seemed like they were laughing with her, but in the cold light of day she realised that perhaps they had been laughing at her. Then, she had thought Stacey was encouraging her to have fun, cheering her on, but now she thought perhaps Stacey had been ridiculing her. They had finally left her collapsed on her bed, face down and fully clothed, at 3am. She had woken up in the same position, hardly able to breathe because her face had been pressed into the pillow, the creases branded into her skin.

Yesterday she couldn't stop throwing up, her throat burning and her stomach muscles aching with every heave. Someone had held her hair back at one point – Bev possibly – and Paula had run her a bath. Later, when she could finally face some food, Bev made them all a late dinner of pasta. Bev was clearly the mother of the group, but Paula had also checked in on her and brought her some water during the day. The only one who hadn't bothered was Stacey who, other than asking her how she was feeling when they had passed in the corridor, had not really taken much interest in her.

Valentina turned towards the kettle and busied herself with her cup of tea as they carried on talking behind her. It sounded like someone they knew was having a party tonight. She wondered if they would invite her to join them. When the tea was made, she went to sit with them, but Stacey was taking up all of the seating space on the bench on one side of the table. Valentina hovered awkwardly while they talked about someone called Kevin who Bev had seen yesterday when she was in town. Valentina felt embarrassment flush over her as she realised Stacey was ignoring her standing there expectantly. The table was littered with crumbs and tea stains. Last night's dinner plates and pans were still in the sink.

Finally Bev said, 'Stacey, shove up and let Val sit down.'

Stacey grunted and slid across so that Valentina could

perch on the end of the bench next to her. 'Who's Kevin?' Valentina asked.

'He was in our uni res in first year,' Paula replied.

Someone else Valentina didn't know and frankly wasn't the least bit interested in knowing.

'So what is everyone doing today?' she said instead.

'I've got a load of books to source for next week in town,' Stacey said.

'I'll come with you,' Paula said.

'And don't forget Kev's party tonight,' Bev said to them. 'I said we'd go at about 8 p.m.'

'Ugh, do we have to?' Paula moaned.

'Well, no, but it could be fun. His parties usually are,' Bev said, 'and we don't want to let him down, now that I've said we'll come.'

'He won't notice either way, Bev. Okay, let's see what the cards say,' Stacey said.

Paula rushed into Valentina's room and came back with the pack of cards that had been spread out on the coffee table when she moved in.

'Go on then,' Stacey urged.

Paula shuffled the cards, her hands lightning quick and well-practised.

'What's going on?' Valentina asked, confused.

'Oh, it's nothing. It's stupid really, a sort of superstition we have,' Bev replied.

'Yeah, it started in first year when we couldn't decide what to do one night and Paula was playing solitaire. So we picked two options and asked the cards, then did whatever the cards told us. It's kind of stuck since then,' Stacey explained. 'Fate decides for us.'

Paula placed the cards in a pile face down. 'Okay, black we go; red we stay in,' she said. Then she addressed the cards, her face serious. 'Cards, should we go to Kevin's party tonight? Bev, you make the cut.'

Bev leant over, cut the cards and turned them over.

The seven of spades.

'Right, we're going. I better get some drinks in then, because someone drank all of ours the other night,' Stacey said, looking at Valentina.

She looked sheepish. 'It wasn't just me!'

'I need to get dressed, so move,' Stacey said pointedly, glaring at Valentina.

'Oh!' Valentina slid out of the booth to let Stacey out and then the others disappeared too. Valentina was left sitting alone with her tea in the dirty kitchen.

No one had invited her to go to the party.

Later, there was a lot of slamming doors as they took turns rushing in and out of the bathroom, borrowing clothes, discarding them again, discussing their insecurities and throwing compliments around like sweets.

Valentina sat in the lounge, listening to it all unfold around her. The air was toxic with perfume and hairspray, the different fragrances fighting over each other. Eventually they were throwing on their coats and heading for the door.

'What are you up to tonight, Val?' Paula asked as she chucked keys into a small bag.

'Oh, I don't know, maybe have a bath and get an early night,' Valentina said quietly.

'So if you're here, I don't need to take keys? They won't fit in this bag.'

'Um, yeah, that's fine – I can wait up.'

'That's not fair, guys. Who knows what time we'll be home? She wants an early night,' Bev said.

'It's fine, really. I don't mind,' Valentina said hastily.

'You're an angel, thank you,' Paula replied.

And then Valentina was left alone in the hairspray smog of their departure.

She got up and walked out onto the balcony. The evening air was definitely getting chillier. She could see them walking away towards the path that ran through the woods, a shortcut into town. Their arms were linked and she could hear their laughter. She watched them until she couldn't see them anymore, the trees closing over them, swallowing them whole. She watched them until it was as though they were never there at all.

The sky was darkening, the clouds hanging low. They would probably get wet later when they were making their way home, she thought and smiled to herself.

She walked into the kitchen, thought about ordering in pizza, but decided she wasn't that hungry. She felt restless, not able to concentrate on anything, not wanting to either.

The cards were still on the table, cut into two piles. She picked them up, tried to shuffle them, but they flicked out of her fingers and scattered, spilling onto the floor. She tried again and wasted a good half an hour shuffling the cards over and over, wanting to be able to do it as well as Paula. She remembered playing solitaire on her computer a while ago, could remember the broader rules of the game, so she dealt out the cards and played a few rounds. She lost every time.

Sighing, she wandered into the hallway, then found herself in Bev's room. The bed faced the door. It was unmade with clothes scattered across it. A lacy, violet bra dangled from the desk chair. This was a paradox of Valentina's room, which was impeccably tidy, the bed made, her clothes put away in the wardrobe. She was conscious that since it was also the lounge, she was sharing her bedroom with the other three, although no one had been in to use it uninvited since she had moved in. They tended to sit around the breakfast bar instead.

Valentina picked up one of the tops tossed on the duvet. It was a lovely teal colour, silky beneath her fingers with shoestring straps and lace edging. Not something Valentina could see Bev wearing. Valentina lifted it to her nose and breathed in deeply. She could smell floral notes, maybe a citrus undertone. The lemon shower gel in the bathroom maybe.

She looked around the rest of the room. There was a wardrobe, a small chest of drawers and a bedside table squeezed into the room, alongside a desk covered with books, pens and files. The bedside table had a towering pile of books on it that threatened to topple over. A mix of romance novels and celebrity autobiographies. There were a number of crumpled tissues tossed next to the books and a jumble of necklaces and earrings.

She opened the drawer in the bedside table and saw a row of glasses cases, each with a different loud, outlandish pair inside. The next drawer down had a stash of chocolates and biscuits inside. There was an open packet of chocolate-covered toffees and Valentina took one out, unwrapped it, savoured it on her tongue. She took another one, then closed the drawer.

The chest of drawers had a heap of make-up scattered across the top in front of a small, free-standing mirror, along with more tissues stained with lipstick marks. She tried a berry-coloured lipstick but it wasn't her colour, so she wiped it off with a tissue, which she tossed into the overflowing bin on the floor.

Valentina opened the wardrobe, but it was mostly jeans and jackets. She turned to leave, then opened the bedside table drawer again and stole another toffee, stuffing the wrappers into her jeans pocket.

She walked into Paula and Stacey's room next, which was as untidy now as it had been on the day she had arrived. Their room had two single beds at opposite sides of the room, a bedside table each and two desks. One wall was taken up with two wardrobes pushed together. She wasn't sure which side of the room was Paula's, but looking at the books on the desk, she could make a fair assumption. Paula was studying physiotherapy and there were a number of biology and anatomy books on the desk beneath the wall of anatomy posters.

She opened one of the wardrobes and was bombarded with colour. This was Stacey's without a doubt. She pulled out a bright pink, Sixties-style shift dress with a white collar. Pushing her jeans down to her ankles, she tried it on. Stacey was smaller than her and the dress strained across Valentina's boobs, but the fuchsia pink made her olive skin and raven hair stand out in contrast. If she lost a few pounds, she could ask to borrow this.

She tried on some more outfits, finding some that just about fit, but others that certainly did not. The last outfit she tried on was a khaki jumpsuit with gold stripes down the legs. She could just about do up the zip, but again it was tight over her boobs. Valentina considered herself in the mirror on the back of the wardrobe door, feeling like Maverick from *Top Gun* in it, but a little ridiculous as well. She could see Stacey in it though, who would probably team it with trainers, her long blonde hair piled into a high ponytail, and she would look amazing.

Valentina reached behind her to unzip the jumpsuit, but the zip was stuck. She could only just reach it with her fingertips and could feel her shoulder straining painfully as she tried to get a better grip. Suddenly, the material along the side hem tore with a sickening rip. Valentina stopped breathing. Her fingers gripped onto the zip and she gave a hard tug until it finally opened. She tore off the jumpsuit, shoved it to the back of the wardrobe and slammed the doors shut. She sat on one of the beds.

Stupid, stupid, stupid.

She slapped at her head with her hands to make the voice stop.

Her eyes wandered over to the bedside table. The drawer was open and she could see a packet of birth control pills, make-up and cigarettes inside. Again, this would be Stacey's – she was the only one Valentina had seen smoking so far. Yesterday when she was sticking her head out of her window for some air in between bouts of nausea, Stacey had been leaning out of her own window smoking. Stacey had put her finger to her lips conspiratorially, then stubbed out the cigarette on the window ledge and ducked back inside.

Valentina grabbed the packet of cigarettes. It was half full and there was a lighter tucked into the box. She took out a cigarette, went over to the window and leant out, just as Stacey had. She lit the cigarette and breathed in deeply, then started to cough and gag. She tried again, feeling the nicotine pull into her lungs this time, then the rush of dizziness as her brain processed the toxins. It felt a little like a tequila buzz, but less unsteady.

She looked out over the woods. There was a full moon riding high in the now ink-black sky and she gazed at it, looking for a face in it. She didn't see anything initially, but the further down the cigarette she got, the more she saw it. A vague outline of eyes, maybe a nose. Watching, menacing.

She shivered, stubbed out the cigarette and added the end to the pile Stacey had collected in the corner of the window ledge. Her mouth tasted awful now, coated in fur, and the smoke clung to her hair, but the next time would be easier. She could start taking cigarette breaks with Stacey, bonding over a shared vice. The idea made her smile. It looked cool when Stacey did it.

Her mother had smoked. She thought she remembered seeing her sitting in the sun with large sunglasses covering her eyes, and she had looked glamorous, untouchable. Or was this one of her made-up memories? She had those sometimes.

Thinking about her mother made Valentina want to call her father suddenly. He hadn't phoned to make sure she had settled in okay. He sent money, arranged gifts through his PA, never answered the phone when she called. So what was the point?

Instead, she opened Paula's wardrobe, which was just as cluttered as Stacey's, with a shelf just for toiletries. Valentina took out a bottle of bubble bath and went into the bathroom to turn on the taps of the bath, pouring some of Paula's lavender bubbles into the steaming water. She returned the bottle to the shelf, making sure it was facing exactly the same way as before, then rummaged through the magazines on Paula's bedside table. They were mostly editions of *Women's Health*, which Valentina wasn't particularly interested in, but she took one to read in the bath anyway.

The magazine slipped out of her fingers and slid under Paula's bed. Valentina reached down to get it and her fingers caught on something else poking out from under the mattress. It was the spine of a book. A diary.

Paula's diary.

Valentina lay in bed staring at the ceiling and processing everything she had learnt about her new housemates. Turns out it was a blessing that she didn't get invited to the party after all. Paula's diary made for much more interesting reading.

Valentina could hear Paula's voice in her ear when she was reading it, as though she was sitting in front of her, curled up on her bed, confiding in her. Valentina liked the idea that she was probably the only one who knew about the details of the diary.

She heard a knock on the door, then whispers and giggles. Valentina threw on her dressing gown and opened the door. They stumbled into the flat, drunkenly loud, and disappeared straight into the kitchen. Someone turned on the radio and it blared suddenly before being turned down to a rumble.

Valentina went to join them, a wide smile on her face.

5

PRESENT DAY

The open-plan office was mortuary quiet as usual. Stacey found it odd that people didn't talk much at work. Even Brian, who sat on the other side of the partition between their desks, would rather send her an email than lean over and talk to her. Every phone call was conducted in hushed tones; mobiles were set to silent, punctuated by the occasional vibrating hum as a phone stuttered across a desk.

Stacey sat at her desk desperately resisting the urge to put her head on her forearms and go to sleep, still deep in the fight against waves of nausea, not helped by the stale air in the room. She had a pile of reports to process and the minutes from a recent management meeting to circulate, but she could feel the life draining out of her with every minute that passed. Once she had had grand ambitions of being an architect, but those dreams crumbled after the mess around graduation and now she was stuck working as an administrator for a building control office, processing planning applications for loft conversions and side extensions that she could've designed better.

That was Valentina's fault, of course. If she hadn't moved in with them, Stacey would probably be running her own architectural firm now instead of typing up reports on the tiny faults the inspectors had found with the specifications of Mrs Jones's home office.

She felt weirdly removed today, as though experiencing everything from outside her body. She stared into space, thinking again about the letter burning a hole in the lining of her cheap handbag. Derek, her boss, stopped at her desk to deposit another pile of reports in her in-tray. His round face filled her field of vision. He was a balding man with glasses that never looked clean and a remarkably bushy moustache considering the lack of hair on his head. He smelled of cheap aftershave that made Stacey's nose twitch and he walked on the balls of his feet so that it looked like he was bouncing, the heels on his shoes never really wearing down. He was also a pedant for punctuation and punctuality.

'Stacey, those minutes won't email themselves,' he said.

'Sorry,' she mumbled in reply. 'A bit of a headache brewing.'

'And here I thought you had just fancied a lie-in this morning,' he said sourly and bounced away. She flipped her middle finger at his retreating back, then noticed Simon from Accounts leaning back in his chair, scratching his crotch and watching her with amusement, so she flipped him off too.

She had often wondered about Simon's fascination with his crotch area, to the point where Linda from Accounts had nicknamed him 'Gonads' behind his back because his fingers were always adjusting, repositioning and scratching away. Stacey had first-hand experience of what was in his trousers and it wasn't substantial enough to need such constant adjustments.

She grabbed the letter from her handbag and her mug from her desk and staggered to the break room. It was a small, windowless room at the far end of the office floor with a small, round, permanently stained table and four plastic chairs, an under-counter bar fridge that largely smelt of Haroush in HR's pungent homemade lunches, a kettle, and a sink that was always full of dirty cups and spoons.

Brenda from the Survey Planning team was sitting at the table with a Tupperware in front of her, her substantial bottom and thighs spilling over the sides of the chair. Stacey lifted the kettle and noticed it was empty. Brenda had a full mug of incredibly milky tea in front of her with steam still rising from its murky surface, but she hadn't refilled the kettle after emptying it. Stacey always thought this was poor etiquette and never left a kettle empty after she had used it – a habit from back when she had lived with Bev, who would go mad if the kettle was left empty.

She gave Brenda a pointed stare as she filled the kettle, but Brenda was too busy prising the lid off her Tupperware. The sulphuric stench of hard-boiled eggs wafted over to Stacey and she felt her stomach lurch. Brenda was oblivious as she tucked into her mid-morning snack, licking her fingers in between bites.

Not for the first time in the last two days, Stacey wished she was still a smoker so that she could go and stand in the fresh air and breathe toxins into her lungs.

While she waited for the kettle to boil, she opened the letter.

Dear Stacey,

The funeral will be over now.

I hope it was good, as far as these things can be. Were Bev and Paula there? It's okay if they weren't. You are the one I wanted there the most. You were always the one I wanted to notice.

I need your help.

A favour, if you will. You owe me that after everything.

I need you to find out what happened to me. I'm scared.

I think I know what's coming.

Don't let them tell you it was an accident.

It wasn't an accident.

Find out the truth.

Love,

Valentina xx

The kettle clicked off loudly, but it was only when Brenda's chair scraped against the linoleum that Stacey jumped and landed, back in the room. Brenda was packing away her Tupperware, her meaty hands fumbling with the lid. Her dress had wormed its way into her bum crack as she bent over the table, but Stacey watched her leave the room without saying anything. She made her tea on autopilot and slumped into the still-warm chair that Brenda had vacated, spreading the letter out in front of her.

'God, it stinks in here.' Gonads burst into the room, his voice jarring. He was young and callous, but they had had some good laughs in the pub after work sometimes, despite his fascination with his own bits, and had that one quick and unsatisfying (for Stacey anyway) shag in the back of Simon's Ford Fiesta at the office Christmas party a couple of years back. The fact that he was half her age and very laddish in his humour meant that this sexual encounter would never be repeated unless there was substantial alcohol involved, but Gonads still tried it on when the drinks were flowing on a Friday night in the bar across the street from the office.

'It was Brenda,' Stacey replied.

'Jesus, has that fat cow been eating eggs again?'

'Don't call her fat,' Stacey said distractedly. 'She's on a keto diet or something.'

'No, you're right, she not fat. She's gargantuan.'

Stacey wasn't listening. She was reading the letter through again, her eyes picking out phrases like 'I'm scared' and 'not an accident'.

What was Valentina trying to tell her?

And why her? They hadn't spoken in thirty years and even when they had lived together, Valentina had been much closer with Bev than her and Paula. So why hadn't she written to Bev?

She had expected the letter to contain confessions, accusations, reparations. But this was about something else.

Simon was still droning on, talking about a gig he was going to that night at the Brixton Academy to see a band Stacey had never heard of. She picked up the letter and her tea and left him hanging mid-sentence as she walked out.

'Charming,' she heard him mutter.

She fell into her desk chair and stared at the letter, willing it to give her some answers. She grabbed her phone from her desk and started punching out a message to the funeral WhatsApp group, but before she could send it, a shadow fell over her and she turned to see Derek standing next to her again, his hands on his hips.

'Something more important to do, Stacey? Those minutes should've been circulated an hour ago. Please don't make me report this to HR. You are on thin ice as it is.'

He was of course referring to the unfortunate recent incident in which he caught her swigging from a half-bottle of vodka in the lift. It was after hours – 5.02pm to be exact – and the lift doors had glided open to reveal him standing there just as she had raised the bottle to her lips. He had reported her to HR for drinking on the job, despite her protestations that she was on her own time at that point, albeit still on company property.

The truth was Derek had been trying to get rid of her since the Christmas party three years ago when she and Simon had been filmed drunkenly impersonating the management team, including her incredibly accurate rendition of Derek's bouncy walk, which had received rapturous applause. Someone had uploaded the video to the office WhatsApp group and he had been particularly salty with her ever since. Stacey had her suspicions about who had uploaded the video. Her money was on Elaine, the receptionist, who had a weird crush on Gonads. Frankly, Elaine was welcome to him.

'Fuck off, Derek.'

He paled, said, 'Excuse me?'

The office hum quietened even more.

'I said fuck off.'

Simon had reappeared from the kitchen and she could see him gaping at her over Derek's shoulder.

'How dare you talk to me—'

'We all know you're the one who's been drinking from the office bottle of schnapps in the fridge and filling it up with water. It wasn't Sharon, even though she was pushed out for it. Next time, remember that water freezes but alcohol doesn't – and that there is a glass panel in the kitchen door. Anyone can see in at the right angle.'

Derek looked ill. 'I don't know what you're talking about.'

'Of course you don't. You also don't know anything about the small envelope of money that Mrs Jones attached to her building application last week. She called to ask if you had received her card. Nice new watch, by the way.'

'I... I...'

'Now I have had a really shitty week. As you well know, I attended the funeral of an old friend yesterday and now I have just found out she may in fact have been killed. So I will ask you once more to *fuck off*.'

Stacey swivelled around in her chair and stared at the pile of reports in front of her.

Despite its mind-crushing monotony, Stacey really needed this job, especially after how her marriage had ended. She put her head down and started working, ignoring Derek as he bounced off, probably straight to HR.

She waded through the pile of reports, not allowing herself to think about the letter any further. Her eyes constantly flicked to the clock as she mentally counted the minutes until 5pm.

However, an hour later she was called into the boss's office. Haroush was there too. Never a good sign.

'Hi, Haroush, how was your lunch today? It smelled nice,' she said.

'Um, good thanks. My wife's leftover chickpea and butternut curry,' he said without making eye contact.

'Yes, I know. I can still smell it.'

Haroush subtly sniffed at the air, blushing.

Fifteen minutes later she was gathering up her stuff after being advised that some time off may do her good, that perhaps she should take a few personal days in order to come to terms with her loss. She knew the only reason she hadn't been fired outright was because of what she had disclosed about Derek in front of the entire office floor. She actually wasn't sure about either of the things she had accused him of – she hadn't actually seen him swig from the schnapps bottle at 10am, but had seen him putting it back in the ice box and it was most definitely predominantly water when Simon had brought it out for everyone to have a drink to celebrate Elaine's birthday last week. Mrs Jones had asked about the card, but it was her nervous, quivering voice that had made Stacey wonder if there was more to it. Even so, Derek's reaction meant she had in fact been spot on.

She ignored the curious stares and hurried out of the office into what was now a soaking drizzle. She typically had no umbrella with her after this morning's panic and the thin jacket she had grabbed provided very little protection. She huddled into the bus stop, squeezing past two giggling teenagers who were bent over TikTok, and pulled out her phone to send the group message she had composed earlier. She stared at the little bubbles, willing them to reply. Rain dripped off her nose. Then she saw that Bev had started typing. She waited, but no reply came. Bev stopped typing.

By the time the bus pulled up at the stop down the road from her flat, Bev still hadn't sent a reply and Paula hadn't even read the message.

Bev sat at her kitchen island, perched on the edge of one of their incredibly uncomfortable but effortlessly stylish bar stools. She could hear the television blaring from the lounge where Malcolm was watching *Question of Sport* and another fighting to be heard from the family room where Bethany was watching Netflix. There seemed to be a lot of swearing coming from whatever she was watching, but Bev didn't have the energy for a fight about the suitability of Bethany's entertainment choices.

She was still a little hungover and worn out from yesterday's activities. The dinner dishes sat around her, congealed lasagne sticking to the oven dish and plates stacked near but not in the dishwasher. She'd made the lasagne earlier to make up to Malcolm for his cheese and biscuits dinner the night before, but while Jasper had eaten it greedily, Bethany had complained about the mushrooms she'd found in it and Malcolm had been annoyed because he'd apparently already had pasta for lunch that day at work.

She was nursing an ill-advised coffee, despite it being way too late in the evening for her to be able to metabolise caffeine, as she stared at the message she'd received earlier from Stacey. It was a little garbled – something about another letter from Valentina and that her death may have been suspicious.

She wasn't sure what to say – or even what to think about all of this. She had started to reply earlier, but then Malcolm had arrived home and now she was pondering what it was Stacey would want to hear. The truth was they hadn't spoken to Valentina for decades and knew nothing about her life – or death. Bev knew very little about Stacey these days too. She hadn't given very much away yesterday. She knew something had felt *off*, but she also realised they wouldn't all slot back into friendship as though thirty years hadn't passed, as though they hadn't all parted ways after something despicable had happened. None of them could expect to walk away from that and just get on with their lives. There was always a price to pay.

She would admit to no one but herself that she had been overwhelmingly relieved to hear about Valentina's death. She trusted Stacey and Paula to keep their promise, but Valentina had always been the unknown entity, the stray thread that could lead to it all unravelling. With her gone, it meant that what happened could stay firmly in the past, buried where it belonged, and no one would find out about what they had had to do, the lies she had had to tell.

Yes, dead and buried. Just like Valentina.

Paula grabbed an ice pack from the box she kept in her bedside table and waited for it to grow cold enough to rest on her rapidly swelling knuckles. There were only two ice packs left in the box. She would need to order some more. At this rate, it might be best to set up a recurring order on Amazon.

Sue had just left for the gym, a kick-boxing class tonight, so Paula had an hour or so to herself. She winced as she flexed her left hand. Sue had told her not to be so clumsy, said that she was possibly the most injury-prone person Sue had ever met. She'd just had her hand in the wrong place at the wrong time when Sue had pushed past the drawer, when it had slammed into her knuckles with enough force to leave painful bruising.

She lay back on the bed and sipped at a bottle of beer. She knew she had to reply to Stacey's message, but she had lacked the energy all day. Thinking about it hurt her head.

Paula had to admit the letters were creepy, but the Valentina that Paula remembered had always had a proclivity for melodrama. What Stacey expected them to do about it now was anyone's guess – and Paula was at a loss as to why Stacey wanted to do anything at all. They were all very clear when they parted ways that what they had done would never be spoken of again.

She sent back a brief 'lovely to see you' reply to the group, completely avoiding the issue of Valentina altogether, then lay back against the pillows and grabbed her beer again, her brain whirling.

She flexed her fingers and looked at the aubergine bruises thoughtfully. The little nest egg she had been collecting quietly over the last year needed to grow a bit quicker. It was time she disappeared for good.

It's easy to find people these days. Not many can resist the pull of social media. The opportunity to tell a story, to create a version of yourself that you wish was true when in reality your life is a shit show of disappointment. And then you die.

Their Facebook pages haven't been updated in a while, but no one uses Facebook any more. It's all about Instagram these days for the forty-somethings. Tiny little squares; snapshots of a perfect life. You can glean a lot of information from those profiles. A door number and a location from an 'outfit of the day' snap. The logo on a child's school uniform. Tagging their favourite local restaurant in a 'date night' post. A birthday when they post about that beautiful bouquet of flowers delivered to their door to brighten up an otherwise grey and rainy Monday. Even down to the street they live on and the name of their first pet when they are filling out those pointless quizzes to see what their porn star name would be.

It all makes it easier for a stranger to build up a picture of their lives from the details they don't know you have.

Facebook may not be their first choice of socials, but they created their profiles when they were less worried about security, so the old camera roll can be a treasure trove of hidden snippets of information.

I scroll through each social media page, writing down the little details that will be useful, and I notice patterns emerging. When they tend to take their holidays; what their daily routines are; if they are still in touch with each other. Apart from an annual 'happy birthday' post and a few likes, they are not in touch.

Paula is the hardest to read, the least likely to share, but even she is not a closed book. I know which hockey team she plays for, the name of her wife's drumming workshop business and that she likes to share memes that make her sound like she is hilarious and a joker rather than actual photos of her reality. Like a comedian hiding their depression behind a stand-up routine.

Yes, I found each and every one of them – and it was actually fun.

But not as much fun as what's to come.

6

AUTUMN 1992

Valentina sipped at her tea in the intense, early-morning quiet. She was the only one awake. When she had come out of her room, she noticed that Bev had left her bedroom door ajar. Valentina had crept in and watched her while she slept, her mouth open, one arm flung above her head and a foot sticking out of the duvet. She looked so peaceful. Valentina had reached out, let her hand hover over her face, a moment in still life. Then Bev had snorted, a half snore half cough, and rolled over, and Valentina left. The door to Paula and Stacey's room was closed, but she imagined them in their single beds – Paula laid out like a starfish and Stacey curled into a tight ball maybe.

A couple of days had passed since Kevin's party. They had sat up talking until the early hours that night, the three of them telling Valentina about all the cool people they had met and sharing snogging stories – well, Stacey anyway, who Valentina was starting to realise didn't think it was a good night out unless it ended with her tongue down someone's throat. They finished each other's sentences, speaking in partial phrases, a shared history finishing their thoughts for them. Valentina felt like she was poking at their bubble from the outside, hoping that it would burst so that they would let her in.

Last night Stacey had gone out with someone she had met the other night, but Bev and Paula had stayed in. Valentina made dinner for them – chilli, rice, all the extras to go with it – and they ate together, laughed, chatted. She was annoyed with herself for burning the onions because she could taste a bitterness in the background of the chilli, but the other two seemed to enjoy it, ate all of it.

They'd chatted easily, the conversation evolving naturally when Stacey wasn't there to make everything about her. Valentina had kept quiet while they talked about their families, where they'd come from and the people who were most important to them, but she thirstily soaked up the details of what they had shared. The fact that Paula had controlling, conservative parents with whom she had very little in common and had used running from an early age to find her freedom, but Stacey came from a tight-knit family with protective brothers and working-class parents who were beyond proud of their only daughter going to university. Bev came from a more affluent family, with an uptight older sister and a childhood of family holidays in the south of France. She was still close to her mother in particular and spoke to her nearly every day. Valentina had heard her on the phone, telling her the most mundane details of university life while her mother lapped it up.

So Valentina had created a rich childhood tapestry of her own that included a caring mother who had taught her to cook when she was little, letting her stand on a stool to see into the pan, or would brush her hair endlessly, her hands gentle and soothing. When Paula had spoken about her father's disinterest in her choice of university course, Valentina had painted a caricature of an overprotective father who supported her financially so that she could focus on her studies.

She found it was easier to lie than to tell them the truth. The truth would only make them pity her. And the more she lied, the more she believed it was actually true. The image of an Italian mother wearing an apron stained with tomato holding her up as she stirred the pasta sauce was one that had played in her mind so many times that she was almost convinced it had become reality. They didn't need to know the truth, did they?

Stacey's name had come up time and time again, even though she wasn't there. Stacey had been the catalyst in the three of them becoming friends when they were little, stopping someone from bullying Bev for her glasses and playing football in the boys' team with Paula so that she wasn't the only girl. They sanctified her – and it made Valentina surly. She had snapped at them, saying that Stacey must have some faults, that no one was as perfect as Stacey appeared, and the atmosphere had cooled. Bev and Paula had made excuses, saying they both had reading to complete before lectures started next week, and had withdrawn into Paula's room, closing the door on her so that she was left with just the sounds of them laughing, playing music and talking through the wall.

The problem was Valentina understood why they were so smitten with Stacey. It wasn't just her dry, northern humour. She had an allure that Valentina could only dream of having, a way of making everyone in the room notice she was there, as though she glimmered with possibility. Valentina had caught herself overcompensating around Stacey, trying to outdo her or draw the attention away from her sparkling cerulean blue eyes. But she needed to tone it down a bit.

Valentina took her mug of tea back to bed with her and curled her toes into the sheet, needing to feel the comfort of the still-warm cotton.

She heard the toilet flush. Someone was awake.

She threw on her dressing gown and headed back into the kitchen. She had already washed all the dishes from last night and put everything away.

The perfect housemate.

She grabbed a clean mug from the draining board.

Paula walked in, her hair on end, yawning widely but already in her running kit.

'Oh, hey,' she said, pulling up sharply. 'God, you're up early.'

'So are you. Cuppa? Lovely morning, isn't it?'

'Why are you so chirpy?'

Valentina had worked out which were their favourite mugs. Paula liked a big, chunky mug in the morning but a thin, porcelain one in the afternoon. Bev used the same mug all day, liked to save on the washing up, while Stacey wasn't fussy about the kind of mug she used, but would only use it once, leaving the dirty ones on any available surface.

Paula propped herself up in the corner of the breakfast bar, her lily-white legs spread out on the bench in front of her. Valentina could make out the palest of fuzz on them, so different to the dark brown fur on Valentina's legs that she had to shave every couple of days to keep tamed.

She put the cup of tea in front of Paula. 'Did you sleep well?'

'Yeah, not bad, got a bit of a headache though. That's what woke me up. And Stace was ranting in her sleep again. Don't know who she was fighting in her dreams, but whoever it was took a good kicking last night.'

'I don't mind swapping and sharing with her if you want your own space.'

'Oh, no, I don't mind. I'm used to her,' she said quickly. A flush crept into Paula's cheeks.

Valentina sat down opposite Paula, the bench cold beneath the backs of her legs. 'You two have been friends a long time.'

'Yes, we have.' She slurped at her tea.

'It must be nice to know someone so well, be so close to someone,' Valentina said.

'I guess.' Paula frowned, stared into her tea.

'She sure likes the boys though, huh?'

Paula looked up sharply. 'What do you mean by that?'

'I dunno. She just likes meeting boys...'

'Yeah, well, it's just a bit of fun. It's harmless.'

An awkward silence fell between them. 'I was thinking that maybe we should go out tonight – to the pub. What do you think?' Valentina said hastily.

'I don't know, I've had a full-on week and lectures start up again on Monday. I've got loads of pre-reading to do.'

'It's my birthday.' The lie jumped into her mouth before she knew she was going to say it.

'Is it?' Paula broke into a smile. 'Happy birthday!'

'What's going on?' Stacey sloped in, her long hair coiled into a messy bun on the top of her head like a pineapple crown, her mouth pulling wide in a yawn. 'Put the kettle on, Val.'

'It's Val's birthday! We are going to the pub tonight,' Paula said.

Stacey started bouncing on her toes, her pyjama top lifting in time. 'Damn right we are!'

Valentina smiled. Telling the lies was easy. The difficulty came in keeping track and maintaining all of them.

The pub was loud, smoky, perfect. Paula flung open the double doors like she was entering a saloon. A wave of heat engulfed them. It was packed with students getting to know each other before lectures kicked off. A band was setting up to the right of the bar on a tiny, raised platform that wished it could be called a stage. A man in a leather waistcoat and too tight jeans was plugging in an amp, a cigarette dangling from his lips. He looked up at the sound of the doors banging open and caught Valentina's eye, then noticed Stacey behind her, threw her a wink and went back to fiddling with the cables.

Valentina stared at him for a moment, as though imprinting him on her memory. 'So he's creepy,' she said to Stacey.

'Harmless and old, I reckon,' she replied, completely unfazed by his attention.

Paula strode straight over to the bar and ordered a round of shots. She handed them out, saying, 'Let's get this birthday party started!' and knocked it back. She was in a strange mood, prickly and contrary. The walk through the woods had been tense, with Stacey talking endlessly about her date the night before until Paula had told her to shut up about it, about *him*. The conversation had then ground to a halt, with only the trees whispering at them in the breeze and the water laughing and gurgling at their awkwardness. Paula was scowling when they emerged from the trees, but Stacey had prodded her sharply with her elbow, stuck out her tongue and made Paula laugh, her annoyance forgotten as quickly as that.

Valentina could feel the tequila shot burn her throat and her eyes start to water. Someone shoved a wedge of lemon in her hand and she sucked on it, the sourness making her wince.

Bev, Paula and Stacey cheered and threw their arms around each other. Valentina muscled in next to Bev and they all danced on the spot for a minute.

'Right, my round. Wine? Or something else?' Valentina said. She whipped out her father's credit card. He had told her it was for emergencies only, insisting now was the time for her to learn about money and independence. But surely your pretend birthday with your friends constituted an emergency, right? He wanted her to fit in, find her place. He wanted things to work out this time. Mostly so that he could wash his hands of her with a clear conscience.

'Wine! Definitely. I don't think I can handle pints today – I am so bloated with my period,' Stacey said. Valentina had noticed this need for the three of them to share even the most intimate details about themselves. They didn't even close the bathroom door, just shouted out conversations while they peed. She couldn't fathom it. She had never been that open with anyone. Then again, no one had ever been that open with her either.

'Ugh, I know, me too,' Valentina said, although her period was still two weeks away. Stacey smiled at her in solidarity.

Valentina ordered a bottle of pinot grigio. She didn't think they were fussy about what they drank, but her father had at least taught her some things about wine. Of course, the choice in a place like this would be limited, but the pinot looked like it was the best from a bad list. He would be horrified. But she hadn't spoken to him in weeks, so what did it matter.

She left the credit card behind the bar as a tab and ducked and swerved back to where the girls were standing. 'I've started a tab – tonight is on me. I phoned my father earlier and he insisted on paying for our drinks. A birthday treat. He's very generous that way,' she said.

'Bloody hell, if I'd known that, you could've bought that first tequila round!' Paula said. 'Cheers to Mr... hang on, what's your surname again?'

'Mackenzie,' she said in a quiet voice.

'That's not Italian.'

'My mother was Italian. My dad is Scottish.' That was the first time any of them had actually bothered to ask her surname.

'Ah, hence the accent. Right, well thanks, Mr Mackenzie. And happy birthday, Valentina!'

Bev was looking around. 'We need a table.'

'We'll never get one tonight,' Stacey said.

Bev looked pained. 'I don't want to stand all night.' Valentina was quickly realising that Bev was not one for overexerting herself physically.

Valentina noticed two girls sitting at a large table next to where the band was setting up. She passed the wine bottle to Bev and said, 'Wait, I'll sort it.'

She walked over to the girls. 'Hey,' she said. 'Um, I was wondering if I could ask you a favour.'

They looked at her curiously, but said nothing.

'My friend over there—' She pointed at Bev, who was wearing another pair of ridiculously large glasses that made her eyes look huge like Bambi and was clutching her waist like she had a stitch. 'She's just found out she's... well, she's not well. It doesn't sound good – operations and stuff – so we've brought her out with us tonight to try and distract her, but she's struggling with standing up for so long. I was wondering if we could use this table, you know, since she's not feeling great after her – *chemo*.' She whispered the word and tried to make her eyes as big as Bev's.

'Oh my God, I'm so sorry to hear that. Of course, take it! The poor thing,' one of the girls said, her hand clamped to her heart. They scrambled to their feet and Valentina called the others over.

As Bev walked past them, one of the girls grabbed her arm and said to her, 'I hope you're okay. Be strong. Nothing is permanent and this will pass. You'll be okay.'

'Er, thanks,' Bev said, confused.

As they sat on the still-warm seats, Bev said, 'What did you tell them?'

Valentina shrugged. 'I may have implied that you were ill, might have mentioned chemo.'

'What? Bloody hell, that's not funny!' Bev looked horrified.

'No, but they gave up the table, didn't they?' She thought they'd be pleased, but Bev looked shocked.

'Oh lighten up, Bev,' Stacey said. 'It's just a little white lie.'

'Yeah, but you don't joke about that kind of thing.'

Valentina put a hand on Bev's arm. 'It's fine, my mother died of cancer, so I have a free cancer card to play anytime I want. Wine?'

Bev frowned, but before she could say anything else, the man in the leather waistcoat was tapping on a microphone. The feedback screeched through the room, raising a loud groan from the audience.

'Alright, alright, settle down, you fuckers. So you have the pleasure of our company for tonight. We'll do requests, but only if we like them – and only if we know the words.' He chuckled. 'But first we'll start with one we've chosen.'

A bald black man slung a guitar strap over his shoulder and a man with long, dirty-looking brown hair sat down behind a mixing deck. They broke into a loud version of 'Living Next Door to Alice' and a small crowd cheered.

Valentina looked at Bev. She was no longer frowning. She was singing along loudly, the little lie forgotten. Valentina relaxed and started to sing along too, pretending to know the words.

She felt like she was being watched. Her eyes scanned the bar and came to rest on a blond-haired guy standing on the far side of the bar with three friends. He was openly staring at their table, a half-smile on his face as people talked around him, clapped him on the back, bought him a drink. Valentina was thrilled to realise he was looking at her. Then a group of people moved into her line of sight and when they'd passed, the guy had turned away.

Long before she wanted it to end, the lights had come on and the chairs were being stacked onto the tables. Leather Waistcoat Man was unplugging his kit and the barman was going around telling everyone to 'finish up, come on, we've all got homes to go to' and 'fuck off home, you lot'.

Paula groaned and pleaded for one more round, the syllables of her words slurring together, but he laughed and said, 'Next time, darling. Finish those and get yourselves off home.' She'd had a lot to drink tonight, had constantly egged the others on. Only Valentina had matched her drink for drink in solidarity though.

Valentina shared out the last dregs of the wine. Bev said, 'Ugh, no, I can't,' and poured the last few mouthfuls into Valentina's glass instead. Stacey did the same until Valentina had a fuller glass than anyone else.

'Anyway, it's your birthday,' Stacey said when Valentina started to object.

'Yes – and I have chemo tomorrow,' Bev said and everyone laughed raucously.

'Just you and me, kid,' Paula said and picked up her own glass, which had only a mouthful in it.

'Ladies, come on,' the barman said again, sounding annoyed. Valentina saw they were the only ones left. Even the band had packed up and was ready to go. Leather Waistcoat Guy was leaning against the bar, watching them with a creepy smile on his face. His bandmates were heading out the door.

'Right then, down in one,' Paula said and stood up.

Valentina stood too quickly, felt everything tilt and staggered against the table.

'Whoa,' Bev said. 'Maybe you shouldn't.'

'Oh come on, Bev, if you can't get pissed on your birthday…' Paula said and turned back to Valentina.

Valentina felt like her face was melting and drooping. Paula was swimming in front of her, like someone was adjusting the focus on the room. She looked down at the three glasses she could see in front of her and reached for the middle one. It turned out to be the right one. She necked it back. They all cheered and clapped, even Bev, who said, 'You are insane!'

Valentina felt special, accepted, loved, sick.

She turned and vomited on the floor under the table.

'Shit, time to go,' Stacey said and grabbed Valentina's arm as they all raced from the bar before the barman saw the surprise she had left for him.

The cold night air slapped Valentina across both cheeks, clearing her head a little. Stacey and Paula were cackling with laughter while Bev held Valentina up as they weaved down the street. Then Paula said, 'Bugger, your card is still behind the bar. We'll have to go back.'

'I'll go,' Stacey said. 'I'll just scribble any old thing – they can see I'm pissed. They won't check the signature.'

Valentina leant against the cold brick wall, then slid down to the pavement, her legs flung out in front of her. Bev and Paula were laughing about something someone had said, but Valentina couldn't focus on the words, which darted around like obscure song lyrics.

After five minutes Stacey had still not returned. 'Where the hell is she?' Bev muttered.

'Maybe she's been done for forging a signature,' Valentina said and giggled, then hiccupped.

The doors to the bar opened and Stacey emerged, but she was not alone. Leather Waistcoat Man was with her, his arm around her shoulder.

Stacey was smiling, but to Valentina his arm was a lead weight on her shoulder, compressing her while Stacey twisted to get out of his grip.

'Hey there, ladies. How about I walk you home?'

'No, thanks, we're okay,' Paula said, rolling her eyes. 'Come on, Val, up you get.'

'Need a hand there?' he said, smirking.

'No,' Valentina said and stumbled to her feet, using the wall for leverage.

He turned back to Stacey. 'Come on, let's go back to mine. My flatmate has some friends over – we can carry on the party.'

Stacey looked over at them, but Paula shook her head subtly. 'No, thanks, we're done for the night,' Stacey said.

'Well, I think I should make sure you get home safely at least.'

Valentina could feel familiar, red-hot anger build inside her, the redness rushing over her skin and in front of her eyes. She lurched at him and pushed him hard. Caught by surprise, he fell onto the pavement on his back.

'She said no!' she shouted at him, punctuating every

word with a hard kick to his ribs with her pointed boots. He rolled around, crying out in pain, then covered his head as she aimed a kick at his face, but she was off balance and stumbled backwards before her foot could connect.

'Val! Val! Stop!' Bev was pulling at her, hindering her from getting another kick in.

'Crazy bitch!' Leather Waistcoat Man said from where he was still in a foetal position on the pavement.

She lunged for him again and he flinched just as the barman came out of the pub to see what the commotion was. He initially looked in the wrong direction, away from them, so Paula grabbed Valentina's arms and said, 'Run.'

And they did. They ran until their lungs burned. Valentina's head cleared a little, the red fog retreating. Sweat prickled the skin beneath her sparkly top and her breath was acidic and hot in her throat. They ran until they were safe under the cover of the trees, until they could lean against a tree trunk, panting and sweaty, camouflaged by the darkness of the woods.

Stacey was the first one to laugh. And once she started, she couldn't stop until they were all laughing.

When they caught their breath, Stacey looked at Valentina and said, 'You're mad, but thanks.'

Valentina smiled. 'I've always got your back.'

7

PRESENT DAY

Another day, another morning waking up on the lumpy sofa with the cat sitting on her chest and her head thumping in time to her racing heart. Palpitations; swollen tongue; the smell of stale cigarettes tainting her hair.

Stacey groaned, pushed Nemo aside and sat up. Her foot kicked an empty vodka bottle and it rolled away under the coffee table. She squinted at the greasy pizza box, Coke cans and overflowing ashtray on the table, felt her stomach lurch. She closed her eyes, breathed deeply and slowly. Satisfied that her stomach seemed to be okay again, she opened her eyes once more. She was still fully clothed. Her mouth was like sandpaper, her throat scratchy from the cigarettes, her eyes dried into husks.

Nemo had moved to curl up next to her, his tail wrapping around him and his face tucked into his paws. She reached out a shaky claw of a hand and stroked his soft fur. The cat ignored her; if anything, he curled up even tighter. She went into the bedroom with heavy legs, took off her clothes and tossed them into the pile on the carpet. She needed a shower. A cold one might shock the hangover out of her. It had worked yesterday. The tiles were blissfully cold beneath her bare feet, but she resisted the urge to follow Nemo's example and curl up on them. She sat heavily on the toilet and rested her head in her hands. Her hair was pungent with stale smoke.

Flushing the toilet, she stood in front of the basin and stared at the woman glaring at her from the mirror. She had to stop doing this. The drinking. The junk she was putting in her body. She had spots on her chin and there was nothing on earth that would convince her to step on a scale because she knew from the roll above the elastic of her knickers that she would be even more disgusted at herself if she did. Every morning she swore to herself in this very mirror that today would be different, that she would take back control, and every night she berated herself for failing again.

She went to sleep last night with images of Valentina tattooing the inside of her eyelids. She knew what she had done, had managed to squash the guilt into a tiny box and put it high on a mental shelf, but the box had fallen off the shelf and the guilt was seeping out.

She sighed, washed her hands and splashed cold water on her face, then grabbed her dressing gown from the back of the bathroom door and went to make a strong coffee. The shower could wait.

The milk was sour. She could smell it as soon as she took the lid off the bottle. What day was it? Had the milkman been? She went to the front door, slid the chain back and looked out onto the front step. Her milk bottles were there, but one had been knocked over and there were tiny holes pierced in the foil cap where a bird had taken the opportunity to steal the unclaimed milk.

As she bent to pick up the bottles, she noticed someone standing across the street in a baseball cap and a baggy hoodie, watching. She pulled her stained, threadbare dressing gown a little tighter, even though it didn't close properly anymore, grabbed the milk bottles and slammed the door on the spectator.

She went over to the lounge window and peeked through the blinds. The person was walking away casually.

With a cup of coffee in hand, Stacey sat at the kitchen table and opened her laptop. The battery was flat. Of course it was. The last time she'd used the laptop was when she had been drunkenly stalking Alan and his girlfriend on Facebook last night and it had died before she could post an ill-advised comment on their latest #datenight post. The charger was plugged into the socket next to her bed. She decided to have that cold shower instead. It might clear her head a bit.

The water was ice cold when she first stepped under the spray. It pelted her upturned face like hailstones, making her inhale sharply. She turned around and allowed her back to be attacked, feeling the fog in her brain begin to clear. After a few minutes the water warmed until it was almost too hot. She washed her hair and took her time getting dressed, her movements hindered by long periods of staring into space.

Eventually she opened the blinds and pushed up the sash window in the lounge, letting in the warm air and the cacophony of the street outside. This wasn't a quiet, middle-class end of town like she imagined it was where Bev lived.

This was a busy, loud, caustic part of town where children cried, sirens screamed and car horns were thumped in anger. She wanted to be outside in the noise, not in here, alone with the quiet. She threw on the first pair of shoes she could find, a tight-fitting pair of dirty trainers that lay stranded in the hallway.

There were people everywhere. She weaved between the bodies, bumping elbows, avoiding pushchairs. She passed a stall on the pavement selling coffee and sausage rolls. She bought both. Next to it was a flower stall, full of yellows and purples and pinks. She couldn't afford flowers right now. Instead, she pulled out her phone and took a photo, smiling to herself. Then on a whim she sent it to Bev and Paula, wishing them a lovely weekend. She wanted them to think she was okay, not splintered into tiny pieces.

Besides, now that Valentina was gone, there was nothing to keep them from staying in touch surely? The threat had passed. The witch was dead.

The bright yellow and blue of a Lidl logo loomed ahead of her on the other side of the road. She had no real food in her flat, could do with buying something vaguely healthy, especially if she actually wanted to make good on her promise to sort herself out. Her phone buzzed – Bev had responded to her photo with a red heart and a hug emoji. She glanced to her right while taking a big gulp of her coffee before stepping out into the road. At once she heard the screech of brakes and turned to see a bicycle swerving around her, missing her by centimetres. Stacey jumped back onto the pavement, her heart pounding. Her coffee cup fell at her feet, coffee splashing onto her trainers.

A skinny man in Lycra, his eyes obscured by dark,

alien-shaped sunglasses beneath the cycling helmet on his head, started swearing loudly at her. She could feel the anger emanating from him in red-hot waves as he shook his glove-encased fist at her.

'You fucking bitch! Look where you're going! You'll hurt someone. Jesus Christ! What's the matter with you?'

'I-I'm sorry,' Stacey said. 'I didn't see you.'

'Fuck's sake. Too busy looking at your fucking phone. Stupid bitch.' He tore off again.

An elderly woman standing next to her said, 'You alright, love?'

Stacey could feel unnecessary tears hovering on her eyelashes. 'I... I didn't see him,' she said lamely.

'Don't worry, love, he was going a hundred miles an hour on that thing. Way too fast in my opinion. No harm done, eh?' She smiled at Stacey kindly, her grey hair framing a soft, round face. Then she looked both ways and crossed over the road in a slow shuffle, heading towards the supermarket.

Stacey stood for another moment, still shaken and now embarrassed, her earlier momentary contentment shattered. She looked down at the spilled coffee and reached down to pick up the cup. She threw it in the bin next to her and took a deep breath before checking a few times that there was nothing else coming.

In the supermarket, her hands shaking, she filled a basket with fruit and vegetables that would probably go off in the fridge long before they were eaten, wholemeal bread, a chicken to roast and a few ready meals, before throwing in some chocolate and crisps, because everyone deserved a treat. Her hand hovered over the bottles of wine, her fingers even curling around the neck of one, but she let go, walked away. She was peering into the ice cream freezer trying to decide between cookie dough or caramel swirl when she noticed the elderly woman reaching into the freezer next to her for a packet of frozen Yorkshire puddings.

The woman nodded at her and said, 'Ice cream makes everything feel better,' before wandering away with her basket. Stacey smiled and exhaled, noticing how tense she was holding her shoulders. When she was younger, she would've taken the cyclist apart with her razor-sharp tongue, maybe even have stepped out into the street and pushed him off his bike for calling her a bitch. But these days, she was left a quivering mess, tears in her eyes and shaking like a frightened puppy.

It was pathetic. She was pathetic.

It made her think of Valentina again, of the four of them and how full of life they had been, all big dreams and unstoppable spirit. How Valentina could turn volatile at the snap of her fingers.

Then of course there was yesterday when she had told Derek to fuck off. Channelling her inner Val after all this time.

She went back to the wine section, grabbed two bottles of cheap rosé and headed for the tills, hoping her credit card wouldn't crack under the strain.

Valentina's Facebook page could've been anyone's for what little information there was. Stacey sat with a glass of the wine at her elbow, loose tracksuit bottoms on and her feet now bare. She'd taken off her bra and tied up her hair, then settled herself on the couch. The volume on the television was turned down low, just enough to keep her company but not enough to distract her.

The profile detailed the university Valentina attended, which she knew of course because she had been there too, but it didn't detail the one she had gone to before joining them in their last year. It had seemed curious at the time that someone would choose to transfer in their final year or that someone with that much family money had chosen to flat-share, but they'd never pushed her on it. The profile then went on to say she had worked for a small PR company shortly after she graduated, but there was no other work information after that. Considering the PR agency had Mackenzie in its name, she assumed her father had owned it as part of his portfolio of companies and had given her a job.

There were a number of photos posted sporadically over the years of various places she had visited: Dubai, Bali, Singapore, Australia. All of the beautifully captured photos were of landscapes and famous landmarks or carefully placed cocktails; no faces and no names tagged.

On occasion, various men featured but rarely the same man twice. There was a Greg, Justin, Paul – all young and good-looking in a suntanned, sporty way. Then there were photos of her race numbers for various half and full marathons, which baffled Stacey, who couldn't imagine Valentina doing anything sporty. She had never seemed the type – could dance for hours but wouldn't run to catch a bus.

Still, people can change, can't they?

Some more than others.

Thinking about Valentina now, Stacey realised what little they had known about her, how everything about her seemed to contradict itself, like she was one of those folded paper fortune-teller puzzles. If you lifted one corner, there would be a different answer to what was under the next.

After the last holiday in Australia some years ago, the photos on Facebook stopped. Not unusual – most people had stopped using Facebook and moved on to other social media platforms, their profiles left behind like memorials.

Then posts began again just after she died. Apparently grieving friends heartbroken by her passing, hoping that she was finally at rest, complete with angel emojis. If they were so heartbroken, why weren't they at the funeral?

One post in particular caught Stacey's eye. Someone called Tania Bennett had posted:

Valentina was a force of nature who will be missed by all of us. I hope whoever did this is found and punished. Rest in peace, angel.

Stacey looked at Tania Bennett's profile, but it was private. The name seemed vaguely familiar though. Then she checked her phone and saw that Tania Bennett was the person who had sent her the details of the funeral. Still, there was something about the name that bothered her – a connection that was just out of reach like a forgotten song lyric. Stacey zoomed into the profile photo, but couldn't see the face close enough to identify them. Valentina had had occasional friends from her classes, but not many. Her primary social group had been the three of them.

It was a weird thing to say though, wasn't it?

What the hell had happened?

She thought about sending Tania a message, but didn't know what to say.

Hello, you don't know me but how did Valentina die? Seemed a bit blunt and upsetting if Tania had been a friend.

Valentina's Instagram was more of the same nondescript posts – no selfies but a lot of photos of local scenery, a few shots of meals out and random items of interest, like a heart-shaped rock, a carrot that looked like it had a willy, that kind of thing. Valentina didn't seem to have a Twitter account, unless she had a random username that Stacey couldn't identify.

Stacey then did a quick Google search for Valentina Mackenzie, but nothing came up other than a short news post the year after they graduated about her father passing away. Her father had bankrolled everything – her education, her living costs, giving her an allowance. She could've afforded somewhere much nicer than their cramped and damp flat. She had thrown cash at them like sweets and they had gratefully accepted, especially Stacey who didn't have the luxury of a rich daddy.

But all the money in the world won't make someone genuinely like you. In the beginning they had actually liked Valentina for who she was, not because of her generosity with her father's money, and by the end it wasn't money that had caused their happy foursome to implode.

It was Valentina herself.

Bev wiped her soapy hands on a tea towel as she spoke

quietly into her airpods while she tidied up after dinner. She had called Stacey, worried that she was still fixating on Valentina's death.

'Stace, have you had anything to eat today?'

'What's that got to do with anything?' Stacey's Geordie accent was more astringent when she spoke to Bev, familiarity stripping the artifice from her voice.

'I just...' She couldn't say she thought Stacey was pissed again, although her words were softened and rounded, running into each other.

'Yes, I had a sausage roll with my wine, Bev. Okay?'

Bev sighed. 'You should come over and have dinner with us one night, meet the kids.' She watched the bubbles swirling and popping, swirled her index finger through the white foam as she listened.

'What? Now that the wicked witch is dead, we can come out to play?'

'No, that's not... hold on a minute.'

Bethany had strolled into the kitchen, her eyes barely lifting from the screen clutched in her hands. She shuffled over to the fridge in chunky, pink, fluffy slippers. She pulled a tub of vanilla ice cream from the freezer and grabbed a spoon, using her tiny hips to slam the drawer closed. Bev narrowed her eyes. Bethany had exams coming up, but there seemed to be no revision going on. A lot of screen time, her face glued to her phone as she chatted away on Snapchat, posing and pouting for the camera. Bev had tried to talk to her about it, find out who she was talking to, giggling with, sending posed photos to, but there was no discussion to be had. Just a lot of sighs, withering glares and slammed doors. Jasper had said something about her 'linking' with someone new, which he explained meant she was chatting to someone she liked online, but that they hadn't actually met up yet. It was all so alien to Bev now, the language, the dating rules, the technology. A reminder of just how old and out of touch she was.

She wanted to tell Bethany not to make the mistakes she had made, to make something of her life, to not end up forever wondering what might have happened if she had made different choices.

But when did a teenage girl ever listen to her middle-aged mother? They always knew better.

Once Bethany had shuffled from the room again, Bev said, 'I'm just worried about you, that's all. I don't understand why you aren't letting this go.'

There was silence from Stacey. Except for the sharp inhalation of a cigarette, Bev would think she had hung up. There was definitely something going on with her. Bev had been surprised at the physical change in her. She'd always been a bit rough around the edges, not surprising considering her childhood, but she'd hidden the crassness behind a pretty mask that she put on from a jar every morning. Now though, there seemed to be a sense that the seams had unravelled.

The Stacey of their younger years was always so confident, funny, sparkling, the centre of attention. She had thrived on it, loved having everyone dancing to her tune. She'd hidden behind the party girl persona, never really letting anyone but Bev and Paula get close enough to know her.

The Stacey of now had collapsed in on herself, quieter, the sparkle diminished. Bev had seen that at the funeral, not to mention noticing the amount she had drunk. Bev had had a lot herself and had felt terrible on it; Stacey had seemed comfortable with the overindulgence.

Then Stacey said, 'These days vodka is the only thing that helps me sleep,' in a quiet voice. 'I say sleep, but I pass out really, like a sad alcoholic. It's still rest, I suppose. I've been like this since... *then*. There were pills for a while, but I... well, *Alan* thought I was taking too many.'

Bev thought she was finished, but she wasn't.

'It's the images,' she continued. 'I can't get the images from my head, Bev, can't wash the blood from my hands.'

Paula wandered along hand in hand with Sue, their palms sweating uncomfortably, but it was Stacey she was thinking about. She'd seen Stacey's message with the flowers and was pleased to think she was in a better frame of mind today. Yesterday Stacey had sounded a little unhinged. Paula had just dismissed her, but maybe she shouldn't have. The idea of spending time with her again after all these years made her feel equal parts nervous and hopeful.

Sue was saying something to her. 'Sorry, what did you say?'

'I said do you want vegetable fajitas or tofu stir-fry tonight?' Sue said impatiently. The vegan market was busy, with hipsters wearing floaty yoga pants selling everything from cheese to bamboo toothbrushes. Sue was in her element, tasting this and buying that, handing the bags to Paula to carry. The truth was Paula wanted a burger with fries and lashings of ketchup, but Sue's latest obsession with veganism meant that no meat would be passing her lips anytime soon. She certainly wouldn't be pointing out to Sue that she had actually put on weight since they had adopted veganism, all that fake cheese, avocado and almonds proving rather calorific. And the fact that when Paula told Sue she was at the gym, she was actually sitting in a MacDonald's, relishing the burger as much as the peace and quiet.

'Let's go stir-fry,' Paula said. Fajitas would mean more avocado and she didn't think she could take any more.

Sue stopped in her tracks and turned to glare at her. People had to navigate around them, but Sue stood rooted to the spot. 'What's going on with you? You've been weird ever since that funeral.'

Paula frowned. 'Nothing, I'm just not feeling myself. Might be coming down with something.'

Sue glared for a few seconds more, then sighed dramatically and carried on walking, her grip tighter. Paula's phone buzzed from her back pocket and she pulled it out to see another message from Stacey on the group chat.

Been looking at Val's socials – do either of you remember someone called Tania Bennett? xx

Paula glanced at Sue, then slid her phone back into her pocket. The name Bennett seemed familiar, but she couldn't think why. She chewed on her lip, throwing the name around her head. Then Sue was pinching her on the arm to get her attention and dragging her towards a stall selling tie-dyed kaftans, so she put it out of her mind. She was yanked past someone in a Boston Red Sox baseball cap and a baggy hoodie, despite the warmth of the day, and the hair on her arms stood on end as the stranger's hand brushed hers. Paula stopped in her tracks and turned back, but all she caught was the retreating back of the hoodie as it disappeared into the foot traffic.

Sue was talking in her voluminous voice to the stall owner about her recipe for baked tofu with sweet chilli sauce, so Paula pulled out her phone again and checked the home screen. The message was still there, willing her to answer.

As she chewed on the inside of her mouth, a series of notifications rattled through from Instagram. Odd in that she hadn't posted anything in a while. She glanced over at Sue, who was still deep in conversation. Paula opened Instagram and saw that someone had liked a series of old posts one after the other. Then she saw the comments that had been posted too. All from the same username.

The words stung like tiny poison darts. Comments about her hairstyle, her dress sense, telling her she looked like a ridiculous dyke, questioning whether she was actually a man in drag, telling her that immoral people like her didn't deserve to live. Spiteful, horrible vitriol dripped off the screen and into her brain.

'Babe, I think I'll go for the blue one – what do you think?'

'Um, yeah, the blue one,' she said quietly. She clicked on the username and pulled up their profile, but it was someone who had posted nothing, had no followers and followed only her. She blocked them straight away with trembling fingers.

'Babe! Here!' Sue was holding out the paper bag with the

blue kaftan folded neatly into it. Paula shoved her phone into her pocket and took the bag as instructed.

Stacey almost saw me earlier. I wasn't expecting her to open the door. I let my concentration slip and mustn't let that happen again.

She was wearing a flimsy dressing gown and the front was gaping so that anyone who was interested had a pretty good view of what was underneath. Thankfully, that is not what I'm interested in. She looked terrible, like she'd had a rough night, her face as puffy as her body.

I moved on then and took up a position further up the street. There's a small park at the end of her road with a few memorial benches dotted around overflowing bins. If I sit on the middle bench on the far side of the park, I can still see her front door, can see if she leaves.

She did leave and headed towards the shops, but I didn't follow her this time.

Instead, I went back to her house, knocked on her door, listened. No one else was in there, although I could hear a cat mewling. I know hers is the ground-floor flat, with another two on the floors above. I was hoping someone would arrive, maybe open the door so that I could worm my way inside, but today was not my lucky day.

A small window was open to the lounge, probably for the cat to come and go, but it was too small for a body.

I'll come back. Patience is required. She'll leave the back door open one night when she passes out on the couch and then I'll be in. After all this planning, I need to be patient as good things come to those who wait.

I moved on to the other one then. Paula. It was easy to follow her to the market, to keep a distance while she was dragged around by her partner. She kept looking at her phone, which gave me an idea. It took mere moments to set up an account and comment on some of her social media posts. Then all I had to do was sit back and enjoy the look of shock as her face paled when she read them.

I want her to feel persecuted, like they persecuted me.

8

Valentina headed out of the flat and along the long corridor to the stairs. The flat was on the third floor, but the lift hardly ever worked. She could see a group of three men standing outside the flat a few doors down, clearly students too. They were leaning on the wall, looking down onto the road, smoking cigarettes and letting the ash rain down below. Their words were mumbled in between nicotine puffs. Valentina recognised one of them from the pub the other night. The blond guy. Interesting.

They looked up as she got closer. 'Hey,' said the one nearest to her. He had bright red hair that hung in unkempt curls past his ears and had fashioned a perfectly shaped ginger goatee beard on his pimply chin.

'Hey back,' she replied, her eyes on the blond, who had already turned away in disinterest. The redhead stepped in front of her.

'We're neighbours if I'm not mistaken. The name's Stu.'

'You are not mistaken.'

'And you are?'

'Valentina.'

He nodded in approval. 'Nice to meet you, Valentina. This is Rob, Mike and Sean.'

She looked at the other three and nodded in greeting. Two of them nodded back. They were clones of each other, dressed in slogan T-shirts and scruffy jeans with their long fringes hanging like curtains across their eyes. They leant nonchalantly against the wall in a pose she could only assume was supposed to look cool. The blond had a completely different style. His hair was neatly cut, his jeans relatively clean, his plain white T-shirt sporting a small South African flag on the sleeve. He was casually barefoot, the soles of his feet dark with dirt. He remained looking through his cigarette smoke to the street below.

'You a student then?' Stu continued.

'Last time I checked.'

'Let the lady get on with her business, Stu,' the blond said.

Stu shrugged and stepped aside. 'See you around.'

'Maybe,' she said and continued down the stairs.

She emerged from the stairwell on the ground floor and paused to look up at the third floor. The other three were out of sight now, but the blond was still there, leaning on the wall, now looking down at her.

She could feel his eyes on her as she walked away.

Valentina pushed open the door to the bakery and was immediately assaulted by the smell of bread, pastries and sugar. She would have to walk past this place pretty much every single day as it was located at the entrance to the car park for their block of flats. She'd need an iron-clad will if she was to stop herself from venturing inside all the time, but today she allowed herself to go in.

She bought a box of custard slices, doughnuts, carrot cake and iced buns, but stopped herself from buying volcanically hot pies as well, despite how delicious they looked and smelled. She didn't want to seem overly keen.

When she returned to the third floor of the flats, bakery box in hand and out of breath from the stairs, her four neighbours had disappeared, leaving behind only cigarette butts. She let herself back into the flat.

Paula materialised from the bathroom in a scented fog after one of her very long soaks in the bath, the fragrance now familiar to Valentina as it was a ritual that Paula followed most days after going for a run through the woods and beyond. It was like she was running from demons that only Paula could see, punishing herself. Valentina couldn't understand the motivation to run for the sake of it.

'How was your run?"

She shrugged. 'Quiet, just how I like it.'

'I should join you sometime. You seem to really enjoy it.'

'What you got there?' Paula asked, her surprisingly unkempt eyebrows raised. Valentina itched to get a pair of tweezers on them.

'I thought I would treat us all since lectures start tomorrow. Got some goodies from the bakery. I'll put the kettle on.'

'Very generous of you,' she said, frowning. Paula had a knack for making Valentina feel like she was suspicious of her. Maybe it was just the eyebrows.

Valentina put the bakery box on the kitchen table and filled the kettle. As if drawn telepathically, the others emerged one by one until they were all huddled around the table.

Stacey chose a jam doughnut and tucked straight into it, oblivious when sugar smeared her nose and jam dripped down her T-shirt. Paula reached over and gently wiped away the sugar.

'Look at the state of me.' Stacey laughed and scooped up the jam with her finger.

'I met the neighbours when I went out,' Valentina said.

'Oh, the guys from a few doors down? Yeah, they're nice enough. I know some of them from lectures last year,' Bev said.

'They were in the pub the other night, weren't they? I recognise the blond anyway. Two of them were properly full of themselves, but he was really rude. Cute though.'

'Sean? He can be really intense, but he's actually got a dry sense of humour when you get chatting to him,' Stacey responded. 'Definitely cute in a brooding way.'

'He's always brooding around you anyway, Stace, after that one night last year,' Bev said.

'And with Stu,' Paula added.

'That was stupid with Stu. I was so drunk. Don't even remember it, but it must've been good because he's been keen for round two ever since,' Stacey said with a grimace. 'Sean was also a vague memory, but I remember he at least hung around for a bit afterwards. Couldn't get him to leave the next morning. He's a bit needy, I think, wants a cuddle afterwards.' She rolled her eyes.

'So you've slept with half of their group? Is there anyone on campus you haven't slept with?' Valentina said.

'Oi, don't say it like that!' Stacey responded, blushing slightly.

'Hey, I'm not judging.' She was though. She was thinking that if that was her, she would've been called all sorts of unsavoury names and yet Stacey could wear casual sex like a coat that everyone admired. How was that fair?

'I don't like Sean. He's always watching – *you* anyway,' Paula said to Stacey.

'He's harmless. Just a bit smitten, I think,' Stacey replied with offhand arrogance.

Everyone streamed around campus, elbows out, heads down, rushing to get to their first lectures on time.

Valentina kept bumping into people, always seemed to be heading in the wrong direction against the flow of traffic. She was on the end of some sharp looks and even sharper elbows. The corridors were a maze, all painted the same colour, rows of heavy wooden doors and an unfathomable numbering system. The steady thrum of conversation carried her along, but she was stressed. Her lecture was about to start and she had no idea which lecture hall was the right one. She stepped to one side and took a deep breath, consulted the map again. She was sure this was where she was supposed to be, but the room number in front of her wasn't the same.

The traffic was starting to slow, the corridors emptying. She looked around, panicked and pulled open the door in front of her with crossed fingers.

There were still some stragglers taking their places, throwing down their bags and flopping into the stiff-backed seats. She saw a space at the end of the back row and headed that way, happy to be out of sight.

'Hurry up, people. I need you to be here on time. And if you're on time, then that means you are ten minutes late to me,' the lecturer said from the lectern at the front of the room. She was a tiny, round woman and had chosen to wear a long, flowing skirt that made her look even smaller and rounder. Her hair was a flaming red colour that almost perfectly matched the colour of her skirt, which was cinched at the waist with a wide white belt, making Valentina think of a traffic cone.

Valentina shoved into the seat and thrust her bag down at her feet. She pulled her notebook from her bag and shuffled uncomfortably, breathing heavily and feeling clammy. She fanned herself with the notebook. A man with tanned arms and neat blond hair sitting along from her looked over briefly and she noticed with a jolt that it was Sean. He didn't indicate he had recognised her. She looked away quickly, bent down and rummaged in her bag for a pen.

She observed the others sitting near her. A man in the row in front of her was sniffing loudly and occasionally scratching at his head, peppering his shoulders with dandruff. The woman a few seats up from him had her hair piled up in a Sixties-style beehive and had what looked like an inch thick of make-up on her skin, but Valentina could still make out the hills and craters of her acne. Further along, a skinny guy kept blowing his nose in loud honks into a tissue.

She glanced sideways at Sean again. He was staring

straight ahead, but was resting his arm along the back of the chair next to him as though he was relaxing at the pub. His hair was smoothed into place and he was wearing the same T-shirt as yesterday.

She looked to the front again. The lecturer was droning on about the work they would be covering and throwing dates for assessments around. Valentina sat back to keep Sean in the corner of her eye, taking note of how he scratched at his arm, twiddled with his pen and scribbled little doodles on the paper in front of him. She reached up and pulled her hair free from the hairband, shook it down her back.

He turned to look at her and she blushed as their eyes connected. She flicked her eyes away, but he leant over and said, 'You alright?'

'Um, this is sociology, right?' she stumbled.

His lip raised in a half-smile. 'No, it's social anthropology. Think you're meant to be on the next floor up.'

'Oh God.' She looked next to her, but the row was now full of students and it would be very embarrassing and disruptive for her to try and sneak out now. She was trapped.

When the lecture was over, she packed up hastily, then stood huffing and puffing at the guy next to her as he faffed on. He eventually took the hint and shuffled along the row of seats to leave. She was conscious of Sean standing right behind her, waiting patiently.

'You're the neighbour,' he said in a low, gravelly voice over her shoulder, his breath ruffling her hair. He had an accent that she couldn't quite place, but it certainly wasn't northern.

She now feigned casualness and flicked a glance over her shoulder. 'Yeah. Scott, right?'

'Sean,' he replied.

'Right, yes, of course.'

'So, sociology huh?'

'Yeah, if I ever find the right lecture hall,' she replied as he stepped into sync next to her at the end of the row.

He nodded, looked away, nodded again. She was hoping he'd offer to show her around, but instead he said, 'Right, well, I've got a lecture over on the East Campus now so...'

'Yeah, okay, see ya,' she said.

He peeled away into the foot traffic. She stopped in her tracks and watched his head bob away, oblivious to the shoves and pushes as people moved past her.

So that could've gone better. Her head was already tossing around all sorts of witty things she could've said, conversation starters, clever observations, but in the moment she had been practically mute. Idiot.

She had some free time before her next lecture and wasn't sure what to do with herself. There wasn't enough time to go back to the flat and her stomach was rumbling, so she wandered in the direction of the student café, hoping for a cup of tea and maybe an iced bun or something. In the distance she spotted someone who looked like Stacey. Valentina quickened her pace.

It was Stacey. She was walking with another girl who Valentina didn't recognise, but she had incredibly long, jet-black hair and caramel skin. They were chatting, occasionally laughing, their bags over their shoulders and their coats bundled into their arms.

Valentina hung back and followed them. They were in no rush, so they must have some free time too. Valentina made a mental note of that.

The girls headed into the café and Valentina paused outside, letting a few minutes tick over before she entered behind them. She looked around nonchalantly at everything and nothing before joining the queue. Stacey and her friend were a few people ahead, still chatting. The girl with the black hair reached out to pick up a bag of pretzels with an incredibly slim arm. She was wearing a heavy man's watch that looked like it could slide straight off her tiny wrist. She read the back of the pretzels bag, clearly decided the calories weren't worth it, and put the bag back. Valentina looked at the display case next to her and grabbed a packet of the pretzels for herself.

Stacey was now at the front of the queue, placing her order. Her friend was laughing loudly, making Valentina's skin crawl. Stacey was offering to pay for her. They received their order and moved away, neither looking around. There was still one person in front of her as she watched Stacey move to a free table in the far corner of the room.

Then it was her turn. She ordered a tea, paid for the pretzels and took the tray offered to her. Once paid for, she casually strolled around as though looking for a free table. It was looking like Stacey was never going to notice her, so Valentina said, 'Stacey!' with feigned surprise. 'Yay! So pleased to see you!'

Valentina noted the look of inconvenience that passed between Stacey and her friend before Stacey smiled at her as Valentina weaved between the tables.

'Hey!' she said warmly, then glanced at the girl with Stacey.

'Hey, Val, how's lectures going?' Stacey did not introduce her friend.

'So far terribly. I ended up in a social anthropology lecture instead of sociology,' Valentina replied, balancing the tray on one hand and adjusting her bag on her shoulder with the other. There were three chairs at the table, but they had dumped their bags on the third and they were showing no sign of moving them so that she could sit down. 'What about you?'

'Yeah, okay so far. Same crowd as last year, same lecturers. Nothing new yet.'

'So you have some free time now too then?' Valentina nudged.

'Yes and no, we have about half an hour before we have to head to a tutorial, but we've also got stuff to do.' Stacey was looking everywhere but at her.

'Oh God, the tutorial with the worst professor – very creepy,' Stacey's friend said. Up close, she was very pretty with smooth skin and intense, dark chocolate eyes.

'God, yes! So it's not just me then?' Stacey replied animatedly. 'He has a way of looking at you like he's working out what you would look like with no clothes on. Totally creeps me out!'

'Who's this then?' Valentina asked, balancing the edge of her tray on the table, but neither seemed to hear her.

'Have you seen the way he watches Louise when she walks in? Someone should complain. His eyes never leave her chest.'

Valentina pushed her tray further onto the table, catching the edge of Stacey's coffee cup and upending it. Coffee splashed everywhere, mostly into Stacey's friend's lap, and they both jumped to their feet.

'Shit, I'm so sorry!' Valentina said, trying not to smirk.

She grabbed a napkin and patted at the rapidly spreading pool of coffee. The girl shrieked and grabbed her bag to pull it out of the way of the river of coffee running off the table.

Stacey rushed away and returned with a pile of napkins. She pushed Valentina and her one soggy napkin aside to dump the pile in the puddle.

'I'm so sorry,' Valentina said again.

'No harm done,' the girl said through clenched teeth. 'I'll get another coffee.'

Stacey pushed the wet napkins to the centre of the table. 'We should get going,' she said. 'Val, you take the table though and I'll see you later.'

Valentina could tell Stacey was annoyed. They walked away and Valentina sat at the vacated table, the air bitter with milky coffee. She watched through the window, sipping on her tea, as they stopped outside chatting for a moment. Stacey was rolling her eyes, her hands gesticulating wildly. Her friend put a hand on her arm, said something and they both laughed. Valentina could imagine what they were saying – how stupid and clumsy she was, how pathetic and desperate for friends, how annoying. All stuff she had heard before. She thought of her father then, how he would say similar words when she demanded too much of him. How he stopped saying anything at all to her after her mother died.

Stacey and her friend began to walk away, then stopped and turned around. Sean was walking over to them, a wide smile on his face. Valentina sat taller in her seat. Stacey's friend looked thrilled. She smoothed her hair and tilted her head to look at him from under her eyelashes, her fingers fiddling with a strand of her dark hair. He leant in and kissed her in greeting on the cheek. She blushed, giggled, flicked her hair.

But it was Stacey that Valentina was really watching – how her eyes never left Sean's face, how her lips tightened and gaze narrowed as he flirted with her friend, how Stacey's fingers had rolled into fists at her sides.

9

The remnants of a Pot Noodle, toast crumbs and the wrapper from a large slab of chocolate lay scattered around Stacey as she lay on the couch under a blanket, flicking through the options on Netflix, with Nemo at her feet. She felt like she was coming down with a cold – shivery, her body aching, her head thumping. Either that or she was having withdrawals after deciding to not have a drink at all today.

If it was withdrawal, she should be worried, but she wasn't. She didn't have the energy for worrying about this on top of everything else. She struggled to focus on the screen, changing her mind between a romantic comedy and a documentary about Pamela Anderson and then again to a Harlan Coben series. Finally she flicked onto a true crime documentary as a woman ran through some woods barefoot in the dark. It made her think about the woods behind their flat, the many times they had cut through there. She could suddenly see the shards of light piercing through the threes, could smell the damp coming from the river, could feel on her fingertips the cold moss coating the rocks at the edge of the water.

Then her brain leapfrogged onto a still-life image of Valentina being chased through the woods. It played on a loop in her brain and she knew she needed to find out more about Valentina, to understand her, to figure out why she had chosen her instead of Bev or Paula to contact. The starting point had to be finding out how Valentina died.

She pulled up Tania Bennett's Facebook post on her phone again, reading the words over and over until they blurred in front of her eyes, but there were no obvious clues, no details on the profile. She did a search on TikTok to see if Valentina had an account. It would've been the kind of thing she would've loved if it had been around when they were friends. All that performing and parading. Stacey was pleased there had been no such thing as social media back then. If you did something stupid, made a poor choice, passed out in a heap with vomit down your front, there was no video evidence collected, then thrown in your face when you least expected it.

If there'd been social media, their secret would not have stayed hidden for thirty years.

Stacey thought back to the funeral. She had been given an order of service, which had been printed by a funeral company. They might have more information on how she died. She could phone them tomorrow.

She rested her head against the cushion and closed her eyes for a second, but the image of Valentina barefoot in the woods was still there, like a ghostly transfer. She desperately wanted a drink, but also wanted to prove she could go just one day without one. The urge was so great though that she could taste the tannins on her tongue, could smell the fruity acidity, could picture the beads of cold condensation on the glass.

She grabbed her phone and dialled Bev's number.

Bev's voice was a calming tonic as soon as Stacey heard it. 'Hi, Stacey – you okay?'

Stacey's voice was barely above a whisper. 'Not really. I keep thinking about Valentina; can't get her out of my head. What if something did happen to her?'

'Oh, Stacey, you know what this is.'

'Do I?'

'Yes! It's guilt, pure and simple.'

'But we did what we had to do—'

'Not that,' Bev cut her off. 'I mean guilt at how you treated her. How we all treated her. She didn't deserve it, did she?'

'Oh come on, it wasn't that bad. I just – she got on my nerves, that's all!'

'You bullied her – you know you did. And now you feel bad because she reached out to you and you don't deserve to be her hero.'

Stacey's silence spoke volumes.

Bev continued, 'Look, there's nothing you can do now that will make up for how you treated her back then. So leave it alone. It can't do any good poking around. You'll just stir up old memories.'

'Maybe.' Stacey sighed. 'I miss you two. More than you realise.'

She heard a male voice in the background, insistent, rumbling. 'I know, me too. Look, I have to go – Malcolm needs me. You sound tired – get some rest. It might look different tomorrow.'

They hung up. Stacey got to her feet, swayed on the spot, as though letting her feet decide if she was going to go into the kitchen for wine or into the bedroom for sleep. She forced herself to bed.

A noise jolted her awake. She peered at the clock on her bedside table. It was 2.40 a.m. She hadn't closed her curtains before climbing into bed and the moon was a washed-out silver sphere in an otherwise cloudy sky.

She sat up, listening hard, wondering if it had been a noise or her dream that had woken her. Nuggets of the dream were still floating in the air – the woods, branches cracking underfoot, the smell of rotting leaves and deep red blood. Valentina's perfume.

Then a screech cut through the night, followed by the clatter of a bin being upturned. Foxes.

She sighed. Sleep was always elusive for her and she knew she would struggle to get back to sleep with the foxes throwing a party outside. She threw back the covers and got to her feet, exhaustion weighing down her muscles. She would need a sleeping pill. She dragged her feet across the thinning carpet, felt along the wall for the bathroom light and flicked on the switch. She flinched, the light making everything blurry and indistinct. She kept her eyes shut as she felt her way over to the bathroom cabinet above the sink. Blinking, she looked up at the mirror on the front of the cabinet.

Valentina was staring back at her.

Stacey stopped breathing and spun around, but there

was no one there. A flash of movement in the darkened bedroom. Nemo making himself comfortable in the warm spot she had vacated.

She exhaled, splashed some water on her face and inspected the shelves for the sleeping pills. She swallowed a whole pill, desperate to get back into bed and pull the covers up.

Another noise. This time like a thud and sounding closer than where the foxes were flirting in the street. A thought slammed into her brain. Had she locked the back door when she came to bed? She couldn't remember checking it.

She crept from the bedroom and along the hallway into the darkened kitchen, hardly daring to look around. The moon was brighter now, the clouds pulling back momentarily, and she could see the lounge and kitchen, which were empty.

No intruders here.

She checked the back door. It was closed, the deadbolt drawn. She chuckled, berating herself for her nerves, and shuffled back to bed.

Five minutes later she was asleep again, her gentle snores obscuring the sound of the front room sash window sliding shut.

Stacey felt marginally better the next day after some medically induced rest, but her head was thick and woolly, a headache flirting at the edges. As she wandered into the kitchen yawning, she grabbed her phone and checked her notifications. There was a WhatsApp from Alan asking her to stop logging into his Netflix account or he would change the password. She ignored it. Considering the short but scarring time they were married, he at least owed her a Netflix subscription. It probably meant his girlfriend didn't appreciate that Stacey had added a whole heap of documentaries about country singers and wrestlers to the profile, just to mess with the algorithms a little bit.

Besides, she knew his threats were mostly hot air. He had loved her, but couldn't understand her tendency for self-sabotage. If things had been going well, she would pick a fight for no reason, which would swell until it engulfed them. He had initially blamed her dependency on various emotional crutches, like the drink and the pills, but eventually he had to accept that they were just a symptom. The root causes were not something he could ever comprehend. He just wasn't going to be enough of a reason for her to change – and she also suspected he didn't have the energy to stick around to see if she would – so he left.

But he'd never changed the Netflix password. Just like he'd never changed the payment details on their utility bills on the flat. Sometimes she wondered if he loved the new girlfriend, if she made him happy.

Now she sounded like an Adele song. She needed coffee.

There was also a message from Bev, checking in on her. She tossed the phone onto the kitchen counter without replying to either message.

She made a coffee and sat at the kitchen table, listening to the silence in the room, the clock ticking, the fridge humming. When she'd drained her mug, she pulled her bag towards her and rummaged inside for the pamphlet from the funeral, even going so far as to tap the number for the funeral home into her phone, but she hung up. What would she say exactly?

Her feet were cold against the linoleum floor. She opened her laptop and Valentina's Facebook profile filled the screen. She zoomed into Valentina's photo, ran her eyes over the familiar face – familiar and yet so much like a stranger.

A red notifications icon showed where it hadn't been yesterday – or not that she had noticed anyway. She clicked on it and the Messenger app opened. Despite having not reached out to Tania Bennett, Stacey fully expected a message from her. Her body went cold when she saw who it was actually from. She placed her hands flat on the kitchen table to ground herself, concentrated on the crumbs below her toes.

The message was from Valentina, sent over a week ago. Must've been just before she died. Stacey hadn't noticed it because she hadn't opened Facebook in quite some time, and even then it was only to look at Alan's latest post. #soulmates

The message read:

Hi Stace, I know we haven't spoken in a very long time, but I need help and I don't know who else to talk to. I'm scared. He's coming for me and I don't know what to do. I don't really want to drag you into this, not again, but you would know what to do. You did back then. He's back. It's not over. Love Val x

Stacey read the message again, her mouth gaping, but those words shouted at her from the screen.

He's back.

*

Paula sat on the edge of the bed, listening to Sue clattering dishes in the kitchen. Sue was in a good mood today and making a head start on Sunday lunch by whipping up a vegan sticky toffee pudding for dessert. Paula was relieved that the day had started well. Yesterday's trip to the vegan market had ended up in a sulky Sue for the rest of the afternoon. Then Sue had accidentally knocked Paula's dinner plate out of her hand after she'd dished up so that Paula's stir-fry ended up on the kitchen tiles and she'd had to watch Sue eat hers alone while she ate toast. That didn't bother her so much – she liked toast – but it was the look on Sue's face when her plate had smashed at her feet, her eyes dancing in delight while her mouth was spouting apologies.

She was pleased when she'd awoken to the sound of Sue singing in the kitchen this morning. If she kept her cool, this good spell could go on for some time. It had in the past. Weeks of calm and serenity would go by and just when Paula started to feel comfortable, she would do something silly, let her mouth run on, maybe act clumsily, resulting in a bruise here and a welt there. Sue was always telling her how inept or forgetful or stupid she could be and she was right.

Paula heard her mobile ring from where she had left it in the lounge. She slid her feet into her slippers and went in search of it.

She pulled up short to see Sue standing in the middle of the lounge, still in her apron, with Paula's mobile phone in her hand and her forehead wrinkling as she stared at the screen.

Wordlessly she handed the phone to Paula and left.

Paula's stomach dropped. She glanced at the phone and saw she had missed a call from Stacey. She listened to the voicemail – Stacey telling her to call her back. She sounded awful – hyped and pitchy.

Frowning, Paula dialled the missed number. Stacey answered almost immediately.

'Hi, Paula.'

'Hi, Stace. You okay? You sound terrible.'

'Maybe a cold.'

'I bet your lovely husband is looking after you though.'

'Yeah, well… Anyway, that wasn't actually why I was ringing you.'

'Oh?' Paula sat on the edge of the couch. From here she could see Sue pottering around, but by the increased volume of the pans banging against the countertops, Sue's good mood had already vanished.

'Look, this is going to sound… weird. You know I got that letter from Valentina before the funeral, then another one afterwards, right?' Stacey was saying.

Paula leant back against the couch cushions, put her feet up on the coffee table, then dropped them immediately and threw another glance at the kitchen. Sue had her back to Paula, but the way she was standing, alert and with her back arched slightly, Paula knew she was listening in.

'Well, I've just noticed that she also sent me a DM through Messenger a week before she died. And it's really creepy,' Stacey continued.

Paula turned to look out of the window into the street and dropped her voice. 'Anyone using Messenger these days is creepy. Look, Stacey, I don't really know what you're hoping to achieve. We put all of that behind us years ago

– for very good reason. Nothing good can come of bringing it up now.'

'I know, I know, but hear me out. In the DM, she says, *He's back*.'

'What?'

'That's what it says.'

'Maybe someone is pranking you. Maybe *she* was. You know what she could be like. She wanted people to stop and notice her, particularly you. Maybe this was just an elaborate way of reaching out after all this time.'

'Maybe – but she's the one who forced us all into isolation from each other.'

'Let's remember that with Valentina there was no rhyme or reason to anything. Look, there's nothing we can do about it anyway. You should just forget about all of it. Leave it alone. Leave her in the ground.'

'Paula, I can't help thinking that something happened to her – and that it's our fault. After that night—'

'Stacey, leave it. Please. Forget about the letters, about her, all of it. Get on with your life. It's over. It was thirty years ago.'

She could hear Stacey exhale. 'Yeah, maybe you're right.'

Paula paused, looked over to Sue again, then said, 'Would it make you feel better if we met up? Talked in person?'

What are you doing, Paula? Don't do it.

'Yes, yes it would.' She sounded desperate, like she was grasping at nothing. Paula felt it like a tug.

What Stacey didn't realise was that she was a drug that Paula had had to wean herself off over time – and here she was, thirty years later, offering herself up again like a relapsed alcoholic.

After arranging to meet, Paula hung up and sat for a moment, then heard a pan lid clatter and went through to the kitchen reluctantly.

It was a bright room, painted a lovely shade of yellow, with a window that caught the sunlight and scattered it in shards across the walls. Paula had always loved the light in here. Sue was standing in one of these shards of sun, her back still to Paula.

'Something smells good,' Paula said brightly.

'Who was on the phone?' Sue's voice was razor-thin.

'It was Stacey, my friend who I went to the funeral with? She's having a hard time, I think.'

'Is that all she is?'

'What do you mean?' Paula couldn't gauge the level of accusation in Sue's voice because she still had not turned around.

'You seem to be getting a lot of messages and calls from her since you went to that funeral. So is she really just an "old friend"?'

'Yes, of course she is,' Paula said firmly.

Sue turned around then, a strange half-smile on her face.

'Okay then. Pass me that, would you?' she said, pointing to the pan on the stove next to Paula.

Paula reached for the pan handle and grabbed it firmly. Ferocious heat from the handle seared into the palm of her hand. Paula cried out and dropped the pan at her feet, her skin already starting to sting. Boiling water splashed everywhere and she jumped backwards.

'I said it's been in the oven. Be careful,' Sue said, still with that strange half-smile.

'What? I didn't hear you,' Paula said, aghast, through the tears that had sprung to her eyes. She dashed for the sink, but Sue was blocking the way. She reached out and grabbed Paula's wrist. 'If I find out you are lying to me, I will not be happy.'

'I'm not lying,' Paula said through gritted teeth.

'Good.' She stepped aside. 'You should get some cold water on that in case it blisters.'

The ice-cold water from the tap did little to quell the pain in the palm of her hand.

'Let me have a look,' Sue said, coming up behind her. Paula flinched as Sue reached for her hand, but allowed her to unfold it. She held it gently under the running water, her thumb stroking the back of her hand. 'You really are the clumsiest person I know. Always getting yourself into these scrapes. Thank goodness you have me here to keep an eye on you. I told you that pan handle was hot, but you just didn't hear me the first time.'

Did she tell her? Paula had been preoccupied with Stacey's call, so it was possible she hadn't heard what Sue had said.

'Go and put an ice pack on that and I'll make you a jasmine tea,' Sue said and leant in to kiss her on the cheek.

Bev looked at the table setting and nodded. She was happy with the end result. Lots of colourful napkins, some lovely little blooms in the tiny vases dotted along the middle and a variety of wine glasses to cover every eventuality. Malcolm's elderly parents were coming today, along with her own parents, for a long-overdue Sunday roast. This was the kind of situation that Bev tended to avoid at all costs. Having both sets of parents in the house at one time was usually a recipe for disaster because they were very different people.

Her parents, Neville and June, were sweet-natured and only wanted to please everyone. They were firmly in the 'everyone's a winner' camp of thought, while Gloria and Ralph, Malcolm's parents, had very high standards and expected everything to be perfect. They had never liked Bev, had always thought their Malcolm could've done better. They were the same with the kids and asked for constant updates from Bethany and Jasper on how they were doing at school, and could be quite brutal in their criticism if they thought the teenagers weren't performing well enough, were spending too much time on their phones, socialising on a school night. If they were to be believed, Bev let her children run riot in the streets, practically barefoot, thus raising a couple of hoodlums. In contrast, Neville and June believed that Jasper and Bethany were spectacular at everything and were overflowing with positivity.

It would prove to be a challenging afternoon by all accounts, not least because Bethany was refusing to speak to Bev after she confiscated her phone when Bethany was rude to her earlier. Her Snapchat was bursting with unread messages and Bethany had raged at Bev over the prospect her friends might think she was ghosting them, because apparently that was a crime against humanity these days. Bev picked up Bethany's phone now and saw a number of Snapchat messages from one name in particular, a boy who seemed to be very keen, but she couldn't read the content of the messages without logging into Bethany's phone and she didn't have the code.

She shoved the phone back into the pocket of her apron and adjusted the cutlery in front of her, making sure it was straight. Satisfied, she went back into the kitchen to finish making the cheesecake. The kitchen already smelled amazing, with a garlic-studded lamb slow-roasting in the oven. She must remember to make the Yorkshire pudding batter ahead of time and put it in the fridge to get cold because she could not serve Gloria a flat Yorkie today. She had done that two years ago and it was still mentioned at any opportunity.

She picked up a whisk and got to work on the cream just as her phone began to ring from her apron pocket. She put the whisk aside to answer it and was surprisingly delighted to hear it was Stacey calling.

'Stacey, hi, what a nice surprise!'

'Hi, Bev, how are you?'

'All good, thanks, but I've got my parents and Malcolm's parents coming for lunch so a bit busy to be honest.'

'I won't keep you then.'

'You okay?' Bev leant heavily against the counter, sending the whisk flying.

'I'm okay, just really tired and I have a headache,' Stacey said.

Splatters of cream had dotted across the floor as the whisk landed. Bev sighed. Now she would have to add washing the floor to her to-do list. There was a moment of awkward silence and Bev was about to tell her that she had to go and she would call her another time when Stacey said, 'I got another message from Valentina.'

'Another letter?'

'No, a DM through Messenger. She sent it before she died but I never look at Facebook, so I didn't see it until today.'

'Wow, that's… creepy.'

'Yeah, it is.'

'What did it say?'

'That she was scared and that he was back.'

'Who was back?' Bev rubbed at her arms as goose bumps sprung out on her skin.

'You know.'

'No, I don't.'

'Oh, come on, Bev. You can't really be trying to pretend nothing happened? It did. It's real.'

'No, I think all of this is just Valentina being a bitch again.'

'That's what Paula said. But what if it's not? I might just look into her death a bit, see if there is anything weird that comes up.'

'Is that really a good idea? If you poke around too much, it might… you know, *draw attention*. Listen, I have to go – a cheesecake to make and things. Just leave it alone, okay? Lovely to talk to you though. Bye.'

She hung up abruptly.

Thirty years later and Bev was still reliving that night every single day, could feel the dirt of it on her skin, no matter how many baths she took, could taste the metallic fear in her mouth and the bitter guilt on her tongue. She had thrown herself into her family, going above and beyond in order to prove mostly to herself that she wasn't a bad person.

She just did a bad thing.

'Bev! The pan!' Malcolm shouted from the doorway as the cream on the stove started to boil over.

'Oh!' She grabbed at it and pushed it off the heat, but could see the bottom had caught and the cream was ruined. 'Oh no, that's the last of the cream. How stupid of me. I'll have to go and buy some more.'

'Can't you make something else? My mother isn't a huge fan of cheesecake anyway.'

'I have an apple crumble too, but my mother loves cheesecake so thought I would do both. It's no problem, I'll just pop to the corner shop.'

Bev grabbed her coat and shoved her feet into her shoes. She needed to get outside, to breathe as panic tightened her chest. Stacey was asking too many questions. Questions she must never find out the answer to.

Another unexpected surprise. I'm just casually standing a little way down the street, obscured by the trunk of a large oak tree, when the front door of her house opens and vomits her onto the street. She looks stressed, her brow knitted, her hands clasping at the lapels of a coat she doesn't need in this weather, as though she is wrestling with herself.

She is clearly distracted, so I follow her, keeping a safe distance anyway. She's never noticed me following her before though and today she is way too distracted to care. She is going at a quick pace, her feet slapping the pavement in simple black ballerina pumps.

She lives on a beautiful, albeit very middle class street, with tall houses behind iron gates and Range Rovers parked in wide driveways. The street leads up to a small terrace of shops that includes a newsagent's, a wine merchant and a bakery. I follow her as she heads into the newsagent's and I hover outside the door, reading the headlines on the Sunday papers.

She is standing in front of the fridge section, her hand reaching out but not taking anything, as though she is frozen in time. The hand is trembling and pale.

Something has rattled her.

I'm tired today. I yawn into my gloved hand. It was late – or rather early in the morning – when I slid shut the other one's sash window behind me. Doing her a favour, really, as she'd left it open earlier. Practically inviting anyone in.

I want to laugh out loud when I am watching them. They are so oblivious, so caught up in their own self-centred bubbles that they can't see what is right in front of them. But their loss is going to be my gain.

10

They piled out of the flat. Valentina was last as she teetered on her spindly heels.

'Keys, Val?' Stacey sniped over her shoulder, clearly in a mood. Valentina checked she had them before closing the door. She wasn't sure when it had become her job to carry the flat keys when they went out, but she felt pathetically warmed at the responsibility.

The other three linked arms and trundled ahead, filling the corridor. Valentina had to trot to keep up. The balls of her feet were already hurting in the shoes and her low-rise jeans were cutting into her. Bev and Stacey were both wearing platform trainers; Paula was in her usual bovver boots. It was too late for Valentina to go back and change her shoes now.

As they reached the stairwell, a door opened and Stu, Rob, Mike and Sean pushed and shoved their way out of their flat, jostling with each other like ten-year-olds. They halted when they saw the girls.

'Ladies, looking fine tonight. Where are you headed?' Stu said.

Bev giggled. 'Starting at the White Horse, then we'll see – 101 is playing tonight.'

'Well, as fate would have it, we are also heading in that direction. May we escort you lovely creatures into the night?' Rob said. This was the first time Valentina had heard him speak. His voice was surprisingly high-pitched and she fought the urge to laugh out loud.

'You may indeed,' Bev flirted back and they filed down the stairs.

Valentina noticed the way Stacey had perked up when she saw Sean. She grabbed onto Stacey's arm to hold her back and said in a whisper, 'Didn't I see Sean on campus with your friend?'

'Yeah, so? They're sort of chatting a bit, not really going out or anything though.' She shook Valentina off impatiently.

They all headed through the car park and out onto the street, turning left towards the path that would take them around to the shortcut through the woods. It was a clear night, no clouds, and Valentina could smell the river on the breeze, metallic and alive as it snaked along the edge of the path through the woods, hugging it, holding it close, the ground soggy and mossy under foot. Valentina looked down at her shoes and knew they'd be ruined if they took the shortcut.

'Guys, can we go the long way? My shoes.'

'Val, the long way takes ages. We always go this way,' Paula said. 'Just take them off and go barefoot if you need to.'

It didn't take that much longer to go the long way – it only added ten minutes onto the walk – but those ten minutes were apparently crucial when heading to the pub. And there was something edgy about walking through the trees at night. They all did it, despite the obvious safety concerns.

'I'll go barefoot and you can borrow these if you want,' Sean said and pointed to the flip-flops he was wearing. Did he actually own real shoes?

'But your feet will get muddy,' she said.

'Doesn't matter to me.' He shrugged. 'It's either my feet or yours.'

'Come on, you two, let's go,' Mike said over his shoulder. 'I'm so thirsty I'm seeing camels.'

Valentina and Sean looked at each other and he shrugged again. 'Offer stands.'

'Thanks,' she said and bent down to slip off the heels. He flicked his flip-flops at her and she slid her feet into the warm imprints. They were way too big, like clown shoes. He carried on walking, veering towards the grass next to the path, seemingly quite comfortable in his bare feet.

She grabbed her shoes by the heels and followed him.

'Don't you find it uncomfortable being barefoot? I saw you weren't wearing shoes the other day either – in the hallway.'

'You're observant,' he replied and she flushed, although he wouldn't have noticed in the fading light. She wanted to say she wasn't taking notes or anything, but before she could explain herself, he said, 'It's my South African heritage.'

'What is?'

'The barefoot thing.'

Now that he'd said more than a few words to her, she could hear his accent, the way he shortened his vowels, clipping the ends off his words. 'Oh?' she said.

'We spend a lot of time running around with no shoes on in Africa. We like to feel the ground beneath our feet. Shoes and socks feel like they're too constricting, you know?'

Valentina thought about the heels she was carrying and the way they pinched and nipped as she walked, but how beautiful they made her feel. 'Yeah, I get that.' They walked on, the others in front of them laughing loudly and the boys flinging banter at each other. Bev, Paula and Stacey were still walking with their arms linked, Stacey in the middle. Valentina looked away.

'So South Africa, huh? How long have you been here?'

'My family moved here the year before I finished school, so a few years now. The politics and all that just got a bit much for my parents, you know?'

'Do you miss it?'

'So much. The sun, the outdoors. There's something about Africa that gets into your bloodstream. It's a living, breathing part of you.' His voice was animated like she hadn't heard it before.

'I'd like to go someday,' she said, although it had never crossed her mind before. All she'd heard was the snippets on the news, the violence, the political upheaval, and even then she hadn't taken any real notice because it had no real bearing on her life. But she knew it was what he would want to hear, so she said, 'I believe it's an amazing place despite the troubles.'

'I'm going back for a couple of weeks as soon as exams finish. There are so many different parts to it – the bush, the mountains, the vastness of the Karoo. It's all so epic and it breaks my heart what that country and our people have been through, but now that Mandela is free, there's change coming and I'd like to return to see that change for myself sometime.'

Valentina had to rack her brain to remember what she had last heard about South Africa. She was saved from her embarrassing ignorance by him saying, 'That's why I'm studying political science and history. It's an era-defining time.'

'Yeah, absolutely,' Valentina said, 'so era-defining.'

'What are you studying?' he asked.

Valentina thought about her humanities degree and how it had stemmed from a need to do something but no idea what, preferably something that didn't require too much work. That wasn't what she wanted to admit to Sean after his impassioned speech though. 'I'm doing humanities, hoping to go into charity work, maybe travel to less fortunate countries and do my bit.'

'Amazing. What kind of charity work?' They were at the edge of the woods now, the path growing thinner and darker as the trees reached over them. She could hear the leaves whispering above them, inviting them in. Here and there they could still see lights shining through the branches, illuminating their way in fits and starts like someone was flicking a light switch on and off.

'Um, well...'

Stacey's voice cut in then, saying, 'Come on, you two, you're falling behind.' And then Stacey was in front of them and looping her arm through Sean's, pulling him away. 'What are you two talking about so seriously anyway?'

A shape appeared next to Valentina and she jumped. She had been so focused on Sean that she hadn't noticed Stu come up next to her. 'Alright?' he said.

'Yeah, you?'

'Didn't want you back here on your own. It gets dark really quickly.'

'Yeah, I can see that.' The light was fading fast and tonight for some reason, maybe because she felt on edge, Valentina felt claustrophobic under the trees, like they were closing in more than usual. The moisture in the air from the river was making her coral-coloured top stick to her skin.

'What were you and Sean talking about?' He was walking very close to her side, their arms brushing, his aftershave filling the breathing space between them.

'Just South Africa and stuff.'

'He gets a bit riled up about it. Can get really serious. Also, the chicks dig him talking about it – Johnny Foreigner and all that.' He sounded sulky.

Valentina could feel her feet sliding around in the flip-flops, could hear the slop and sludge of mud in places, and felt a stab of guilt again at Sean walking barefoot on the cold ground, despite his affirmations that he was used to it. 'I should go and see if Sean is okay – since I'm wearing his flip-flops,' she said, as much to put some distance between her and Stu as it was to catch up with Sean and Stacey.

'He's in good hands, don't worry. He won't be focusing on his feet.'

Valentina couldn't make out his face, but the envy in his voice was clear. 'There's a bit of history there, is there?'

'Just like a one-night thing – with each of us,' he replied proudly.

Up ahead, they heard Stacey cry out and a dull thump. Stu surged forwards, leaving Valentina standing alone. She hurried after him, but found herself bogged down in a particularly gloopy patch of mud that sucked the flip-flop off her foot. She balanced on the other foot and yanked the flip-flop free before rushing after everyone else.

When she caught up with them, they were huddled around Stacey, fawning over her.

'Are you sure you're okay?' Stu asked.

'Yes, I'm fine, really. It's nothing, just kicked that tree trunk, that's all.'

Sean was holding her up like she had lost a limb. 'Here, lean on me,' he was saying.

'What happened?' Valentina asked.

'Poor Stace hurt her leg on a tree trunk, might leave a nasty bruise,' Bev said.

'For God's sake, she said she was fine,' Valentina said a little too sharply. There was an awkward silence.

'Seriously, I'll be fine. Let's keep going,' Stacey said.

Valentina hung back as they set off again. The trees were thinning out up ahead and she could hear car horns in the distance. They would be clear of the intimacy of the trees soon, back into the artificial light of the town. Her opportunity to speak to Sean alone had passed with little to show for it, all because Stacey had interrupted. Stacey had had her chance with Sean, but it was starting to look like she didn't want anyone else to have him either.

The path ran out and the river disappeared under a cobblestoned bridge. Sean and Stacey stopped to one side at the foot of the bridge. Stacey was giggling like a kid at something Sean had said, her injured leg quickly forgotten. He was looking at her bemused. Valentina approached them and slipped off the flip-flops. Not waiting for Sean to stop speaking, she thrust the flip-flops at him.

'Thanks so much, Sean, you're a real sweetie,' she said. 'I owe you a drink. Let me buy you one tonight.'

'Yeah, whatever,' he said, his eyes never leaving Stacey's face.

'Come on, people, let's get going. Much faffing tonight,' Paula said from halfway over the bridge. Sean followed after Stacey like a puppy. Valentina felt her fists clench at her sides and forced herself to relax them.

Patience, Valentina. Breathe. They will see you. Give it time.

The whole night was ahead of them. Plenty of time. Sure, Stacey was monopolising him now, but things may well be different by closing time.

Still barefoot, Valentina followed them over the bridge and onto the cobblestoned streets of the town centre. This side was very much geared towards the university students, with bars, takeaways and clubs rubbing shoulders with each other. You had to go further into the old town to find the quaint market square, posher shops and restaurants.

The group headed towards the White Horse, which sat between a kebab shop and a tiny crystals and incense shop that smelled heady and pungent despite being closed, like the smell had seeped into the wood grain. In contrast, hot air, cigarette smoke and the smell of stale beer hit them as Paula pushed open the pub door. Valentina's feet were cold against the pavement as she watched the others go in. She knelt down to put her shoes back on, trying to regulate her breathing and push back the angry heat she could feel hovering at the back of her head.

When she finally went in, the group had split into two. The boys were at the bar, shouting greetings in response to excited calls of, 'Sean! Mate, good to see you!' and 'Hey, lads, come and get a pint in.' They were clearly a popular group, mostly driven by a weird fan base that seemed to follow Sean around, made up predominantly of rugby-playing lads and girls drawn to his intense, brooding persona. Stu, Rob and Mike were in their element, lapping up the scraps of attention that fell from Sean's plate, pints in hand and cigarettes dangling from their lips.

Valentina stood in the doorway, watching as the room swelled and moulded around them. On the whole, she wasn't one for fawning after the most popular boy, but there was something about Sean, she had to admit. But for every person who greeted him audibly, his eyes would flick over to where Stacey was now sitting at a booth with Bev to see if she had noticed how popular he was.

Stacey had not noticed. She had already flicked her attention away from him again, now relishing in the little posse of fans mingling around her – people she knew from lectures or parties, in the halls or just from being Stacey around campus. They came over to the table, made conversation, looked like they were settling but were then seemingly moved on swiftly by Paula who, after wading through the bodies laden with drinks for them, was acting like Stacey's personal bodyguard.

Stacey was putting on a show for everyone, an actress filling a role. Valentina hadn't quite figured out who Stacey really was yet. She watched her from across the room through narrowed eyes. She'd never experienced that level of worship from anyone and yet Stacey was generating it without even trying. The heat was rising up the back of her neck again. She looked back over to Sean, who was also watching Stacey with narrow-eyed interest. Then Stu leant over and subtly pressed what looked like a box of matches into Sean's hand, which he accepted with a nod before turning back to the bar.

Valentina slid into the booth next to Bev and accepted a pint of cider from Paula. She drained a quarter of it in one large gulp as Stacey laughed loudly at nothing in particular. She tossed her long blonde hair over her shoulder, then rested her head on the side and twisted a chunk of hair around her finger. Valentina envied her long, lemony hair, which was in complete contrast to Valentina's dark mass of unruly curls. Valentina had tied her hair up into a ball tonight, but reached up and undid the tie, letting the curls fall beyond her shoulders. She sat back, attempting to mirror Stacey's casual demeanour.

The pub was close to full now. A tall, skinny man with dreadlocks and a patchy beard was setting up electronic equipment on the stage, but the band hadn't started yet, so the soundtrack playing was one of excited student voices, all talking over each other and laughing loudly, which drowned out whatever actual music was playing over the sound system.

The girl Stacey had been with in the café the other day wandered over to say hello. She greeted Valentina warmly despite having been on the wet end of her coffee spillage. Valentina smiled back coolly, her fingers twisting her hair nonchalantly. The girl wandered away then and went to talk to Sean, who was still at the bar in the middle of the group of boys, punching each other on the arm and spilling their pints in excitement. Mike was handing around shots of tequila.

Bev noticed Valentina watching them and rolled her eyes. 'They never know when to pace themselves. They're like children.'

By 10 p.m., they were all shoulder to shoulder on the small square of carpet that had been cleared as a makeshift dance floor as the band 101 belted out student classics. Valentina bounced in a tight huddle with Bev, Paula and Stacey, their handbags banging at their hips, all singing loudly and off key for the most part. Valentina was drunk; she could feel it. There was a fog to the room, like she was seeing everything through gauze, and the air felt out of sync, tilted, soupy.

She had taken her shoes off again and left them on a table somewhere. The soles of her feet stuck to the carpet and more than once someone stood on her toes, but she was immune to it all as she bounced and laughed and sang. A sweaty dew clung to her top lip and her hair was stuck to the nape of her neck, but she felt alive despite the discomfort. This was what she was here for. She had never felt like this, like she belonged. She could feel an inky sadness creeping over her suddenly, like a shroud, but then Stu sidled over and put his arm around her, pulling her in. They began to dance and sway together, laughing, singing off-key, their hip bones close.

Paula and Stacey were jumping, their hands in the air,

splashes from their glasses raining down on all of them, while Bev was stuck to Mike, barely moving amongst the heaving bodies. Sean was avoiding the dancing, choosing instead to watch from where he was still propped up at the bar. Valentina noticed Stacey's friend was no longer with him. She had left with a bunch of girls in a gaggle of talk about going to a nightclub.

Before long, the band was playing its last song, and the crowd was groaning and booing in disappointment that it was throwing-out time. The lights were turned up bright and glasses were drained. It was like someone had pulled the plug on the night and the energy was slowly swirling out of the door as small groups peeled off to find a nightclub or more drinks to be had elsewhere.

Valentina gathered up her shoes in her hand and weaved towards the door, using one hand on Paula's shoulder as her guide. The cold air hit her full in the face and she reeled backwards, but Bev caught her. 'Whoa, Val. Steady, yeah?'

Sean emerged into the night and immediately lit a cigarette with a shiny silver lighter, the end glowing angry and orange. He walked over to Stacey and hovered next to her.

'So where are we going now, lads? A few of the others have gone to Razzles. Fancy it?' Rob said.

Stacey said to Sean. 'You could come back to ours?' She was swaying a bit herself, her words blurred and running into each other, but she somehow still managed to look attractive rather than a drunk, sweaty mess.

'Yes! We have beer, I think, and if not, we definitely have tequila. And crisps! Bloody love crisps,' Bev said, hanging off Mike's arm.

Sean considered the end of his cigarette, flicked ash onto the pavement casually, and said, 'Could do, I guess.'

'Great, let's go,' Stu said. Valentina started walking, then pulled up sharply as pain shot through her feet. She cried out and dropped to the ground. Blood started to seep from a deep cut in her foot where a shard of glass was piercing the skin. She looked down at the blood with fascination.

'Bloody hell,' Stu said. 'You can't walk home like that. Anyone got a tissue or anything?'

Stacey sighed and rummaged in her bag. She pulled out a loose tissue that may or may not have been used before and handed it to Rob, who crouched down next to Valentina. He pulled out the shard of glass and pressed the tissue to the wound.

'Jesus, Val, that looks deep,' Paula said.

Stacey looked annoyed. 'How the hell are we going to get her home?'

'I can give her a piggyback – she won't be that heavy,' Stu said.

'I'll help. We'll take turns,' Sean said. Stacey turned away.

Bev pulled her hair band from around her wrist and said, 'Use this to tie the tissue to her foot until we get home.'

The tissue secured, Paula helped her up and she felt herself hoisted onto Stu's back. His strong arms pinned her legs and she giggled. She felt like she was flying. She buried her head into the back of his T-shirt. He smelled like smoke, beer and sweat. She could feel the sharpness of his shoulder blades digging into her.

They looked a strange mix as they weaved back over the cobble-stoned bridge and onto the woodland path. The river ran loudly alongside them, following them as they were swallowed up by the trees. Valentina relaxed into Stu, but before long he was panting and pulling behind the rest. Their voices started to grow quieter as they drew further away.

Valentina could feel herself dozing off, the swaying motion coaxing her into sleep. Then she was flying again as she was passed over to a taller body, differently shaped, the muscles more defined, the edges softer. She opened her eyes and saw that Sean had taken over from Stu to carry her the last bit of the journey. She snuggled in again, smiling into his back. 'My knight in shining armour again,' she whispered into his ear.

'Just don't throw up down my back,' he said in a growl.

He picked up the pace and closed the gap on the group in front.

Stu had caught up with Stacey and Paula and was making them laugh. Bev and Mike were walking hand in hand, with Rob next to them like a third wheel.

A noise, like a squeal, pierced the night and they all stopped abruptly. Sean spun around to face the way they had come, but it was dark, with very little moonlight to illuminate the path behind them. 'This place gives me the creeps,' he said in a quiet voice.

'I like it,' Valentina mumbled. 'It's cut off from everything.'

'That's why I don't like it. Anything could happen and no one would find us until tomorrow.'

The squeal came again, this time closer. 'Just a fox,' she heard Paula say in a no-nonsense voice a little in front of them. 'It'll be more scared of us than we are of it.' She heard their footsteps start up again, the crackle of leaves and squelch of mud. Sean started walking again, but quicker now until he was overtaking the front group. They emerged from the woods to see the car park of the flats in the distance, a patchwork of sparkling lights.

'Thank God,' Sean said, his breath thick and heavy. 'I'm not carrying you up three flights of stairs though.'

When he set her down at the foot of the stairs, the tissue was soaked through with blood, but she could just about put her weight on the ball of her foot and managed to hop up the stairs slowly. By the time they reached their floor, she was the one panting and her vision had cleared, the drunkenness pushed back a bit.

Once Stacey had rummaged in Valentina's bag for the keys and opened the front door, Bev and Paula hooked their arms under her and helped her straight into the bathroom before plonking her on the edge of the bath. Bev set about removing the tissue while Paula ran a basin of hot water to wash the wound.

'Stace, get the drinks poured,' Valentina shouted towards the kitchen. 'Won't be long.'

'You've probably had enough,' Bev said.

'God, no, the night is but a foetus, Bev,' Valentina replied, then started to laugh loudly, nearly sliding off the edge of the bath. 'Foetus – ha! I've had an abortion, you know.'

They looked at each other warily.

'Yeah, my lecturer at my last uni. Dad paid for it of course. That's as much as he does really. Writes the cheques.'

Paula rolled her eyes and said, 'You're talking nonsense. Sit still while I sort this out.' She hoisted Valentina's foot into her lap and gently cleaned away the dirt and blood. The wound was still bleeding, but slower than before.

'No, it's true. Ouch!' Valentina hissed and glared at Paula.

'Sorry, I think there's still glass in it.'

'Just leave it, I'll be fine. I just want to join the others.' Their voices were carrying through from the kitchen and someone had turned on some music.

'Plenty of time, let's get this sorted first,' Paula said, hanging onto her foot in a vice grip.

'Stacey doesn't seem very concerned about me,' Valentina said, her voice needling.

'Because you're fine – it's just a cut,' Paula replied.

'So is she really into Sean? I can't really tell because she seems to like… well, everyone.'

'Val, stop talking.'

'I just think she's not as invested in this group as the rest of us are. And she'll get a reputation for being a slut if she's not careful.'

'Val, you've known her weeks. We've known her years, okay?' Bev said.

'Exactly! You can't see it! You guys are my best friends – I'm just looking out for you.'

'Bev, pass me the first aid kit from the cupboard.'

Bev practically threw the kit at Paula and stomped from the bathroom. The first aid kit had one large plaster in it and Valentina squealed when Paula smeared antiseptic cream on the cut and slapped the plaster on.

'There, now you can go,' she said, as if to a toddler. 'And Val, be careful – we're quite a loyal group. If there's a choice to be made, it would be Stacey.'

'Would she do the same for you though?' Then Valentina smiled and hopped out of the room, leaving Paula on her knees with bloody tissues scattered around her.

Valentina hopped into the kitchen where Stacey, Sean, Stu

and Rob were sitting around the table, bottles of beer open in front of them. Bev and Mike had disappeared behind Bev's closed bedroom door.

'Where can I sit?' she said.

'Here,' said Stu and patted his lap.

'Come on, let's go in the lounge – sorry, Val's bedroom,' Stacey said instead.

They moved like a long conga line into the lounge and flopped down on the couch and floor around the tiny television set. The music was coming from the stereo in the lounge and Stu flung himself down by the CDs and started rifling through them.

'What's this?' Mike asked, indicating the solitaire laid out on the coffee table, which Valentina had used to decide what to wear. She was officially obsessed with it – using it to decide everything for her now.

'Just a game. Helps us to decide what to do sometimes.'

Sean was sitting on the couch very close to Stacey and whispering in her ear. Paula walked in, saw the two of them and walked out again.

'What's up with her?' Rob asked. 'I'm happy to keep her company if she's feeling lonely.'

'I don't think you're her type,' Valentina said loudly. 'Your boobs aren't big enough.' Rob looked confused, while Stacey glared at Valentina.

'What? It's true, isn't it?'

'What is?' Rob said, looking from one to the other.

'Nothing, Val's had too much to drink, that's all,' Stacey said.

'Then maybe I should be putting you to bed, Val,' Stu said with a smirk.

Sean was whispering in Stacey's ear again, his hand wandering up her thigh, but Stacey was starting to look annoyed and shuffled away. He moved in again. Valentina watched them, could feel red heat crawling over her skin.

'Yes, come on then, Stu,' she said with false bravado.

He looked unsure. 'You what?'

'Come on,' she said and nodded at the bed. She got to her feet and staggered over to her bed.

'Now you're talking,' Stu said, his face lighting up.

'Val, stop teasing him,' Stacey said.

'I'm not. Clear out, you lot, unless you want to watch of course?'

There was silence. Rob shrugged, grabbed his beer and stood up, looking ready to do as he was told.

'Val, enough. You're drunk.'

'And you're jealous, I think. But you've already been there, so there's nothing to be jealous about, right? Oh, apart from my rich daddy – 'cos you don't have that, do you?'

There was silence. Stacey turned to Stu, who was looking amused at what was going on. 'I think you should go.'

'But I haven't finished my drink yet,' he said indignantly.

Stacey grabbed his beer and went over to the glass door that opened out onto the tiny balcony facing the woods. She opened the door, stepped up to the railing and poured the beer out over the wall.

'What the fuck?'

'Now you're done.'

Valentina started laughing and hopped off the bed to join Stacey on the balcony.

Stu reached for the beer bottle, but Stacey was too quick

and threw it over to Valentina, who caught it, but only just. Valentina dangled it over the balcony. He lurched at her and she darted out of the way. He fell against the balcony railings, embarrassed, as Stacey started to laugh.

'Fuck this,' he muttered.

'Ah, did you miss?' Valentina said in a needling voice. 'Would you miss if it was me?' Suddenly she hiked her leg over the railing and started to scramble over to the other side.

'Val! What are you doing?' Stacey said, not laughing any more.

Valentina swung her other leg over until she was standing on the wrong side of the railings over the carpark three floors below, clinging on with one white-knuckled hand, the beer bottle still held aloft. Then she let the bottle drop. It fell as if in slow motion and all eyes followed it down until it smashed onto the windscreen of a car parked below, leaving a cobweb of fractures in the windscreen and setting off the car alarm, a loud siren in the night-time quiet.

'Fuck, you're crazy,' Stu said as he leant over and peered down. The indicator lights on the car below were flashing in anger as the siren blared. A light came on one floor down.

'I'm outta here,' Stu said. 'She's all yours.'

The boys left one by one, leaving Stacey still gaping at Valentina on the other side of the third-floor balcony railings.

'Val, please climb back over. This isn't funny.'

'Okay, okay,' she said and went to slide her leg over, but shouted in pain as she bumped the cut on the sole of her foot. She looked to be falling backwards, as if in slow motion, her fingers slowly losing their grip, but Paula came out of nowhere and grabbed onto the front of her top to steady her.

'Come on, help me!' They got their arms under her and hauled her back over the railings until they all fell in a pile on the cold balcony tiles, breathing heavily.

Valentina started to laugh, her voice alone in the night.

Valentina woke to a belting headache and a red-hot foot. She had passed out long before the car alarm finally wore itself out in the very early hours. She limped through to the kitchen, made some tea and went back to bed with it, but kept her bedroom door open. After a while, Bev wandered past, her dressing gown pulled tight. 'Bev!'

Bev stuck her head around the door. 'Yeah?'

'I'm sorry – about last night. I just… drank too much.'

'Why, what happened?' A floppy-haired head appeared over her shoulder. 'Hi, Val,' Mike said, looking pale.

'Oh, hi, Mike.'

'God, did anyone hear that car alarm last night? Fucking annoying,' Mike said and sloped towards the kitchen.

Bev followed him, leaving Valentina nursing her tea and her head. She put her earphones in and listened to her Nirvana CD at a deafening volume, but after another ten minutes or so, she tossed the earphones aside, threw on a pair of leggings and a sweatshirt and went to face the others.

Bev and Mike were sitting together at the table in silence.

'Where is everyone?' Valentina asked.

'Gone out for a walk to clear their heads,' Bev replied. 'About ten minutes ago.'

'Maybe I'll see if I can catch up with them.'

'They headed towards the woods and the river, I think.'

Valentina threw on her trainers, wincing when she put pressure on her sore foot.

The air was chilly with a greyness hanging over everything. October had come in thick and heavy, as it always did in the north. Valentina hopped along the corridor of the flats and down the stairs as fast as she could.

She limped through the car park, past the shattered beer bottle shards on the ground and the fractured windscreen. As she limped quickly towards the trees, she saw Stacey's friend from the café heading towards their flat.

Valentina paused and called out to her.

The girl turned to look at her, gave a slight wave and approached cautiously. 'Hey,' she said.

'Hi, you okay?'

'Yeah, just thought I'd pop up to see Stacey. Is she in?'

'Oh, um, yeah she is, but... um.'

'What?'

'Well, she's with Sean. He stayed over last night, so they're... you know...'

'Oh.' The girl looked annoyed, then sad.

'Oh wait, were you...? Sorry, maybe I shouldn't have said. I mean, it's not like Stacey is keen on him – God, she'll basically sleep with anyone, but he was dead keen. Has been for ages. Anyway, I have to go. See ya!'

Valentina limped away, a large smile on her face. She peeked back and saw the girl slope away, her shoulders drooped, her head hanging.

The woods towered ahead of her and her breath was coming in gasps as she followed the path. The branches shifted and moved as the gloom enveloped her, the river whispering at her side. She followed it along, the smell of moss and mud filling her nose and clearing her head a little. Then the whispering voice of the river became the louder voices of someone talking. She slowed down, listened, then crept forward some more.

Stacey's voice, the unmistakable rasp of it, the blunt Geordie edge. Valentina veered off the path and climbed up the bank over rocks and branches, heading up and away from their voices. Below her she could make out a red jumper. She scrambled along a bit further until she reached a long, flat rock set into the steep bank, but hidden from below by an ageing, wide tree trunk. She hauled herself up onto the rock, feeling the rock scratch at her shin through her leggings. She looked below her and saw Stacey and Paula sitting on a fallen tree trunk, set back from the path.

'She's a liability,' Stacey was saying.

'Yeah, but we can all get a bit lairy when we've had too much.'

'There's something about her though – something… unhinged. I could've killed her when she said that about you. She can be really nasty.'

'I've never said I didn't want it to be common knowledge though?'

'You're too nice, Paula, always wanting to see the good in people, give them the benefit of the doubt. I don't feel the need to. I think we should tell her to move out.'

Valentina felt cold. Goose bumps stood out on her arms and she wrapped them around herself.

'You're jealous, that's all. And she called you a slut.'

'Jealous of Stu? I don't think so! She can have him.'

'Well, sloppy seconds 'cos you already have.'

'And all I remember is how bad his feet smelled when he pulled off his boots!' They both laughed. 'Come on though, you've got to admit it's a bit weird how she can just snap like that – fine one minute, then completely different the next. That's not normal. And she seems proper needy, like she's always there. The other day I caught her watching me as I came out of the bathroom in a towel. It was creepy.'

'None of us are normal, Stace. That's why we're still friends. Yes, I agree she's a bit of a troublemaker, likes to stir things up, but maybe she just really wants a friend. I think she's lonely. She doesn't seem to have made any new friends from her courses. We're lucky – we have each other, always have done. This is a new place, new people. She went to boarding school, so is probably used to having loads of friends, don't forget.'

'You and your bleeding heart, Paula. I think she's trouble and she should go before she gets too comfortable. Bev found her, so she should tell her.'

There was a moment of silence, then Paula said, 'Look, maybe let's see how she gets on in the next few weeks, yeah? There's only one year to go – we need the rent paid and with lectures now starting up and all the exams coming up, she will likely settle down a bit.'

'Did you see the way she was flirting with Sean too though?'

'You are jealous! Ah, that's so cute! You know he's not interested in her. None of them are – she's just something they haven't seen before, new and glossy. Besides, you aren't interested in Sean either. You just don't want him to like her.'

'He is so not my type, so intense. Did I tell you I think he's following me on campus? I keep seeing him everywhere. It's creepy. Between him and Valentina, I can't get a moment to myself. Every time I turn around, one of them is there.' Stacey leant down and grabbed a stick that she picked at distractedly before throwing it into the rapidly running water.

'You weren't finding him so creepy last night. You were flirting as much as she was,' Paula said, a soft sulk hanging onto the words.

Stacey shrugged. 'Sometimes it boosts my ego a bit, alright? To have him falling over me, you know? And he's very popular, so it does my reputation good.' There was silence again for a moment. 'I'm horrible, aren't I? And a slut.' Valentina could hear the smile in the words. 'If you want Val to stay, you need to keep her in check. Otherwise, she's out. I don't need two psychos around me.'

Valentina sat long after Paula and Stacey had left, tears stinging her eyes.

11

PRESENT DAY

Stacey put the phone down and slumped back against the couch cushions, her mouth dry from talking, her throat raspy. She was sweating and the migraine drugs she had taken earlier were starting to wear off. Her headache hadn't been that bad, but she had wanted the fuzziness.

She tried to have a nap, but tossed and turned, dozing off then lurching awake, leaving her feeling fuzzy and disorientated. She sat up in bed and opened her laptop, deciding to indulge in her guilty pleasure of looking at houses for sale near to where Bev lived that Stacey would never be able to afford. Those with a price tag of over two million pounds with vulgar furnishings and random art. Huge gardens and in/out driveways. But even that didn't hold her interest for long.

She got up and went to find Valentina's letter, held it, turned it over, as though she would find a hidden message on the other side, like it was an ancient treasure map.

She picked up the phone a few times to call the police, but decided against it every time.

The lid of the red wine bottle was cold in the palm of her hand as she twisted it off. Two glasses went down in quick succession as she tried to find out more about Valentina's life over the years. There was very little online about her family and her father's PR business, but there was mention of his having won awards for campaigns he had created for a large wine import client. Ironic that Stacey was drinking cheap plonk while she read up on him.

The PR business looked like it had been wrapped up shortly after his death, which was a few years after graduation. Stacey knew Valentina had worked for her father's PR firm, but there was no indication of what she had done after that. Maybe she hadn't needed to work after her father died. This was a time before social media when people were less inclined to document every aspect of their lives like they would today, so it was so much easier to disappear from view.

Two glasses of wine turned into the entire bottle and by the time it was empty, Stacey had convinced herself that she should talk to the police after all, that something terrible had happened and she owed it to Valentina to fix it. Stacey's guilty conscience was always at its clearest at the bottom of a bottle. She searched up the website for the local police service and went through all of their questions about whether the crime was happening now, if someone was in danger, was the perpetrator on the scene, but none of it was relevant and she didn't actually know anything at all.

It would be easier to call them. She struggled to focus on

the numbers that swam in front of her as she called the local police station. Explaining that she had information about a friend's death, she was put on hold for quite some time. The tinny music was making her head spin, then someone else was on the phone, trying to palm her off, convincing her to report it online, then suggesting she come down to the station and report it in person. Attempting to keep her voice calm, she explained that she was ill and needed to do it over the phone. Her head was thumping again. More tinny music followed and she almost hung up.

Then a new voice came on the line, thin, high-pitched and sounding like it was coming from a thirteen-year-old girl. She introduced herself as PC Julia Banks and Stacey suspected she was a junior officer who had drawn the short straw. Stacey resisted the urge to ask her how old she actually was.

'My friend died recently and I'm worried that something bad happened to her,' Stacey said instead and felt like a child herself saying it.

'Okay, let's start at the beginning. Can I have your name please?'

'Valen— Oh, sorry, Stacey Maxwell.'

'And your friend is...?'

'Valentina Mackenzie – at least she used to be. I assume she still is.'

There was a pause and Stacey could imagine PC Banks scribbling notes in big, round letters with a long, thin, sparkly pen with a pink pom-pom on the lid.

'And what happened to your friend?'

'Well, I don't know. I found out recently that she died – I

don't know how – and I went to her funeral and everything, but I've been getting these letters and messages from her and she is making it sound like she was scared, that maybe someone was trying to hurt her.'

Another pause as PC Banks probably drew doodles on her notes. 'When last did you see your friend?'

'Thirty years ago.'

PC Banks coughed – at least Stacey hoped it was a cough and not a snort of derision. 'Thirty, did you say? As in three zero?'

'Yes, we haven't spoken for a very long time,' Stacey admitted.

'And she sent you a letter?' PC Banks didn't sound like she was taking notes or doodling or anything anymore.

'Yes, just before her funeral I got a letter asking me to make sure Paula and Bev were there and then I got another letter after the funeral. Look, the point is that she said she was scared and it sounded like someone might be threatening her.'

'Do you have any idea who might want to harm your friend?'

There was the issue. Stacey couldn't tell her what she really knew, who had the best motive for hurting Valentina – because he was dead already.

'No, I... er...'

PC Banks exhaled audibly down the phone line. 'I appreciate your posthumous concern for your friend's welfare, but I don't see what we can do without more information.'

Teenagers didn't use words like *posthumous*. Maybe

Stacey had been wrong about PC Banks. Maybe she had been wrong about lots of things. 'But what if he hurt her?' Her voice was small now.

'Who? Who do you think may have hurt her?'

'I... I... don't know.' Stacey wanted to scream his name. It sat on the end of her tongue like a pill, dissolving into bitterness. But he couldn't hurt anyone else. They had made sure of that.

'Ms Maxwell,' PC Banks said and Stacey pictured her putting the pom-pom lid on her pink sparkly pen, closing the folder and pushing the notes away from her, now no-nonsense. 'Have you had anything to drink this evening?'

'What's that got to do with anything?' Stacey's eyes flicked to the empty bottle on the coffee table next to the cold medication, the glass with the shallowest of maroon dregs at the bottom.

'Perhaps you have taken something? Are you alone? Is there someone there with you – or can you call someone to come over and sit with you? It sounds like you have had a nasty shock with your friend's passing and may be struggling to come to terms with it. Perhaps I can suggest—'

'NO! I have not had a nasty shock – and okay, I may have had some wine, but I'm serious about this!'

There was suddenly a burst of background noise, shouting and doors slamming in the police station, a heavy thud. Stacey imagined it like it was portrayed on the television, with drunks raging, blood pouring from a bar fight, and chairs being flung. Prostitutes dressed in tiny dresses and ripped fishnet stockings, looking like Julia Roberts while they pulled each other's hair and scratched at heavily made-up faces with false nails. In reality, it was a Sunday evening in northern England and PC Banks probably spent her time on car break-ins and inappropriate graffiti or the occasional champagne-fuelled brawl at the races.

'How about I take your details and you can call us if you hear anything or think of anything else that may help us to open an inquiry? Perhaps if you get some rest and drink some water? And if you still feel there is cause for concern, give us a call back or come in to see us,' PC Banks said. 'There's also the Samaritans that could help—'

Stacey hung up. She could imagine PC Banks sharing a giggle with her friends in the station about the drunk crazy lady on the phone who thought someone had murdered her friend who she hadn't seen in thirty years, all because the Royal Mail had delivered a letter to her.

So now what should she do? Ignore it like Bev and Paula seemed to want to do? Did she need this aggravation in her life? Probably not. She thought about calling Alan and talking to him about it, but knew she would come away from the conversation feeling unworthy. The days when they could talk about anything, would put the world to rights over a glass of wine and a takeaway were long gone. In fact, those days had been short-lived. The demons playing around in Stacey's mind had made sure of that. Her need to implode anything good in her life.

Bev and Paula were right. She certainly didn't need the police digging into their past. What had she been thinking? If PC Banks had taken her seriously, then all the time spent trying to keep it all buried would've been pointless.

Not that Stacey could forget about it. There were some

things she couldn't put aside or move on from, even after all this time.

That weekend was one of them.

She's a mess. Look at her, passed out on the couch again, her mouth slack, drool pooling on the cushion under her head. This time she left the back door open. It squeaked on its hinges as I pushed it open and a cat charged out into the night. I left it ajar in case the cat found its way back.

She is lying on her back, one arm flung above her head, the other hanging low to the carpet. It would be so easy to finish this now, a hand over her face, watching her eyes bulge as she struggles to breathe, as panic rips through her and her arms start to flail, only for the life to drain out of her and her body to lie still again.

And the whole time she would be looking at me.

I reach out a gloved hand, hover it over her open mouth, pull it back again.

Her phone is on the coffee table. I hold it under the hand dangling to the floor and gently use her thumbprint to access it.

I read the texts that have passed between them with interest, then scroll through other messages, the drunken texts to her ex, the suggestive messages to someone called Simon who seems capable of only conversing in emojis. Aubergines, peaches, that kind of thing. Juvenile.

She snorts and turns her head away, pushing it into the cushion. I am again tempted to put my hand on her skull and push her face into the upholstery, but I put the phone back where it was and leave. The cat is sitting on the path outside the back door. It watches me with judgemental eyes. I reach down and pick it up, stroke it gently, then push it back into the kitchen and close the door.

12

WINTER 1992

Valentina closed the window in Stacey's room, cutting off the cold draught that had carried out the smell of cigarettes. She had seen them coming across the car park, their laughter reaching all the way up to the open window, but she didn't want them to catch her in Stacey's room. She'd taken to hanging out in there when everyone else was out, wearing Stacey's clothes, trying on her make-up, lying in her bed. It was like she was trying Stacey on for size, figuring out what it was about her that everyone gravitated towards, like a magnet.

The dynamic had changed in the last few weeks since she had overheard Stacey and Paula. She'd been giving them space, tried to fit herself into the box they had designed for her. It was a tight squeeze, with much of the Valentina in her wanting to burst out at the seams. Her charm offensive had been impressive. She either turned them down when they invited her out, telling them she was having a quiet night in to study, or she went and made sure she didn't drink too much, keeping herself alert and in control. She needed to make this work. She needed to keep the Other Valentina on a leash.

Stacey had met a new guy on campus. Peter had swooshy hair, ocean blue eyes and a shaving rash on his neck. Valentina had subtly informed Sean of Peter's existence when she had seen him in the Student Union the other day, relishing how his face fell as she dropped into conversation how funny Stacey's new boyfriend was. He wasn't funny at all, in actual fact.

Sean wasn't the only one wounded by Stacey's new fling. Paula had reached a new level of grumpiness. It became commonplace to see Peter emerge from the bathroom in just his boxer shorts or for Stacey to slope in the next morning wearing the same clothes as the day before. Paula tended to be sullen and quiet on those days when Stacey was with her new boyfriend, closing herself in her room, saying she had to study.

But Bev was almost oblivious to the drama – or choosing to pretend like none of it was happening. She had the approach that everything was okay if she closed her eyes and pretended it wasn't happening. Bev and Valentina had spent a lot of time chatting at the kitchen table while Paula sulked and Stacey shagged. It made Valentina very happy that one of them was accepting of her.

And then Stacey would come home for a few days, the frost would clear and Bev would abandon Valentina once more, choosing to close herself into Paula and Stacey's room, with giggling coming through the walls along with the smell of the pizza that Valentina had ordered but they had eaten.

She heard their voices on the stairs now as she removed the traces of Stacey's lipstick from her lips, heard the key in the door as she remade the bed, darted into the bathroom and emerged just as they stepped over the threshold.

'Hi, everyone, good afternoon?' she greeted them warmly.

'Yeah, not bad,' Paula said.

Stacey wasn't with them.

'Stacey not with you?' she said to Paula. 'You hardly see her these days. You must miss hanging out with her.'

Paula narrowed her eyes. 'Actually, she's outside talking to Sean.'

'Oh, right.'

On campus, Valentina had long ago worked out what Stacey's timetable was and was still keeping an eye on her in between lectures, keeping to a safe distance, then casually bumping into her every now and again. Stacey was right. Sean was definitely following Stacey around campus. Valentina had intentionally bumped into him on several occasions too. She started asking him for coffee and walking with him to lectures with the dual purpose of getting to know him better and keeping his attention diverted away from Stacey. He was nice, but very intense. Not much made him laugh and he was always drawing her into deep conversations on topics about which she knew very little. He had a way of making her feel vacuous.

She thought she'd been making ground there, but Stacey was an ever-present threat.

She was also proving a tough nut to crack and one that Valentina had pretty much given up on. She remained resolutely distant from Valentina, disengaged, indifferent. Valentina would always be the outsider as long as Stacey was the favourite. Sure, the other three had years of history and friendship, but Valentina didn't even think Stacey was particularly nice to them. She never helped with tidying up the place or washing dishes; she would happily ditch them to go out with other friends, especially if there was a new boy involved; and she never bought her fair share of drinks.

So why did everyone worship Stacey? And why did no one see Valentina?

The flat was empty. The other three had gone out to yet another party to which they had not invited Valentina. She had picked up whispered snatches of conversation about it while they were getting ready and it sounded like Stacey had told the other three not to invite her. Valentina opened the door to the balcony and watched them wander into the night, with their arms linked, Stacey in the middle as always.

She really was getting in the way.

Valentina had a bottle of beer dangling from her hand and she swigged from it as they disappeared from sight. It was a clear evening, stars at full brightness, the moon large and round. She leant on the balcony, fighting the urge to scream into the silence.

'Nice night, isn't it?' she heard a voice say. She looked to her right and saw Sean leaning over the balcony of his flat further along, mirroring her with a bottle of beer in his hand.

'Yeah, it is,' she said back.

'So where are they off to?' He'd been watching them too then.

'Some party – someone Stacey knows. Probably one of

Peter's friends. They're getting quite serious now,' she lied. His lips pursed. She smiled sweetly back at him.

'You didn't fancy going with them?'

She wasn't about to admit to him she hadn't been invited, so she replied, 'Nah, fancied a quiet one. Been out too much lately. And besides, Stacey and Peter can get quite *physical*, which is awkward sometimes.'

Silence fell uncomfortably. Then he said, 'Fancy some company?'

Valentina thought about how captivated he was by Stacey, how they all were, and how she was there alone, and she heard herself saying, 'Sure, why not?'

She woke to the sound of the front door closing and the loud stage whispers of the intoxicated. She tried to move, but felt pinned down. There was an arm flung over her, dusted with blond hair and wearing a leather bracelet with a charm in the shape of a rhino. She turned her head to the side and saw Sean fast asleep next to her. Clothes were strewn across the floor and a number of empty beer bottles littered the coffee table.

There was a weird blank in her memory. One minute they had been chatting on the sofa, listening to CDs, drinking the beers he had brought over and then it was like someone had pressed the delete button. When she tried to remember what came next, there was just white space and static.

Sean needed to go. The others couldn't find him here. It wouldn't go down well. Last night she had thought this was a good idea, but she'd meant a drink, a flirty chat. Not this. They would never understand that this hadn't been planned.

She listened carefully. The girls weren't sitting in the kitchen chatting because there was no dull sound of music, no lowered voices. They must've gone straight to bed. She shook Sean until he groaned and opened one eye. 'You need to go,' she said.

He groaned again and closed his eyes. She kicked him hard on the leg under the covers. 'Go! Now!'

'What time is it?'

'I don't know – one o'clock maybe? Just go.'

He sat up slowly while she started gathering his clothes together for him. She bent down to grab his T-shirt from the floor and noticed what looked like the little plastic casings of a headache capsule on the carpet under the couch. She frowned, picked them up along with the wrapper from a condom and tossed them into the wastepaper bin before grabbing Sean's flip-flops. By now he at least had his underwear on. She shoved the rest of his clothes into his arms and pushed him towards the closed lounge door. She paused again, listening, her ear to the glass. It was quiet.

'Listen, don't tell anyone about this, okay?' she said in a whisper.

He shrugged and said, 'Fine by me.'

She opened the door and shoved him into the hallway.

As they reached the front door, Stacey emerged from the kitchen with a glass of water in her hand.

They all stared at each other, then Sean said, 'Night, ladies,' with a smirk and wandered off into the dark in his pants with his clothes still bundled together.

13

PRESENT DAY

The doorbell was insistent and shrill. Stacey swore loudly and threw back the duvet. A shadowy figure hovered behind the glass of the front door and she pulled the cord of her dressing gown tight around her.

Clive the postman was standing on the other side of the door, a tall and thin man whose dark hair was mostly obscured by a baseball cap that was pulled low against the pouring rain.

'Morning, love,' he said in a gruff voice. 'Sign here.' He shoved an electronic handpiece at her. She scribbled something indecipherable in the box on the screen and swapped him the handpiece for a letter.

The letter looked official. Her heart dropped into her feet when she saw a solicitor's office stamp in the top corner of the envelope. Was it work firing her after last week? Or Alan? Either of these was plausible at this stage. Her phone buzzed in her hand – she'd ignored a call from one of her brothers yesterday and he was texting to check up on her. She wanted to text back to tell him to fuck off – they would all love it if they knew she had been fired. The favourite daughter falling from grace spectacularly – no job, no husband, no prospects. Family bonds weren't as close as they used to be since she'd started pushing them all away from her.

She walked back into the kitchen, tearing at the envelope. The letter inside politely informed her that Valentina Lucia Mackenzie had instructed them to pass a bequeathment on to her. Stacey wanted to laugh out loud at the idea that Valentina had a last will and testament in place, then figured that was inappropriate, even if she was standing in her own flat in her dressing gown, alone.

Stacey read the letter again. Yes, Valentina had left her something and she had to contact the solicitor's office to collect it. Stacey really hoped it was a large wad of cash – it would make her life a hell of a lot easier. She thought of Stacey's wealthy father and this time she did laugh out loud. At the irony of it – how Valentina had managed to ruin her life, but was now likely to be the person to save it after all. How Stacey had treated her like shit when they had lived together and yet she was going to be rewarded for it.

She got into a hot shower and stood for a moment, her face turned up to the spray, relishing in it peppering her skin, allowing herself a moment of hope. Dressing quickly, she made a cup of tea and tapped the number for the solicitor into her phone.

An efficient receptionist answered the call in clipped tones.

'Hi there,' Stacey said breezily. 'I received a letter from your company this morning about needing to collect a cheque that has been left to me by a dear friend who passed away recently. How do I go about arranging this?'

The receptionist informed her that all she needed to do was come to the solicitor's office if it was local to her and she could collect in person. It was indeed local and Stacey said she would be there within the hour.

Her good mood continued as she stepped out into what now looked to be a bright morning, with a cyan sky that stretched for miles. The earlier rain had cleared, leaving only damp streets and a metallic smell in the warming air. She walked with purpose, avoiding the puddles and feeling a lightness she hadn't felt in some time. Shops were quietly open and commuters rushed to work with reusable coffee cups in hand. She had the luxury of not needing to worry about being late.

She walked past a small bookshop and saw in the window the novel that Elaine had been reading on the reception desk when Stacey had left last week in disgrace. The book was about a murder in a blended but dysfunctional family by an author who was unfamiliar to her, but she went in and bought it anyway, feeling frivolous.

The solicitor's office wasn't far from her work and it felt surreal being here on a Monday but not turning right to walk past the small greengrocer's, the deli sandwich shop and the estate agent's, as she normally would. Instead, she turned left towards the KFC, dodged around a woman walking a chihuahua that was dressed in a pink hoodie, and stepped over the protruding legs of a homeless man bundled into a stained tweed coat and a grey beanie. She stopped, retraced her steps and put a couple of pound coins in his used coffee cup, feeling magnanimous.

A man was standing outside the KFC with a box of chicken nuggets on offer. Assuming they were free samples, she reached out for a nugget and said, 'Thanks.'

He looked at her in disbelief and said, 'What the fuck?' which she thought was a bit strange until he closed the box of nuggets and rushed away, scowling, and she realised that he wasn't offering free samples after all, but actually eating his breakfast, to which she had just helped herself.

She was mortified and could feel the angry heat of shame wash over her as she started walking again. She skirted around the edge of the pavement to avoid a woman with a pushchair just as a double-decker bus drove past, its front wheel splashing dirty brown rainwater all over her legs.

The reception for the solicitor's office was stylish and modern, with sterile white walls and black leather chairs. A smartly dressed woman looked up as Stacey stepped up to her desk. She slowly took in Stacey's damp legs and the brown marks on her trainers.

'I'm Stacey Maxwell – here to collect an envelope? I called earlier?'

'Of course, take a seat and I will be right with you,' the receptionist said politely.

Stacey sank into the low chair, hearing the leather squeak and fart as she adjusted her position.

The receptionist disappeared beyond a glass door, only to return moments later carrying what looked very much like a shoebox and a paper file.

She approached Stacey and handed her the shoebox. 'Here you go,' she said with a distanced smile. 'Would you mind signing this as proof of receipt please?'

'I'm sorry?' Stacey said, taking the surprisingly heavy box. 'I don't think this is right.'

'Stacey Maxwell?'

'Yes, but I was expecting a cheque?'

The receptionist consulted the paper file, then shook her head and said, 'No, this is what you are here to collect – from Ms Mackenzie.'

She held out the paper again, along with a pen. Stacey paused, then thought maybe the cheque was inside the box. Signing the form, she struggled to her feet and gathered the box up under her arm.

This was not what Stacey had been expecting. She had fully expected to be handed a cheque, hopefully large, that she would immediately take to the bank to deposit. Instead, she sat at a table in the sunshine outside a coffee shop with the box in front of her. She ordered a coffee and pulled the box closer for inspection.

It had once housed a pair of size-six black patent leather heels from Jimmy Choo apparently – and Stacey had a momentary thought that they would be too big for her size-five feet if that was what Valentina had left her – but there were no shoes inside the box.

Instead, it was full of envelopes, notebooks and photographs. Hoping that one of the envelopes contained a cheque, Stacey started to go through it all paper by paper, but could feel the rest of the air deflating from her initial bubble of hope. The waitress brought out her coffee, but Stacey ignored her as she opened a letter addressed to Valentina Mackenzie from what appeared to be her local GP, detailing an appointment with an oncologist.

Valentina had been diagnosed with cancer two years ago.

Was that what had killed her in the end then? Not some knife-wielding stalker or an unwelcome blast from the past?

Stacey sat back in the metal chair and felt tears start to build along with the realisation that she had heard what she had wanted to hear, jumped to conclusions. Valentina hadn't left her any money after all.

Going back to the papers in the box, she tried to make sense of them, find a purpose behind them. It was a paper trail of Valentina's last two years. Why?

Stacey could feel a darkness settling over her as the disappointment won out over any sense of curiosity. She pushed the box away.

Fuck Valentina. Manipulating her again.

She sat, her back rigid against the couch cushions, her feet dangling like a small child's. It was quiet in the flat but outside the evening symphony of car horns, dogs barking and kids shouting had begun. Stacey heard none of it. She stared at the wall in front of her, letting her disappointment manifest and evolve into something that felt less immersive. The daylight was started to lose its shape when she finally moved.

She grabbed her phone, ordered the cheapest and greasiest takeaway she could find and sat back on the couch with the shoebox in front of her once more. She needed to know why Valentina had sent this to her, needed to understand.

The letters from Valentina's doctor detailed her breast

cancer treatment and various appointments, but why did she want Stacey to know that? Because it was what ultimately killed her? Then why the message about being scared? Why mention *him* again?

She had a sudden mental image of Valentina sitting in a hospital bed, a scarf tied tightly around her head, alone and terrified, and she felt guilty for having reacted so strongly to the news that there was no money in the bequeathment.

Shameful, Stacey.

There was an academic diary with a black cover and the year 1992-93 embossed in small gold numbers. Stacey paused, feeling the weight of it in her hands, as though expecting it to be so much heavier considering the relevance of that year.

She flicked through the pages, noting the scribbles about Valentina's classes, assignment due dates and various appointments with her tutor, as well as occasional doodles. So many entries suggesting her father was visiting or dates to have dinner with him, all crossed out, the pen tearing the paper in places. Stacey couldn't remember him visiting even once that year. There were many evenings when Valentina had dressed to go out and then had changed her mind at the last minute. Stacey now realised that for what it was – a daughter desperate to see her father, only for him to have something more important to do instead. She always had an excuse as to why he couldn't make it.

She remembered Valentina had loved to doodle, like her fingers couldn't keep still. Her notes for classes had been covered in random hieroglyphics. She'd draw caricatures of the people she saw and the diary had little characters and images drawn into the corners of the pages.

The day she had moved in with the three of them was marked in red pen with exclamation marks and little stars around the words. Similarly, Stacey's birthday was decorated with balloons. Stacey couldn't help herself from flicking forward a few months. Seeing all the arrangements for that weekend carefully detailed on the page in front of her left her feeling chilled, like there was a ghost sitting next to her, breathing on her neck and stroking her hair, whispering, 'Do you remember?'

Then the entries stopped.

She flicked back again, a realisation jumping into her brain. They weren't just the details of Valentina's classes; they were also the timings of Stacey's classes, where she had gone, who she had been with. She had occasionally suspected Valentina was watching her, but this was actual proof. At the time, she had been more preoccupied with the idea that Sean was following her. That feeling of being watched had become a constant coat she wore. But now she started to doubt whether it had been him at all. Maybe it had been Valentina she had sensed all that time.

There were notes on the others too – Stu, Sean, Paula, Bev, even someone she called 'coffee girl', who had apparently spent time with Stacey on campus, mostly having coffee together and hanging out. Stacey didn't recall the girl. It was thirty years ago, after all.

The diary was a stalker's paradise and a snapshot of a twisted mind. But it was also like a book of love letters. When you read between the lines and actually looked at the notes and doodles, there were comments on what Stacey had been wearing on a particular day, for instance, and a note about how good it had looked. She'd then tried to find the dress herself, scribbling questions about where it came from. More notes about a certain hairstyle Bev had tried or a meal that Paula had cooked for them.

None of the notes were nasty or malicious. It was just someone trying to fit in, to be like them. Creepy nonetheless, but Stacey was ashamed to think she may have misunderstood Valentina.

Stacey set the diary aside. Underneath it was a random collection of what looked to be receipts for various things – drinks, food, cigarettes. All dated for the same few days. Stacey realised with a jolt that Valentina had kept the receipts from that last weekend.

Next came a pile of photographs of the four of them, smiling, happy, drinks in hand and their arms around each other. She couldn't help but smile when looking at their fresh faces, all of their hopes and dreams drawn on in blue eyeliner and the blackest of mascara. This was before selfies and smartphones. These were the days of disposable cameras and taking them to be processed at the one-hour photo booth. The excitement of opening the little folder and discovering that your finger had been over the lens for most of them. The joy at finding that one perfect picture in amongst the blurry ones.

Stacey remembered Valentina's bedroom wall. Despite only knowing them for a few months, she had Blu-Tacked a collage of photos to one wall and was constantly snapping away on a disposable camera that she kept in her handbag at all times.

The photos fit with the entries in the diary as visual evidence of Valentina's point of view.

At the bottom of the box she found an A3 piece of

paper folded numerous times until it was about the size of her overworked credit card. She unfolded it to discover a hand-drawn map of the university and the surrounds, with various places circled in red and symbols drawn on it. On the reverse side someone had scribbled more symbols down, like shorthand. Stacey frowned, looked closely at the circled locations, trying to fathom the significance. The university was on the left-hand side of the map and there were places marked all the way over to the right by the river and the woods.

Then she realised what it was.

It was the location of the flat and the itinerary they had followed that weekend. The places they had been to – and that one final destination, like the X on a treasure map, except this was a red circle right over the river.

In the very corner of the map was a message written clearly in longhand.

> *Stacey,*
> *He's coming for you too. He's going to find you and then he's going to tell the police everything.*
> *Stop him. Don't let him get you too.*
> *Follow the trail, retrace our steps and you will get to the truth.*
> *V x*

Paula stifled a yawn. The television was blaring a replay of a David Attenborough documentary about penguins and she had to fight to keep her eyes open against his soporific voice. Sue was glued to it. She loved a nature documentary, but Paula would've preferred to watch the Tom Hardy film that was showing on Channel 4. She had set it to record and hoped she could watch it sometime when Sue was out. If Sue ever left her for long enough, that is.

Since her phone call from Stacey yesterday, Sue had essentially been supervising her, giving her no room for any apparent infidelity. She had no workshops booked in today, so every time Paula moved, she could feel Sue's eyes on her.

She suspected Sue had taken to deleting all of Paula's series-linked favourites because none of them had recorded lately. Another way to punish her. Of course, it could also just be that the system had glitched and the series links hadn't renewed. She shouldn't jump to conclusions.

Sue was lying against Paula on the sofa, but instead of it feeling intimate and cosy, Paula felt claustrophobic. Sue's arms were entwining her. She felt like a spider trapped in a web. The more she moved or twitched, the tighter Sue seemed to squeeze.

Paula yawned again and felt her eyelids droop. She was about to succumb to blissful sleep, hoping that if she did fall asleep here, Sue would leave her on the sofa for the night, when her phone erupted with a shrill, jarringly jaunty ringtone.

Paula jumped, as did Sue.

'Who the hell is calling you at this time?'

It was just after 9pm, hardly the middle of the night. Paula clamped down the sigh that nearly escaped her mouth.

She tried to grab her phone from the coffee table, but Sue's hand shot out and reached it first.

'Stacey again. She just can't leave you alone, can she?'

Paula's stomach plummeted. 'Just let it ring,' she said quietly.

'No, I think you should answer it and tell her not to call you anymore.'

'I've told you she's just a friend. An old friend.'

'And I've told you that you don't need people like her in your life. You have me. That's all you need.' Sue sat up and Paula acknowledged the relief at the weight lifting from her lap. 'Unless I'm not enough for you?'

'Of course you are.'

'Then tell her not to call you again.' Sue was brandishing the still-vibrating phone like a weapon.

Paula reached for the phone, but it stopped ringing before she could answer it.

'I'll call her later. Come on, let's carry on watching.' She leant back against the sofa cushions and pointedly stared at the television, ignoring the angry warmth that spread across her cheeks.

The phone began to ring again almost immediately. They both stared at it like it was the timer on an unexploded bomb.

'Maybe she's in trouble,' Paula said. 'That's why she's phoning back. Maybe I should answer it.'

Sue huffed and puffed her annoyance. 'Do what you want,' she said and got to her feet. She stalked off into the bedroom, slamming the door behind her.

Paula exhaled and answered the call resignedly. 'Stace, what's up? Are you okay?'

Stacey was talking at her, but the words were jumbled, rushing into each other. 'Stacey, slow down. I don't understand.'

'Paula, she's trying to tell us something. She left me this box and there's a map. It's like a weird treasure map, but I think she's trying to tell me how to find out what happened to her.'

'What do you mean, she left you a box?'

'A solicitor phoned and told me she had left me something. I stupidly dared to think it was money for a moment there, but it was just a box of papers and letters and stuff. Details about her breast cancer treatment. But then under a pile of old photographs of us, I found this map and she has written on it, telling me he's coming for us.'

Her words were dodgem cars bumping into each other and rebounding away.

Paula slowed her own down to compensate. 'Stacey, back up. You said cancer? Valentina had cancer?'

'Yes! But that's not important.'

'Of course it is! That will be why she died, not something more sinister. Look, I can't talk about this now—' Her eyes flicked to the closed bedroom door. 'Let's meet tomorrow, talk about it in person. Okay?'

'Okay, okay. That's good,' Stacey replied. 'I'm going to call Bev too.'

'Yes, good idea.'

Paula hung up, satisfied that she had calmed Stacey down a bit, but the conversation had bothered her. When they had been friends, Stacey had been the calmer one, the one who didn't get rattled by exams and pressure. Now she sounded like she was just gripping on, but her fingers were slipping. Paula had noticed a rigidity about her at the funeral, had assumed it was because of the occasion. Maybe she had misread the situation.

Another part of her recognised how pleased she felt now that it was Stacey chasing her.

Thank you, Valentina.

Bev was asleep on the sofa, her mouth hanging open slackly, little snorts coming from one blocked nostril. Malcolm was in his armchair, his slippered feet propped up. Every time Bev snorted, his eyes flicked at her in distaste. He nudged up the volume on the television by another two points.

Bev's phone started to ring, sending vibrations through the sofa cushions.

'Bev! Your phone,' Malcolm said firmly and Bev lurched awake, feeling gritty and off-centre. Her eyes were blurry. She couldn't remember where the phone was for a second, then felt the vibrations and slid her hand down the side of the sofa cushion.

'Hello?' she croaked.

'Bev? Is that you?'

Bev frowned, still not connecting the dots. 'Yes?'

'It's Stacey. Listen, I'm meeting Paula this week and I want you to come too. It's Valentina.'

'Val's dead, Stacey,' Bev said, rubbing at her eyes. 'We've talked about this.'

'I know, but what we need to work out is *why*. She's sent me a map and some clues.'

'Seriously?'

'Yes, I know it sounds mad, but there's something there, I know it. She says he's coming for us next too.' Her voice was a low, conspiratorial whisper.

Bev paused, felt the tiredness sitting on her. She wished

it would all come out into the open. She didn't know how much longer she could go on with all of this. 'Fine, let me know the details and I'll meet you.'

After Stacey hung up, Bev dragged herself to her feet, said goodnight to Malcolm and the dog, and slowly climbed the stairs, her legs heavy and her knees clicking. She passed Jasper's room, which was suspiciously in darkness, and then Bethany's room, which had a blue glow coming from under the door. She was still up and on her phone despite the rule that there were to be no phones in their rooms after 9pm.

But Bev didn't have the energy for an argument tonight. She felt tired in her bones and just wanted to crawl into bed and sleep, so she ignored it and kept walking, up another flight of stairs to the loft room.

The Peloton loomed large in the window and she reached around it to draw the curtains.

By the time she had brushed her teeth, smeared anti-ageing moisturiser into her rapidly sagging skin and changed into her nightgown, her earlier exhaustion had disappeared and she lay in the dark on her back, now unable to drop back into sleep. This was why she shouldn't sleep on the couch. She tossed and turned, trying to find a comfortable position, but lying on her front hurt her back and lying on her side hurt her arm. God, she felt old.

She stared into the dark, thinking about the people the four of them had become, where all those dreams had evaporated to, what they looked like now. She thought of the husband downstairs and the daughter in her room, both of whom she barely spoke to these days. Just who was Bethany talking to? She thought of her son, who she felt she didn't really know anymore. A polite stranger. She thought about her own life and its lack of purpose.

And then she thought about the years ahead, when the kids had gone to university and it was just her and Malcolm in their big house, barely speaking, moving around each other and apologising for getting in each other's personal space, and she knew that sleep wouldn't be visiting again tonight for quite some time.

I say goodnight in the chat and watch as the three dots show she is typing again. We have said goodnight at least three times now, but she is reluctant to let me go. I've told her I'll miss her when she's asleep, that I imagine what she looks like, what she's wearing. I have actually enjoyed these interactions with her, like playing a role in a film. This is the joy of modern technology – you can be anyone you want to be.

You can be anyone *they* want you to be.

Then the message comes that I have been waiting for, planning for. She wants to meet. I smile. Oh, I love this game. And they are making it so easy.

It has to be her idea for it to be plausible. Her friends will warn her off, will question my authenticity, but she will defend me, say it was her idea to meet, not mine.

I start typing again, planting the seed, watching it grow.

14

WINTER 1993

Valentina drove around the car park looking for a space. Her dad had bought her a new car for her birthday and this was her first opportunity to drive it back to university after the end-of-semester break. He hadn't actually been there to present it to her. It had been dropped off by someone at his office. She was excited to show it off to the others though, knowing how thrilled they would be that they now had a designated driver.

The heater was blasting out hot air in an attempt to combat the January chill. She had missed them all over the Christmas break, had wondered what they had been doing, who they had been seeing. Apart from a few days over Christmas, they had all stayed in the flat while she had stupidly travelled back to Scotland in the hope of actually seeing her father. He'd made yet more promises and had broken every one of them. The house had looked magical though, just like she imagined her mother would want it. He'd paid a company to come in and decorate. There had certainly been no heart-warming trip to choose a tree or evening in front of the fire with Bailey's while they decorated it.

So she had packed up early and travelled back to her new family.

Stacey had been furious after seeing Sean leave in his underwear that day before Valentina left and there had been a few angrily whispered conversations behind closed doors, the hissing and spitting reaching Valentina's ears anyway. It sounded like Bev had been the one to convince Stacey to let her stay because she had nowhere else to go and they would never find someone else to take her place and pay for the rent this far into the year. Valentina had gone back home then, giving them all some space and hoping it would be forgotten by the time she got back. She'd also transferred the rest of the year's rent over to Bev in one payment as insurance.

There was more to her going home though. She had been looking for clarity. Something wasn't right about that night with Sean and every time she thought about it, she felt cold and off-centre, like she couldn't find the missing piece of a puzzle.

She had never intended to sleep with Sean, so why had she?

And why couldn't she remember it?

Still, she had invited him in and knew she had been flirting with him as they drank a couple of beers. Her own fault, really.

She had called the flat a few times, hoping to talk to Stacey, but only Bev ever answered and was politely friendly, said she would pass on the messages. She'd be curious to see if the messages were written down on the notepad by the phone.

She even tried calling Sean to find out if anyone had said anything to him, but the phone in their flat had rung for ages, then Rob's high-pitched squeak had finally answered and she'd hung up, not actually sure what she wanted to say.

She'd been here before though, the gaps in her memory, the black spaces of time that seemed to break off in her mind and glide away, like a released balloon floating off into the distance. It had been like that during that incident last year when they'd accused her of obsessing over her lecturer, following him, calling him, hanging around outside his rooms. He'd really got annoyed when she had started following his wife, tried to have conversations with her, but Valentina couldn't remember a lot of that. The memories of the abortion were there though, particularly late at night. The smell. The cold steel. The cramps.

That hadn't been a lie.

Still, if he hadn't slept with her in the first place, she wouldn't have become so attached, right? Wouldn't have realised how desperately she wanted what he already had. Completely his fault and he knew that – the pay-off was not just to keep him quiet about her issues, but also an admission of guilt on his part and an acknowledgement that Valentina's dad would take no further action with the university. Win-win. Sometimes her father was a handy man to have on her side.

A freezing rain was falling, making visibility really difficult and the roads slippery, but she finally found a parking space on the other side of the car park to the stairs. She scrambled out of the car, grabbed her bags and ran through the rain to the shelter of the stairwell. She stood at the foot of the stairs, dropped her bags and shook the rain out of her hair.

'Woof,' someone said.

'Excuse me?' she snapped.

'You look like a dog after a bath.'

She turned to see Stu standing behind her, smirking as usual.

'You're calling me a dog?'

'Only joking, Val, relax.'

'Not exactly a compliment, is it?'

'Nice motor,' he said without apologising.

'Thanks,' she muttered back.

'Gonna take me for a spin?' Everything that came out of his mouth sounded weirdly creepy lately, like he was trying too hard, but not quite hitting the mark.

'Probably not, Stu, no.'

'Oh, come on. It'll be fun – we can go get a drink, maybe park up at River's End to watch the sunset or something? I've got a couple of bottles of red wine upstairs.' He was leering at her in a way that she assumed he thought was sexy, but looked to her like he had trapped wind.

'Nah, you're okay.'

'You know Sean and Stacey are back on.'

She stopped in her tracks. The way he said it – with the utmost delight at sharing the news, a trick she had learnt well – meant that Stu knew about her and Sean. So much for Sean not saying anything to anyone. 'Oh? What happened to Peter?'

'Well, I say back together... more like he's trying really hard after Stacey and Peter broke up. She's playing hard to get, but I think he's wearing her down. Anytime now, I reckon.'

'Because that's the kind of foundation a good relationship is based on – wearing the other one down.'

'Some people are harder than others to get into bed, I guess.'

Ouch.

'She was dead easy the first time around,' Valentina said.

He smiled. 'Anyone would think you're jealous. Anyway, she loves the attention, so...' He shrugged, but Valentina could tell he was still mildly annoyed that Stacey had never been that interested in him. 'So how about it? Later?'

'Don't hold your breath.'

She struggled up the stairs with her bags. He didn't offer to help, just stood watching her, amused.

She unlocked the door and fell into the flat. 'Hello? I'm back!'

She could hear muted voices, but no one came to greet her.

'Hello?' she called again and followed the voices.

She stuck her head into Stacey's room and found her sitting on her bed smoking a cigarette out of the window, with Paula and Bev at her feet. They were nursing cups of tea.

'Hi,' Valentina said.

'Hi, Val. Did you have a nice break?' Bev asked.

'Yeah, thanks. I called out when I arrived – guess you didn't hear me.'

'Oh, did you? We were talking,' Stacey said coolly without looking at her.

'Oh, what's the gossip? What have I missed? Saw Stu

outside and he said something about you and Peter breaking up? Sorry to hear that.' she said to Stacey.

'Yeah, I just wasn't feeling it.' She shrugged, but didn't elaborate. An awkward silence ensued. At least she was talking to her though, even if it was without eye contact. The thing about Stacey was if you paid her enough attention, she'd lap it up. Valentina just had to persevere, pander to her for a while.

'Right, well, I'll get my bags into my room then. I've brought presents!' Valentina said and walked out. The mumbled voices started up again as soon as she left.

After she had dumped her bags, she went back to join them, a box of cigarettes and a lighter in her hand.

'It's just creepy sometimes, but he is useful to have around – he was really good to know when I was doing my last research paper on Cape Dutch architecture.'

'Who's this?' Valentina asked as she perched on the end of the bed.

'Near the window, please, Val – and since when do you smoke?' Bev said disapprovingly. Valentina moved to hover next to Stacey. She offered Stacey another cigarette, which Stacey considered, then accepted.

'She's talking about Sean,' Paula said pointedly. 'Stacey is keeping him hanging like a maggot on a fishing line.'

'Paulie!' Stacey swiped at her with her foot.

'What? It's pathetic. You're using him and he knows it. He must do.'

'Are you sleeping with him?' Valentina asked in a frosty voice.

'What do you care?' Stacey replied very quickly. 'And for your information, no, I am not. I'm choosier than that.'

Valentina shrugged.

'He wishes she was though,' Bev said with a giggle. 'That's why he keeps coming back.'

'No, that's just my magnetism and allure,' Stacey said with a cheeky grin. 'Right, I need to go. I said I would meet him on campus.' She stubbed out the hardly smoked cigarette and jumped off the bed.

'Are you in later?' Valentina asked.

Stacey stopped and turned to look back. 'Probably not, why?'

'Just because it's my first night back – and I brought you all Christmas presents,' she said in a quiet voice.

Stacey laughed bitterly. 'You only went home for a couple of weeks, not to Africa on sabbatical or something.'

Valentina flushed.

'The two of us are out tonight too,' Bev said. 'Mike and Rob are taking us to the cinema later.'

'It's not a date,' Paula was quick to add.

'See ya,' Stacey said and left.

'Right, I have to get ready too,' Bev said.

Valentina slunk back into her room, but kept the door open. She could hear the other three laughing, talking, and she felt alone. Still a stranger among them. Still no closer to feeling included.

The front door opened and closed as Stacey left. Then Bev and Paula were slamming the door on their way out. Valentina watched them all from the window. She saw Bev and Paula walking towards the river with Mike and Rob, the four of them laughing about something, the boys jostling each other. Bev jumped on Mike's back and he gave her a piggyback for some of it, then he dropped her and she

WHEN WE WERE YOUNG

chased him. Valentina could hear their laughter filtering in on a tiny draught of air through the window. She watched them until the woods ate them up.

Then she sat on her bed and let the silence swallow her whole.

The room smelled like stale cigarette smoke under a layer of floral perfume. They'd been using it since she'd been gone.

She looked over at the pile of presents in the corner and calmly got to her feet and began to kick out at them, flinging them around without a sound.

Out of breath, she stopped and flopped onto her bed, feeling a little better.

She took a moment, then wandered into the kitchen and peered into the fridge. Someone had put a 'Don't touch' label on a tub of leftovers, but apart from milk and some mouldy cheese, it looked like no one had done any shopping the whole time she was away. To be fair, in recent weeks, she had been the only one to do any shopping at all – and she had paid for it too.

The realisation came at her like a hard slap. They were all using her and she was lying back and letting them. She had spent most of her time at home thinking of ways to impress Stacey, ideas to get them to like her, and none of it would work in the end because they were laughing at her behind her back, thought she was needy and spineless. They hadn't missed her. They hadn't even thought about her in the weeks she was gone. It was almost as if they were sad to see her back. She was just the rent cheque to them.

The crux of it was Stacey. Everyone was so caught up on her. What the hell was so great about her anyway? She was a toxic friend, happy to toss you aside for a better offer. She was self-centred, opinionated and lazy.

The only one who had seemed happy to see Valentina today was Stu.

She sniffed at the milk, thought it smelled okay and thumped it onto the counter before slamming the fridge door hard enough to make the magnet holding the chores rota fall onto the floor. The rota floated from the fridge door like a huge piece of confetti to land on the linoleum. She watched it dispassionately, then stepped on it. She opened the cupboard, found a box of Rice Krispies but no bowls. A glance at the sink told her where all the dishes were, so she grabbed the last mug from the cupboard, the handle of which was missing, and the last spoon from the drawer.

There was no way in hell she was doing their washing up.

She carried her mug of cereal back into her room and sat heavily on the couch. This other half of the room was as much of a mess as the carnage she had created with the gifts. More cups and plates were left on the coffee table. Someone had tossed their shoes and socks off and they lay abandoned on the carpet like the leftover evidence of a car accident. There was an apple core left on top of the television with a fly sitting on it. No respect for the fact that this was essentially Valentina's bedroom, that she was expected back from her break and they could've tidied up their crap before she arrived.

The pack of cards was laid out on the table, a half-completed game of solitaire on the go. Putting the cereal to one side, she picked up the cards and shuffled them to the rhythm of the snap, crackle and pop from the mug of Rice Krispies.

Before she started playing, she asked the cards if she should go out with Stu tonight instead of staying in on her own.

The cards said yes.

A few hours later and her head was spinning like she'd spent too long on a merry-go-round. The rain had stopped when she knocked on Stu's door and suggested they went for that drive after all. His face had lit up like a Christmas tree and he had happily obliged. He'd disappeared back into the flat and reappeared minutes later with two bottles of cheap red wine. He seemed nervous when they headed down to her car. She thought it was sweet.

She hadn't intended on drinking more than two glasses. She was driving after all, not that it was far. River's End was on the far side of the woods, beyond the footbridge into town. She had just wanted to get away from the whispers in her ear, telling her how pathetic she was, to give herself room to breathe away from the flat and the constant reminders that she didn't even qualify for a room, but had to share the lounge space like a squatter. She wanted to drive away from the voice in her head telling her to tear the place apart, to burn it to the ground with Stacey, Bev and Paula in it.

They'd driven out along the edge of the woods until they reached a car park where people stopped to appreciate the view. There were benches and picnic tables set up in appreciation of the view over the river as it ran down out of the town itself and beyond. At this time on a cold night, there was no one else there.

They had parked the car and sat on the top of a picnic

table, their feet on the seat with the night sky above them and the bottles of wine between them. The sky was overcast with very few stars to be seen. It would've been a lovely place to sit if the wood hadn't felt wet and cold beneath her bum and the sky wasn't such an ominous, heavy weight above them. The air was very cold and they could see their breath in front of them. The heavy jumper she was wearing didn't help with the cold at all, but she hadn't thought to bring a coat.

One of the wine bottles had no label on it. Stu had unscrewed the cap and handed it to her. He drank from the other bottle, a cheap Australian red. Valentina had taken a sip from her bottle. It was cheap, bitter and warm, but one sip turned into two or three as the heat of it travelled through her, which had now turned into the rest of the bottle very quickly. She was still angry, but the wine was helping.

The bench started to slide around underneath her, tilting her this way and that like she was on a funfair ride.

They laughed and talked about all sorts of things. He seemed to be holding his wine better than her. His voice wasn't slurring and slipping like hers was. He reached out and rested his fingers on hers, subtly, very gently, like an innuendo. She looked at his fingers stroking the back of her hand and wanted to move it, but she couldn't get her hand to do what her brain was instructing. Stu was now looking at her with that familiar expression of intent that said he was perhaps not into talking any more.

But she wanted to talk. She was waffling on about Stacey and Sean and how ill-suited she thought they were, when he leant in mid-sentence and tried to kiss her. Initially, she kissed him back, then a sense of alarming panic came over her and she pulled back, roughly shoving her hand at his chest to push him away.

'No.'

He looked completely taken aback, as though this was inconceivable. 'What?'

'I'm not into this tonight. I just wanted a bit of friendly company, nothing else.'

He was looking at her in bemusement. Then his expression changed and he said, 'It's because of Sean, isn't it?'

'What?'

'You haven't stopped talking about him all night. You're just like everyone else. You're caught up on him, hoping he'll notice you.' His voice was acidic. 'Well, he won't, you know. And you have no idea what kind of person he is.'

He turned away from her in a sulk.

'No, I'm not after Sean. Where did you get that from?' Her words were thick and woolly, the bitterness of the wine coating her tongue. 'Besides, he's clearly obsessed with Stacey.'

'She should be careful. He's not who she thinks he is.'

'What do you mean?'

'Nothing,' he said petulantly.

'If there's something I need to know, you better tell me.' The conversation was jumbling together in her head.

'There isn't. It's... nothing.'

'Stu, you're a mate, okay? I like that we can have a laugh like tonight and not have to complicate things. But you don't need to be jealous of Sean.'

'Who said I was jealous?'

Valentina looked at him, his bottom lip protruding and

his hands hanging low between his legs, the bottle dangling from his loose grip. He lifted the bottle to his lips and took a long swig.

She wanted to laugh. Instead, she snatched the bottle from him and drank some more herself. 'I get it. I have the same thing with Stacey. Everyone loves her – they practically fall at her feet, and I don't get why. She can be a real bitch. You should hear some of the stuff she says about Sean. About all of you, in fact. You know, she said you have a bit of a teeny one down there—' she nodded with her head at his crotch '—and that your feet really stink.' She laughed raucously. 'And she says Sean is pathetic and not that good in bed. She's not into him, but she strings him along.'

'You didn't mind giving him a go.'

'I don't remember it. Ha!'

He looked sideways at her. 'Really?'

'Yeah, my mistake for drinking too much too quickly, I guess. It's a bit of a joke with the other three how sad and pathetic he is.' Valentina took another drink, then handed back the bottle. She didn't know why she was saying all of these things, but she couldn't get her mouth to stop.

They were quiet for a moment. The wind was picking up and the trees were groaning and flexing their muscles around them. Her bum had gone numb against the cold wood and she shifted her position. Her foot connected with the empty bottle and it fell and shattered on the ground. She watched with the mild fascination of the intoxicated.

'Do you really not remember?'

'Nope, not a thing. One minute we were talking and the next he was leaving in his pants. I wouldn't have slept with him if I was sober. I didn't want to. I just wanted a friend.'

She surprised both of them by starting to cry in big, ugly sobs. 'And now Stacey thinks I did it on purpose to get to her and they don't want me around anymore,' she said in between gulps. Her nose was running as much as her mascara. He looked around, horrified, as though hoping for backup. 'And now I just feel like a big, ugly slag,' she wailed.

He put a tentative arm around her. 'We should go. We should get you some water.'

He went to stand up, but she pulled him back down onto the cold table. 'No, no, I'm fine. I just feel... sick.' She launched from the table over to the bushes and threw up.

She staggered back to the table, her hysterics over as quickly as they had arrived. She wiped her eyes, then her mouth on the back of her hand and sat back down before grabbing his wine bottle and drinking deeply again.

'What did you mean – about Sean?' she said.

'He's just... if he has his eye on someone, he can be a bit... full-on. I just wouldn't want Stacey to get hurt or anything, even if she is a bitch as you say.'

'Oh, God, you too! You're all so worried about Stacey. What about me?'

He was going to reply, but the rain started up again, heavy and stinging. He grabbed her by the arm and bolted for the car.

By the time they reached it, they were soaked through, but laughing. Stacey climbed into the driver's seat and turned the key. The wheels screeched on the wet ground as she pressed too excitedly on the accelerator. The car lurched.

'Are you okay to drive? Maybe I should,' Stu asked. He was still swigging from his wine bottle.

'You're not driving my new car, forget it! I'm fine – and it's not far.'

'You sure you're feeling okay?'

She just smiled in return.

She peered through the windscreen at the dark ahead of her, but it was difficult to make much out. There were no streetlights and the headlights of the car only reflected back the raindrops. She breathed deeply, trying to steady herself, but her head was oscillating, and everything was coated in such darkness that she had to concentrate really hard to follow the gravel road out of the car park and back onto the tarmac.

Stu wound down his window and roared into the night as she turned onto the road too fast. They felt the car tilt, then steady itself again. She laughed and pressed the accelerator even harder as they sped along the road. The lights of the block of flats in the distance beckoned them home. She kept the wheels on the cat's eyes in the middle of the road to keep herself straight, using the thumps and bumps to correct herself when she veered too far to one side or the other.

A car passed them travelling in the other direction and Valentina thought perhaps she was a little too far over the white line this time. She corrected just in time and the car hooted as they shot past. Stu leant over and hooted the horn in return. She looked over and saw he was laughing.

Ahead of them was another car, this one travelling much slower than them. Valentina drove right up behind it, flashing her lights. Now was not the time for travelling at the speed limit. The rain lashed through the open window on Stu's side and she could feel it peppering her face, refreshingly cold on her hot cheeks.

Then Stu was leaning out of his window, unbuckling his trousers as he went. He was shouting at her, 'Overtake! Overtake!'

So she did. He turned in his seat and dropped his trousers as she drove parallel to the other car, showing them his bare butt and howling with laughter. An older couple were in the car. The woman looked away in disgust; her husband shook his head in disapproval. They braked and let Valentina's car shoot past. She overcorrected again as she pulled back in front of the other car and felt her car tilt once more. This time she had to reach out and grab onto Stu's wet shirt as he looked dangerously close to falling out of the open window.

He flung himself back into his seat, his hair soaked but his smile wide. 'Fuck, you are insane!' He began to buckle up his jeans again.

They were fast approaching the entrance to the car park for the flats and she was going to miss it, so she slammed on her brakes. They were both flung forwards. Stu slammed his hands against the dashboard, but Valentina felt her forehead hit the steering wheel hard. Tiny flashes of light exploded behind her eyes. She turned sharply into the car park, then slowed right down in order to find a parking spot. There was one, but it was quite far from the entrance, so she kept going. It was soon apparent that there wouldn't be a better space on this side. She slammed the car into reverse and floored the accelerator. They shot backwards and were both catapulted forwards again as the car collided with something.

'Whoops,' Valentina said with a giggle, put the car into first gear again and drove off. 'There'll be something further around.'

She found another space, parked the car as best she could and they scrambled out, running into the stairwell. Her shirt clung to her, transparent from the rain. Stu was transfixed, but she charged up the stairs and collapsed, panting, at the top.

'Bloody hell, that was the most fun I've had in ages! You are brilliant,' he said, following her up. His eyes were shining, but all Valentina could think about was what Stacey had said about his smelly feet. She laughed out loud.

Stu grabbed her and pulled her towards him. 'Are you sure you don't want me to come in?' he said. She could feel his breath on her face, could make out bits of skin flaking on his lips, and she felt a surge of nausea.

She swallowed and said, 'No, I need sleep. And water.'

'You can sleep – afterwards.' He smirked as his hands grabbed onto her waist.

'Sleep in your own bed, Stu, alone.' Now she just wanted to get away from him. She pushed at him ineffectually, her hands lacking any sense of strength or coordination.

'But Val, come on, I adore you,' he crooned, his hands wandering. 'You're breaking my heart. We could be beautiful together, like a symphony. You know you want to.'

This time she shoved him harder, her eyes steely. 'NO.'

He looked taken aback, then amused, like she was teasing him. Without warning, he flung his leg over the balcony wall overlooking the road, then followed with his other leg until he was dangling over, holding onto the bricks with just his hands, his body suspended above the three-floor drop down onto the tarmac. 'You're breaking my heart. Save me, take pity on me.'

Valentina watched him coldly. 'I tried that trick for

attention a few months back and it didn't work for me, so it's not likely to work for you.'

'Let me in, Val, let me in or I'll jump!' he wailed.

She rolled her eyes.

'Oh, Val, I can't bear to be without you!'

She stepped forward and said, 'So jump,' her face blank.

He looked unsure then. 'What?'

She leant into his face and said in a low voice, 'Jump if you want to. Don't let me stop you.' She still had her car keys in her hand and she poked at each of his fingers with the sharp end of her front door key. 'Eeny, meeny, miny, mo.'

'Ow! Stop it. Help me up!' he screeched.

'Oh, so you're joking then?'

'So were you!' His voice was tiny now and quite frightened.

'Was I? How do you know? You see, I'm not sure anyone would miss me if I did fall. Sad but true. What about you? Would anyone miss you? Do you want to find out?' She poked again, harder. One of the keys left a tiny bubble of blood on his finger.

'Fuck, Val, this isn't funny.' He went to pull himself up, but his hand slipped and his body tilted backwards. He managed to get his hand back onto the wall. 'Help me back up.'

Valentina stepped back and crossed her arms. 'You got yourself into it; now get yourself out,' she said coldly and walked away.

'Fuck, help me!'

She weaved as she tried to slot her key into the front door, ignoring Stu's pleas over her shoulder.

Footsteps clattered up the stairs. Mike and Rob emerged

from the stairwell, followed by Bev and Paula. They stopped short at seeing Stu dangling from the wall, his eyes wide like dinner plates. They rushed towards him and grabbed onto him.

Bev and Paula both shouted out in fright as the men dragged Stu over the wall and they collapsed in a heap on the floor.

When they got their breath back, Rob said, 'What the hell, Stu?'

'It was just a laugh. A stupid prank,' he said, but his eyes were wide and his skin was pale and clammy. He flicked his eyes warily at Valentina as she disappeared into the flat without a backward glance.

15

PRESENT DAY

Stacey jumped when a toddler in a high chair at the table next to them bashed her spoon against the plastic tray. The busy restaurant seemed to be heaving with children and mothers oblivious to the noise. Bev frowned at the kid but said nothing. Paula merely wiped up the last of her egg yolk with a corner of toast. The plate in front of Stacey was untouched. She pushed it away.

'You okay, Stacey?' Bev asked.

'It's just really noisy in here. I can't think straight. This is why I don't have kids.' She pushed her hair out of her face, feeling heat building in her cheeks. 'God, it's hot in here too.'

'Stace, what's going on?' Bev said.

'I don't understand any of it and it's tormenting me. He's dead. We all saw that.'

The women at the table next to them fell silent and threw shocked looks. Stacey glared back at them and they looked away hurriedly, signalled for the bill.

Bev sat forward, her face grey beneath the layer of foundation, and said in a bitter whisper, 'I can still remember that night so clearly. Some nights I wake up and I have to check to see if I still have dirt under my fingernails, if I can smell the stagnant river water. If she is dead because someone killed her, that's just karma for that night frankly. And I don't want to go back there ever again. I've moved on.'

'Have you, Bev? Have you really? I can't. I don't sleep. I haven't slept properly since that night,' Stacey said. Bev looked down into her cappuccino. 'We were all involved; it wasn't just her fault,' Stacey added.

'You've changed your tune a bit. I seem to think we all agreed we were only there because of her,' Paula said. 'Look, I get that this has rattled you, but I don't know why you are so obsessed with pursuing it. Bev is right, we should leave well alone. What does Alan think?'

'I've hardly told him that when I was university I just happened to kill someone after my last exam, have I? Are you telling me you've both confided in your partners?'

They didn't need to shake their heads. They all knew this wasn't the kind of thing you brought up in conversation over your morning cornflakes. Stacey watched a woman across the room pack up colouring crayons and teething rings, plant an innocent kiss on a chubby toddler cheek.

'It was thirty years ago. This is just Valentina messing with your head again, like she used to do. She couldn't open her mouth without a lie tumbling out. She knew she was dying, she had unfinished business with you, so she decided to fuck with you. It's sick, but that was her all over. You

WHEN WE WERE YOUNG

need to let it go. Get on with your life,' Paula said. 'We all do.'

It was blissfully quiet for a moment, then the toddler in the highchair screeched until her mother passed her a soggy stuffed giraffe.

'All I am asking is that we take one weekend to look into it. Follow the map, retrace our steps and see what's there. If at the end of the weekend, we have found nothing new, I will drop it. If we do find something, I'll take it to the police, but will keep you out of it.'

'You can't keep us out of it. If there is something there, we will all be implicated. You do realise that, don't you?' Bev hissed.

Stacey leant forward. 'But, Bev, if someone hurt Val, then I assume they know what we did and they could be coming for us next. Have *you* thought about that?'

Stacey sat on the edge of her bed, the weekend bag open behind her. Clothes were piled up around her; more were discarded on the carpet.

What exactly did you pack for this kind of thing?

She felt more than a little bit sick at the idea of the weekend now. Not spending time with Bev and Paula as such, although she would need to watch what she was saying, not let them get too close. She'd already revealed too much. It left her feeling exposed and naked.

It was the idea of reliving that weekend though. She didn't want to go back there, but she also knew she had to finish this once and for all, had to lock it away for good before all the secrets and guilt swallowed her whole. Bev wasn't the only one who was haunted by what they had done.

A sudden memory of Valentina the day she moved into their flat blindsided her. Valentina's scared eyes, the nerves evident in the way she clasped her hands as they pranked her with the party poppers, the amount of alcohol they ended up drinking that afternoon, sitting around that tiny breakfast bar where your ankles were always cold from the draught coming through from the hallway. How much Valentina had vomited the day after, to the point where Bev seriously contemplated phoning an ambulance because she was still throwing up at 7 p.m. That was the first of many epic hangovers for Val. She never could hold her drink. Thought she could though and would do anything for a reaction, but always paid for it the next day.

Stacey felt tears tickling her eyes just thinking of the girl who had moved in and how quickly she had morphed into someone else in a few short months. Which version had been the real Val?

Thinking back now, she could see how Valentina had tried them all on for size in a bid to be just like them so that they would like her, accept her. How wrong she had been. They had all had their *things*, that one part of their personality that made them unique, kept them sane, set them apart – except for Valentina. Paula had her running, all those endless miles of pavement that put distance between her and her disapproving family. Bev had her love of colourful glasses that set her apart from the crowd so that she wasn't just another boring, invisible geek. Stacey had had her love of architecture, her drawings and plans, her constant interior design ideas that were going to put her on the map one day.

But what had Valentina had? She couldn't think of anything.

But then, she hadn't really given Valentina much of a chance to express herself, had she? She had been petty, had felt threatened by Valentina. She could see that now. And why? Because she was worried her friends would like Valentina more than her? She'd had a lot of time to think about this in the last few days and she was ashamed of herself. And looking at the hand-drawn map Valentina had made, along with the doodles and caricatures in her diary, Valentina had been talented.

Why hadn't they noticed?

Stacey picked at a piece of skin around her fingernail and looked at the chaos around her. Thank God she lived alone. No one to be annoyed at the clothes tossed about. No one to talk her out of this. No one to worry if something happened to her.

Nothing to lose.

Sue hovered in the doorway as Paula packed her bag. In the years that they had been together, Sue and Paula had rarely spent a night apart and Paula was looking forward to being on her own, even if it was under these circumstances.

'Don't take that one, the colour looks awful on you,' Sue said as Paula packed the light blue shirt she loved and wore constantly.

Paula removed the shirt and put it to the side.

'You know, I still think you shouldn't go. We could go to the new vegan market in Alnwick on Sunday instead. There's a great Caribbean restaurant there that's just opened.'

Paula smiled tightly. 'I have to go. It's work.'

'No, you don't.' Sue sat heavily on the bed, making the suitcase bounce so much that a pair of Paula's sensible knickers flipped out of the suitcase and onto the blue-striped duvet.

Paula tugged on the sleeves of her hoodie, trying to filter out Sue's words as she subconsciously rubbed at her arm where bruises peppered her skin so that she looked like a Dalmatian. All those little nips when she came up to hug Paula, telling her she loved her, then pinching her like a toddler – they all left a mark.

So Paula had lied and said she had been called away on a work trip to a conference as a replacement for someone who had dropped out at the last minute. She'd had to leave Sue with the name of where they were staying, but thankfully Bev had booked them into a hotel just outside the grounds of the university that coincidentally had conference facilities. It was somewhere they would never have gone to in their student days. The carpets had to be sticky and the walls grey with cigarette residue for them to even consider a place worthy of visiting back then. If Sue were to check – and Paula had no doubt she would – she would find a website for a beautiful manor house in manicured gardens near to the university where a medical conference was taking place. Sometimes luck was on your side.

Paula had originally met Sue at a drumming workshop that she had been running when Paula was at a particularly low point in her life. Paula had split up from her previous girlfriend and had just learnt that her mother was ill, even though she hadn't seen her mother since the day she came out, the day her mother wept over apparently never having grandchildren and her father had told her to come back when she had 'grown out of it'. That had been just after graduation, when so much had already happened to her and she had needed the support of her family. Instead, Paula had run out of their small, terraced house in 'Shitbottle' and never looked back.

The first thing Paula noticed about Sue at that workshop was her voice, which commanded everyone in the room. So different to the northern accents of her friends and family, Sue had a voice like spiced rum with the lilts and tilts of the Caribbean running through it. Paula had since learnt that that hot-rum voice could also scald.

Paula had moved in, even though they hadn't been together long. She'd been moving from place to place without really feeling tethered since they had graduated and had needed something to feel more permanent. The truth was the place she had felt most at home was that little flat above the bakery, with the woods watching over them and the river whispering into the night. She would lie awake some evenings with the window open, Stacey snoring lightly in the bed across the room, and she's listen to the river talk to her, hear the trees singing in the breeze. That had been home – and Valentina had taken that away from her.

She'd been trying to recreate that homely feeling ever since and she thought that she had found it with Sue. But as the weeks wore on and the novelty wore off, she realised that she and Sue were very different people.

She packed a bag one day when Sue was at work. The

irony was she had one hand on the latch of the front door, ready to leave for good, when Paula's brother had phoned to say her mother had died. Paula hadn't had any contact with her family for some time, hadn't even known she was ill. The grief that hit her was mostly about what she hadn't been able to say to her, interwoven with a deep-seated guilt. She'd put the suitcase back in the cupboard and that's where it had stayed until today.

Sue had said it was for the best, that all Paula really needed was her. She'd talked her out of going to the funeral and within days she had proposed and Paula had said yes. They were married shortly afterwards, with no one there but the two of them in a tiny register office.

Since then, Paula had spent many nights lying awake, thinking of ways of escaping. Paula wasn't stupid. She knew that this was a toxic relationship, one where Sue was in control, from what they did to what they ate (Paula missed bacon sandwiches) to who they saw. And if things didn't go in Sue's favour, she would say nothing until the lights were turned off and they lay in bed. That's when she would whisper in Paula's ears – not words of affection, but all the ways in which she was a disappointment: her failures, her weaknesses, her ugliness. The things she'd done wrong that day. The ways in which she needed to do better tomorrow.

After a while you came to believe those whispered words in the dark. You came to wear them like a second skin. When you had no one else to contradict them, those words stuck.

The words telling her no one else would love her. That she was lucky she had found Sue. That she was undeserving of anything better.

Then Sue would roll over and fall into a peaceful slumber while Paula lay awake, staring at the shadows as they danced across the Artex ceiling, berating herself and promising that she would do better tomorrow because deep down she knew Sue was right.

All Paula wanted was a few nights without that voice in her ear, that grabbing hand on her arm, those pinching fingers leaving red marks that stung when Paula voiced an opinion that hadn't been Sue-checked first.

She wanted the river and the trees.

The truth was she wasn't going on this trip for Valentina or to make amends.

She was going back to the past to escape her present.

Bev set the weekend bag by the front door. She had checked the satnav route and knew where the traffic would be heaviest since she was going to be driving them all, picking them up one by one, all of them together again. She looked up at the photographs on the wall, the smiling faces of when Bethany and Jasper were younger and still needed her attention and love. Things were simpler then. Now it was slammed doors or silence and nothing in between.

She checked the shepherd's pie baking in the oven and tossed a salad in balsamic dressing. Earlier she had heard Bethany on a call with someone in her bedroom. She had tried to listen in through the bedroom door, but the words were muffled and spoken in low voices. Was this the boy that Jasper had mentioned? Just one more thing to add to her endless list of worries – whether her seventeen-year-old daughter was courting danger by meeting men on the internet.

Jasper was due home any minute from football, dragging mud onto the carpet no doubt, and Malcolm was on the train from work, probably dozing until his in-built alarm woke him as the train pulled up to his stop.

She had Walter keeping her company though, her constant shadow. He snuffled at her feet, contemplating whether the piece of cucumber she had just dropped was suitable fodder for dogs. She liked to be needed, to know that her husband and children could concentrate on excelling while she made sure everything behind the scenes ran smoothly. Her job was to look after them. She'd learnt from the best. Her own mother had been a typical Seventies mum with a helmet of hair and chops for their tea, the ironing board constantly set up in the corner of the sitting room.

When they were younger, Bev had found Stacey's house fascinating with its noisy chaos, washing hanging off radiators, Stacey's brothers shouting constantly and her dad walking around in a vest, moaning about the Tories. Stacey had been the baby girl of the house, pandered to by her dad and brothers, coveted by her mum who relished her one moment of pink in a very blue house. In contrast, Bev had come from a place of calm, everything neat and in its place, polite dinners and no conflict or raised voices.

Bev had wanted to recreate that kind of home when she married Malcolm, but it had become a place of stilted conversations and televisions in separate rooms. Even so, she tried to live up to her mother's standards and create a home she was proud of. Now it could all be taken away.

The front door opened and Malcolm shuffled in, shaking the rain from his hair.

'Darling, you're home,' she said, wiping her hands on her apron as she rushed to where he was throwing off his coat.

She gathered up the coat and took his briefcase from him before giving him a kiss.

He looked over at her packed bag. 'What's this?'

'Remember, I told you I'm going away tomorrow?'

'Oh, is that this weekend?'

'I reminded you as you left this morning,' Bev mumbled.

'Right, right, yes, mustn't have heard you.'

'You don't have to worry about anything. I've cooked some dinners and made sure Bethany and Jasper have everything they need.'

'Excellent, because I am exhausted so will need to rest this weekend myself.' He kissed her lightly on the cheek and she blushed in delight. 'Fetch me a whisky, would you?'

She retreated into the kitchen and poured the whisky. When she returned, Malcolm had already kicked off his shoes, tossed his socks onto the carpet and reclined in the leather chair that she hated but from which he couldn't bear to be parted. His toes fidgeted and flicked at each other, like they were dancing in celebration at finally being free from the confines of socks and shoes. She looked away.

'Here you go, darling,' she said, holding out the glass.

He reached for it, took a sip, then recoiled. 'There's no ice in it.' He held it out at arm's length.

'Oh, sorry.' She scuttled away, tripping over his shoes.

The ice machine clattered, the ice tumbling into the whisky.

'Mum?' Bethany stood in the kitchen doorway, her hair piled into a lopsided ponytail, her feet in childish socks covered in pictures of dancing llamas.

'You okay?'

'Can I have a hug?'

Bev paused, taken aback. She couldn't remember the last time Bethany had needed anything from her, let alone comfort. She folded her into her arms and said into her hair, 'Do you want to talk about it?' She felt Bethany's head nod against her chest.

Bev closed the door on the sounds of journalists arguing with politicians coming from the television in the other room and indicated for Bethany to sit with her at the kitchen island.

'I don't understand, Mum. It was going so well.'

'What was? Is this something to do with your friendship group? Or a boy? Or girl of course.' Bethany rolled her eyes. 'Sorry, I just don't want to say the wrong thing,' Bev stumbled. 'Just tell me everything from the start.'

Bethany stopped and started a couple of times before she found the right words, and then it was like the tap had been opened. Bethany told her about the boy she had been talking to – or 'linking with', as was the lingo these days apparently.

He'd slid into her DMs on Snapchat a few weeks ago, claiming to be a friend of someone at her school, but she hadn't managed to work out the connection yet. None of her friends knew who he was. Still, he was cute in a mop-haired way and his Snap stories were mostly of him playing sport or photos of his dog, who looked very similar to Walter. Bethany showed Bev the profile pics that looked harmless enough, but Bev felt a gaping hole of dread open in her stomach all the same.

The boy said his name was Ben Tannet and he went to a local sixth form college. She'd checked some of her friends' Snapchats and he was in their friends lists despite not really knowing him. But that was how things went these days. Ben started asking Bethany questions about herself, but she'd had the forethought to be choosy in her answers initially – because despite what Bev may fear, she was not naïve and gullible. And Bev wasn't so out of touch to know that you could never be too careful. That blue-eyed boy could easily be a hairy, unwashed, fifty-year-old man sitting in a council flat in Oldham with an unnatural taste in young girls.

Bethany picked at her fingers, wouldn't look Bev in the eye. 'It's okay, sweetie, carry on. I won't judge.'

Bethany took a deep breath and continued. 'We flirted a bit, you know, messages and stuff, then voice memos. He kind of got me, understood about stuff that I don't think you and Dad would understand. He wants similar things to me, has a similar family life – a brother who he has nothing in common with—' Bev went to interrupt, but stopped herself. Now was a time for listening, not correcting. She felt like there was so much more that Bethany could be telling her as it was.

Bethany continued. 'We talked about university and applying to the same ones. It just all sounded great. Too great.'

'So what happened?'

'I don't know.' Her eyes filled with tears that stung Bev to the core. 'We talked about meeting up, going on a date maybe. Then, he asked for… photos. He said he had loads of sport on, so couldn't meet me for a while and wanted something to look at. I wasn't sure initially, but then I....' Bev could hardly hear her, her voice was so low now, so full of shame and embarrassment. 'I know I was stupid and I felt ridiculous taking them. Just underwear though – nothing worse,' she added hurriedly. 'I mean, why would anyone want to look at me as it is? With the cellulite and my massive hip dips.' She started to cry properly then and Bev folded her into her arms again.

'Oh, baby girl, you are beautiful. Don't ever think you are not.' Bev wanted to shout and rage and scream at the images in her head of Bethany trying to find the perfect lighting, filter or angle to make herself more perfect than she already was, just for some hormonal little shit with spots and a bad haircut. 'So you sent them – there's nothing we can do about that. But he may not show them around. If he's as nice as you think he is, then he will keep them to himself.'

Then she really started to cry. 'He's ghosted me, Mum,' she wailed. 'He got what he wanted and now he's not replying to my messages or anything. He's blocked me on Snapchat and all my friends. And I don't know if he's shared the photos or what he's done with them. He could've shared them millions of times by now. I'm so stupid. How can I have been so stupid?'

Bev cuddled her closer just as Malcolm stalked into the room. 'Where did you get to with that whisky?' He took in the state of Bethany and the look on Bev's face and scurried out, not wanting to get drawn into any teenage dramas.

Bev consoled Bethany until the timer on the shepherd's pie broke them apart. Then after a quiet dinner during which no one spoke very much, Bethany curled up in Bev's lap and they watched a Disney film together in the family room, her baby girl back where she belonged.

The aching void Bev had had in her gut all day, the feeling that something was coming, was now amplified until she could recognise it for what it was. It was the feeling of inevitability.

So much could happen this weekend. So much could go wrong. And she had so much to lose. She stroked Bethany's hair, relishing the feeling of holding her close, not knowing if she would get the chance again.

Bev didn't want to go, but knew she had to.

It felt like the last thirty years had just been a long spell in a waiting room and her number was about to be called.

I look at the photos one more time. Tastefully taken, I'll give her that. I wonder if she has told her parents about her ridiculously stupid lack of judgement. How all it had taken was a few carefully chosen words for her to confide so many of her secrets and bare so much of herself.

I swipe across to the next photo, taken against the backdrop of a messy teenage bathroom, with wet towels on the floor, make-up spots in the basin and a pair of straighteners plugged into the wall, dangerously close to the bath. A full bath and a little nudge is all it would take for her future to come to a very sudden end.

For her parents to know the pain of immeasurable loss.

For a door to close on a different chapter.

I set the phone aside. I don't have time to ruminate over the photos like I have done over the past few days. I have a bag to pack and a train to catch. I think I knew they were coming before they did. I have seen all the little preparations they have been making. The trips to the pharmacy to load up on travel-size toiletries. The supermarket expedition where family-sized ready meals and pizzas are thrown into the trolley along with snacks and sweets, as though prepping for a road trip. The lengthy visit to the off-licence for bottles of wine that would be drunk in the hotel bedroom while reminiscing in pyjamas, sitting on the floor and giggling.

All those little things we do that are a change to the normal routine, of which we think nothing, tell a story to a not so casual observer.

They don't notice me as I watch from the vitamins aisle of the pharmacy or stand in the frozen food section, my head hidden behind the ice cream tubs.

I am hidden in plain sight.

But not for long.

16

WINTER 1993

Valentina woke to bright sun and the sounds of the rubbish truck outside, the shattering of glass and the squeal of the truck's brakes piercing her fitful and intoxicated sleep. She blinked to clear the dehydrated grit from her eyes, realising she hadn't removed her contact lenses before she had passed out. She turned onto her back and peeled the lenses from her eyes, turning the irises from blue to brown. No one had noticed that she had started to wear coloured lenses in the same shade as Stacey's blue eyes. Stu certainly hadn't noticed last night. That just showed you.

She swiped at the dried drool on her chin and sat up slowly, feeling her brain clatter against the inside of her skull. She touched her forehead gingerly and the large bump that pulsated, hot and bruised. How the hell had that happened? When had she fallen over? Getting into bed? She tried to remember what had happened towards the end of the evening, but the details were coming in small shards of clarity.

She hadn't closed the curtains and last night's rain had been replaced with bright light that hurt almost as much as trying to remember did. She got up. The world tilted like she was going to pass out. She stumbled to the balcony door, threw it open, lurched to the railings and threw up onto the tarmac three floors down. Her nostrils filled with the smell of regurgitated wine and she retched again. She remained leaning over, her eyes closed, her breath coming in pants and gulps, her eyes watering and her head pulsating.

When she opened her eyes, a dark red puddle of vomit stared back at her from down below, splattered like a modern work of art. She swiped at her mouth and turned to go back inside, then noticed the car parked behind the vomit. It was standing at a strange angle, as though someone had abandoned it rather than parking it in the space. She realised with a sickening lurch that it was rammed up to the car next to it, which was in turn rammed up against the next car along.

She had a vague recollection of hitting something when she was reversing last night. That recollection became a certainty that she had in fact reversed into a parked car, which had then ricocheted into another two cars, before she had driven off and parked around the other side. She could just make out her car on the other side of the car park, parked awkwardly and taking up two spaces, the back end looking crinkled even from this far away.

She sighed and sloped back to bed.

When she came around again, the flat was eerily quiet. She sat up, feeling slightly more human but still as though there was a large animal riding on her back, hugging her chest with its tight arms and breathing rancid breath in her face while it poked at her bruised forehead with an insistent finger. She swung her legs out of bed and took gentle steps towards her bedroom door.

She opened it, then paused upon hearing muffled voices from behind the closed kitchen door.

'She was just standing there, watching him with this weird look on her face,' Bev was saying.

'What do you mean?' Paula replied.

'I don't know, like she was *wanting* him to fall. It was really creepy. Then she just unlocked the front door and went to bed. Lucky we came when we did. He could've fallen. He could've died.'

'I told you she was odd,' Stacey said in a stage whisper.

'She was telling me that her mother was ill and she had a lot on her mind – maybe it's just worry,' Bev said.

'When did she tell you that?' Stacey replied sharply.

'When she was away. She called the flat a couple of times to talk to you – I told you she had called, but you were always out with Sean. Did you ever call her back?'

'No, it wasn't going to be anything important, was it? She's obsessed with me – I still say she's been in my room.'

'It was important if her mother was ill. She was obviously looking to talk to someone,' Paula said.

'Then she had Bev to talk to. Besides, she's lying. She told us ages ago that her mother died when she was young – cancer, wasn't it? – so her father sent her to boarding school.'

They were quiet then and Valentina thought the

conversation might be over. Then Paula said, 'She likes you, Stace, but you...'

'I what?' Stacey was getting annoyed.

'You don't see what's right in front of you sometimes,' Paula said in such a quiet voice that Valentina had to lean forward to catch the words. 'You're too busy using people, soaking up their attention, that you sometimes forget that others have feelings too. And you like it, all the attention, the adoration.'

'Wow, Paula, tell me what you really think!' Stacey's voice rose.

'Shush,' Bev said anxiously. 'She's asleep.'

'So what are we going to do?' Stacey said insistently. 'I want her out. She's a manipulative, lying bitch.'

Valentina felt cold, not from standing in the draught in her pyjamas but from the words lashing her skin like hailstones.

'We can't chuck her out with nowhere to go,' Bev pleaded. 'Exams start soon and she's paid all her rent. We can't pay that back.'

'Let's just keep our distance then. There's only a few more months to go and then we're done,' Paula compromised.

'Fine, but she's your responsibility, not mine,' Stacey said tightly.

Valentina closed her eyes against the sinking feeling of her lies catching up with her. She stepped back and the floor creaked loudly.

She froze, then stepped into the hallway, adjusting her hair over the still-pulsating lump on her forehead and rearranging her face into an expression of innocence.

'Oh, hey, guys,' she said brightly as she pushed open the kitchen door. 'Didn't realise anyone was in here. Cuppa?'

She went straight over to the kettle, her back to them.

Only Bev replied with: 'Not for us, thanks. We've just had some.'

'God, my head is banging after last night,' Valentina said over her shoulder.

'You had a big one,' Bev replied.

Valentina glanced at them. Stacey was staring into her mug, twirling her hair around her finger. Paula was scowling at her, her forehead wrinkled with thunderous thoughts. Bev looked sad, as though Valentina had disappointed her by not living up to her potential.

'Stu and I ended up going on a spontaneous night out, just a couple of bottles of red wine sitting out at River's End, but the wine knocked me for six. I don't normally feel that drunk so quickly, but it really hit me last night. It was weird – I felt completely spaced out. Can't remember most of it.'

'So you don't remember leaving Stu dangling over the wall?' Paula said.

Valentina frowned as she turned towards them. 'No? What are you talking about?'

'Last night, Val. He said it was a prank or something. It was scary, seeing him like that.'

'I don't remember that at all. I remember drinking red wine, then getting back here and going to bed. What was he thinking? Such an idiot!'

Bev's eyes narrowed. 'What happened to your head?'

Valentina put her fingers up to her forehead and brushed

the hair further across to disguise the bruise. 'I must've hit my head on something – I don't know. Explains my headache though.'

Stacey got to her feet and walked from the room. All eyes followed her.

'Is she okay?' Valentina said.

'I've got to go,' Paula said and followed Stacey.

Bev smiled weakly at Stacey and followed the others, leaving Valentina alone with her stewing teabag.

She did remember the incident with Stu, mostly for how cold she felt towards him and how she had wanted to shock him, maybe even wanting him to fall, but she wasn't sure why. The image of him hitting the pavement, the dull thud he would make, the rapidly spreading pool from his splattered skull... These thoughts weren't shocking to her. Sometimes she had this disconnect between her thoughts and her feelings, like she was the passive dealer in a massive game of cards playing out in front of her. It was Stu's turn to either stick or twist last night. What she couldn't work out though was whether he had stacked the cards in his favour or not. She shouldn't have been as drunk as she was, but he'd supplied the booze, encouraged her to drink it. So it was his fault if he'd fallen, his choice to climb over the wall, his mistake to hope she would help him.

Her brain was hammering in each thought, making it difficult to see properly. She took her tea and went back to bed. She was restless despite her hangover, her legs twitching and wanting to move. Before long, sitting in bed became an annoyance. She dressed quickly in sports leggings and a sweatshirt, slurped back the still-hot tea and left the flat, slamming the door so that they would all know she had left.

She wanted them to wonder where she was going, wonder if they were missing out this time.

She shoved her hands in her pockets against the cold. A biting wind made the leaves swirl at her feet. She stepped out of the stairwell and straight into the path of her dark red vomit. She saw the cars, the damage. She needed to assess her own car, break it to her father. She could tell him Stu was driving, that it was raining and visibility was bad. Her father wouldn't care anyway. He'd just pay the bill and go back to ignoring her. And now the girls upstairs had washed their hands of her too. She'd done it again, pushed too hard to get people to like her and ended up pushing them over the edge instead.

Why didn't they like her? How come everyone else got to be unapologetically themselves, but she had to mould and adapt to suit? Stacey could be as selfish and narcissistic as she liked and everyone still hovered over her like she was coated in honey. Paula could be as prickly and as grumpy as anything and everyone just smiled and said, 'That's Paula.' And Bev, who was so desperate to please everyone that she didn't do anything for herself and could be the most judgemental of them all, yet they still rallied around her.

At what point would she be accepted enough that they would say, 'Oh, that's just Valentina – she can be quirky and odd sometimes, but we love her just the way she is'?

And who exactly was she these days? Which version was reality?

She looked over to the woods, wanting quiet anonymity. She sprinted along the path, letting the air darken to the level of her mood and feeling the cold air sting her lungs as she breathed shallowly. Moisture from the river cooled her flaming cheeks as she neared the trees and dropped back to a walk. After a moment she could feel herself coming back down to ground, her steps growing lighter, her breath regulating. She headed to the flat rock again, now her favourite place to hide, and sat, letting the sounds of the woods calm her. She lay back along the rock, despite it being icy to the touch, and stared up at the bare branches swaying in front of a clear, crisp sky.

She tried to empty her mind, but it kept coming back to the three girls back at the flat and how badly she wanted them to accept her, to welcome her in and treat her as one of them. She had thought this was it, that she had found her tribe, the family she craved, but she'd been wrong. She was always wrong. No one wanted her, no one needed her. Not her mother who she couldn't quite remember any more, her father who had discarded her, or her best friends who were flinging her aside. She wanted to shout out to them to see her, hear her.

It wasn't until she heard voices that she realised she had dozed off. She looked at her watch. She had been lying there for half an hour. Her back was cold, but the inside of her head was feeling clearer, even if her forehead still hurt.

She listened hard to determine what had disturbed her and heard male voices approaching. She immediately recognised Sean's accent and leaned over to see him walking with Stu below her by the river. Unless they looked up through the bare tree branches, they wouldn't know she was there.

'Mate, she's insane.' They stopped and leaned against a tree.

'You gave it to her though?' Sean said.

'Yeah, but only half. Not as much as you said I should. I didn't have much time. She took me by surprise.'

Valentina leaned over even further and strained her neck to see them. At first she could only make out dark-coloured hoodies and jeans, then she recognised Stu's red hair. They each held orange-glowing cigarettes in their fingers, the smell of which floated up to her. It was not nicotine but had the unmistakably sweet tang of weed.

'It was weird – she was fine, laughing to start with, then she switched and she went proper psycho on me. Hysterics, crying and all sorts.'

'Next time you'll have to give her all of it.'

'I didn't expect her to knock on the door, did I? I just threw in what I had. Anyway, she was properly upset, talking about how she wouldn't have done it – with you, I mean – and she was acting properly freaky.'

'They don't know anything about it afterwards, you know, so there's no harm done. They really can't remember. They think they just drank too much and it's their own fault. It's win–win if you ask me.'

'She knew something had happened and said that she wouldn't have done it if she'd been sober.'

'Rubbish, she still would have. They all would. They don't actually mean no when they say it. They want you to pander to them, convince them that they aren't being little sluts. All we're doing is cutting out all that bullshit.' Sean's voice was like a flint on a stone, striking cold and hard.

'Nah, I dunno.'

'Listen, you can't say anything – to anyone.'

They started walking again and were slowly swallowed by the trees as Stu replied, 'I said I wouldn't, didn't I?'

What had Stu given her? Was he talking about the wine? That didn't fit though. But then, he never did drink from the same bottle as her, did he? She remembered drinking from his at one point, but not vice versa. Her bottle had had no label on it either. Was that deliberate? To make sure she drank from it? She needed to talk to him, to get Stu on his own and find out what they were talking about. Then she remembered Stu saying last night that Sean wasn't who Stacey thought he was.

And completely out of the blue came an image of an open capsule case, one half red, one half yellow, tucked under a couch, out of sight, then casually tossed into a bin without a thought.

17

PRESENT DAY

Bev parked in the car park at the train station as instructed and could see Paula in the distance, sitting on a bench with her bag at her feet. It was strange that Paula hadn't wanted her to pick her up at her flat, but she'd been quite insistent.

She climbed out of the driver's seat and waved. Paula jumped to her feet and hurried over.

'Hi, thanks for picking me up.' Her words were rushed, her eyes darting around. She threw her bag in the back of the car and climbed in after it.

'You can get in the front. I haven't picked Stacey up yet,' Bev said.

'No, no, that's okay. Let's get going.' She looked anxious, on edge. As they all were, Bev supposed. This was a weird thing they were doing.

Bev put the car into gear and they pulled off. She flicked her eyes to the mirror, could see Paula sitting low in the seat.

'You okay?' Bev asked.

225

'Yes, fine.' She didn't sound fine.

They drove in silence until Bev turned on the radio and chose a station that played mostly Nineties music. 'To get us in the mood,' she said with a smile and a glance in the mirror.

Paula smiled back thinly.

Bev tapped her finger on the steering wheel and hummed to herself, then started chattering to Paula in an attempt to relax her. 'I wasn't sure I should come since the kids have only just gone back to school, but Malcolm was insistent. He said I needed a break and he's right. We haven't had a holiday for a while and even this is getting away, isn't it?'

Paula nodded in agreement, but she looked like she was starting to relax a bit as they travelled closer to where Stacey lived. The buildings were getting more familiar to those they had grown up amongst. Stacey really hadn't moved too far from where they'd all been to school together. The estate she had lived on with her brothers was about ten minutes from her flat and Bev navigated the streets without needing the satnav.

She indicated and pulled over outside a scruffy-looking front yard with overgrown grass and a torn bin bag, its contents spilling out onto the path. There was a cat in the front window, the curtain twitching in time with the sway of its tail, then Stacey was struggling out of the front door with a suitcase and a frown. She threw the bags in the boot and climbed into the front passenger seat.

'Alan needs to mow your front lawn, Stacey,' Paula said in greeting.

'Is that a euphemism?' she replied and laughed.

Stacey rummaged in a plastic bag she'd shoved in the footwell and cracked open a can of pre-mixed gin and tonic.

'Started already?' Bev said.

'It's a road trip!' She pulled out another can, which she passed back to Paula.

Paula reached out for it, exposing a hand that looked scabbed and sore.

'Ouch, what did you do to your hand?' Bev said, noticing the red burns that had only just scabbed over.

'Stupid really. Grabbed the handle of a pan that had been in the oven. Just wasn't thinking.'

'Oof, yeah, we've all done that.'

Paula smiled thinly. 'So how is the family, Bev? You were saying they're back at school?'

'Oh yeah, good. Bethany is in Lower Sixth and Jasper is in Year 10. They will need lots of emotional support in the next few years with all the pressure kids are under these days.'

'That's good that they have such a close and open relationship with you though, that they ask for that support? Most teenagers don't talk to their parents. Everyone I know with teenagers seems to put up with silence or resentment and are treated like glorified maids, quite frankly. Good for you. You've done something right,' Paula said. Bev didn't correct her. She focused on the road ahead as she pulled out into the traffic and followed the robotic voice of the satnav. Her conversation with Bethany still left her feeling cold to the pit of her stomach when she thought about it. She'd given her an extra hug before she left that morning, but the shutters had come down again and Bethany had squirmed out of her hold.

'I can't believe we all live so close still – to each other and the university,' Stacey said. 'Do you see your family much these days, Paula?'

'No, I didn't really get on with my parents after I came out. They were – well, you know what they were like. They thought I would grow out of it, that if they ignored it, I would suddenly not be gay. My mum has passed away now and I have no urge to get in touch with my brother or father.'

'Oh, come on! They weren't surprised, surely? You were always so obviously gay, no offence.'

'None taken,' Paula said with a smile.

'Do you remember when you used to try and convince me and Stacey that Nicole Kidman was hotter than Tom Cruise?' Bev said with a giggle.

'I still stand by that, even today.'

'Brad Pitt and Gwyneth Paltrow.'

'Also still true.'

'The Nineties had some beautiful Hollywood couples.'

'Oh yes. Something for everyone.'

Paula opened her can, the sound joyous. Stacey turned around in the seat and smiled at Paula. 'To travelling back to the Nineties,' she said. They clinked the cans together.

'That's not fair – I want one,' Bev said, trying to ignore the chill that passed over her.

'We'll save you one,' Stacey said, then added with a wink, 'Maybe.'

Before long, the car headed out of the dirty town and away from the grey streets towards fields and trees and long stretches of hedgerows. Bev turned up the song on the radio and they sang out loud, all of them reluctant to talk about what they were really doing, what lay ahead of them.

'Why did you both never really move away from here? Down south maybe?' Stacey asked.

'Never fancied London myself. Too busy, too... *southern*,' Paula replied.

'A lot more gay than up here though,' Stacey said.

Paula laughed.

'We talked about it when Malcolm had the chance to move quite a few years back, but we like where we are and, like you say, London seems so ruthless, so fast-paced, so *modern*. Besides, we are all within a twenty-minute car journey of each other, which is nice.'

'Yeah, nice, except it's been thirty years – and you're not that old, Bev. Stop sounding like you're a pensioner,' Stacey said. Bev could hear the annoyance in her voice.

'It doesn't feel that long though, does it? I guess time goes by quickly, especially if you have kids because frivolous nonsense gets pushed aside for responsibility,' Bev said.

'Paula and I don't have kids. That doesn't mean we haven't had a full life or responsibilities.' Stacey was on edge.

Bev frowned at her. 'I know. I wasn't saying... Sorry, I—'

'Stace, back off. Just calm down, okay? She didn't mean anything by it,' Paula said. 'Remember, we had each other's backs once and we have them again this weekend, whatever happens.'

'Sorry, Bev,' Stacey said.

Bev frowned. 'Are you okay?'

'I just... I don't know. I think someone was watching me at the station. It just felt – you know, hairs on the back of your neck stuff. I couldn't see anyone though. It's just been playing on my mind, that's all.'

Paula paled. They fell silent as Bev turned the radio up another notch.

The hotel was beautiful with brightly coloured window boxes and painted shutters over a garden bursting with roses and foxgloves. There were tables outside in a courtyard where people enjoyed pots of tea and ploughman's lunches in the sunshine. Stacey imagined Poohsticks on the bridge over the river and croquet on the lawn at the back. Bev fit right in, but Stacey felt ill at ease, like a bottle of cheap Cava at a sophisticated dinner party.

'Don't worry about the cost,' Bev was saying as they walked into the reception area. 'Malcolm has said he will cover it as a gift to all of us.'

'That's very kind,' Stacey said, exhaling in relief. She wasn't sure her credit card would've stretched to cover it and she had already started concocting some sort of plan to skip out without paying the bill. She had been banking on Bev being too polite to ask for the money back later.

The woman behind the reception desk was in her fifties, her grey hair cut in a short bob that curled neatly under her double chin. She wore round glasses that perched on the end of her nose. A scarf was knotted at her neck above a dark blue cardigan that was buttoned severely to the top. She smiled widely as they approached, her face cracking in two.

'Hello there, I'm Joan. And you are?'

'Bev Lawson checking in.'

Stacey still couldn't get used to Bev's married name. Stacey hadn't taken Alan's surname straight away and the marriage had ended before she'd got around to doing anything about it.

Joan began to explain about breakfast times and asked if they wanted to eat in the restaurant that evening. Bev looked at them for an answer.

'Um, well, we have places to go, don't we?' Stacey said.

'Tonight? Can we not do it tomorrow?' Bev asked.

'I think Stace is right. We should get it done tonight.'

Bev looked disappointed, but declined Joan's offer to book a table, saying, 'Maybe tomorrow night.' The woman handed over old-school keys with the name of the B&B printed on huge, thick leather tags.

'You are all on the top floor and the lift is straight through there,' Joan said, her smile even wider than before.

They trotted off in the direction she was pointing. Stacey's suitcase had one wonky wheel and it kept toppling over so that her arm twisted unnaturally behind her. It made a clattering sound across the parquet floor and she felt like all eyes were on her.

Bev giggled. 'No offence, Paulie, but I reckon Joan thinks we're a group of lesbians on a dirty weekend.' They all looked back at Joan, who was watching them curiously. Stacey lifted her hand and waved. Joan looked away quickly.

Paula laughed. 'You wish, Bev. I reckon you've always secretly fancied me. I've told you, Gwyneth over Brad, every time.'

Their bedrooms were all next to each other. Stacey's key was stiff and she had to use two hands to turn it. Behind the door was a room straight out of a period drama. A huge four-poster bed dominated and there were heavy, floor-length curtains at a wide bay window. There was an ornate desk in one corner and a heavy oak wardrobe, with prints of English country flowers dotted along the pale cream walls.

In contrast, the small ensuite bathroom was modern and eye-wateringly clean, with beige tiles and glaring white porcelain. A large, claw-footed bath took pride of place instead of a shower.

Stacey threw her suitcase on the bed and walked over to the window. Below her was a large, rose-bordered lawned area with tables and chairs dotted about, and through a small, hedged border she could see a vegetable patch.

And there in the distance were the woods. Her eyes were drawn to them after all this time. Like a familiar friend she hadn't seen in some time. A friend that was very good at keeping a secret.

She turned away at the knock on the door. Paula stood on the other side, waving a bottle of wine at her. 'Let's have a look at your room then.' She walked in without invitation. 'Nice, I think you have the biggest one.' She peeked into the bathroom. 'And I don't have a bath like that. I have a shower. I think we've found our base. I'll go and get Bev and then you can show us this map, get this thing going. Here, put this in an ice bucket.'

'There's an ice bucket?'

'Bound to be somewhere. This looks like an ice bucket kind of place.'

Stacey closed the door on Paula and quickly moved her suitcase. She was gagging for a cigarette but would wait until they were outside. She opened her tote bag and necked a few gulps of vodka from the half-bottle hidden inside, tucked next to the shoebox.

Paula walked in without knocking. Bev followed behind. Stacey stashed the vodka away and pulled out the shoebox.

'Did you find that ice bucket?' Paula said.

'Oh, er, no.'

'That's okay – I'll call down to reception for one,' Bev said. She grabbed the telephone and dialled a number.

'Is this it?' Paula asked, pointing at the shoebox.

Stacey nodded.

'Jimmy Choos, huh? Nice. Although I prefer trainers myself.'

Bev had finished speaking into the phone. She flung herself onto the bed. 'Joan says she's got one ready to bring up. Oooh, Jimmy Choos!'

'Val had expensive taste,' Stacey replied. She sat cross-legged on the bed next to Bev and pushed the box into the middle between them. Paula lifted the lid and spread out the letters, reading them and passing them on. When the knock came at the door, Stacey jumped up and opened it. It was Joan, the smiling receptionist.

'Here you go – for your celebration. A special occasion? How lovely.' She was holding out an ice bucket with a champagne bottle sticking out of the ice and four glasses.

'Oh, I'm not sure—'

'Yes, we are celebrating *special friends* reconnecting,' Bev said from behind Stacey.

'Well, that's just super. Have fun and let me know if there is anything else you need.' There was that smile again, wide and carnivorous.

'Thanks,' Stacey said and closed the door on her.

'Is that on the house?' Bev said. 'How lovely. Do the honours, would you, Stace?'

'I brought wine from home too,' Paula said.

'Sorry, I didn't think to,' Stacey admitted.

'No need, I was being purely selfish,' Paula replied.

Stacey put the ice bucket on the desk and removed the bottle. It was real champagne, not cheap prosecco. Stacey hoped this was on the house and not on her room tab. She tore off the foil and got to work on the metal cap. The cork popped obscenely to a little cheer from the other two. Stacey wanted to shout that this wasn't a party or a celebration, but she kept her lips pinned together and poured the champagne.

Paula and Bev spread out the letters and papers in front of them and Stacey gave them time to look them over as she sipped. She had a notebook in her tote bag and she opened it to show them the notes she had taken over the course of the last few days. Thoughts, ramblings, questions.

'Apart from the obvious receipts and things, there isn't anything unusual here. It all matches what I remember us doing. There's nothing different. But she was with us the whole time that night anyway,' Stacey said.

'Yes, we were all together, apart from after we got back to the flat of course.'

'So I don't get it. The map is the same – just a route of the places we went to. All I can think is that she wants us to revisit these places for some reason.'

'The notes in her journal are interesting though. It's an indication of what she was thinking, of where her head was. It's like she was studying us, making notes on our routines, our outfits, everything,' Stacey said. 'It's quite sad, really.'

'She wanted to be like you, Stace. You could never see it, but I could. The way she changed her hair, started wearing clothes similar to yours. She even started wearing blue contact lenses, do you remember, Paulie?' Bev said.

'Yeah, I noticed, but you were quite oblivious, Stace. You decided to freeze her out and you were very good at it. She was invisible to you after she slept with Sean.'

Stacey looked deflated.

'I'm not criticising,' Paula said quickly. She looked back at the map. 'Maybe we are missing the point after all. Maybe she just wanted to concoct a reason for us all to get together again. Felt bad that we all went our separate ways because of her and this was her weirdly Valentina way of making amends.'

Stacey turned the map over. 'Then what do you make of that?' She pointed at the message. Stacey drank more champagne, ignoring the bubbles popping in her nose.

'I don't buy it. He was dead,' Paula said. 'What does the shorthand say?'

'I haven't managed to work that out yet,' Stacey replied. 'What do you think, Bev?'

She shrugged, but stayed silent.

'Okay, but the letter clearly says that Val had cancer and had missed some of her appointments for whatever reason. Sounds to me like the Big C got her in the end,' Paula said.

A phone started to vibrate somewhere and they all reached for their pockets simultaneously. Stacey knew it wouldn't be hers, since no one really called her anymore, but she checked anyway. Bev looked disappointed to see it wasn't hers. Paula paled.

'Sorry, I have to get this,' she said and dashed from the room.

Bev and Stacey looked at each other. 'Is she acting weird, do you think? Jumpy?' Stacey asked.

'Honey, I think we all are. It's like we've forgotten how to do this. How to be friends. Maybe we need to put this aside and just have a few glasses of fizz to relax.'

'Yeah, maybe you're right.' She drank some more, but could feel Bev's eyes on her.

'And maybe the fizz will help us be a bit more truthful with each other,' Bev said quietly.

'What do you mean?'

'I think that maybe we all have a few secrets and that it might be about time we were honest with each other.' Bev was staring at her. 'Starting with you.'

Paula paced around the reception, conscious of Joan watching her like a hawk. She kept her voice low as she replied to Sue's questions. The others in the reception certainly didn't fit with Paula, with her short hair, ears ringed with piercings and heavy bovver boots. This was a place for romantic weekend getaways, long walks in the countryside and wandering around the market square, tasting local honey and spending lazy Sunday afternoons by the river.

She leant on a table at the side of the room, but it tilted and a pile of tourist information leaflets cascaded to the floor. Joan leapt up and scurried over to pick them up.

Paula blushed and mouthed an apology before moving over to a couch set beside a stone fireplace. She didn't want to have to answer all the questions Sue was still throwing at her.

'Listen, Sue, I have to go. My boss is calling me over. We're on a quick coffee break and I can see him waving at me. Can you hear him? He's the loud one in the background.' She moved to stand closer to another guest who was preaching to his companion about the health benefits of hiking. Sue said a terse goodbye.

Paula stood for a moment, staring at the phone, her mind whirring. Someone brushed past her on the way to the reception desk and the phone fell from her hand onto the floor. She scowled at whoever had bumped into her, but they had moved away without apology and were talking to Joan, whose wide receptionist smile was back in place.

My gamble has paid off. I tried calling a few hotels in the area with a little white lie about not being able to remember what hotel my friends had booked into. I wasn't getting very far until I changed tack and mentioned to the receptionist here that I was booked in with my friends and it was a celebration, so could she send some champagne up to my friend Stacey's room. She happily obliged and I knew I had the right place.

Then I called back and booked in myself. As soon as I step inside, I can see I was right. I hesitate and almost walk out again when I see her on the phone, but then I pick up the tension in her shoulders, the way she is gesticulating as she talks and I recognise the signs of an argument. She will be too distracted to take any notice of me.

I have my cap pulled low, a heavy coat obscuring my body, despite the warmth of the day. I walk straight past her, even brushing arms with her, but she doesn't look up.

Only when the phone falls from her hands does she look up, but I have moved past her already and am engaging the receptionist in dreary small talk.

Does the receptionist know she has checked in a room full of murderers? Does she have any idea about who will be sleeping upstairs?

Except they won't be sleeping.

By the time I get my key, she has gone again, back to her room, I expect.

I take the stairs to my own room and settle myself in, not noticing the furnishings or the décor.

I pull the desk chair up to the window, which fortuitously overlooks the front entrance to the hotel, and I sit down, ready to wait.

18

Valentina kept some distance between her and Stu as he walked around town. He ducked and dived, carrying a takeaway coffee in one hand and his rucksack over his shoulder. Occasionally she dared to get close enough to him to smell his cheap aftershave in the breeze, but he remained oblivious to her. He ducked into a clothes shop and she hovered outside for about twenty minutes until he came out with a shopping bag replacing the coffee cup.

She'd been watching them all for a while now, figuring it out, trying to get to the bottom of what Stu and Sean were up to. Detailing their movements, writing them in her notebook alongside the notes she was making on Bev, Stacey and Paula. She wanted to understand her housemates, get a better sense of how she could fit in with them before presenting them with whatever it was Stu and Sean were guilty of – a sort of grand gesture for which they would thank her profusely and beg her forgiveness for jumping to conclusions about her.

She really did have the best of intentions. She simply wanted to be their friend, wanted to protect them from people like Sean and Stu. That's what friends did for each other.

She should've been studying. Finals would be upon them soon and she had a final thesis to hand in. The others were hard at work, closed behind bedroom doors, their heads in their books. But some things were more important than exam results. Her friends were more important.

Her friends who weren't speaking to her.

The more she had followed Sean and Stu, the more she was convinced that her friends needed to be protected. So she had created a profile for each of them, working out what their routines were, what they liked to eat and drink, who they were friendly with. She hadn't bothered with Mike and Rob as they were inconsequential in all of this, just hangers-on, circling the main players, hired extras.

The other two had starring roles, but she was still trying to figure out the details of the script.

She had followed Sean a few weeks ago when he had been to a nightclub with that girl from campus that Stacey had been friends with before Valentina had lied about Stacey and Sean. She had hung out in the back of the nightclub, dancing quietly in the shadows until the girl had left with Sean. They'd gone back to his flat – she'd needed a fair amount of help from him to get up the stairs – and the next morning Valentina had seen her leaving, looking more than a little distressed, her face pale, her eyes red. The walk of shame indeed.

She hadn't seen her around campus after that though.

There had been some other interesting observations too, such as Stu's predilection for eating large meals, then disappearing into the nearest bathroom soon afterwards. She thought only girls had problems with eating disorders, but Stu was surreptitiously vain, constantly checking his appearance in windows as he walked past, sucking in his non-existent belly, his neatly groomed goatee that was perfectly trimmed to sit above his sharpened cheekbones. These little habits were not something you would notice during a night out, but were painfully apparent when you studied him closely.

Then there was the curious change in Sean when you actually watched him move about campus now. Earlier in the year, he had been the centre of attention with guys greeting him warmly and girls openly flirting with him. But now many of the girls gave him a wide berth. They moved around him as though he had a weird aura, not in anger or distaste but with a sense of fearful confusion.

Stacey was still reeling him in, then pushing him away. At once friendly and meeting him for coffee in between lectures and then playing hard to get when he suggested going out. She had exams as her excuse for now, but that wouldn't hold for much longer.

And unbeknown to Stacey, as much as Valentina was observing her, so was Sean. He was a constant presence in the background of her life, watching from afar, soaking it all in. Valentina had even noticed him lingering behind her in the supermarket when she had gone out to buy cigarettes and milk the other day.

Back at the flat, the others were keeping their distance

from Valentina. There were no more invitations out or nights sitting at the table eating dinner together. Now they ate together in Stacey and Paula's room while Valentina made herself a sandwich or a bowl of cereal alone at the table. If she made a pot of chilli and offered it around, they were always full from their own dinner, even though no dishes had been used. It was as though they were all counting the weeks until she moved out.

But that was okay. Valentina knew she would change their minds before they went their separate ways. She knew that in thirty years' time, they would still be friends, once she had shown them how much they needed her in their lives, the lengths she would go to to protect them. They had to see it.

They were fiercely loyal to each other and she desperately wanted to know what that felt like, to know that someone cared enough to fight for you. Like she was doing for them.

They would be grateful. They would be indebted to her. And she would finally have what she craved more than anything else: to be needed; to be wanted.

The smell of chip fat hung like a vapour over the doorway of the takeaway as Stu stood at the counter and considered the menu on the wall. He ordered, then looked like all of his Christmases had come at once when the server handed over the tray of chips dripping in vinegar and loaded with salt, along with a miniature wooden fork.

He shovelled them in greedily, his focus entirely on the chips and not on Valentina watching on. Afterwards, as he threw away the tray, a look of self-disgust crossed his face. She'd seen that look before at boarding school when girls had eaten entire slabs of chocolate in frustration, only to then flagellate themselves in shame afterwards. He stood, staring into the bin where he had thrown the tray, his eyes narrowed and his shoulders slumped.

He turned suddenly and rushed towards the large department store further down the parade of shops, grease still coating his lips. She followed him as he made his way through the menswear section, apparently following the signs to the toilets. She pretended to inspect a rather ridiculous jumper that looked like it was painted in chevrons while he carried on along the corridor to the bathrooms.

She followed. At the end of the corridor were two doors. An elderly woman emerged from the women's, wiping her hands on the fabric of her sensible navy slacks. The door to the men's bathroom was still swinging closed from where Stu had shoved at it in self-repulsion. She could see in just enough to determine there was no one at the urinals and just one large, balding man at the basins, who emerged belly-first a moment later.

She pretended to check her watch as he waddled past, then she ducked into the male bathroom behind him.

The air smelled of bleach and air freshener covering a very subtle undertone of urine. Tinny generic instrumental music played from hidden speakers. The room was empty with only one cubicle door closed. She crept into the cubicle next to it and silently locked the door behind her. Through the thin partition, she could hear a subtle retching, pitched at the volume of a practised regurgitator. Valentina lowered the lid of the toilet and stood on it. She was just tall enough to rest her arms on the top of the partition and peer over. Part of her still expected to look down on a complete stranger, but she recognised the red hair and broad shoulders immediately. He'd flung his coat on the floor and a line of sweat ran down the back of his T-shirt.

She waited patiently for him to finish, watched as he panted and wiped his mouth with toilet roll, still bending over the toilet, then said over his head, 'Better out than in, hey, Stu?'

He shot up, his eyes wide, the colour draining from his face.

'What the…?' Then his face burned red. 'What the fuck, Valentina?'

'So this is your dirty little secret, huh?'

'Don't know what you're talking about. I ate something funny, that's all. Been feeling shit all day, maybe too many beers with the lads lately. What the fuck are you doing in here?'

'Oh, right, so it's not your eating disorder then?'

He laughed hollowly. 'What?'

'Your eating disorder.'

'Fuck off, Valentina.' He slammed out of the cubicle and went to wash his hands.

'Oh, Stu, I've been following you for some time now and I have quite a few photographs of this so-called tummy bug of yours. You should really go to a doctor because you've had it for ages now.' She was enjoying messing with him. She could feel a buzz under her hairline, like an electric current that ran along her scalp and down her spine. 'Or should we just tell the truth for what it is and say that you have the most girly of ailments? Bulimia, is it?'

He was quiet as he stared at her through the mirror. It crossed her mind that he might lash out at her, but she wasn't afraid. 'What do you want from me?' he growled.

'Nothing really,' she said haughtily. 'Other than to know what you and Sean have been doing – and what you gave me that night.'

He looked confused for a second, then realisation kicked in, like the turn of a page.

'I don't know what you're talking about,' he said unconvincingly.

Valentina sighed dramatically, leant against a sink and crossed her arms. 'You see, the thing is you either tell me what I want to know or I start to paste photocopies of your bathroom antics all over campus. You'll be the laughing stock of the rugby team, probably tossed out even, but worse than that, everyone will know your dirty little secret after I plant a few well-placed rumours in the right ears. That disposable camera of mine is so handy sometimes.'

She waited as every single one of his thoughts played out on his face. Then he deflated in on himself and she knew she had him.

19

Paula stepped back into the room to find Bev and Stacey glaring at each other. Stacey was clearly struggling to keep her anger in check.

'Why don't you tell Paula what you've just implied, Bev?'

'Wow, this has escalated since I left,' Paula said and sat on the bed between the two, like a mediator at a family counselling session. 'What's going on?'

'I merely implied that perhaps Stacey is drinking a bit too much. She's had double the amount that we've had. And sometimes when she phones me, she sounds like she's drunk. That's all I'm saying.'

'That's enough, don't you think?' Stacey was livid, could feel a heat in her ears. Bev didn't know anything about her or her life. How dare she judge her?

A small voice in Stacey's head reminded her she was only annoyed because Bev had touched a nerve.

'Okay, I'm sorry, I'm just worried about you. I'm sure

Alan would've noticed if you were drinking more than you should.'

'Oh, fuck off about Alan! There is more to life than being married, you know, Bev.'

Bev gaped at her.

'That's all you ask about – Alan this and Alan that. Not about *me*, what I'm doing with my life.' She took another drink of the champagne, realised her glass was empty and gesticulated for Paula to fill it up again. Paula obliged, but Stacey saw the raised eyebrow and quick glance at Bev, heard the sigh.

'He left me, okay? Are you happy now?'

'Who? Alan?' Bev asked.

'No, Vladimir Putin. Of course Alan!'

'When?' Paula asked.

'A few months after we got married.' Stacey let out a bitter laugh. 'It would seem that you two are the only ones who can stomach living with me.' She accepted the now full glass from Paula.

'What happened?' Paula pressed.

'Nothing – and everything. He wanted a little housewife who would make his dinner and do his washing while he put his feet up. Turns out we were oil and water. And I have a tendency for self-sabotage. I wonder where that came from?'

'But why didn't you tell us?'

'Because I was embarrassed. The truth is everything I have done since the last time we were here has been a failure. I have been sacked more times than not; I fell out with my family and can't bear to see them; I failed at my marriage, mostly because I was out every night in bars while he was at home watching the news – oh, and I slept with Simon at work, so there's that. I have absolutely nothing to show for the last thirty years.'

Bev thrust her own glass at Paula to refill and pulled Stacey in for a tight hug. When she released her, Stacey said, 'I was the popular one back then, do you remember?' She looked at each of them in turn and they both nodded. 'I had all those guys wanting to walk me back from lectures, buying us drinks, the girls asked me where I bought my clothes, copying my hair. I had my parents and brothers proudly telling anyone who would listen that I was at university, the first one of the family. And I loved it. I loved all of it. I know you used to get annoyed by it, all those hangers-on,' she said to Paula, 'but it made me feel... important, I guess. Successful. The only ones who really knew me, knew where I had come from, were you two. Then I lost you too.'

'It was useful sometimes having those boys hanging around you,' Bev said with a cheeky smile.

'And the girls,' Paula added.

'That's all Valentina wanted though. She so desperately wanted to be you,' Bev said.

'I know, but there was something about her that was so desperate, so needy, and I found that threatening and at the same time annoyingly pathetic. I don't know why – maybe because I always *demanded*, but I was never *needed* until she came along. It was too much pressure, too much responsibility maybe. I'm selfish. I don't want to have to think about someone else, to have to consider their thoughts and feelings. Alan figured that out long before I did,' she said. 'You guys were different. You didn't depend on me to make you feel more worthy. She did – and I couldn't handle it.'

'So do you and Alan still speak?'

Stacey shuffled uncomfortably. 'I didn't take the break-up too well. There may be a restraining order against me. I can't actually come within a few feet of him now.'

Paula giggled. 'Bloody hell, Stace.'

'I find new ways of tormenting him and his lovely little girlfriend.'

'Like what?'

'I still have the Netflix password so I mess up the algorithms on their profile by liking really violent programmes or random documentaries, that kind of thing. Or I watch later episodes of something he is watching so that it messes up where he's up to when he logs back in. The other day I logged into our old Amazon account and ordered a shitload of hen party supplies, like inflatable penises and stuff, to be delivered to their house that he paid for. That kind of stuff helps me get over the pain.'

'Oh my God, that is genius,' Paula said, laughing.

Bev looked shocked, but amused. 'I never had you down as a petty criminal mastermind,' she said.

Stacey shrugged.

'Well, I for one am pleased you told us the truth,' Bev added.

'You're still wearing your wedding ring,' Paula noted.

Stacey looked down at her ring finger. 'Yeah, can't seem to take it off. Not just because I don't want to – and that's because I know it was my fault we failed – but also because my fingers are way fatter than they were when I got engaged. You'd have to cut my finger off to get it off.'

'Don't joke about cutting things off,' Paula said quietly without a trace of humour.

'Why was it your fault though? It takes two in a marriage,' Bev said. Stacey recognised the Bev swerve – she should've gone into diplomacy.

'I've struggled. Can't seem to get past what we did. I don't sleep; I drink too much; I can get abusive, I guess. He was trying to get close to me, understand where it was all coming from and I couldn't tell him. That kind of secret has a way of eating you up from the inside if you can't share it.'

Paula was nodding. 'I guess the only ones who understand what we've gone through is us,' Paula said.

'And Valentina,' Bev added.

'Yeah, Valentina.'

They sipped at their glasses, no one saying anything for a moment.

Then Bev said, 'Well, since we are confessing our sins, I guess I should confess mine.'

'Okay,' Paula said, frowning, 'although I can't imagine you would have any sins, except for that haircut.'

'Oi!' Bev punched her playfully. 'Well, how about this? My kids hate me and my husband doesn't see me anymore. He didn't offer to pay for all this. The truth is he wouldn't notice if he did pay for it all. He sits in his fucking recliner chair, flicking his toes and holding out his hand for his whisky and I fetch for him like a good little doggy,' she said, the bitterness audible. 'My children don't talk to me. They treat me much the same, like the hired help who does their washing and cooks for them. We eat separately most nights;

we do nothing together on the weekends. And I'm lonely – and bored. My own fault too though – I met Malcolm shortly after graduating and never did follow my dream of a career and seeing the world. Just like you, I was in a weird place and I wanted to hide away, scared of anyone ever finding out what we did essentially. I put all of my energy into proving I was a good person and trying to build the perfectly happy family, all the while expecting it to be taken away from me. And then when enough time had passed and I could start to believe we were in the clear, my life had passed me by.'

'It's not too late to make some changes though?' Stacey said. 'For all of us.'

'Yeah, we just need to get through this weekend, see where it takes us – and if we come out the other side in one piece, let's make a pact to sort ourselves out,' Paula said.

'Sounds like you might have some things to get off your chest too, Paulie?' Bev said.

'Um...' She looked at the scabs on her hand and thought about the bruises that were covered with unnecessarily long sleeves. 'No, I just could be doing more with my life too, like everyone else, I suppose. There's always room for personal growth.'

'How's married life for you?' Stacey asked, getting to her feet and opening the bottle of wine Paula had brought in with her.

'Lovely, great fun. Sue is a larger-than-life character, runs drumming workshops and is an amazing cook.'

'Any kids in your future plans?' Bev asked.

'God, no! I mean, I don't think I want them.' She sounded very defensive to Stacey and there was a shiftiness about her. Stacey had the distinct feeling she still wasn't being as honest as she and Bev had been. But then she had a similar feeling about Bev.

They were still lying. She could feel it.

'Loo break,' she said and shut herself in the bathroom, the champagne making her suddenly light-headed as her thoughts bounced around.

What if she couldn't actually trust either of them? Bev had been lying about herself as much as Stacey had. Maybe she should be looking closer to home – and specifically inside this room – for answers. Maybe this was all set up by one of them. Besides, who better to want Valentina dead than the people in this very room? The people who had the most to lose if the truth came out.

The idea chilled Stacey to her core.

She splashed some cold water on her face, took her time to get herself together before she returned to the bedroom. It was starting to get darker, the shadows lengthening across the carpet. 'We should think about getting changed and heading out at some point,' she said.

'So where do we start?' Bev said. 'Where did we go first that night?'

'Where we always went. The White Horse,' Paula replied.

'Then that's where we start.' Bev grabbed her phone and pulled up a map. 'It's not too far a walk from here actually. Maybe twenty minutes? Can you both handle that?'

They nodded.

'So let's get changed and get going. It's now or never really.'

'Now or never,' Stacey echoed.

She watched them through narrowed eyes as they left the room.

I watch as they leave the hotel and walk out towards the street. They are arm in arm, stretched across the path like a fortress. I can hear the gravel crunch beneath their feet and their muted laughter as they walk and talk. I can't make out what they are saying, so I lean over and open the window, but their voices are lost in a light breeze that is blowing in from the sea in the far distance.

They reach the gate and turn left towards the woods. Exactly where I want them to go.

Back to where it all happened.

We will all find out the answers tonight, one way or another.

The question is whether we will all make it back alive.

20

SPRING 1993

Valentina had gone to a lot of trouble. She'd bought a chicken and had roasted it in garlic, lemon and Italian herbs. There were creamy potatoes baking under the chicken and a salad ready to go. The smell coming from the kitchen was one she would like to think her mother would be proud of. She didn't know that exactly, but the mother she had created in her mind was an excellent Italian cook with warm, open arms that were always ready with a hug and a smile that lit up a room. The one she actually remembered had always been too ill to see her or sleeping, so she'd created her own memories of the things they had done. Memories she had come to believe because they were more pleasant than those of a skeletal woman sniping at her to let her rest when she was in pain or the smell of hospitals and disinfectant replacing that of her perfume.

She'd set the coffee table in the lounge as best she could for four of them, complete with little tea lights and paper serviettes. She'd even bought custard tarts from the bakery for dessert. All of that and the wine in the fridge would go a long way to getting them to hear what she had to say.

Weeks had gone by since she had heard Stu's confession and she had consulted the cards numerous times to decide how to tackle the issue. In the end, telling the girls had won out over any other form of action, so she'd listened in on their plans and knew they would all be home later tonight because their final exams began next week. Stacey had cooled things with Sean as the threat of exams loomed, but Val was certain she had been keeping things firmly in the friend zone with him anyway. None of them had been socialising all that much. They'd closed themselves into various rooms or hidden in the libraries on campus while they crammed and squeezed as much information into their heads as possible.

Valentina was the least concerned about her exams. She was likely to fail, but she was okay with that because she would come out of this experience with something more valuable than a degree. She would have won the gratitude and loyalty of the girls. She knew now that their friendship was what she wanted. Nothing else mattered. She had money, so she didn't need a career. What she didn't have was right in front of her.

These were the people that were now the most important to her.

But the exams would be over at some point and then they'd be back to going out, celebrating, and she knew Sean would set his sights on Stacey once more. He would run out of patience. She had to protect her. But she had to do it in the right way. She needed to make Stacey listen.

Valentina looked around her bedroom, which was

spotless. Then she grabbed the small hammer and knocked a nail into the wall directly above the coffee table before hanging a print in pride of place. It was a framed print of the four queens in a pack of cards and she thought it represented the four of them perfectly.

She stood back and admired it, then heard the front door open and the sound of three voices all talking over each other.

'Hiya,' she said brightly as she walked towards them. 'So I know you've all been working hard over the last few weeks and we haven't really seen much of each other, so I've made us all dinner and I thought we could hang out, drink some wine? What do you think? Take a break from studying?' She clasped her hands together expectantly, feeling like a schoolkid, practically bouncing from one foot to the next.

'Thanks, but I've got loads of work still to do before Monday,' Stacey said without really looking at her. Stacey hadn't actually looked her in the face in weeks. She tended to look beyond her or through her, but never at her.

There was an awkward silence, filled by Paula saying, 'It smells amazing though.'

She tried to catch Bev's eye and eventually did. Bev crumbled almost immediately, as Valentina knew she would.

'You know, guys, it would be a shame not to eat with Valentina after she went to so much trouble. And I for one am starving, so what do you say we take an hour off for dinner and pick up the books again afterwards? Everyone needs a break from studying once in a while.' They looked from one to the other, until Paula said, 'Sure, why not?'

'I've set the table in my room, thought it would be a nice change of scenery. And these are my mother's recipes.'

Stacey begrudgingly followed as they all filed into the lounge, kicking off their shoes as they went. Valentina rushed into the kitchen, grabbed a bottle of wine from the fridge and came back to see them settling in around the coffee table.

'I can't believe how much trouble you've gone to, Val,' Bev said. 'This is really thoughtful.'

Valentina beamed back at her. 'It's the least I can do really. You've all been so good to me and I've just messed up time and time again. I wanted to do something nice in return.' She poured generous glasses of wine, emptying the bottle.

'Cool print,' Paula said, indicating the frame Valentina had just hung.

'Thanks – it reminds me of us.'

'Why, because of the solitaire thing?'

'No, the four suits – Bev is the Queen of Hearts, the one always going out of her way to help everyone; Paula is the Queen of Clubs, no-nonsense, reliable; Stacey the Queen of Diamonds, beautiful and yet strong and resilient.'

Stacey looked at her puzzled. 'Which makes you the Queen of Spades then?'

'I guess so – dark and in your face, but always there in the background, the ace in your pocket. Or ready with a spade to bury the body for you.'

'Riiight,' Paula said, frowning.

'No, I think she has a point,' Bev said.

'You just like being the Queen of Hearts, you softie,' Stacey replied and everyone laughed, which warmed

Valentina. It felt like the world was tilting on its axis and finally coming back in line. She could feel the frost that had layered over the walls over the last few months starting to melt.

'Um, this is… nice too,' Paula said. Rows and rows of photos were stuck on the walls above her bed and desk, many of them taken without their knowledge. It was a like a shrine.

'Thanks,' she said, not noticing Paula's frown and worried glances at the other two. She went back into the kitchen to carve the chicken and could hear snatches of their conversation coming through the thin wall.

'Bless, she's trying really hard,' Bev said. 'You have to give her that.'

'This is quite something though,' Paula said.

'Stace, you can't stay mad at her forever – and there are only a couple of weeks left as it is before we all go our separate ways. It might be nice to feel like the place is harmonious, especially since stress levels are going to be so high over exams. Please, Stace, for me – even just for one night, yeah?' Bev added.

When Valentina returned with the platter of chicken and the salad bowl, it was Stacey who got to her feet to take them from her and said, 'Smells delicious, thanks.'

They piled their plates high and Valentina spent more time drawing pleasure from watching them eat than from eating herself.

'God, these potatoes are amazing! Where did you learn to cook like this?'

'My mother – she used to let me watch her in the kitchen

and she was an amazing home cook. Her Italian upbringing, I guess.' She noticed Stacey glance at the other two and the slight shake of Bev's head as Stacey went to say something, but Valentina jumped up and went to get more wine before she could.

'And I've got homemade custard tarts for dessert afterwards,' she said as she returned.

'Bloody hell, Val, you should be spending your time revising, not baking.' Bev's disapproval was loud in her ears.

'I'm kidding, I bought them from the bakery,' Valentina said.

'Oh God, for a minute there I thought you were telling the truth,' Bev said laughing.

'As if she would,' Stacey muttered.

There was another stilted silence, broken only by the sound of Paula scraping the last of the potatoes onto her plate.

'You're right, Stacey, I haven't always been honest with you all – and I guess my biggest problem is saying things for attention and then lashing out. I've always been volatile – that thing with Sean was me lashing out, I guess. But there is something I do need to tell you all – about Sean.'

Stacey's lips drew in so far, they disappeared. 'For fuck's sake.'

'Just hear me out please, Stacey,' Valentina said.

Bev put a hand on Stacey's arm. 'Fine, let's hear it.'

Valentina took a large drink of her wine. 'So you remember that night ages ago when I went out with Stu and I ended up vomming off the balcony?'

'God, that tiger lay on the pavement for days – that's the

longest it hasn't rained in ages. I swear there's still a stain there now,' Paula said with a snort.

Valentina smiled. She drank some more. 'So Stu said something to me that night – about Sean – that I only really remembered later. It was a weird night because I was really drunk, like properly wasted, but I didn't have as much as I would normally have. I kind of put it down to stress or my period or whatever, but it still just didn't seem right. Anyway, long story short, Stu told me that sometimes Sean puts stuff in girls' drinks to get them extra wasted so that they won't necessarily remember what they are doing afterwards.'

Her words were met with silence.

Then Stacey said, 'Oh come on, you expect us to believe that?'

'It's true! Have you not noticed how some girls steer clear of him now? If you were to ask them, they probably couldn't tell you why. Like your friend, the one I spilled coffee on that time? I saw her and Sean go out together a little while ago, but she hasn't spoken to him since.'

'Oh please. I've heard enough of this. Bev, I'm sorry. I gave it a go, but I can't.' She started to get to her feet.

'Wait, let me get this straight,' Paula said. 'You're saying that Sean and Stu are some sort of double act going around drugging girls to sleep with them? But that's absurd! He doesn't need to.'

'Stu pretty much admitted it! I think Stu had put something in my drink that night too. I overheard him and Sean talking about it the next day and it sounded like that was his intention, but that maybe it didn't work or he didn't give me enough or something.'

'And why would Stu tell you this, Val? Sean is his best mate. Not to mention that he is incriminating himself by the sounds of it,' Paula said.

'Because I may have found something else out about him, something he doesn't want everyone to know, so I've kind've used it against him.'

'Found what out?' Bev asked, but Stacey interrupted from the doorway.

'This is just more of your lies, isn't it? You're making it up just to cover up the fact that you slept with Sean, even though you knew me and him were getting close. But the truth is you wanted him because he wanted me. What? Did you feel guilty afterwards? Or like the slut you are? So you thought you'd make up this elaborate story? Make us feel sorry for you?'

'Wow, Stacey, if anyone is a slut, it's you,' Valentina spat back.

She had the distinct feeling that the evening was slipping out of her grasp.

Stacey stormed over to where Valentina was still sitting on the carpet. She towered over her as she said, 'These two convinced me to let you stay, but I think your time is up. I want you out.'

'I'm the victim here, not him.'

'He's my friend. You are not.'

The words stung like tiny, poisoned barbs.

'But I am your friend. You three are my best friends and I wanted you to know, to protect you.'

'Oh yeah? And how long have you known?' Stacey said, her voice steely.

'What?'

'How long have you known about this? That night with Stu was weeks ago, wasn't it?'

'Um, yeah, I guess.'

'And you're only telling us now? When I've been hanging out with him, we all have? You didn't think you should tell me straight away? Or is it that you'll now say anything because you are that desperate for attention, that lonely?'

'Well, at first the cards said not to say anything—'

'The cards?' Paula said incredulously. 'Val, that's just a stupid game. It's not real; it's not magic or voodoo or anything.'

'Ruining a good guy's reputation just for your own alibi, to make yourself into some poor victim for attention. That's sick.' Stacey flung the words at her.

'No! It's not that at all! It's true – all of it. He drugged me to sleep with me. They both did!'

'Just like it's true your mother was ill recently and you were so worried about her when the truth is that she's dead,' Stacey said. 'Look at this, look at all of it.' She swept her arm across the room, indicating the wall of photos. Valentina flinched, convinced Stacey was going to lash out at her. 'This is just weird. You're weird. You need help. Your constant lying, your obsession with all of us. We can't believe a word you say. I think we're done here. I'm going to bed.'

She stormed out. The walls of the flat vibrated as she slammed her bedroom door.

Paula and Bev sat with rigid backs. 'Why, Valentina?' Paula asked. 'Why do you feel you have to lie to be friends with us? We would like you just as you are if we thought we actually knew the real you, but I don't think we do. Everything is fake. You do realise that this isn't the way to get Stacey's attention, right?'

'Like you would know? We all know you're in love with her, Paula, but don't have the guts to tell her. Now that's pathetic,' she spat at Paula.

The words landed like boulders on the coffee table. Paula looked like she was going to throw a punch, then she calmly got to her feet and left the room. Bev shook her head at Valentina and said, 'Low blow, Val. You didn't need to say that,' and also left.

Valentina sat in the quiet, hearing only the clock tick and the fridge rumble into life. Then she grabbed the platter of chicken, screamed in frustration and propelled the platter at the lounge doors.

The platter struck the glass and exploded into a million pieces.

21

PRESENT DAY

The White Horse hadn't changed a bit. If it had had a coat of paint, the owners had chosen exactly the same shade of what could only be described as blood-clot red as before. Stacey had never noticed how womb-like the bar was until she stepped back into it thirty years later and the memories came rushing back.

It was busy, the Friday night crowd the same age demographic that it had been when they were regulars. But the students were more woke these days, it would seem. The menu on the chalkboard at the side of the bar no longer advertised curly fries and toasted pitta bread drenched in cheese sauce. Instead, there were tofu bites and sweet potato chips.

The air was noticeably cleaner too, the no-smoking rule making it an easier place to breathe, but strangely stripping it of some of its atmosphere. The carpets were still sticky though and there was the obligatory band setting up on the small stage. Certainly not 101 – who knew how old those men would be now, Stacey thought.

'Oh my God, it's like stepping into a time machine,' Paula said with a laugh.

'Isn't it just?' Bev agreed. 'I can't see the cheesy pitta on the menu anymore.'

'Oh God, that stuff was brilliant for soaking up the alcohol. The way they made a pitta bread and cheese sauce into such a monumental meal was genius.'

'What are we drinking? Pints of cider like the old days? Or are we too grown up for that now?' Stacey asked.

'Cider it is. Stacey, you get them in. I'm going to wrestle a table from someone,' Paula said and headed over to where a young man wearing a bucket hat was nursing a pint on his own. Stacey watched as Paula leant in to talk to him, then saw him get up reluctantly and move off to perch against the bar.

'Here, use this,' Bev said and thrust her card at Stacey.

'No, we'll split it.'

'We bloody won't. Malcolm can pay, the lazy git. He owes me more than a few date nights anyway.'

Stacey waved at the young girl behind the bar, a tiny slip of a thing in skin-tight jeans and a crop top that exposed the tiniest waist Stacey had ever seen. 'Three pints of cider please,' she said loudly to be heard over the conversations going on around her.

'What kind?' was the reply.

'Don't care.'

'Cool.'

Bev had now joined Paula at the table and they were laughing between themselves. The man in the bucket hat was watching them with a piteous expression on his face.

Whatever, mate.

Three pints appeared on the bar in front of her. She handed Bev's card to the girl and asked her to run a tab on it.

The girl nodded and wandered off.

Stacey balanced the glasses between her hands and wormed to the table.

'What did you say to him?' she asked as she sat down.

'I told him that we used to come here when we were at uni and now Bev has cancer and we are here for one last trip down memory lane. Do you remember when Val used that lie that time?'

'Oh God, yes, wasn't it her birthday?' Stacey said.

'Well, we thought it was but I wouldn't be surprised if she'd even lied about that. And why am I always the one to have pretend cancer?' Bev said.

Stacey raised her pint glass. 'Well, here we go. Let the journey begin.'

'Let the journey begin,' Paula and Bev said in unison.

The band started to warm up. 'What do you think? Some Nineties classics or not?'

'No chance!' Stacey said to Paula.

The band began to play 'Should I Stay or Should I Go' by The Clash and all three of them laughed and cheered. A few people looked at them curiously, this bunch of old girls sitting in the corner of a student bar with their pints of cider and middle-aged haircuts.

'Okay, so now that we are here, what are we looking for?' Bev asked when the song ended and the band started on a newer tune that none of them knew.

'No idea,' Stacey said. She looked around at the bar, the people, the walls. Nothing seemed to jump out at her. It all looked like it had back then. She drank from her pint. 'It's like looking for something you don't know you've lost.'

Paula started laughing and pointing at a framed newspaper clipping on the wall over Bev's shoulder. 'Oh my God, I remember her!'

'Who?' Bev said and swivelled around in her chair.

'She was in my psychology class, I think, or maybe anatomy, I can't remember, but she was obsessed with aliens, even back then. We used to tease her about it behind her back, saying she was wearing metal underwear and stuff because she was convinced that we would all end up being abducted by aliens. Turns out she became a bestselling author! Look!'

The article was a write-up on her as a local author of science fiction and how she'd graduated from the university and went on to write a number of *Sunday Times* bestsellers.

'Oh, I read one of her books once. Really mad, but strangely good. Almost like *A Hitchhiker's Guide to the Galaxy* in style. Good on her,' Bev said.

'Wait...' Stacey said, looking around.

'What?' Bev was frowning and scanning the room herself.

'Look at the pictures on the walls,' Stacey said.

Paula looked around too. 'They're all newspaper clippings.'

'Exactly! When we used to come here, they were posters for gigs mostly. Now they are newspaper clippings from old newspapers. Maybe we need to be looking at more of them.' Stacey could feel a weird excitement building. The first piece of the jigsaw was falling into place. 'And not just any newspaper clippings. They're old articles from the student newspaper.'

Paula got to her feet and started to make her way around the room, leaning over tables and ignoring the complaints from their occupants. When she reached a table at the far side of the room, she reached over and grabbed the small frame from the wall, said something to the couple sitting there and returned looking triumphant.

'This is it.' She clattered the frame onto the middle of the table.

The article was short, a small piece running alongside the main article about students dressing up as political figures and staging a mass protest on the main campus.

Student Missing After Night Out

Campus security is asking for anyone with information on the whereabouts of Sean Cross, 22, to get in touch after his housemates alerted campus security that he didn't return home on Friday after drinking in town. He was last seen leaving Razzles nightclub alone in the early hours, but failed to return to his flat. He is believed to have consumed a large amount of alcohol and his friends and family are concerned for his welfare.

He was wearing blue denim jeans, a black Metallica T-shirt and flip-flops, one of which was found near the river's edge. Campus security is urging anyone who may have seen him to get in touch on 0899-442-2424.

There was a small, grainy photo attached. A face they all recognised.

They were silent as they passed the article between them.

Stacey felt like she couldn't breathe. The last time she had seen that face, it had been leering down at her as she scratched and shoved at him.

Paula put it back on the table. 'Let the treasure hunt begin,' she said finally.

'But this doesn't really tell us anything, does it? It could be a coincidence,' Bev said.

Stacey saw how Bev's hand trembled as she drained her pint, how her eyes were wild, flicking around the room. Paula seemed calmer, less shocked.

'You're right, Bev. We covered our tracks. It was like the article said – he had too much to drink and fell in the river. The fact that they never found him is neither here nor there. If there was any connection to us, the police would've come knocking some time ago.'

'I know. I've spent the best part of the last thirty years waiting for that knock on the door,' Stacey said.

'It was your idea,' Bev said quietly.

'Oh no, don't do that. It was all of us,' Stacey said.

Bev sighed, drank some more.

'The point is that this is Valentina making trouble, not

the police. She just wanted us to know she hadn't forgotten maybe. Sean is dead.'

They sat in silence until Bev said, 'Sometimes I feel like someone is watching me.'

'That's just paranoia,' Paula replied, but she didn't sound convinced.

'Maybe – or my guilty conscience, but sometimes I feel like there is someone there when I leave the house, watching, following...'

'Don't dismiss her, Paulie. Maybe the person who got to Valentina has been watching all of us too. Do any of us know what happened to the others? Rob, Mike, Stu? Maybe they had their suspicions or something,' Stacey said.

'Mike is happily married and has a couple of very cute kids, according to Facebook,' Bev said.

They both looked at her, surprised. 'What? So I might have kept an eye on him a little over the years.' She looked sheepish.

'Wow, okay,' Paula said with a laugh.

'I used to be on Mike's friends list, but he binned me a few years back, so I just look him up now and again to see, you know. Nothing weird or stalkerish. Anyway, it wouldn't be him. I never found a profile for Rob though or Stu,' Bev said.

'We didn't really know Rob that well, did we? He was just a hanger-on, wanting to be like the others, but never quite getting it right. Can't even remember much about him other than his weirdly high-pitched voice,' Paula said.

'Like Mickey Mouse,' Bev said with a snort.

'But we didn't know Valentina either,' Stacey said. 'So maybe he was more of a threat than we thought.'

'Fair point. Maybe they were with Sean at the club and we didn't see them? But they saw us?' Bev was growing paler by the second.

'I'm not convinced about Rob, but what about Stu?' Paula asked. 'He may have assumed Valentina told us about what him and Sean were up to, in which case he may have had his suspicions. Has anyone else seen anything of him online?'

'I've never looked, to be honest. Knowing Valentina had exposed the whole eating disorder thing would give him a motive,' Stacey said.

'But Valentina said she didn't start those rumours – and that was so long ago. If he wanted to hurt her, he would've done it that night when he confronted her in the bar,' Bev said.

'That doesn't mean she was telling the truth about the rumours, does it? You know how she disliked the truth. She was a gold-standard chaos neutral.'

Paula grabbed her phone and opened the Facebook app. 'What was his surname again?'

'Oh God, I can't remember – something German-sounding maybe?' Stacey replied.

'Without a surname, I can't look him up – Stu just won't cut it!'

'Another dead end then,' Bev said disheartened.

Their glasses were empty. Stacey went to get refills.

'Does she seem okay to you?' Paula asked as they watched her walk to the bar. Stacey was wearing ill-fitting black trousers and a T-shirt that had little holes in it by her belly button. Her once long and beautiful blonde hair was lank, the ends crispy with split ends.

Bev was thoughtful. 'I don't know. Could be the strain of this and the divorce? I think she's been quite honest about what has happened in the last few years, but maybe not about how hard it has been. She doesn't say much about her work, but she never did become an architect. But then I never became a teacher, did I? And not being on speaking terms with her family will have hit her hard too.'

'Why didn't you become a teacher?'

She shrugged. 'I met Malcolm shortly after I graduated and he became my priority. I was at my first placement and I realised that I didn't like other people's kids. Everything was such a mess back then – after you know... I didn't want noise and responsibility and stress. I wanted a quiet life, to keep my head down, and he offered me that. Very boring. You've done the best out of all of us though – a lovely wife, a cool job doing what you always wanted to do.' She fell silent again. 'Does it not bother you – what we did? Play on your mind – the guilt?'

'Yeah, but I'm very good at closing myself off from things I don't want to think about. I put it in a box and put the box on a shelf. That's how I cope.'

Stacey returned with the drinks.

'So what next?' Paula asked her.

'Well, where did we go after here? Did we go straight to Razzles when we got thrown out of here?' She pulled out the map and Paula laid it out on the table, moving the glasses aside so that they could see. There was a big red circle over where they were now along with the number 2.

The number 1 was where the flat had been. Numbers 3 and 4 were circled a few streets away. The sketches were exact mini replicas of the buildings, drawn in black ink. 'Yes, looks like it was Razzles. So we go and see if it's still open. It's a long shot though after all these years. Drink up, girls.'

'No, we went for chips first – number 3 is the chip shop; number 4 is Razzles,' Paula said.

'You're right – and you were throwing chips at each other. I was getting really annoyed because they were such nice chips and I really wanted to sit down and eat them. We sat on the square of grass and Valentina spilled vinegar on herself. Every time I smell vinegar, it reminds me of that,' Bev said sadly.

'Well, I'm starving. I could do with some chips,' Stacey said. 'So let's go.'

The bar is full enough that they don't see me standing in the corner, a beer in front of me and a bag of salted peanuts, just like any other punter. I keep my head down, would love to get closer to hear what they are talking about, but I don't want to risk it. Especially since everything is working out perfectly so far.

They can't see how they are being manipulated, directed into position, pawns in a game.

All will become clear soon enough though.

I sip at the cold beer, trying to ignore the urge to get closer. It is like an itch I can't reach.

There is a dartboard on the wall near to them. I walk over to it and grab the darts from the board. One by one I throw them at the target, my ears straining to pick up their conversation. I get snatches of words, occasional phrases and can get a sense of what they are saying. They still seem to have no idea what is waiting for them at the end.

I draw my arm back and lob the dart through the air at the board, imagine it piercing a cheek, maybe an eye, the resultant squeal of pain as the nerves fire in response.

Nothing less than they deserve.

22

Valentina closed the door and leant against the back of it. She dropped her bag at her feet and had to fight hard against the urge to slide to the ground. So the last exam was written, the last page turned on this chapter, and now they could pack up and go their separate ways.

Stacey hadn't followed through on tossing Valentina out on the street, but only because of exam distraction. But now that the exams were over, there was nothing stopping her.

A burst of laughter exploded from the kitchen. Valentina pushed away from the door, stepped over her bag and followed the sound. Stacey and Paula were sitting at the table, Bev was standing by the sink, and it was like that first day all over again. Valentina felt tears prickle at the back of her throat. She had been so optimistic just a few short months ago – and now she felt more alone than ever.

'Hey, how is everyone?'

'All good,' Bev said brightly. 'How was your last exam?'

'Oh you know...' The truth was she had probably

bombed all of them, but that didn't matter to her anymore. Nothing did.

Valentina leant against the fridge and said quietly, 'Listen, I just wanted to apologise. I think I wasn't quite what you were expecting and I've made some mistakes. We'll all be going our separate ways in the next few days, so how about we go out tonight, one last blast like at the beginning? Have a bit of fun – drinks on me? Well, my dad anyway. Make the bastard pay one more time.'

The girls were silent. 'I don't know, Val, there's always something kicks off when we all go out,' Paula said honestly. 'We were just going to have a couple of drinks at the White Horse, then maybe grab a pizza or something.'

She knew Paula was lying. She had heard them making plans to meet up with a few others at Razzles later.

'Oh, okay, that's... sure, no problem. I have packing to do anyway. Well, no hard feelings, yeah? And good luck with your results and stuff.' She kept her head down and her shoulders slumped as she walked out.

She could hear them muttering behind her and counted to ten before she knew Bev would cave and convince them into letting her join them.

'Val! Wait!' It was less than ten seconds this time. 'Let's ask the cards. It's a tradition now – let the cards decide Valentina's fate one more time.'

Valentina felt like she was in the dock waiting for a guilty verdict as the cards were shuffled and dealt. Apparently cutting the cards wouldn't be enough for this kind of decision. It required the full solitaire. So the task was given to Stacey, but they all leant over and followed her hands as they flicked, twisted and turned.

Eventually the game was won and Valentina exhaled in relief.

'Right, let's get ready,' Bev said, clearly happy with the result. 'I have a feeling this is going to be fun.'

They were shiny happy people heading out for their last night before joining the real world. Under a cloudless sky, the night was one long, endless possibility. Before they left the flat, Valentina opened a bottle of champagne. The real stuff again – to remind them of her when she first moved in. It made Bev hiccup as the bubbles popped in her throat. They raised their glasses to what had gone before and what was yet to come.

Valentina looked around at the three people she felt closest to in the world at this moment. It was like the stars were aligning for something big tonight, a sense of expectation, anticipation, but of what she wasn't sure. As they drank their champagne, Valentina looked at each in turn and could see they'd all made an effort, a little more sparkle here, an extra dab of colour there. She smiled over the rim of her glass.

This time they all linked arms as they walked towards the woods. Valentina was on the edge, her arm slotted through Bev's, and it felt natural. They chattered and laughed about everything and nothing. A fox screeched through the trees, disturbed by their happy voices. The trees creaked and groaned, as though making room for them to pass. Celebrating their journey.

And the river escorted them along, joining in their conversation.

The woods thinned and the voice of the water was replaced by car horns, a siren far in the distance, an aeroplane overhead, unnatural noises drowning out the natural.

They reached the bridge and crossed over, the White Horse in their sights. There were plenty of people out tonight, now that exams were over. They stood in groups in the night air outside the pub, drinking pints and smoking, the puffs circling up into the night.

Paula stopped them before they walked inside, saying, 'Look, let's make a pact, just for tonight. No guys to ruin it for us, okay? Just us four tonight. No arguments, no snogging, no nonsense. Just a girls' night out. Are we agreed?'

They all nodded.

The pub was noisy, with everyone trying to talk over the music bellowing at full volume. Voices sang along to the choruses of songs they all knew and laughter rang out in fits and bursts. The girls ordered pints of cider and hovered near a booth at the side of the room. As luck would have it – the stars aligning? – the occupants of the booth got up shortly after the girls arrived and they slid into the vacated seats. Valentina felt on top of the world, sandwiched between Paula and Bev. Stacey was on the other side of Paula.

The doors of the pub ricocheted open and Mike, Stu, Sean and Rob walked in. A cloud fell over Valentina's mood. She looked away as they surveyed the room. She noticed Stacey look at Sean, then look away too. Even Bev seemed uninterested. Maybe what she had said had actually registered?

'Bev, there's Mike,' Valentina said.

'Yeah, so?' she said.

'Oh, are you two not...?'

'Turns out he's been seeing someone else at the same time as me. I saw her out of the window the other day. He didn't even have the decency to move out of eyesight when he snogged her goodbye.'

'I'm sorry, I didn't know.'

Bev shrugged. 'We need tequila! I'm going to get some.'

'Are you sure, Bev? Not sure if you can handle it,' Paula said, frowning.

'Of course I can.' She got to her feet and strode to the bar with purpose, pointedly walking directly past Mike without acknowledging him. The other two men looked over to their table and a surge of energy passed between them all. Mike followed Bev to the bar and Valentina could see him trying to talk to her, but she kept turning away from him.

He reached out and grabbed her arm. She tried to snatch it back, but he held his grip.

'Should we go and help her?' Valentina asked.

'Bev can look after herself, don't you worry,' Paula said.

Valentina watched as Bev pulled free, then pushed through the crowd of people and headed for the door, with Mike hot on her heels.

'Where is she going?' Valentina didn't like this one bit. Her happiness was starting to slide into the red zone.

'She hates confrontation, but when she gets angry, she can properly overheat. My guess is that Mike is trying to explain himself and she's going to give him a piece of her mind. She'll be back in a minute,' Stacey said.

Valentina kept her eyes on the door, ready to go after Bev

if she didn't return soon. The minutes ticked over, then the door was thrown open with such force that it swung back against the wall and the glass cracked loudly, like ice on a lake. The volume in the pub dropped off completely as all eyes turned to see Bev walk in, her head held high, followed some way behind by Mike, who was sporting one bright red cheek.

A cheer went up around the pub.

'See? Told you,' Stacey said.

Then everyone returned to their conversations and Bev headed to the bar. Minutes later she was back at the table with a tray of tequilas and a glint of steel in her eyes.

'What happened? Where did you go?' Valentina asked.

'Bloody hell, Bev, you broke the door!'

'So he says he wants to go outside so that he can explain. Then he says she means nothing, it was a one-night thing. I'm like how is that making it okay? Did she know about me? Probably not. Did she know she was a one-night stand? Probably not. Then he starts saying that he'll buy me a drink, we can hook up for the last time because they're all leaving tomorrow and I lost it. Like I'm a toy he wants to play with. Nah, so I slapped him and came back inside.' She smiled proudly.

'I didn't know you had it in you,' Valentina said.

'What is it with men thinking we are their possessions and playthings? That they can pick us up and drop us again when they feel like it? I want a man who sees me for who am, not what I can do for him,' Bev said. She grabbed a , raised it high and said, 'To the girls!'

the girls!' They knocked back the shots and Valentina heat rush all the way to her feet.

'This is why I'm a lesbian,' Paula said.

They all stared at her, open-mouthed. Stacey suddenly cheered and whooped. 'She said it out loud!'

Paula blushed, but she was smiling broadly.

'I get it,' Bev said. 'Maybe I should switch to the other side too.'

'Sorry, I still find Nick Berry sexier than Sharon Watts,' Stacey said.

'That's who you've picked? I'm gay and I find Nick Berry sexier than Sharon Watts,' Paula said, laughing.

'I'm sure if anyone could turn you, Paula could,' Valentina said to Stacey.

There was an awkward pause before Paula said, 'She's right, you know. I am awesome. Here, I'll show you.' She leant into Stacey, aiming for a kiss, but Stacey swerved and Paula latched onto her neck. Stacey looked surprised, then horrified. Paula showed no signs of letting go, so Stacey pushed her away roughly.

'Oh my God, Paula, that is so gross and disgusting!' Stacey said loudly.

'Ha! She gave you a hickey!!' Bev declared loudly.

It was true. There was now a small but distinct mark on Stacey's neck.

Valentina noticed how hurt Paula looked before anyone else did. 'I'm not disgusting,' she said in a low voice.

'No, Paulie, I didn't mean you. I meant *it*. I'm not into… you or any girls for that matter. You know that. You're my friend, my mate, my sister. And I definitely like boys.'

'It was just a joke anyway,' Paula said, but the hurt cast a shadow over her face.

'More drinks,' Valentina said, not wanting the night to

be ruined by anything. 'I'll go.' She got up and felt the heat rush through her body at the sudden movement. She had to jostle and elbow her way to the front of the bar and when she got there, she realised she was standing across from Mike, Sean, Stu and Rob. Mike and Rob were deep in conversation, screwing their eyes up at the smoke they were both exhaling in between syllables. Mike kept rubbing at his cheek, which was still red.

Stu and Sean were talking, their heads bent in close. Sean looked annoyed; Stu looked almost tearful. They hadn't noticed her watching them, but she saw Stu palm something into Sean's hand, which Sean deposited straight into his back pocket. Stu turned away and began talking to Mike and Rob, but he was pale. Sean leant on the bar and waved his hand to get the attention of the barman, who went straight over to him despite the many others waiting their turn patiently.

Another barman nodded at Valentina, but she ignored him and moved past the people to her left, swerving and ducking until she was close to where Sean was. As he turned with his pint, she stumbled and fell onto him. Beer flew over anyone standing nearby. A loud shout of consternation erupted as Valentina looked straight at Sean and said, 'So sorry! Someone pushed me! Oh, Sean, shit, your drinks. Can I buy you another round? I am so sorry.'

He looked at her narrowly for a second, then said, 'It's fine, no harm done. I know the barman – he'll get me some more.'

'Are you sure? I feel really bad.'

'Yeah, it's fine.' He turned his back to her and leant over

the bar again. She brushed past him and headed into the corridor that led to the toilets.

She locked herself in a cubicle, put the lid of the toilet down and sat on it, then pulled out the little matchbox she had lifted from Sean's pocket when he had turned his back on her. There were two capsules inside the box.

She sat for a moment, thinking, until someone hammered on the door. She shoved the box deep in her pocket and headed back to the table.

A few more rounds of drinks and Bev was starving. 'I want chips,' she said sulkily.

'Then let's get chips,' Stacey said. 'We can get some down the road, eat them on the square, then head over to Razzles.'

'Yes, let's do that!' Bev clapped her hands together and bounced in her chair.

Paula laughed. 'I love Tequila Bev!'

The chip shop looked like it was about to close. A rotund man in an apron and a paper hat was wiping down the counters and turning off the fryers. He had a ring of sweat soaking through the paper hat, grease smudges on his white apron and an air of exhaustion about him. Bev charmed him with a few bats of her Bambi eyes behind her fuchsia-framed glasses and he succumbed, handing over polystyrene trays of steaming-hot chips. He gave her tiny packets of salt and vinegar along with little wooden forks, and the girls filed out of the shop, ridiculously happy with their late-night supper.

They found a bench on the square and Bev and Stacey sat

on it, with Valentina and Paula at their feet on the grass. Bev looked completely besotted with her chips. She peered at them in adoration, inhaling deeply before sinking her fork in one. 'Oh my God, these are good. Needs salt and vinegar though. Pass it over.'

Paula threw some sachets at her. Valentina helped herself to some too, but when it came to opening the vinegar, she squeezed too hard and it squirted out all over the front of her dress. 'Dammit! I'm going to stink now!' She patted at herself with a serviette.

'Idiot,' Stacey said and threw a chip at her. Valentina wasn't sure how to act at first, this being the only time tonight when Stacey had addressed her directly. She paused, then grabbed a chip and threw it back.

Then Paula lobbed one at Stacey and a full-out war began. Bev sat passively, then grew annoyed. 'Guys, come on, these chips are so good, so if you're not going to eat them, don't waste them. Give them to me.'

'Sorry, Mammy,' Paula said with a giggle and settled back into eating again.

This is going to be okay. Everything is going to be okay.
Valentina smiled to herself.

23

PRESENT DAY

The streets were busy with students milling around as the night wore on. There was the occasional well-dressed couple, winding through the students to the better part of town, but on the whole, it was like being back in 1993. It was a nice evening, the sky clear and a large full moon of cheese hanging low above the buildings. Stacey walked in between Paula and Bev, feeling a little like time had wound backwards to those days when they would walk arm in arm everywhere, like they were physically joined in some way. Like the way they had left the hotel earlier, automatically slipping back into old habits. It's funny how quickly you could cut yourself off from someone when you needed to – and how quickly you could reconnect too.

The weeks after they went their separate ways were a haze, a mix of loosely formed memories and feelings. Many days spent in bed, sleeping, Stacey's parents convinced she was catching up after revising hard for her finals, not recuperating after a trauma. Her brothers had given her space for a while, then had grown annoyed at her immobility while they went out to work every day.

On a whim, she got up, went out and cut her hair short, right up to her ears in a weird sort of bob that made her face look too round. It had taken ages to grow out again and was never the right shade of blonde after that, growing mousier with every passing year. Bev and Paula weren't there to tell her she looked stupid. That had made it worse to bear. Those had been dark days, but the years that followed were arguably darker.

Now, walking with the two of them again, she could see glimpses of her younger self, the confidence she had had, the lack of responsibility manifesting in a general sense that she couldn't give a shit about the world. She linked her arms between them now and smiled at each of them in turn, feeling a sudden surge of love and nostalgia.

'It's actually great to be back here with you two, you know? I haven't felt this good in quite a while – since the divorce actually. After that, I kind've lost myself – but now, us three back together, it's nice.'

They walked without thinking, muscle memory guiding their feet. They rounded a corner and found themselves outside the Vinegar Splash fish and chip shop, which still existed and was still pungent with malt vinegar.

'Oh my God, my mouth is watering already,' Bev said. 'These were the best chips after a night out, almost as good as the cheese pitta at the White Horse.'

There was no queue and they walked straight in. An indifferent girl in her early twenties stood behind the counter wearing an apron with the shop logo shouting across the front and a hair protector covering her long dark hair, ending in a point where her ponytail was. She was sitting on a bar stool, scrolling absently on her phone. She didn't look up when they walked in.

'What do you want, girls? Bev asked. 'My treat again.'

'Chips, definitely,' Paula said, 'with loads of vinegar.'

'Same,' said Stacey.

Only then did the girl look up. 'Three chips, yeah? Do you want salt and vinegar?'

'Definitely,' Bev said. 'Loads of vinegar.'

She got to her feet and started to scoop hot chips into polystyrene trays before liberally sprinkling vinegar over them. The smell was amazing.

She handed the three parcels over.

Bev paid and they wandered back outside, headed towards the grass in front of the chip shop where they had sat all those years ago.

'We sat right here that night. Valentina was next to you, Stacey.'

'That's right. I threw the first chip – it landed in her lap and then a few more flew and you were properly annoyed.' Stacey laughed at the memory.

'Well, they taste just as good as they did then,' Bev said, stuffing her mouth full of the salty chips. She sighed loudly, closed her eyes. 'Can't remember the last time I had chips from a tray with a wooden fork,' she said.

'That good, huh?' Paula said and rolled her eyes.

'That good.'

'Here,' Stacey said and pulled a couple of cans of gin and tonic from her large handbag. 'I grabbed these on the way out of my hotel room, in case we needed them,' she said and passed them one each.

'Nice,' Paula said and opened hers straight away. She took a deep drink from the can, then leant over to put it down at her feet.

Suddenly she froze. 'Bloody hell,' she said in a strangled voice.

'What?' Bev asked around a mouthful of chips.

'Look.' Paula was bent over, peering under the bench.

Stacey leant over and peered between her legs. Lying under the bench, almost completely obscured by a thicket of grass, was a flip-flop. She reached down and grabbed it.

'Don't touch it!' Paula said loudly.

'Why not?'

'I think it's his.'

Stacey looked at it, turned it over. The sole was worn down, the straps were black, there was no obvious logo. It was dirty, with dried mud clinging to the outer sole. The inner sole was worn down where a foot had pressed down over time.

Paula felt cold, but said, 'This is just a coincidence. Anyone could've sat here over the years and—'

'Left a flip-flop behind? Who does that?' Stacey asked.

'If they were drunk or something, they could have?'

Bev had stopped eating. 'It's another clue.'

'No, it's not,' Paula insisted.

'The article said they found one flip-flop, but not the other,' Stacey said.

'By the river, it said. But he was barefoot. He liked to be barefoot,' Paula insisted.

'Was he? Can you actually remember that?' Bev pushed.

'Well, no, I can't remember – it was thirty years ago!'

They stared at it with pale faces and wide eyes.

'Put it in your bag,' Bev said eventually as their chips grew cold in their laps.

'What?' Stacey asked.

'Put it in your handbag,' she repeated. 'It could be evidence, so we should keep it in case whoever is doing this can use it against us.'

She looked around them, panicked.

'But they wouldn't give us the evidence if they were going to use it,' Stacey said. 'That doesn't make any sense.'

'None of this makes sense,' Paula muttered.

'Maybe they think we won't take it with us. Just do it.' Bev sounded like she was unravelling.

'Bev, this isn't *Death in Paradise*. Have a drink, eat some more chips and calm down.' Stacey shoved the flip-flop in her handbag anyway and opened her can before drinking a large amount in one go. Her hands were shaking.

'I still think it's a coincidence and we are going to laugh at this later when we find out this was all a stupid game arranged by Valentina,' Paula said.

'If she wasn't dead already, I would kill her for this,' Stacey said.

There seemed nothing else to say, so they sat in silence, chewing despite their appetites having vanished into the night.

After a while, Paula said, 'So do you want to carry on or shall we just give up and go back to the hotel?'

They looked at each other, waiting for someone else to make the decision.

Stacey shrugged. 'I say we carry on. If we don't, we will always wonder.'

Bev nodded. 'Agreed. We carry on.'

'To Razzles then,' Paula said and crushed the can in her fist.

'I can't believe I am walking around with a smelly flip-flop in my bag. It could belong to a homeless person who has some weird fungal disease that is slowly infecting the lining of my bag for all I know,' Stacey grumbled.

'Hey, you picked it up!'

Stacey's earlier feelings of warm nostalgia had vanished and she had to admit feeling rattled by the discovery of the flip-flop. It was probably a coincidence, but even so, it could mean something else entirely. It could mean that someone else knew what happened that night. Maybe their theory about Stu, Mike or even Rob was closer to the truth than they thought.

They came to a stop outside a large building that had a broken sign on the front with the name of a bingo hall. The sign was completely broken in places, cracked and fractured in others. The windows and entrance were boarded up, the boards covered in bright, spray-painted graffiti.

Stacey took in the crude, spray-painted art where there was once a bright, lively nightclub with big glass windows that shone fluorescent from the neon disco lights pulsing in time to the Eighties and Nineties music from within as smoke seeped into every fabric and grain of the place. They would've had to have given this place a deep clean before they turned it into a bingo hall for older people, considering how many banned substances were enjoyed in its dark rooms and dingy corridors.

The hefty bouncers at the entrance had been more to stop under-aged kids from getting in rather than from keeping an eye on banned substances. Their pockets were never checked, their handbags never searched. It was commonplace to see white powder on the bathroom counter or to crunch a pill underfoot as they headed to the dance floor. This place had been where the drunks got drunker and the addicts got higher, the walls bouncing with illegal highs and hallucinations.

And now it was just another monument to their youth, an empty shell of a building, probably frequented by squatters late at night who were keeping the tradition of excessive drug use alive while they were slowly killing themselves.

'So I guess Razzles is no more then,' Paula said unnecessarily.

Stacey slumped back against the wall of the building opposite. 'I don't get it,' Stacey said. 'Maybe I am wrong about all of this. Maybe there's nothing to find after all. I guess you're right – she was just messing with me one last time.' She fought the urge to start crying, but could feel the tears tickling the back of her throat, teasing her. 'I just wanted... Oh, I don't know what I wanted.'

'Hey, it's okay, it's good news that there's nothing here,' Bev said, pulling her into a hug. Stacey stood rigid in her arms, refusing to soften. 'If there was something here, then we would have a problem – am I right? This proves the flip-flop is just a flip-flop and that there's nothing here. It is done. That part of our lives is over and we can move on. We just needed to see this, to do this, for all of us to get past it.'

'You're right, Bev. I for one needed to do this to remember what true friendship is and how people are meant to treat each other. I've forgotten that since we were here together and I've let people treat me badly, lost respect for myself, forgot how to fight for myself. This has reminded me of how things should be.'

'What's going on, Paulie?' Bev asked.

Paula paused, thought about what she was going to say, how she was going to say it – the words not quite forming in her mouth, getting stuck in her throat instead, threatening to choke her, cut off her air. She needed to get them out, but once they were out, they were real. But what was she afraid of? That they would say it was all her own fault, that all of Sue's abuse was because she deserved it after what they did? If they said that, it would break her into tiny little pieces that would never fit together again.

Because that is what she had told herself all this time.

And was standing in the street over the road from a boarded-up nightclub really the place to be telling this story?

Her voice was tiny and childlike as she said, 'Sue is abusing me – physically, mentally.'

There was silence and she waited to hear them say what she feared they would say. That they didn't believe her. Just like they hadn't believed Valentina. Instead, Stacey said, 'I'll kill her,' and flung her arms around Paula.

'And I'll get rid of the body,' Bev said and joined in the group hug.

Paula laughed in relief. 'Just like the old days.'

'What is she doing to you? Can you get away? Come and stay with me,' Stacey said, surprising herself at how much she meant it.

'She controls all of our finances. The flat is in her name, it's her bank account – I have nothing without her. I was stupid when I married her. My mother had just died and I was a mess. And alone. Like you, I was adrift, I guess, and she took advantage of my vulnerable mental state. I should give her more credit, actually. She's clever; she makes me feel like it's all my fault, that I deserve it, that I'm clumsy and stupid – and part of me does believe that because it's just punishment for what we did.'

'I get that,' Stacey said. 'You know, one of the reasons I got so mad at Val that night when she told us about Sean was because part of me knew she was right, but didn't want to admit it. Deep down, I knew I was a victim, just like she was. I knew Sean and Stu had both drugged me at some point. I could never remember those nights with them. And yet I told her I didn't believe her.' She couldn't feel the tears running down her cheeks. 'She deserved better than that. If I had properly listened, we could've gone to the police and everything would've been different.' She exhaled, finally releasing the weight of her confession from where it had rested on her back for years. 'I know how hard it is to admit what you have just said, Paula, because I never could. I let my friend down who was also a victim. I let her think I didn't believe her. You're a stronger person than I could ever hope to be.'

'Stacey, she was the girl who cried wolf. We couldn't trust her. We did what we had to do at the time. It's time to forgive ourselves,' Paula said.

Bev had gone pale and was staring back at where Razzles used to be.

'Guys, look.'

Paula and Stacey turned. Neither saw anything immediate, just unfathomable shapes and letters in spray paint.

'What?' Stacey asked.

'Look at the graffiti, look at it carefully – what it says.' Bev looked like she was going to throw up.

Stacey took a step forward and tilted her head to one side. Towards the bottom of the boarded window were the now unmistakable words:

Sean woz here. Then he wasn't.

'I still don't see anything – what are you both looking at?' Paula said.

'There, in the bottom corner,' Stacey said, pointing a vibrating finger at the words.

'Oh come on, you two are now just seeing what you want to see.'

'Are we? One coincidence, fine, but this many, one after the other?' Bev said.

Paula was spinning around, staring at the people passing them, glaring at groups of people. 'None of these people are familiar or paying us any attention. If anyone is watching to see how we are reacting, they are very well hidden.'

'We know where we have to go now,' Stacey said in a low voice. 'Back to the flat.'

'Is that what the map says?' Paula asked. Stacey pulled it from her bag and unfolded it to where the next number was.

'Yes, it's the flat.'

'We'll never be able to get inside though, will we?'

'Let's go and find out.'

'No, fuck them. Let's go straight to where it happened. The woods,' Paula said now, fury fuelling her.

'Shit. Do we have to?' Bev said. 'I don't think I ever want to go back there again.'

They looked from one to the other, then Stacey said, 'Yes, we should.'

They started walking, slower than before, the voices stilled. Thoughts rebounded and bruised the inside of Paula's head. Why had she stayed with Sue? Why hadn't she got away? What kind of sap was she to have been manipulated so easily? Where had the old Paula gone?

Their footsteps were heavy, like they were walking to the gallows, not sure what to expect around the corner, not sure what was waiting for them. Suddenly a phone rang and Paula jumped, realised it was hers, ringing from the back pocket of her jeans. They all stopped and she pulled out her phone. 'It's Sue.'

'Let me speak to her – I'll tell her a few things,' Stacey said.

'No!' Paula held her phone out of the way. 'Just… let me speak to her and palm her off. Shush.' She took the call, saying, 'Hiya,' brightly.

'Where are you?' Sue said without a friendly greeting.

'I'm out with work people – we've gone out for dinner. Why?'

'Because you haven't called tonight.' Sue sounded suspicious.

'I've been busy with everything going on and then we had to get ready quickly to make our reservation.' A group of students walked past, laughing loudly.

'Who's that?'

Paula sighed. 'You don't know them.'

'So why does Find my Phone say you are back where you went to uni with that Stacey? You're with her. You didn't say you were going there.'

Paula almost looked around because Sue sounded so sure of herself. But of course Sue would be checking where she was, stalking her through her app. Why hadn't she thought of that? She should've turned off her location services. On a whim, she decided to play her at her own game. 'I did tell you – I said it was going to be strange being back at the university again, but this is where the conference is. You were so preoccupied with who I was going with that you weren't really listening, to be honest. But that's okay, sometimes you can be a bit forgetful, can't you? We should really look into that for you – it could be the beginnings of the menopause or, heaven forbid, dementia – because I have noticed that lately you are getting quite forgetful, like the time you forgot to tell me you had left the cupboard door open and I turned around into it. God, I had that black eye for ages. Or the time you forgot to tell me the pan handle was hot.' Paula laughed bitterly. 'Anyway, must go as we are heading to a nightclub – going to be a big night and the reception here is terrible. What's that? I can't hear you? You're breaking up...' and she hung up on her, then immediately turned off her phone.

'That's how you do it,' Bev said with a wide grin.

'Oh my God, I'm going to pay for that when I get home,' Paula said, but she was also smiling. 'It was all lies – I never told her that I was coming here, but just once I want her to be questioning herself, you know? Wondering if she is going mad, apparently forgetting the smallest things. Because that's what she does to me all the time.' She felt like crying, screaming, laughing. She did none of these.

'I'm proud of you,' Stacey said and the three of them linked arms again as they walked. 'It used to feel like this, didn't it?'

'What did?' Paula asked, still shell-shocked from what she had said to Sue as nerves started to kick in over the possible consequences.

'Back then, before Valentina, before Sean and Stu and all of them, when it was the three of us – that first year when it was all exciting and new, and we felt we could take on the world. What happened to us?'

'We grew up,' Bev said. 'We realised it isn't as easy as that.'

'But we can take on the world if we are together.' Stacey stopped in her tracks, forcing the other two to stop as well. 'Apart from anything else, I want to be close to you two again. Our friendship is important and we don't live too far away from each other. If nothing else comes out of this, we should make that happen. Forget Sue and her manipulation, Malcolm and his dull existence, me and my path of self-destruction – we can get through all of these things if we are a team, right?'

They hugged again, right there in the middle of the path, as people streamed past them. 'Come on, let's face this thing,' Stacey said boldly.

They reached the end of the path and Bev pulled up.

'Guys, I can't. I don't know what we are going to find in there and I'm scared.'

'Come on, we've got you. There's no one around and we'll stick together,' Paula said.

They took tentative steps into the dark woods, feeling the familiar trees close around them like curtains. Back then it had felt comforting, but now it was undeniably menacing.

'Was it always this dark?' Paula said.

'Yes, it was, but we were so blasé about it,' Stacey said.

The ground was slick with mud and the air was heavy with the smell of the river, which called out to them like an old friend.

After five minutes, they knew they were getting close. They didn't need a map to tell them that.

The last place they had seen him.

It would always be branded into their brains.

It felt like the air dropped another few degrees the closer they got. Paula turned on the torch on her phone and its ghostly light guided them along.

'It was here,' Stacey said suddenly. 'There's the tree.'

They each looked around, not sure what they were hoping to find. But there were no skulls, no bones, no graves. Just the undergrowth, the river shouting at them and the fallen tree trunk.

Paula shone her torch over the water first, then stepped up to the tree and ran the light over it.

And there it was. The next clue.

The Queen of Spades playing card, pinned to the bark.

They heard a noise behind them then, the crack of a stick perhaps or the shifting of the undergrowth. They froze in panic. Seconds passed, in which Paula was convinced someone was going to lurch out of the trees at them.

No, not this time. She grabbed the playing card, then

reached out for Bev and Stacey's hands. 'Let's get out of here.'

They walked quickly, their feet sliding and tripping as the dark weighed down on them. Paula could feel the playing card, cold through her jeans. As they emerged from the trees, the block of flats loomed above them.

'Was it always this ugly?' Stacey asked, voicing what Paula was thinking.

Litter lay at the edges of the pavement – cigarette packets and empty beer cans, the occasional dirty nappy. The corridor to the stairwell and through to the car park on the other side smelled of urine. Somewhere a baby was crying.

A skip sat at the base of the stairwell, a heavy tarpaulin secured over the top. One corner flapped in the breeze, awarding glimpses of the broken furniture and loose bricks that filled it halfway.

They climbed the stairs with trepidation. Outside a flat on the second floor, a man in scruffy tracksuit bottoms and a vest stood leaning over the wall looking down below, his cigarette burning angrily, a beer can dangling in mid-air. He ignored them as they filed past. Someone was cooking onions and burning garlic.

Stacey was panting by the time they reached the top, her heart thudding in her chest. She really needed to start doing some exercise. In contrast, Paula had hardly broken a sweat. Even Bev was only a little out of breath, but Stacey felt like she was possibly in full cardiac arrest.

She paused at the top, pretending to look out over the wall to the street below, but really taking a moment to catch her breath. In the distance was the university, still grand and imposing. Once she had her breath back, she turned to face the other two, who were both staring at the door of their old flat.

'It's open,' Bev said.

The door was open the tiniest bit, as though someone hadn't quite pushed it hard enough.

'Should we go in?'

'Well, that's why we're here,' Stacey said, sounding braver than she felt. 'Come on.'

She reached out and pushed the door open, then stepped tentatively over the threshold and onto what used to be the carpeted hallway but was now a cheap brown laminate. The floor creaked and settled. She froze, listening. There were no other noises to indicate anyone was inside, but the flat had a feeling of occupancy, like the air had moved to shape around someone.

She took another step, felt the other two follow her in, and stopped in front of the glass doors to the lounge. She peeked around the kitchen door, but it was empty of everything. The cupboards stood open, the shelves bare. There were no dishes in the sink and nothing on the countertops – no kettle, teabags, coffee jar.

'I think the flat is vacant,' Stacey said.

'Try the lounge,' Paula whispered over her shoulder.

Someone had put wallpaper over the panes of glass in the door so that you couldn't see into the room. The doors were closed. Stacey reached out and turned the handle, which squeaked loudly in the weighted silence.

Stacey peeked around the doorframe. The room was bare, no furniture. Just dirty marks on the walls and dust on the stained carpet. The carpet was the same colour it had been thirty years ago, with dents in it where chair legs had left an indelible impression over time. The window looking out over the balcony and the woods was dirty on both sides with smears and handprints. The three of them stood in the middle of the room, turning this way and that, trying to fathom what they were looking for.

On one wall, where it had hung all those years ago, was the print of the four queens. Except the glass had shattered and the print itself had been slashed. What looked like old blood dripped down the fractured glass.

Below it, lying scrunched on the carpet, was a piece of paper. Bev went over and picked it up. It wasn't a piece of paper. It was a photograph – of the three of them from behind, their arms around each other in the summer sun, their faces turned to the blue sky. Someone had crumpled it up until it was wrinkled and torn.

'Look,' Bev said and held it out to them.

'Bloody hell, so not a coincidence after all,' Paula said, her voice strained as she took the photo from Bev.

There was a thump from down the corridor and they all jumped.

'Someone's here,' Stacey whispered.

'Probably not, just the wind or something,' Paula said. 'Stay behind me.'

'Why?' Bev asked.

'Because I'm the strongest.'

'Says who? I've done a fair few cardio boxing classes at the gym in my time.'

Stacey looked from one to the other. 'Seriously? This is what you are arguing about? I'll go first because I am definitely the most unstable and therefore the most dangerous, alright?'

She crept to the glass doors and peered along the corridor. The bathroom door was open, but the other two doors to the bedrooms were closed.

She felt stupid and terrified in equal measure as she crept along, with Bev gripping onto the back of her shirt with tight fists. The bathroom door stood wide open and she peeped around the doorframe. 'Oh for fuck's sake,' she said, still in lowered tones.

'What? What is it?' Paula said and rushed into the room.

'This is so clichéd – someone is definitely messing with us.'

The shower curtain was pulled around the bath, obscuring a dark shape in the tub. Stacey stormed up to it, annoyed now, and yanked it back.

She screamed.

Lying in the tub was a man. Blood pooled under his body, red against the white porcelain. A deep gash ran from one side of his neck to the other. His eyes were wide open and staring in shock at her. The left side of his face was badly scarred, the skin buckled and disfigured.

'Surprise,' said a voice behind them.

24

Once the chip trays were binned, they headed to Razzles. It was a gaudy, neon nightclub with ridiculous fake Oscar statues outside the doors and two huge, solid bouncers on guard. Valentina knew what she had in her pocket, but wasn't worried. The bouncers were more worried about under-age drinking than anything else. They probably took more drugs than anyone of the punters inside. True to form, the bouncers looked them up and down, then waved them through.

Inside, the atmosphere was very different to the White Horse. It was dark, with scattered neon lights and lasers rebounding off the walls. The middle of the room was dominated by a dance floor that was already heaving with bouncing, sweaty bodies. The air was thick with smoke and the deep tremor of the bass music vibrated through every surface. On the far side of the room was a long, glass bar that reflected the laser lights in different directions. It was sensory overload on every level.

Initially they stood looking at the dance floor that appeared to be pulsating like the skin of a beaten drum, heads and bodies bobbing in co-ordination. Paula grabbed Stacey's hand and dragged her into the mass. Bev and Valentina followed, and they pushed and shoved and ducked into the middle and began to bounce along with the rest.

When they were sweaty and laughing and exhilarated, they broke for drinks, but otherwise they danced. Their bodies and minds were free. It was early in the morning, but they felt no tiredness. Valentina felt completely liberated, here in the moment, the music pulsing through her skin. She could feel every cell in her blood, every nerve ending alive and firing.

Then all at once she felt cold and the hairs on her arms stood on end as an arm snaked around her waist. Stu and Sean had coiled themselves around them, trying to sidle into their small group. Sean had his arm around Stacey, who was clearly annoyed. She shoved at him, shouted at him to take his arm away. Stu's arm was still insistently taking ownership of Valentina. He leant into her ear and said, 'I need to talk to you.'

'Fuck off, Stu,' she said back.

'I need to talk to you now.' He glared at her. She shrugged and moved to the side, away from the group. They stood, jostled from every angle.

'You told him,' he shouted.

'No, I didn't.'

'Then how does he know – about my *problem*?'

'I don't know, but it wasn't me.'

'Nobody else knew.'

'Maybe you're not as careful as you think.'

'Did you tell anyone about what I told you about him?'

'Well, that would be telling, wouldn't it?' She pushed away from him then and moved back to the group. Sean had gone again – she could see his head bobbing towards a group of girls to their right.

Valentina's hand snaked to her pocket and she checked to see if the matchbox was still there. Frankly, it served Stu right if a few of her carefully planted words had grown in strength and rippled into numerous eager ears. Nothing compared to what he deserved.

This was ruining her mood though. She shouted to Bev above the music to say she was going to get some water from the bar. Bev nodded at her, but kept dancing.

She had to push and shove to get to the front. She asked the barman for a glass of water. He looked disappointed, but shoved a glass at her anyway. She moved away towards the edge of the room and leant back against the wall, watching the mating rituals playing out around her. She could see Paula, Bev and Stacey bobbing and swaying, Stacey with her arms in the air while Paula danced with more intensity, her arms by her sides and her eyes closed. Bev was going all out, jumping, punching the air and spinning around. Her hair was plastered to her forehead with sweat, her glasses fogged, but she was glowing with joy.

Valentina smiled to herself, then the smile froze as she noticed Sean watching the three girls through the crowd. He was swaying in time to the music, but conspicuous because he wasn't flinging himself around like most of the others near him. He kept moving closer and closer, his eyes on Stacey. Stu had vanished, so Sean was a lone predator, his eyes locked in, his mouth watering.

Valentina could feel the anger building from her toes, white hot as it rippled through her body like an electric shock.

No, he wasn't going to get to Stacey.

She wouldn't let him.

25

Valentina stood in the doorway of what used to be Bev's bedroom.

She had a wide grin on her face and a baseball cap pulled down low over her dark hair.

They stood in shocked silence.

'Aren't you going to say hello?' she said enthusiastically, her Scottish lilt so familiar and yet so foreign to them.

Stacey felt Bev slump next to her and automatically reached out to catch her as she fainted.

Valentina rolled her eyes. 'Always was a flake,' she said.

Stacey lowered her to the ground. 'Bev! Bev!' She slapped at her cheek. The shock was wearing off, replaced by rapidly bubbling anger. 'Paula, get Bev out of this room. I need to talk to Valentina.'

Paula reached under Bev's arms and dragged her down the corridor and into the lounge.

Stacey turned to look towards the bathroom door. 'Who is that? What have you done?'

'Look closely, Stace, you know exactly who it is.' Valentina was clearly enjoying herself.

Stacey sickened herself by walking back into the bathroom, one foot in front of the other, until she could peer over the edge of the bathtub. She wasn't going to get any closer than that. Once she looked past the scars down one side of his face, she finally recognised who it was.

'I don't understand,' she said, feeling her own knees weaken.

'Oh God, you're not going to faint as well, are you?' Valentina reached out and grabbed Stacey's arm in a strong grip, her fingers pressing down hard through a pair of black leather gloves, and dragged Stacey from the bathroom towards the lounge. That was when Stacey noticed the glint of a knife in her other hand.

She thrust Stacey into the lounge, then went back to slam the front door and draw the deadbolt across.

Bev was propped up under the window, her colour slowly coming back as she blinked in shock and confusion. Paula had her arm around her, almost holding her up, and was stroking her hair gently. Stacey came to sit next to them on the grubby carpet. The previous tenants must've had a cat or a dog. There were short white hairs sticking to the carpet and dust bunnies in the corners. A tiny spider scuttled past her foot. Questions rattled around her head.

Her brain was refusing to acknowledge what was most important: that there was a dead body in the bath and that Valentina was actually alive. Stacey looked over to where Val stood in the doorway, her hands behind her back, and she felt fear trickle down her spine. 'She's got a knife,' she whispered to the other two.

'What the hell is going on, Valentina?' Stacey said in false bravado.

Paula and Bev were still shocked into silence.

'Well, can I first say that it was a lovely funeral. I could've done with a few more people there, but I didn't have much time to arrange it. The flowers were beautiful though, weren't they? I was hoping you'd say a few words, Stacey. Bit disappointed in you, actually.'

'You were there?'

'Yes, I sneaked in and sat in the gallery until just before the end.'

'That was you?'

'And it was such lovely weather when we were all sitting outside at the pub. Oh my God, did you see that ridiculous French bulldog with the pink rhinestone lead? Hilarious!'

She was toying with them and Stacey could feel the anger creeping further up her neck, red hot in intensity. 'Why? Why would you do that? That's sick,' she said.

'Haven't you ever wondered what your funeral would look like? I thought it would be fun, since I'm dying anyway. And I wanted to know if you would turn up.'

'So the cancer is real then?'

Valentina pulled off her cap to reveal patchy dark curls, bald in places and very thin, the white of her scalp shining through. 'Yeah, it's real – but that's all your fault, Stacey. It's all your fault.' Stacey could now hear how thin Valentina's breath was.

'My fault? How? I haven't seen you in thirty years!'

'Valentina, you have clearly lost your mind,' Paula said, finally finding her voice.

'Not my mind, Paula. No, not that. I have lung cancer.

End stage, sadly. Nothing to be done. But that's what happens when you start smoking in your twenties – oh, and carry around a chest full of anger, bitterness and guilt. It eventually forms a nasty tumour.' She pushed the cap back onto her head.

'How is that my fault?' Stacey asked.

'I started smoking for you, Stacey. I had these sad, pathetic dreams of us sharing smoke breaks together, chatting, hanging out. The guilt? Well, we all share that, don't we? Look at us. Not a functioning adult in the room.'

'Wow, you really want to blame your lung cancer on me? That's quite a stretch,' Stacey spat back.

'We are all doing just fine, Valentina. It's not our fault if you've screwed up your life,' Paula said.

'How is your lovely wife, by the way, Paula? You know, we've struck up quite a friendship in recent months. I went to one of her drumming workshops at the hospital once and it really helps with aggression when you've been told you have months to live. She really doesn't trust you though, does she? I think she's wise not to. I mean, you are on a weekend away with someone you have been in love with for decades, aren't you?'

Paula's cheeks turned a dangerous shade of puce. 'You what?'

'It's funny, but I actually didn't have to plant any seeds of suspicion. It was all there to start with. I just had to support her and tell her she was justified in her feelings, then watch her spin out of control. Fun, but way too easy. Oh, by the way, be careful when you get home. I may have sent her some photos of you and Stacey from earlier today, telling her that I thought I had seen you here and was disappointed not to see her here too. She really can leave quite a mark on you sometimes. Have you two seen the bruises? I'm surprised. I would've put you down as someone who would fight back.' She smiled wickedly.

'Maybe I'll surprise you now,' Paula said in return and looked ready to launch at her.

'Nah ah ah,' Valentina said, brandishing the blade at her. Paula slumped back down onto the filthy carpet.

'So not as together as you'd like us to think, are you?' Then she turned to Bev. 'Now your family, Bev, much harder to crack. Kids these days are much more tech- and security-savvy than we ever were.'

Bev made a strangled noise in her throat. The first sound she'd made since she'd seen Valentina.

'Bethany just wants someone to tell her she is special instead of making her feel like she isn't quite seen or understood. But in the end it was quite easy to slide into her DMs as the lovely young Ben Tannet, local sixth former, very good at listening. Did she tell you about the photos? Those pics she sent him? Sorry, *me*. Would you like to see them? No? Well, *someone* may have circulated them among the boys at Jasper's school. Now Jasper, he's a typical teenage lad and will do anything for a few inappropriate photos. Imagine his surprise when the photos were of his sister! Wow, proper twisted stuff and he may need some therapy after this one.'

Bev looked like she was going to throw up and made to get to her knees, but Valentina moved the point of the knife from Paula to her. 'Oh relax, Bev. We all know you won't do anything. You're pathetic. A quiet little housewife with no real ambition anymore. What the fuck happened to you? Where did the fire go?'

Bev collapsed in on herself and began to weep.

'Stop it,' Stacey said to Valentina, her voice dangerously low.

'And you. The wonderful Stacey – the one we all wanted to emulate, hovering around you in the hope of being your favourite. I was guilty of that myself, doing anything to breathe your air. I am ashamed of myself now, of course.' She started to pace backwards and forwards, the knife brandished like a stick of rock. 'I have to say, it was tough finding anything to hurt you because you're doing it all yourself, aren't you? You sure know how to implode your life. Did you tell these two that you've been given a leave of absence from work for a little outburst at your boss, not to mention drinking on the job? And that's just the days you actually turn up instead of staying in bed with a hangover! Tut tut. Elaine on reception is quite the gossip, by the way. I started chatting to her on the bus every morning and it's surprising how much some people will share when they are bored. She thought the whole affair with Simon was hilarious and weirdly creepy considering how much younger than you he is. Did you tell these two about that too? Oh, Stace, how the mighty have fallen.'

'What do you want?' Stacey asked in a strangled voice, the words thorns stuck in her throat.

Valentina stopped in front of Stacey and crouched down. 'You mean, apart from a cure for cancer?' She barked a laugh. 'That is indeed a good question, Stace. You see, let's not forget that there is a dead man in the bathtub. That dead man was supposed to have died thirty years ago – and yet here he is, freshly dead today. So how come, I ask myself? Someone here has been telling porkies about that night. And I have a feeling it's you, Stacey.'

26

SPRING 1993

Valentina kept her eyes on Sean as he inched closer to Stacey on the dance floor. Then he was next to her, leaning into her ear, whispering. She was initially annoyed, but her face softened as he whispered some more. She smiled slightly and shrugged. They started to dance and sway together. Paula's face was thunderous as she watched, but she carried on dancing with Bev.

Valentina fought her way back through the crowd and shouted in Paula's ear, 'Why is he here?'

Paula shrugged. 'Might be time to call it a night,' she said grumpily.

Valentina looked at her watch. It was nearly 3 a.m. She felt a bit like Cinderella at the ball, with time ticking down on the best night she'd had in a long time.

Bev was starting to run out of dance steam finally, her arms drooping and her body moving less erratically. 'Hey, Bev, I'm shattered. Might want to go soon,' Paula shouted at her.

'Yeah, I'm getting tired too. Val, nearly time to go, do you think?' Bev said.

Paula's eyes were now firmly fixed on Sean and Stacey. 'Sean, leave her alone. Stace, we're going.'

Sean ignored her, carried on pushing up against Stacey in time to the music.

Paula shoved at his shoulder with her hand and he stumbled. 'I said, leave her.'

He glared at her. 'She doesn't look like she wants me to leave her alone.'

Stacey looked from one to the other. 'Paula, leave it.'

'No, he's not putting his grubby hands all over you.'

'What's the problem, Paula? You jealous?' he sneered at her.

Paula pulled back her arm, her hand clenched in a fist, but Valentina positioned herself in between them before Paula could land the punch.

'Sean! Why don't I buy you a drink, yeah? Because I spilt yours earlier.'

'I don't want a drink.' He snaked around Stacey again, but with his eyes firmly on Paula, challenging, taunting.

This time Stacey stepped away from him and said firmly, 'That's a good idea, Valentina, why don't you get Sean a drink?'

He looked at her, his eyes narrowed, but shrugged in feigned nonchalance, although his shoulders were so tense they were sitting by his earlobes. Valentina grabbed his arm and escorted him over to the bar. She ordered two bottles of beer.

Sean watched as Stacey disappeared into the toilets with Paula and Bev. The barman handed her two open bottles of beer. She had a split second to decide, but as soon as she'd led him to the bar, she knew what she was going to do. Loyalty was important. Stacey would see this as a sign of how loyal a friend she was. And evidence that she hadn't been lying.

She looked around. No one was paying her any attention and Sean was still scowling in the direction of the toilets. She turned her back to him, slid open the match box from her pocket and, using one hand, popped a pill open and tipped the contents into the bottle. She dropped the other pill on the floor and ground it down with her shoe.

She gave the bottle a swirl and handed it to him.

'Here you go.' She picked up the other bottle and took a big, encouraging gulp.

He drank deeply. Valentina watched his face for a sign that it tasted different, but he seemed oblivious and went in for another long drag on the bottle.

They stood in silence, drinking in tandem. Then she noticed his shoulders start to droop, as though someone had put two large, heavy bags on each one.

'You okay? You look very sleepy all of a sudden.'

'I feel it, must be the exams catching up with me.' His vowels were less clipped than usual, his words rounder with a slight lisp. The drug was started to take hold.

'It's not the exams,' Valentina said. 'It's the drugs I slipped into your drink.' She smiled sweetly at him.

'Wha—?'

'Those drugs you took from Stu earlier? I don't know who they were intended for this time, but I'm sure as hell not going to let you rape Stacey. I know that's what you did to me – and I have the evidence. You see, you thought

I wouldn't have a clue, so you shoved the empty capsule under the couch, but I found it. It's somewhere safe and I can take it to the police anytime I want. It'll have your fingerprints on it, of course.' She didn't have long, so she spoke quickly. 'So this is how this is going to go. You're going to walk away and never speak to any of us again – and you're never going to do something like this again. All it takes is one word from me to the police and you'll be on the sex register as a rapist. But first, you're going to see what it feels like.'

'You bitch! What did you give me?'

She wasn't sure if he was following everything she was saying.

'You know what it is. Let's not play any more games.' She could see Paula, Bev and Stacey emerging from the bathroom. They'd be making their way over to her in a minute. 'I only did what you've been doing to who knows how many women. You're a sick predator – and I intend to stop you.'

His hands were clenched in fists, rage stiffening his body. His cheeks had red spots of colour high on the cheekbones and he kept shaking his head, as though trying to dislodge an unsuitable thought. She smiled at him again and walked away. She knew he would follow her.

She intercepted the other three and said, 'We need to go. Now. We need to get him to the boot of my car.'

'Why? What have—?'

Sean surged through the crowd at them with a lurching, staggering gait. 'We just need to! Come on!'

The nightclub had emptied out substantially, but there were still plenty of people to fight through in order to reach the exit. The other three picked up on Valentina's urgency and rushed after her, confused.

The air cooled the sweat on their skin as they burst out of the claustrophobic nightclub. In the distance, they could make out a faint orange glow as the sky began to lighten slowly with the dawn.

'What did you do, Val?' Paula asked.

'I just gave him a taste of his own medicine.'

'What does that mean?' Stacey said.

'He was going to slip some drugs into your drink, alright? So I nicked the drugs off him and slipped them into his beer first. That's all. We'll shove him in the boot of my car and dump him somewhere. He'll fall into a lovely slumber and wake up tomorrow with no idea where he is or how he got there. It'll freak him out, teach him a lesson. And it means he can't take advantage of you, Stacey, not again.'

'He was going to do that? Tonight? It was true?'

'Yes, of course it was true! I did this for you, to protect you. And he deserves everything he gets.'

The door behind them slammed open and Sean staggered out, two bouncers attached to him. 'You're drunk, mate, go home,' one said as they shoved him out. He looked awful, pale but with those two red patches on his cheeks, as though he had gone too heavy on the blusher. His eyes were wide and bulging. He was sweating profusely.

He saw the girls still standing on the pavement and lurched at them, roaring in anger. He was surprisingly quick for someone who had been drugged.

'I don't think you gave him enough, Val,' Bev said. 'Forget the car, let's just get out of here. Leave him to stumble around and drop somewhere on his own.' They started to run, past the White Horse, towards the bridge and the river.

By the time they reached the path into the woods, they were all panting heavily. Bev stopped and bent over. 'Aghh, I've got a stitch.'

'Is he still behind us?' Paula asked.

'Surely not,' Stacey said.

'I should've given him both pills. There were two in the matchbox, but I suppose he's bigger than us, he would need more,' Valentina said.

Valentina was peering back the way they had come. 'I can't see him. Come on, let's go home.' They followed the path slowly and carefully in what limited visibility they had. Without the street lights beyond the trees, it was even gloomier than usual and the sun wasn't high enough yet to make a difference. They grabbed each other's hands and snaked along the path, keeping the river to their left and following its voice deeper into the woods.

Halfway along, Bev asked if they could stop so that she could catch her breath. They all leant against a fat fallen tree trunk, its roots dangling exposed into the river like witch's fingers.

'I can't believe it was real – and I didn't believe you,' Stacey said. 'I'm really sorry that you had to go through that. And thank you.'

Valentina shrugged casually, but she felt a surge of joy. This was what she had wanted all along.

'What an utter scumbag,' Bev said. 'I wonder how many times he's got away with it?'

'But not me – the last time, I mean. He hasn't done it to

me before,' Stacey added quickly, denial thick and heavy. 'I chose to last time. And with Stu. It was my choice.'

'But you said you couldn't remember both times?' Valentina said.

'Yeah, I lied, blamed the booze, but I do actually remember.'

Valentina couldn't read her face in the gloom, couldn't decide what was true and what wasn't.

A screech cut through the night-time quiet and they all jumped.

'Just a fox. Come on, let's keep going,' Paula said.

They took a few more steps forward, then heard a rustling from behind them, the snap of a stick. They spun around as a large shape tore through the bushes and launched at Stacey. He knocked her to the ground, towering over her but not seeing her clearly. He was growling like a wild animal, tearing at the fabric of her dress. She pushed and shoved against him, twisting and turning away from his grasping hands.

Instinct took over and Valentina grabbed at his waist from behind, putting all of her weight into her legs so that she could pull him away. He spun around and lunged at Valentina, but his foot caught one of the exposed roots and he fell heavily. The side of his head connected hard with the tree trunk. Like a pinball in an arcade game, he rebounded back, his hands clutched to the side of his head. Valentina felt red-hot rage like a veil over her mind. She grabbed a fistful of his hair and thrust his head at the tree trunk again.

And again.

And again.

The skin on the side of his face ripped and shredded as it

WHEN WE WERE YOUNG

connected with the rough bark of the tree, leaving a bloody mess where his cheek had been.

'Valentina!' Stacey cried. She grabbed Valentina from behind and wrapped her arms around her tightly.

Valentina released him, her breath coming in jagged gasps. He slumped to the ground as Stacey dragged Valentina away.

No one moved. No one breathed.

They stared down on him as he lay face down in the dirt.

The red mist retreated and was replaced by white-cold calm.

'I think I've killed him,' she said evenly.

'No, you didn't. He tripped,' Stacey said in a rush. 'You dodged out of his way and he tripped. It was not you. He went to attack you and he tripped, maybe fell in the river? Yes, fell in the river. We need to get him in the river,' Stacey said in a rush.

'But we can't just leave him there. What if her DNA is on him or yours? You were dancing with him.' Bev sounded like a toddler, her voice high and bubbling with tears and fear.

'Then it'll wash off him. No one will have noticed him leave with us. He looked legless and we ran off. Hundreds of people will have touched him in that club, rubbed up against him. Plenty of witnesses saw us talking to him, dancing. He'll have loads of DNA on him, not just ours. But to be safe, we should dump him in the river, make it look like he fell in.'

'No! We need to do something. Call an ambulance. We don't even know if he's dead.' Bev was now openly crying big, ugly tears.

'He deserves to be,' Valentina said calmly.

'No, to be sure we can't be connected, we need to push him in the river and leave him, before someone comes. He's dead, Bev. There's nothing else to be done. He was drunk and high. He fell. This isn't on us. But we need to fix this before someone comes.' Stacey was glaring at them, willing them to act.

Bev took herself to the side and sat in the dirt, hugging her knees like a child. Paula had said nothing so far, but now said, 'Bev is right, we need to call an ambulance. But we could tell them we found him here.'

'His hair and blood will be on me.' Valentina looked down at her hands, which appeared muddy in the poor light, but she knew it wasn't mud. She could smell the metallic blood in the air, could feel it tacky on her fingers, could feel his hair in her grasp and the weight of his head as it slammed into the tree trunk. Now she felt panic inching up her throat at the mess she may be in. This was something her father may not be able to help with.

Paula was thoughtful, began pacing to and fro. 'Okay, he hasn't moved for a while, so it's not looking good. I'm no doctor, but I can't see his chest rising. Maybe Stacey is right. Let's get him in the river and leave. Someone else can find him. But if we are here, there'll be a lot of questions we don't want to answer. Bev, get up! We need your help.'

Bev was mewling like a small animal and rocking backwards and forward on her haunches.

Stacey and Paula got their arms under his armpits. 'Val, Bev, help!' Paula urged.

Her raised voice spurred Valentina into action. She grabbed onto Bev's arm and pulled her roughly to her feet.

Bev stepped towards the body on the ground and took hold of one of his ankles like a robot.

'We need to turn him over first,' Stacey said, now firmly in control. She grabbed his shoulder and hauled him over onto his back. His face was a mess of blood and what Valentina hoped were leaves but knew with a sickening surety were flaps of skin where his cheek had caught and torn on the bark of the tree stump.

They tried to lift him, but he was too heavy.

'We'll have to drag him.' Stacey said.

'We can't. It'll leave drag marks that will be difficult to explain. It needs to look like he fell,' Paula said.

'We could roll him? If he banged his head and fell, the incline is quite steep, so he would most likely roll into the water?' Valentina sounded like she knew what she was talking about, but she'd never actually got rid of a body before.

'Yes, good plan. Let's roll him,' Stacey said. They dragged and rolled him bit by bit until he was in the river, the water gently massaging his body, the blood rippling out around him.

The sky was starting to lighten quickly now.

Paula grabbed a long, thick branch from the ground and poked at him, pushing him further into the middle of the river. Valentina looked for bubbles in the water under his face, but couldn't distinguish anything in the dark, almost black water.

Paula poked again and tried to wedge the stick under his body, and after a few attempts, managed to flip him so that he was face up. Blood continued to swirl through the water like marbling. They all stared at him.

'What now?'

Bushes moving, branches crackling. Someone was coming up the path.

'We need to get out of here. Whoever that is will likely see his body and pull him out. Nothing to do with us. But if they see us, we'll be in shit,' Stacey said.

Bev had slumped to the ground again, her face sweaty, her hair stuck to her forehead. Valentina stood and watched with wonder as Sean bobbed and drifted down the river, the current grabbing onto him and pushing him away. Paula grabbed Valentina's arm and dragged her away while Stacey scooped Bev up.

'Bev! Come on!' she said in a snarl. 'They're coming! Move your feet.' She pulled at her but Bev remained rooted to the ground, her eyes glued to the tree trunk where a large flap of bloody skin hung obscenely.

The sounds of vegetation moving and low male voices were drawing closer.

Stacey slapped Bev hard across her face, a loud crack that seemed to bring her back to herself enough to get her feet to move.

The four of them ran.

They didn't stop until they reached the flat.

27

PRESENT DAY

Valentina got to her feet, started pacing again. Stacey could almost smell the hyped energy coming off her body in waves.

'You know, when I think back to what we did, it was your idea to dump him in the river, Stacey. And that was fine. We all went along with it. What I'm struggling to work out is how he turned up in my life some thirty years later,' she said. 'Don't get me wrong. I wanted him dead. It was better that way. I thought you did too.'

Stacey kept her eyes on the knife.

'I mean, we were all supposed to leave the next day to head back home, weren't we?' She stopped pacing. Her breath was ragged now. 'You said we should cut all ties with each other. Or that's what was supposed to happen. But what actually happened? And why did you lie?'

'Lying was your forte, not mine.'

'Touché. I may have been economical with the truth sometimes, but all for a very good cause.' She stopped pacing again. A fine sheen of sweat coated her forehead. She licked her lips, which were dry and cracking.

'Maybe we should ask where you found him? For all we know, you were the one who got him out of the water. Maybe you wanted to pin all of it on us somehow,' Stacey said, her eyes following every move Valentina made.

'No, the truth is much more ironic than that, Stace.' She moved to the other side of the room and sat with her back against the wall, facing them. The point of the knife was stabbing into the carpet now, her hand was still tight around the shaft. 'Actually, he found me. There's coincidence and then there's life throwing your past in your face like a turd. I stupidly – and you'll love this, Stacey, because it is so pathetic – I signed up to a dating app. I'd been diagnosed already – the cancer card finally turning up in my hand after all. I knew there was no hope and I wanted a bit of fun before the cancer got too bad, you know? Before the hair that I had always hated was all gone. They say be careful what you wish for. Well, I always wished I didn't have my dark, wiry hair and look at me now! Lost most of it!'

She whipped the cap off again, ran her free hand over the pits and grooves, a bitter chortle escaping from her mouth, and Stacey almost felt sorry for her. 'The mistake I made was using an old photo on my profile from when we were all here. Oh! You'll know it, of course. The one that I put on the coffin. I thought that was a nice touch. Did you like that, Paula?'

Paula looked down at her hand. She was still clutching the photograph that she'd found on the carpet. She opened her fist and threw it onto the carpet in front of her. It landed face-up, their happy faces smiling obscenely back at them from the middle of the room.

'Anyway, one guy liked what he saw, started chatting to me online, and I suppose I was stupid, I let my guard down. He had used a fake photo, of course, disguised his accent, and before long we were chatting online or on the phone every night. I hate to admit it to you, Stacey, but I was lonely. I haven't had much luck with men – or women, Paula, or women.'

Valentina got to her feet again. She waved the knife like a conductor. The light bounced off the silver blade, casting shimmering dots onto the bare walls.

'Then he said he wanted to meet and I thought it might be nice, you know? But he didn't show, started telling me he was ill, had to leave his job, had no money to travel, that he was being evicted from his flat. He was very good at it – I thought I was good, having had a lot of surveillance experience all those years ago. I mean, how else would I have managed to figure out what Sean had been up to? You haven't forgotten how I saved you, have you? Oh wait, I don't think you ever properly thanked me for that...'

She rubbed at her chin, enjoying her moment in the spotlight. 'But I digress. Now, I'm not a gullible person on the whole, am I, Bev? But I fell for his story hook, line and sinker. A bit like your Bethany.' She grinned maniacally at Bev, who looked back at her with absolute horror. 'Yes, that is where I got the idea from, Bev – and Bethany is even more gullible than me! The youth of today, eh, Bev?'

A cough rattled through her body. She put her arm out to steady herself against the wall. Before Stacey could react and launch for the knife, the coughing fit had passed. Valentina crouched down again, still catching her breath around the words. She looked at Stacey. 'Did you like the Tania Bennett detail by the way? Have you figured that out yet? It was that awful girl you used to know on campus. I spilt coffee on her once? She was supposedly your friend, but you can't even remember her name. I thought that was going to be the obvious clue, but I was wrong. Oh and Bev, Ben Tannet is the same person, almost an anagram – do you see what I did there? – they were both me.' She stood and spread her arms wide, the knife dangling from her fingers.

It was exhausting watching her, all jerky movements and exaggerated gestures. She crouched down again, almost fell over, corrected herself.

'Whoops a daisy. Now, I'm embarrassed to admit that I fell for his story – I'm not going to lie. Not this time. It's truth time now. I had all this money from my inheritance. My father came in handy for something. Ha! Do you know, when I got back home, he still would have nothing to do with me? Was so disappointed in me when he found out I wasn't going to be graduating. Threatened to cut me off because, apparently, I had to "learn to stand on my own two feet"! Have you ever? I'd just saved my best friend from rape, for goodness' sake!! Not that she had admitted it. And I was a victim myself! Everyone forgot about that!'

Valentina was veering from topic to topic, her words

becoming difficult to follow. Stacey hoped she was wearing herself out. If she could just find a gap, she could rush at her and grapple the knife from her hand. Stacey fancied her chances – Valentina was clearly unwell.

'I was in a bad place then, I'm not going to lie. And my father was just being so… annoying, you know? So I tried to burn the house down! No, really, Paula, I did! I sneaked into his bedroom when he was sleeping and left a lit cigarette on the pillow. Unfortunately for me, he found it before there was too much damage and I think he knew it was me. He never said anything, of course, but he was different after that. Then he died – not me this time, Bev, don't look at me like that – and the money was all mine anyway.'

'What kind of a monster are you?' Bev asked. 'Or are you lying again?'

'I'm not the monster, Bev! I'm trying to make the world a better place! How many more girls would Sean have raped if I hadn't done what I did?' She pointed over her shoulder to the bathroom.

'Anyway, you're distracting me. Where was I? Oh yes, my father's money. I sent a lot of it to *this man*, thinking I was helping him, but I couldn't understand why he still didn't want to meet up. Then I started to realise what was going on. I mean, come on, right? I was acting as pathetic as you, Paula, letting him make a complete mug out of me. And that's just not on, is it? You get it, right?'

Valentina had put the knife on the carpet in front of her so that she could wipe her forehead. Her skin had turned grey.

Stacey felt nauseous as the words tumbled from

Valentina's mouth. What the hell did she want? Was it revenge? Curiosity? Just a sick game? And was she going to let them out of here alive?

'I decided to get my own back, make him an offer he couldn't refuse. They are all the same, are men. Their eyes are always bigger than their brains. It's all about the chase, the game. I offered him a ridiculous sum of money, but on condition that he collect it in person. Here. In our old flat. Because it looks like the kind of place a drug deal or murder would take place, don't you think?' She looked around at the room. 'When he turned up to collect, I saw who it was. And I tell you what, Paula, you could've knocked me over with a feather because, like you today, I thought he was dead! Of course, he knew who I was all along. My mistake was I didn't give him enough of the drugs that night because he remembered parts. He remembered me drugging him and chasing us. The rest had kind of slotted into place when he'd seen the photo of us, so he *pursued* me. He wanted answers to fill the gaps on how he ended up with a mangled face that was difficult to look at, let's be honest. Turns out swindling money out of lonely women on dating apps was his new career. And someone here let him get away that day.'

She was enjoying herself, that much was clear to see, despite the obvious discomfort she was in. Stacey's brain scrambled to keep up with the details. Part of her wanted to hear the rest of the story, but she also had to get them out of here somehow.

'I mean, I'd stayed in contact with Stu for a bit afterwards, just to make sure there was no connection to us. You see, still looking out for you! He just wanted to put the whole thing behind him. A bit of a coward, that one. He wasn't the one to report Sean missing to the campus police, by the way. That was Rob. But then a few days later, his room was cleaned out and Rob assumed Sean had made it back to the flat, packed up and got on that flight to South Africa he was always banging on about. I told Stu I had seen him leave and he was more than happy to believe me, to draw a line under it all.'

'Wait, you went and packed up his stuff? How did you get in? When did you?'

'We are getting ahead of ourselves, Stacey. One story at a time, yeah? Valentina took a breath. 'Sean didn't really have anything incriminating on us, he couldn't prove anything, but he was still a predator and enough was enough, you know? He had to die. Properly this time. He did, Bev, let's not deny it. He should've died all those years ago for what he had done. Let's not forget he raped me. There was no consent, was there, Bev? No, there was not. And despite what you have made yourself believe over all those years, it did happen to you, didn't it, Stacey?'

Paula was starting to look impatient and Stacey worried that she'd try to do something rash. She went to speak, but Valentina carried on, rambling and ranting.

'So when he turned up here for the money, I—' she grimaced and drew her finger across her throat, then chuckled '—dumped him in the bath and waited for you. To show you, like a gift. It's okay, no need to thank me. I have to say, you three really cut yourselves off, didn't you? You were very good at locking yourselves away from each other.

Now, we could spend some time catching up on the last few decades – you know, about the years I have spent travelling around, trying to find my place, then realising that I don't have a place, that I never will, only to then find myself dying and realising I have wasted all that time – or I thought we could play a game of cards. What do you think? Like the old days. I'll cut the cards and if it's red, you tell the truth; if it's black, you do a dare. It'll be fun.'

She moved to sit heavily in front of the glass doors, leaning her head back against them for a moment, the knife at her side. She was all the way across the room, so no way Stacey could get to her now and grab the knife.

She could feel Bev shaking next to her.

'So who's going to start? Because I really want to find out what happened when we all thought we'd killed this guy. Frankly I'm a little disappointed that we didn't – he's cost me a lot of money and a fair amount of dignity, not to mention all those other women he will have targeted over the last few decades. But we've all lost a bit of dignity over the years, haven't we?' She looked from one to the other. 'You and your drinking, Stacey – and that time you came home from the pub after work and got to the front door and wet yourself a few weeks ago. Yeah, not your finest hour. I was watching you. Did you never notice the man across the street in the cap?'

Stacey blushed a deep red. 'How—'

'Made me laugh, actually. The way you crouched down and just pissed yourself, then fell over into the puddle. Wow!' She turned to Paula. 'And, Paula, how quick Sue's temper is. Is she still upset that you broke her favourite vase? Not that you can remember doing that – because it was me! Ta-da! You did wash up and put it to dry on the counter like you thought, but you also left the kitchen window open and a good, strong gust of wind can knock something like that over – as can a hand through the window. She really took a swing at you that day. I could feel that slap from where I was standing.'

'And Bev, you let a fifteen-year-old and a seventeen-year-old dictate your life. That time you went to the shops three times for Bethany because she wanted a particular kind of spot cream? The cream doesn't exist – I told her (or rather Ben did – you see what I did there?) that it was a small brand only available in that little chemist down your street. You brought back three different types in the end and she still wasn't happy. I admire you for never once telling her to shove it. That's a good mother – I think? Of course, I wouldn't know.' She smirked at them in turn.

Stacey had had enough now. 'You're enjoying this, aren't you?' she said.

'Yes, yes I am. Because the point is that I was trying to do you a favour that night. I was saving your life. And this is how I am repaid? By being stalked and swindled by him? If you recall, you were the one who wanted to dump the body in the river. We should've made sure he was dead,' she repeated bluntly.

She picked up the cards and started to shuffle them with speed. 'I'm so much better at this than I used to be,' she said as her fingers moved over the cards. 'I've played a lot of solitaire over the years. So, who's first? I know, let's start with… Stacey!'

She put the pile of cards on the carpet in front of her and cut them in two. The card facing up was red.

'Truth time, Stace! So what really happened after we all ran back here, some of us still with his blood on our hands?'

'Nothing happened. I packed up and moved out. I never saw him again,' Stacey said. 'I thought he was dead. I left him floating in the river. And that was the best place for him. No one would've connected him to us. Someone must've found him and pulled him out – those people behind us on the path, maybe?'

'No, wrong answer. Because I was watching from this very window to see if they came through the woods. If they hadn't after ten minutes, I knew they had found him. But only a few minutes after us, three guys came out of the woods, chatting and laughing, not looking as though they had found a mangled and bleeding man. So why do I have a man dead in a bathtub who should be a pile of bones by now? Do you like what I've done with the flat, by the way? I bought it a few years back. It's a shithole, but I wanted a memory of how much fun we used to have. Nice, isn't it? Don't you love what I've done with the place?' She was repeating herself, lunacy draped over every word she spoke now. 'Okay, let's try someone else then.' She cut the cards again – it was red again. 'Paula, your turn – tell me the truth about that night.'

'We all came back to the flat and Stacey and I went to bed.'

'Really? You expect me to believe that you just went to bed? None of us would've slept that night. Don't take me for a fool, Paulie.'

She cut the cards again. 'Oooh, black. A dare for you, Bev. I dare you to… tell me the truth about what happened. Do you see what I did there?' She laughed maniacally and picked up the knife again. 'Tell me the truth or I throw the knife!'

Bev stood up then and faced Valentina full on. 'It was me. I went back. I got him out of the water.'

28

Valentina stared at the trees, deep in concentration. She could hear Bev still crying in her room and the low tones of Stacey comforting her. Since the three men had emerged from the trees just after they had got back to the flat, there had been no one else on the path. And now the sun was rising, which meant they may have got away with it. Sean would be floating downriver now, taking any connection to them with him. She felt cold, numb, but also wired. Her foot tapped constantly. She couldn't get it to stop. Justice was served.

How had that escalated so quickly? One minute they had been dancing and singing; the next, they were throwing a body in the river and running for their lives. She had been sitting here expecting a knock on the door ever since, the police, maybe – or worse, Sean.

She looked down at her hands and realised they were still dirty with what could be mud, but could also be blood. Her nails were caked with it, rusty brown. She surged into the bathroom and ran the shower as hot as it would go, then climbed under the spray and turned her face to the scalding water. After half an hour, when the water was starting to run cold, she finally got out, wrapped herself in a towel and headed to bed. She stopped outside Paula and Stacey's room and stuck her head in the doorway. Paula was in her bed, her face turned to the wall, her knees pulled up to her chest, and Stacey had wrapped herself around her protectively. Both were fast asleep, the shock having worn them both out. They looked so peaceful in each other's arms.

Valentina thought sleep would never come for her that night, but it did and she ended up sleeping like a dead person.

Bev heard the shower start and slowly crept from her room where she had been sitting, still fully clothed, contemplating the dirt under her nails and the mud on her hands. She kept seeing Valentina as she bashed Sean's head against the tree trunk, her face gurning, her features pulled out of shape in fury.

It had frightened her to see how quickly Valentina had switched from light to dark. Part of her wanted to understand that level of fury and rage, and could understand that it was seated in not knowing what he had actually done to her and countless other women, but she also couldn't just leave him out there. If he died like this, there would be no justice for any of those women. It was too easy, too simple. And what if Val was lying again? She was confused, unsure what to believe anymore.

She crept out of the flat and into the rapidly lightening

dawn. There was no one around. Birds had started chirping but the song was lost on her as she ran back into the woods. She hid just inside the trees, her breath coming in gulps, and listened. Nothing. She walked slowly, wary of what she would find, keeping her eyes on the river. A large part of her hoped she wouldn't find him, that someone else already had and that he was safe, sleeping it off somewhere.

He wasn't where they'd left him, but the tree trunk showed the signs of their struggle – the rust-brown tufts of hair, skin. Bev nearly threw up at that point, looked away hurriedly, nearly turned around and went back.

She peered up the river. If she couldn't see him from here, then she would turn back, she bargained with herself. Further along she could see a piece of fabric snagged on a tree root at the edge of the river, flapping and floating in the current. She scrambled along the water's edge until she reached it and leant over. It was his shirt. His body had lodged under some overhanging branches. He was face up, his eyes still closed, but his chest was rising and falling ever so slightly and a bubble escaped from his nose.

He wasn't dead. Not yet anyway.

She had a choice – leave him there or fish him out of the water.

The only way she could get to him would be to wade into the river, so she did, ignorant of the numbing cold water, only aware of the need to get him out. She pulled on his leg, but his shirt remained snagged. She pulled again and this time got enough purchase on his trousers for the fabric of the shirt to tear and the body to free itself. She spun him around so that she was now holding him under his armpits and then pulled backwards as hard as she could up the bank. She slipped and fell onto her bum a few times, his wet clothes weighing him down, but eventually he was far enough up the bank. She was sweating, panting heavily, and her back and shoulders ached, but she had no time to rest.

The sun was almost fully up.

She left him there on the edge of the bank and ran back to the flat. She had done her bit.

Her conscience could be clear.

29

PRESENT DAY

They sat, staring at Bev. Even Valentina seemed surprised by her admission. Bev started to cry again and Stacey moved to put her arm around her.

'Well, well, well, I was not expecting that!' Valentina said with a laugh. 'My money was definitely on you, Stacey! All this time I was annoyed at you because I never did think you believed me and it was sweet, lovely Bev who pulled him out!'

'He didn't deserve to die like that. That wouldn't have been justice,' Bev said quietly, 'but I never actually believed I had saved him. I thought I was too late, that he had died anyway, but at least I tried to do something rather than leaving him. It has haunted me ever since though – that I didn't speak up more, that I let you all make that decision for me. I went back again later the next day and he was gone, just the piece of material in the water and the... mess on the tree that didn't even look like blood anymore. I didn't know what had happened to him, but then when we got home and there was nothing on the news about it, I tried to put it out of my head. It didn't really work though.'

'Well, you'll be pleased to know he solved a little of that mystery for me, Bev. You see, I too was curious about what he could remember. A dog walker found him; he was breathing. They called an ambulance, but we wouldn't have seen that because it would've parked on the other side of the woods. At that point, he couldn't remember much except for the drugs and he didn't want to admit that to anyone. He panicked, said he was drunk and fell, just like we had hoped. There was a follow-up article, but just a tiny mention in the student newspaper again, so insignificant that we didn't see it – because who cares if a student got drunk and fell? A waste of everyone's time. Those scars never healed though, as you can see from the mess of him in there. He had a lasting reminder of his crimes and of that I am proud. But when he saw my profile on the dating app, more snatches of that night started to come back to him. The mind is a wonderful thing, isn't it? Self-preservation, you see. One day when you least expect it, BAM! It all comes back like a smack in the mouth. This time he wanted revenge. He wanted to take everything from me.' She sighed. 'I went to such lengths to protect us all – stealing Stu's keys, sneaking into the flat and packing up his belongings so that the others thought he had left after all, loading it into my car and dumping it miles away, replacing the keys. Covering our tracks. Protecting my family. Because that's what families do. They look out for each other. I thought about going after Stu next, but he didn't manage to pull it off with me. He failed – and since you said you remembered everything about sleeping with both of them, I figured Stu wasn't worth it, that he had learnt his lesson. He could've ended up dead too though. Let's hope you were telling the truth, Stacey. Because if not, then you let a predator go free. At least I know I did something.'

Stacey got to her feet. 'What is the point of all of this? Of torturing us? You were as much to blame as we were. You were the one who slammed his face into a tree trunk. You were the one who wanted to kill him. You could've just gone to the police. You had the matchbox.'

'Oh Stacey, I was trying to *save* you. Why can't you get that? All I wanted was a family. You three were my family. But you kept pushing me out. It wasn't about justice, not then anyway. Everything I did was for you, to be accepted by you, to be loved by you. It was all I ever wanted. And how did you repay me? You were the one who stopped me from finishing him off; you were the one who got me hooked on cigarettes. And you pushed me aside, after everything I had done for you. It was all you. You decided for all of us that we would never see each other again afterwards. You split up the band, Stacey.'

30

SUMMER 1993

Stacey sat in her old bedroom, the sounds of her brothers and dad watching football filtering up to her in shouts and roars. Her mother was cooking sausages for their tea, the smell of onions reaching every corner of the house.

Weeks had passed since they'd parted ways. The day after they killed a man. It became easier to hear the more she said it, so she let it run through her head like a mantra. They'd agreed to never talk about it again. To each other. To anyone.

Valentina had begged and pleaded for their phone numbers and addresses so that she could stay in touch, but Stacey had told her flatly and with no emotion that they were done. She would never hear from them again. She still hadn't admitted to anyone that Sean and Stu had drugged her. She couldn't – but the voices in her head reminded her of it all the time.

It was easier to let them believe she remembered it all.

And maybe after a while, maybe she would begin to believe it herself.

When she climbed out of her brother's car, back in the same council house on the estate that hadn't changed, she crawled into bed, pulled the covers over her head and stayed there. Days passed. Her mother came and went, bringing her toast, taking it away again.

Eventually they sent her oldest brother in, who ranted at her, telling her she couldn't be this tired just from a few poxy exams. He wanted answers; she couldn't give them. So she crawled back out of bed, showered and began to make believe every single day that everything was okay, that she was okay.

And the only way she could believe it was to cut all ties with Bev and Paula too. They called the house, they came by unannounced, but she refused to see them.

A month after they left that flat for good, she wrote Bev and Paula each a letter in which she told them not to try and contact her.

She didn't want to speak to them. They should get on with their lives. Seeing them would make it harder to believe the lies she was telling herself every day.

Paula reacted to the letter by coming out to her parents and setting fire to the world she had always known.

Bev met Malcolm and began the process of creating a new family to replace the one she had lost.

Their mistake was forgetting they were stronger together than they were apart.

31

Valentina peeled herself from the carpet and struggled to her feet by sliding her back up the glass doors until she was upright, but still leaning on them. She could feel her energy failing fast, but she needed to see this through.

'You have no idea how I have suffered, what this cancer has done to me. When I should've been enjoying my last few months, I was wasting my time on *him*.' She sighed. 'You know, he went from drugging women to scamming them for money. Have I said that already? Sometimes my brain gets a little fizzy.' She shook her head. 'So once again, I did the world a favour. I got rid of him once and for all this time. But is anybody grateful? NO! Still not! So I'm out. I'm done. I will board a plane to Bali in two days and I will spend my last few months on a beach in the sunshine. And you three ungrateful bitches? What happens next? Hmmm, let me think… I wasn't about to let you get away with just a drinking habit and a spot of loneliness. No, no, no. You need to suffer more than that.'

She grinned, showing all of her teeth, which had yellowed in time. 'I have planted a bit of evidence, framing you for Sean's murder. An anonymous call, a well-placed smidge of DNA – that's all it will take. All evidence I have fabricated over the last few months – a few strands of hair on his body, for instance, and this knife?' She picked up the blade, twisted and turned it in front of them, taunting and teasing with it. 'This is your knife from your flat, Stacey. You have a lovely little cat, by the way. Very noisy though.'

'What have you done to Nemo?' Her voice was like hoarfrost.

'Well, you'll just have to wait and see when you get home, won't you?'

'That's ridiculous, you'll never get away with this,' Paula said.

'Maybe, maybe not, but you will spend the rest of your lives wondering, won't you? Even if you spend the next few days bleaching this place from top to bottom, you have no idea what other bits and pieces of information I may have passed on. You'll always be looking over your shoulders, wondering if I've told the police everything. I will be on a beach, far away from it all, living out my own death sentence anyway. It doesn't matter anymore if they come for me. But you three will forever be in its shadow, jumping every time the doorbell rings, flinching at every siren. It's genius really. I bet you wish you'd been more grateful now.'

Stacey could feel a dark wrath flooding over her like ink. She thought of all the lives damaged, broken and lost in this sick game Valentina had played with them, like she was the dealer and they were the cards, being shuffled, dealt and moved around at her bidding. And she thought about never being free of her.

She launched herself from where she stood and tackled a surprised Valentina backwards, through the glass door. The glass shattered and they fell into the hallway. Stacey kept her eyes on the glint of the knife and managed to clasp Valentina's hands in hers as they grappled on the floor among the broken glass. Valentina was paper-thin under her clothes, the chemo having sapped the muscle tone from her body, but there was an unexpected, adrenalin-charged strength in her that caught Stacey off-guard. Valentina pushed back hard and flung Stacey off to the side. Stacey cried out as a shard of glass pierced the skin on the underside of her arm. She heard a growl and Valentina lurched at her, the knife held high, the blade coming down straight at her face.

This is it, she thought. *This is how it ends.* For a split second, she felt a quiet relief that the fight would be over, that the tiredness would end. She closed her eyes then and waited for the inevitable to happen.

She heard a snarl and opened her eyes to see Paula charge at Valentina and grab her from behind. She flung her back through the glass door like she was a rag doll. Valentina fell, then struggled to get back on her feet, the knife still grasped tightly in her pincer-like grip. She surged back at Paula, but a shape got in the way. Bev's hands wrapped themselves over Valentina's on the handle of the knife and they wrestled backwards and forwards, slicing the air between them. Stacey scrambled to her feet, as did Paula, and they closed the gap on her, ready to overpower Valentina, the three of them acting as one.

Valentina's eyes took in each one of them and it was as though the fight was sucked out of her in an instant. Her body went limp in Bev's arms. Bev was thrown off-guard by the sudden change and she let go of the knife.

Valentina smiled then, a simple, beautiful smile. She turned the knife inwards and plunged it into her own chest. She collapsed back onto Bev, blood pooling from the wound in her chest.

The three of them watched as her eyes fluttered closed, the smile still on her lips.

The woods were dark, the night not dissimilar to another thirty years ago. They made slow progress as they carried the tarpaulin from the skip between them. Bev at one end, Paula at the other, Stacey in the middle like always.

'Here,' Stacey said and they lowered the roll of tarpaulin to the ground. Bev stepped down into the shallow water and waded along the edge some way until she found the spot she was looking for. The exposed roots were still protruding like witches' fingers, the riverbank eroded far enough back that there would be enough room.

'Perfect,' Stacey said. They unrolled the tarpaulin to expose the body, the blood that had seeped from the neck wound long since dried. It took three of them to lower him into the water and wedge him far enough under the root so that he was secure and hidden from view.

Then they rolled up the tarpaulin once more and repeated their journey, this time carrying back a much lighter load, like a pile of sticks.

They laid her in his arms with her head on his chest, like lovers finally at rest.

They walked away without looking back.

When the skip was collected two days later, it had the addition of a knife and a shoebox of papers and photographs, all of which were tossed away with the debris and rubbish.

32

SIX MONTHS LATER

Stacey set the table with three plates and put a jug of water in the centre. She hummed to herself, straightened the knives and forks, then stood back to make sure it was to her satisfaction. She scratched absent-mindedly at the scar on the underside of her arm, the pale jagged line a reminder.

She heard the shower turn off and turned with a smile as the bathroom door opened.

'Hurry up, she'll be here soon,' she said.

She went back into the kitchen and tossed the salad in balsamic dressing, pinching a cherry tomato from the bowl.

She took a bottle of ice-cold rosé wine from the fridge and set it on the counter. She looked at it for some time, ran her fingers through the condensation on the glass, felt her mouth water as she remembered the taste of it on her tongue.

At the sound of footsteps in the hallway, she picked up the bottle and carried it over to the table.

'Smells amazing,' Paula said.

'Thanks. I'm really looking forward to seeing her. I want to hear all about that trip she took with Bethany.'

The doorbell rang then and Stacey squealed. She rushed to the door and flung it open.

'Bev!' They embraced warmly. 'Come in.'

'Look at you, Stace, you look amazing,' Bev said, pushing her bright pink glasses up her nose.

'Thanks – lost another few pounds. It's all this running Paulie is making me do with her. Three times a week before she goes to work – can you believe it?' Stacey closed the front door and ushered her into the open-plan lounge.

'Hey, Bev,' Paula said from behind her. 'You look good yourself. Love those glasses. And the tan is quite something – good holiday then?'

'Oh, we had the best time. I can't believe she is going to university soon. These last few months have been so special. Italy was amazing – the food, the people. All of it.'

Paula opened the wine and handed Bev a glass, then poured one for herself. 'And did Malcolm and Jasper get on alright on their own?'

'Oh, they were fine. Malcolm moved his mother in, can you believe it? I have never seen her so happy to see me when we got home.'

Stacey poured herself some water from the jug.

'How long has it been, Stace?' Bev asked, indicating the water.

'Haven't touched a drop since that night.'

'Good girl. And the new living arrangements? Still happy?'

'Well, we haven't killed each other yet.'

The comment fell between them like a bomb.

'Too soon?' Stacey said and they all laughed.

'I'd like to make a toast,' Bev said. 'To old friends reconnecting – and to Paulie for finalising her divorce and being free.'

'And to being stronger together than we are apart,' Stacey added.

'Cheers!' They looked each other in the eye as they clinked their glasses together.

Epilogue

Howard Archer stepped confidently through the mud. He could feel water begin to seep into his socks and he sighed. Time to get a new pair of walking boots. His chocolate-brown Labrador, Bisto, frolicked at the water's end, running in, rushing out, shaking the water from his thick fur and charging ahead. Howard smiled as he watched the dog and turned the volume up on the classical music playing through his AirPods.

Bisto ran further ahead, his nose to the ground, sniffing enthusiastically. He disappeared out of sight and as Howard rounded the corner, he could just make out the dog rooting around in the ferns at the water's edge. He pulled something free and bounded back to Howard to present it to him.

He dropped it in front of Howard, who stooped to pick it up, thinking it was a twig to throw.

It was a severed finger.

Howard screeched and dropped the finger, feeling vomit rush up his throat. He lurched to the nearest tree and threw up, the force of it dislodging one of his AirPods, which landed right in the middle of what was left of his breakfast.

Bisto looked on in amusement.

Howard paused and wondered if he should just leave

the AirPod where it was. He shook his head in disbelief, wondering how his morning had suddenly veered so far off track, then scooped the AirPod from the puddle of sick.

He retched once more, but fought back the urge to add more to the puddle. He pulled a tissue from his pocket and wrapped the AirPod in it. He'd worry about what to do with that later.

Bisto stood, tail wagging, as Howard walked over to the edge of the river and crouched down to wash his hands. His foot slipped out from under him and he slid down the bank into the river. He swore loudly as he landed in the water. It reached up to his knees and he was no longer fazed by his damp socks.

Turning to pull himself back up the bank, he found himself face to face with the dead body of a man, his arms wrapped around that of a dead woman.

Howard squealed again.

The man had a finger missing from one hand, small bite marks where the knuckle should be. Howard assumed that was Bisto's handiwork. He retched again, clamped a hand over his mouth in horror.

The man's body also had a deep gash running from one side of his neck to the other like a smile and his face was badly scarred down one side.

The woman had a single, deep and bloody wound to her heart.

In her hand she clutched a pack of playing cards.

Acknowledgements

As always, there are so many people to thank for helping me to get this book over the finish line. As they say, it takes a village.

To my agent, Jo Bell from Bell Lomax Moreton, for her encouragement and unwavering faith in me and my little stories. You know how much went into this book, but you never doubted me and I am enormously grateful for that and for everything. You are a powerhouse.

To my editor at Aries/Head of Zeus, Martina Arzu, whose enthusiasm and ideas are immeasurable. It has been a joy working on this one with you.

To the marketing and design team at Head of Zeus, who nailed the cover on very little information from me because even I didn't know where this story would end until the words appeared on the page.

To Alice, Julietta, Heidi, Elin and my friends in the writing community for hearing me out, offering me a different perspective and giving me a benchmark of talent to aspire to.

This story is about old friends, the ones you lose touch with over the years but who would be there in a heartbeat if you needed them. The ones you would call on if you needed to hide a body. You know who you are and I love you.

It's a crazy world where there are still too many victims of abuse. This is for the ones who fought back, the ones who survived, the ones who are thinking about getting out.

And the biggest thanks and appreciation go to my family.

To Ted for his unwavering support, even when the stress levels have reached epic proportions and all he can do is buy the chocolate, pour the wine and leave me be.

I wrote – and rewrote – a large part of this book sitting at the dining room table with my girls either side of me, their noses in books as they studied for GCSEs and A Levels after what have been the most unsettling and disruptive few years of their lives. We've shared the deadlines and the stress, and seeing their determination and commitment helped me to push on. Sharing their worries and doubts helped me to overcome my own. I am immensely proud of you, Paige and Erin, whatever the outcome. This book was a challenge from start to finish, but we helped each other over the finish line, so thank you.

My love for you is limitless.

And finally to you, dear reader. The books are always for you.

About the Author

DAWN GOODWIN's career has spanned PR, advertising, publishing and healthcare, both in London and Johannesburg. A graduate of the Curtis Brown creative writing school, she loves to write about the personalities hiding behind the masks we wear every day, whether beautiful or ugly. What spare time she has is spent chasing good intentions, contemplating how to get away with murder, and immersing herself in fictitious worlds. She lives in London with her husband, two teenage daughters and British bulldogs Geoffrey and Luna.